POOR MAN'S FIGHT

POOR MAN'S FIGHT

ELLIOTT KAY

This is a work of fiction. Names, characters, organizations, places, events, and incidents are either products of the author's imagination or are used fictitiously.

Published by Skyscape, New York

www.apub.com

ISBN-13: 9781477830789
ISBN-10: 1477830782

Cover illustration by Lee Moyer

Library of Congress Control Number: 2014960263

Printed in the United States of America

For Mom

PROLOGUE

At War with the World

"How much debt do you people carry?"

His question stunned *Aphrodite*'s assembled crew. The luxury liner had been at the mercy of this swaggering, self-assured man and his comrades for over an hour. In that time, not one of the crew imagined a pirate asking them how much money they *didn't* have.

"Aw, c'mon now. This doesn't work without some participation from the audience." His gravelly yet cheerful voice dominated the room. Long, straight black hair hung loosely past his shoulders. He wore no eye patch, no tricorne hat or prosthetic limb. Just loose clothes, heavy boots, a day's worth of stubble, and a pair of pistols. "There's a reason we separated you out from the passengers. *You* guys don't have to worry about being hurt or killed, long as you don't do anything stupid."

Faint echoes of crashes, screams, and the occasional discharge of a weapon drifted into the ransacked ballroom through the walls and the vents as if to illustrate his point. *Aphrodite*'s 649 shaken crewmembers—senior officers and much of the security staff conspicuously absent—remained speechless.

The crew vastly outnumbered the dozen or so pirates in the room, but none of *Aphrodite*'s people were armed. Only a small portion had any training or experience with firearms in the first place, and those few knew even better than the others what would happen if they tried to rush the pirates. Many of their captors bore military-grade weapons. The smoldering remains of several people in the port entryway attested to how poorly unarmored humans fared against pulse lasers.

"You there"—the pirate pointed—"Hong. No, don't be so shocked; I only know your name because it's on your goddamn tag there. How much debt do you have?"

"Sixty . . . sixty-seven thousand," answered Crewman Hong.

"Only sixty-seven K, and you look to be, what, twenty-five? Twenty-six? You had longevity treatments yet?" Hong shook his head, and the pirate gave a thoughtful frown. "Well, that'll set you back a good ways, but you must be conscientious about your payments. Maybe did well in school, too, right? Judging by your uniform, I'm guessing that sixty-seven is a little less than four years' income, right? *Only* four years. Shit, crazy as that is, you're a bad example. Never mind."

Hong blinked as the pirate captain shifted his attention. "How about you? In the dress? What do you do here?"

"I'm a hostess," ventured a slender young blonde in glittering black and silver. "I run the b-ballroom here."

"Hah. Sorry 'bout the mess." The pirate shrugged, glancing around at overturned tables and a thoroughly emptied bar. "But then again, none of this shit belongs to you, anyway, does it? You own any shares in this ship or the line?"

She shook her head. "N-no."

"No, of course not. So it's not like it's actually yours, right? It's the company's. You ain't responsible for this, so fuck it. Anyway, what's your debt look like?"

Reluctantly, she glanced at her fellows—most of them in jump-suits or ship's uniforms—and admitted, "One seventy-six."

The pirate whistled. "Maybe not so good in school."

She tried to defend herself. "I had linguistics training!"

"Sure, sure. Hostess. Gotta talk to everybody. Good looks don't always come cheap, either." The pirate winked before pointing to another crewman. "You there! Oil stains! How much? C'mon now, how much debt?"

"Ninety-three thousand . . . sir," the machinist's mate answered nervously.

That got derisive laughs from the other pirates. They all seemed relaxed, yet each held a weapon drawn and ready. Some drank from expensive bottles stolen from the bar.

"Don't call me that, son. I'm a pirate. I'm the captain, sure, but nobody's gotta kiss my ass. Not like *your* captain expects. Don't call me 'sir.' Hell, don't even call me 'captain.' My name's Casey."

He placed one foot on the chair in front of him and leaned forward on his knee. One couldn't help but notice the fresh blood atop the toe of his fine leather boot.

"All of *you* are going to live through this," said Casey, "barring anyone doing anything stupid, of course. But you all did the sensible thing and didn't resist once you couldn't run—and I guess we can't really blame you for running," he conceded amiably. "That was your captain's call, but, well, fuck him.

"I'm here to offer you all a choice of your own free will. Maybe the first truly free choice of your lives. Might seem like there's a gun to your head right now, but we aren't holding it.

"The people who really hold that gun have been there all your lives. NorthStar. CDC. Lai Wa. All those fucking corporations putting all those strings on you ever since you were a shocking disruption in mommy's menstrual cycle. Or a procreation request form, some of you. Those corporations wrote all the rules and they hold all the cards, and you have nothing.

"They put you on your knees and keep you there. And then they go and make it *your fault* by dressing up all the shit you *need to live* as loans you have to pay back. Tell you that you *have* to go to school and then stick you with the bill. Shoot you up with a hundred inoculations for shit that isn't even around anymore and tell you ya can't get a job otherwise, and then they charge through the nose for it, too. Before you know it, you owe money just for being alive. And then you owe money for owing money."

He pulled his foot off the seat and stood tall. "And that assumes you've made arrangements to live that long. Gotta have that gene therapy so you'll live a nice, long life, 'cause if you're gonna be withered and elderly by seventy-five or eighty you sure as hell can't pay back the debts you rack up just making it to twenty-five. Not that longevity's the sort of thing you can pay for out of your pocket, so you owe for that, too.

"They'll never let you get out of debt," Casey said gravely. "You know that, right? Why would they do something so stupid?" He left each sentence hanging in the air, looking from one pair of eyes to the next.

"Used to be, to enslave a person, you had to beat him constantly and take him far from home. Maybe kill a few other slaves in front of him to show what'd happen if he got lippy or tried to escape. Put him in chains. Keep him ignorant. Isolate him. Make him feel less than human. But look at you. Hell, they've got it wired so well now you think you're free. You people are slaves and you don't even know it. They know better than to call it slavery. They just tell you that you owe them money and they set all the rules for how you can pay 'em back.

"So you get a job cleaning up after those rich slobs who were living it up in this ballroom just a couple hours ago. Maybe along the way you can scrape together a few credits to buy yourself some sort of distracting entertainment or drug yourself into happiness for a few hours, but most of that money they pretend they're paying you goes right back into dividends for the stockholders. Then you get up and do it again. And it's never going to end . . ."

A pistol appeared in his hand, drawn in the blink of an eye from his hip. The move startled several crewmembers. Others managed not to show their alarm.

"Unless you pick up one of these, and you tell those fuckers no more. Tell 'em you won't play this game where they make all the rules. Tell 'em you won't follow laws when you didn't get any say in 'em. And give up all that fairy-tale bullshit they feed you where you'll have your own home on a sunny planet and kids growing up healthy and free to choose their own way in life, 'cause I'm telling you, it's never going to happen. *They will never let you go, because there's no money in it.*"

He paused to let it sink in. Then he made his pitch.

"Everyone on our ship gets an equal share of loot and an equal vote. Do well and your shipmates may even vote you up for an extra share. Our chain of command is only for combat and shipboard emergency. Past that, we're all one and the same. Shipboard rules all fit on a single page. No hazing bullshit. We don't care who you fuck or whether or not you pray to whoever the hell you believe in. Anyone gets too hurt to go on, we make sure they get compensated.

"And you're free to go whenever we hit a port, because we don't want anyone who doesn't want to be with us. We know people who can help you disappear. It's affordable, and they're honest enough that they want the money up front.

"It's rough living. Quarters are cramped, and this crew isn't exactly what you'd call culturally enriched. And there's that whole criminal status thing."

Casey paused to scan the crowd. "I'm done. You've got one minute. If you want to join up, talk to one of these fine people with guns. Do it quick if you want to keep any property you have in your quarters.

"Oh," he said, just as he turned to leave. "New recruits get a half share each from this ship. Might want to consider how it'll feel to have more assets than debts for once in your life."

A pair of pirates joined Casey as he walked out of the ballroom. One was a blonde, petite and almost pretty, wearing knives and guns like they were jewelry. The other was a tall young man whose muscles spoke of a great deal of exercise and growth enhancers.

"How was that?" Casey asked as they headed down the passageway.

"I think you're still awfully wordy," Lauren said nonchalantly.

"You mix metaphors," added Carl.

"I what?"

"You mix metaphors. You start talking about the idea of having a gun to their head and then you describe the corps as having strings in their backs, like puppets. And then you talk about playing a rigged game. You've got to pick one or the other. Unless you want them all to see themselves as puppets playing cards with guns to their heads, but that's just stupid. Who shoots a puppet?"

The captain's mouth fell open. "You know, I had teachers who talked like you in school. Pretty sure they're what drove me to a life of crime."

"I thought you were rebelling against the oppressive corporate plutocracy that disenfranchises and enslaves the working class?"

"Lauren, I'm gonna hit him."

"Go ahead." The blonde glanced up at Carl with a smirk. "This is why nobody wants to sit with you in the galley."

Casey forgot about it. The three arrived at a series of offices, all warmly decorated to help wealthy passengers feel welcome. The bloodcurdling screams from within one office hampered the sense of hospitality. Outside the office stood a lone man nervously gulping from a bottle of whiskey. Sweat beaded across his forehead. He looked up to Casey's arrival with partial relief.

"Takashi," Casey said, "what's goin' on? You okay?"

The other pirate opened his mouth to speak, but another anguished scream interrupted him. "It's Turtle, boss," Takashi said. "The guy's just . . . Does he really have to do all this?"

"Hey, hey, chill out. It's okay," Casey counseled. "Takashi, you gotta remember who we're dealing with."

"Well, I've just . . . Casey, I've got my limits, and what Turtle's doing . . ."

Casey shook his head. "You know the only difference between Turtle and these rich fucks is that Turtle robs people up front and with his hands, right? These assholes get you with their interest rates and their late-payment penalties, but it's still robbery."

"Yeah, but it's not like the ship's officers are bankers, Casey."

"It's *all the same*, Takashi," Casey assured him. "They're all the same machine. Otherwise we wouldn't fight 'em like this, yeah? They're only getting what's coming to 'em. Listen, I'll go talk to Turtle. Carl, you wanna take Takashi here for a walk? Maybe find him something better to do?"

"Sure, boss. C'mon, Takashi." Carl nodded, gesturing for him to follow.

Another pleading yelp split the silence as the two left. Lauren and Casey watched them go. "Hell of a thing." Lauren shook her head. "Guy pitches in during a fight just like anyone else. Maybe more. Then something like this happens and he gets all jittery."

"Like he said, everyone's got limits," Casey said. "Just gotta keep reminding them about the cause. He'll get used to this."

Lauren looked at him with a skeptical grin. "Not that many guys on our boat need a cause," she pointed out.

"No, but it works for the ones who do," Casey said with a shrug. "Most folks don't like considering themselves bad guys.

They wanna look in the mirror and see a good guy, no matter what they do. Just gotta make sure they feel some sense of justification is all."

"That what you need?"

"Hey, I feel completely justified," answered Casey. He pounded on the door and waited to be let in.

The scene in the office was nothing short of gruesome. Two men in ships' uniforms sat tied up in chairs, facing one another. Both officers were gagged. The younger one on Casey's right was in far worse shape than the other. Looped around the top of his bloody head was a cord, wrapped around a small dowel at the back. A burly pirate with an open vest and no shirt stood behind him, occasionally twisting the dowel to tighten the cord. Each twist elicited a scream from the victim.

A third ship's officer lay dead between them. A couple of other pirates sat on the desk and on the couch, casually watching.

"We still sorting this out?" Casey asked Turtle.

"Huh?" Turtle blinked. "Oh, I don't actually know. Been a while since I've asked."

Casey sighed. "Bunch'a savages in this crew." He turned to the unharmed officer. "Okay, so you are the ship's purser, right? I mean, we didn't do all this for a case of mistaken identity?"

The officer nodded vigorously. He tried to plead something through his gag.

Casey shushed him. "He can stop hurting people if you'll just agree to unlock the ship's cash accounts for us. All we want is the cash. If you cooperate, we can let you live. Okay?" Again, he was answered with an emphatic nod, but this time the purser tried to communicate something by meaningfully tilting his head and gesturing with his eyes.

"Yes, we can leave your friend here alone, too." Casey sighed. "Turtle. Ease off."

"Guy's fucked up, anyway," grunted Turtle.

Casey turned to Turtle, rolling his eyes. "Do you understand why you're putting the hurt on *this* guy," he said, pointing to the bloody prisoner, "and not the guy with the answers? Do you understand that answer man here doesn't want to see his buddies die and that's why he'll talk?"

Then it was Turtle's turn to sigh. "I'm not a moron, Casey."

"Christ almighty," Casey grumbled, noticing a bleep from the holocom attached to his wrist. "Can you maybe not make such a show of enjoying this in front of the new guys, too? You know some of them get squeamish. Takashi almost puked out there."

He tapped the holocom to open up a communications channel. A screen appeared to reveal the face of a balding man. "Jerry," Casey greeted him, "what've we got?"

"Great haul so far in cargo and ships' stores," answered the other man. "Passengers are mostly wealthy. Bunch of doctors and such, too. Splitting up the loot from this one's gonna be like Christmas morning."

Casey snorted. "Christmas with a couple hundred psychos under the tree."

"That's a good point, actually," said Lauren. "I've seen a pirate crew get *too* lucky on a strike before. That was a luxury liner, too, only half this one's size. After two years of nothing but hits on bulk freighters and mining camps, everyone got crazy. The whole crew cracked under the weight of their own success before we even made it to a friendly port. Half of 'em didn't live to spend their loot."

Casey nodded thoughtfully. Lauren was easily the most experienced among the crew. She was also easily one of the deadliest. "Anyone starts getting too starry-eyed, you take 'em aside and have a talk with 'em. The real money's gonna come from the ship itself, though, assuming we didn't fuck her up too badly. How's the outlook on that?" he asked Jerry.

"We can keep her. Wilson and the other snipes say the FTL generator will be back up in half an hour, maybe less. We can get a short jump out of her to at least get out of this system before a patrol finds us."

"I'm not gonna fret too much about system patrols. How's her armament?"

"That's a kicker. Armaments are solid. She could've put up one hell of a fight if the captain hadn't buckled like he did. Maybe he figured his crew wasn't up to it. Sturdy ship, though."

The door opened again. Carl entered, grinning from ear to ear. "Is that good news you're gonna give me? We got some takers from the crew?"

"Seventeen," answered Carl. "Bunch of non-rates, couple electronics techs, a machinist, and the junior astrogator. A couple of them are ex–Union fleet or system militia vets, too."

Casey shot him a triumphant look. "Fuck your mixed metaphors bullshit." He grinned. "Okay, grab a couple of solid guys and take 'em to their quarters to get their shit. Make sure they get grilled one at a time about the ship. VIP passengers, ship's security, all that stuff."

"You want us to hold the rest?" Carl asked.

"Just until we get the rest of our shit sorted. But make sure somebody from the guard detail knows the way down to the lifeboat decks so you can load 'em up without it turning into a clusterfuck."

"Jesus, Casey, you want to waste lifeboats on these sops?" sneered Lauren.

"Only a couple boats." Casey shrugged defensively. "I'm sure we can squeeze 'em into two. Three at the most. They'll just have to be friendly. Anyway, I said we'd leave them alive."

"What about the rest of the passengers?" Carl asked.

Casey waved a dismissive hand. "Just make sure the ones we plan to ransom don't get too broken. Who gives a shit about the rest? It's not like they're gonna be able to tell anyone what happened to 'em."

ONE

The Test

Tanner's desperate run ended outside NorthStar's district headquarters as he came to the mob of teenagers at the entrance. He nearly collapsed from fatigue, but his arrival brought him no relief from his stress. "Oh God." Tanner shuddered, his despair evident as he caught his breath. "They're actually holding the Test on time this year."

"Wow, did you run all the way here from the depot or something?" asked the classmate standing ahead of him in line. He looked down as Tanner bent over with his hands on his thighs to slow down his breath. "You could've just called me for a ride. We've been waiting out here for ten minutes for them to let us in."

"I would've asked," Tanner groaned, "but my test section started two spots ahead of yours. I'm supposed to be in there already. If you're out here now, I'm at least fifty minutes late!"

Nathan blinked. That wasn't like Tanner at all. The longer he looked at his sweaty, breathless fellow senior, the more his concern grew. "You look like shit," he declared. "What happened?"

Tanner didn't answer right away, still breathing hard as he wiped the sweat from his face. He straightened up to retie his messy black ponytail when he made another frightful discovery. "Oh God, the line's moving. I'm fucked."

Bored, distracted, and nervous students shuffled toward the doors. Some wore body-length micro-smartweave clothes that regulated their temperature and moisture. Others embraced the blazing sun and arid breeze with little clothing and generous applications of protective skin treatments. The wealthier ones, like Nathan, underwent expensive melanin adjustments to address that problem.

Tanner could afford no such options. Normally he dressed in loose, light clothes and used a lot of cheap but effective sunscreen. Today he didn't even have the sunscreen. He wore track shorts that needed to be washed, the first loose shirt he could find, and an awful lot of his own sweat.

"How the hell did you of all people wind up fifty minutes late to the Test?" asked Nathan.

"I couldn't sleep," explained Tanner, "and then I kept looking at the clock thinking about how much sleep I was missing, and the more I stressed about that the harder it was to sleep, so finally I threw a pillow over the clock. When it went off I was so out of it I didn't even recognize the alarm." Tanner caught his reflection in a window. He had the deep tan common in the city of Geronimo, but even so he was in for a nasty sunburn.

"Well, you can calm down now." Nathan shrugged. "You've made it. Look, you lost time, but worrying about it now won't do you any good. Just write it off."

"I'm not ready for this at all," groaned Tanner.

"Oh bullshit. You tutored me. You tutored half the class. You haven't gotten a bad grade on a test since Mrs. Berry when we were little kids, and that was just 'cause she hated you for always correcting her when she was wrong."

"I didn't tutor half the class."

"Hey!" Nathan called out. "How many of you have had Tanner help you in school?"

Heads turned. Hands went up all along the line. Nathan patted Tanner's back. "Come on. Don't worry about this. You're practically the valedictorian."

"Heather Verde's the valedictorian."

"Yeah, and poor Heather's always a bundle of nerves like you are now. She threw up all over the podium at her senior thesis defense panel. Don't be Heather. Settle down and let go of the stress, or it'll just get worse."

Tanner scowled. "How is telling me that supposed to make me feel any better?"

The line moved steadily. Tanner's shoulders sagged. He felt like beating his head against the nearest wall. He had hardly slept. He hadn't eaten or showered, let alone taken any time to collect his thoughts. Before him loomed the Test or, as the illuminated window over the door read, "The Union Academic Investment Evaluation."

His stomach turned. His weary legs carried him toward the inevitable.

A pair of test proctors at the door checked the identities of the arriving students on holographic screens projected by computers on their wrists. Nathan turned to check in with the proctor on the right. The woman on the left looked at Tanner expectantly.

"Name?" she said, her face set in obvious disapproval. Clearly, she knew an unprepared student when she saw one. She stood straight, her businesslike clothing and calm, mature demeanor contrasting against the sweat-drenched boy before her.

"Tanner Malone." The woman's holocom beeped. Tanner blinked with a bit of surprise. "Is that thing reading a voice print already?"

"Do you have your identification?"

"N-no," Tanner stammered, "but if that thing just read my voice print, do you still need it?" His tone was helpful. Polite. Utterly unappreciated.

The woman's scowl deepened. "What school do you attend?"

"NorthStar Educational 772."

She didn't look up from her screen. "Age?"

"Eighteen point five."

"What was the subject of your senior thesis?"

"Xenobiology and ecology."

"You're fifty-six minutes late. This will significantly impact your score." She looked up at him sternly before he could speak. "You may not enter the testing facility with any belongings other than your clothing and any necessary, documented medication. Do you have anything to leave here?"

"No." Tanner blinked. He didn't even have his holocom. He thought of pointing that out, but at this point, she was just an obstacle on his way to a bigger obstacle. There was nothing to be gained in drawing this out.

"Please enter and find your testing cube on the first floor. Follow the yellow track lighting. Your name is displayed on your cube."

Wasting no more time, Tanner stepped inside. He immediately heard another suspicious beep and looked at the plastic framework of the entryway. Obviously he had been scanned. He knew something like that had to be coming, but it didn't make him feel any more welcome or relaxed.

Before him stretched out a wide, open floor filled with two-meter-wide, two-meter-tall opaque black "testing cubes." Each cube was nothing more than a trick of projected light and sound mufflers. One could walk right through any of the cube walls. Most of the cubes had "Testing" posted in red letters on each side. Others bore the Union Academic Investment Evaluation seal and the name of its intended occupant.

Tanner found his cube and stared at the seal while other examinees filed past him. Some wished one another luck. A few sniffled nervously. Most laughed and chattered, either to calm nerves or because they didn't really give a second thought to the gravity of the situation.

He looked around, wanting just one more moment with a friendly face but finding no one he knew. He knew that most of his friends were already sequestered in their black cubes as their scheduled appointments required. Tanner was very late for his. Every minute hurt his score.

A scowling adult stomped up to the cube on Tanner's right and placed his palm on the seal. The cube vanished, revealing a pale, expensively dressed young man sitting on a minimally endowed chair. For a split second, Tanner thought he saw a small holographic screen projected from the youth's left hand, but it vanished almost as quickly as the cube.

"Give it to me," demanded the adult.

"What?"

"The holocom you snuck in here. Where did you hide it? In your ear? Up your nose?"

"I don't know what you're talking about!" the youth protested. He held his hands up, turning away from the adult as if to express his aggravation. The adult promptly grabbed his left arm. "Hey! Get your hands off me!" A small fleck of plastic fell from the youth's sleeve and onto the floor. He stepped on it, but he was too late.

"Get your foot off that."

"Off what? You're crazy! Leave me alone!"

The adult noticed Tanner watching. "Don't you have a test to get started on?"

Instinctively seeking to avoid the man's wrath, Tanner stepped into his cube. Instantly the sounds of the argument not more than a meter away from him diminished. Some invisible sensor kept up with the escalating voices, increasing the sound-dampening effect until Tanner heard nothing. It was just him, his chair, and the screen set within the opaque holographic wall.

"Please be seated," the screen read. A friendly female voice read it aloud. Tanner obeyed. "Please confirm your name."

"T-Tanner Malone," he stammered.

"Please look straight ahead and place your palm on the screen." Tanner obeyed and waited for the scans. "Please hold your hand steady," it said. Tanner took a deep breath to stop his trembling.

"Good morning, Tanner," the cube read to him aloud off the screen. "Welcome to the Union Academic Investment Evaluation. Your academic records have already been processed. Please verify proper record matching by answering the following questions."

The first few questions were identical to the ones he answered at the entrance. Tanner tried to control his irritation.

"Are you rated by your counselors as highly gifted, gifted, above average, average, below average, well below average, handicapped, or nonperforming?"

"Gifted," Tanner muttered.

"Are you a member of NorthStar Education's Society of Scholars?"

"Well, they didn't rate me as 'highly gifted' and I'm not rich, so . . ." He bit back the rest of his response. Being bitter at the computer would make no difference.

"Please answer the question with yes or no."

"No."

"Thank you." The screen shifted to a sequence of corporate and government seals.

"NorthStar Corporation provides a full twelve years of educational services fulfilling the compulsory education requirements of the Union and your home system of Archangel. You have fulfilled the basic average of seven hours per school day through the course of your education. Congratulations on your excellent attendance record! Three additional, optional hours per school day in a variety of subjects have been made available to you as required by law, which you may or may not have pursued by your own choice. At this time, you should be eligible for graduation."

Tanner rolled his eyes. Kids knew all of this from roughly the same time they learned the awful truth about Santa Claus. The countdown clock in one corner of the screen made the whole monologue all the more galling. He had no option to skip the introduction.

"Your education comes at significant expense. The costs of your compulsory education have been fifteen thousand credits per year at three percent annual interest. As you are now a legal adult, you are liable for this debt regardless of whether you graduate.

"NorthStar Corporation, in compliance with the Union Educational Equality Act, has developed the Union Academic Investment Evaluation, or UAIE, to assess your mastery of academic skills and content knowledge. NorthStar, the Union, and Archangel believe that an educated individual is an inherent benefit to society at large. Thus, your performance today on the UAIE may lead to forgiveness of some or potentially all of your educational debts.

"Now, Tanner," the cube said, "are you ready to begin the evaluation?"

"Uh . . . no? No, I'm not!" Tanner told the screen.

"Please choose one of the following causes for exemption," the voice said. For a moment, hope grew in Tanner's heart. Could there be a way out of this, after all?

"Are you bereaved, meaning that you have suffered a death in your immediate family within the last twenty-four hours?"

"No."

"Are you physically ill or in need of immediate medical attention?"

"I—I don't know?" Tanner ventured. "I don't feel well."

"Please stand while I check your vital signs," the cube instructed. Tanner stood and waited through the soft electronic hum. A picture of him appeared on the screen, along with a display of his vitals.

"Your vital signs are all within acceptable parameters," the cube said with a mildly scolding tone. "You are likely experiencing hunger, fatigue, or nausea as a result of poor preparation for the Test. Emotional fitness is the responsibility of the student and his or her family, and is therefore not included as an exempting condition. If you have a cause for exemption other than those listed, please state."

"My parents are basket cases and they've screwed up my whole life," answered Tanner.

There was a moment's pause. "That does not qualify for an exemption. If you have a cause for exemption other than those listed, please state."

Tanner sank into his chair, and hope sank with him. "Well, fuck."

"That does not qualify for an exemption. If you have a cause for exemption other than those listed, please state."

• • •

Less than twenty-four hours earlier, Tanner had felt confident about the Test. It was just one more hoop to jump through. He'd conscientiously saved money over the last two years to cover any shortfalls. Even a single flubbed algebra problem could cost hundreds of credits, but he didn't have much cause to worry. He placed in the top 5 percent of students regionally, planetwide, and even across the system. His course load reached well beyond the Test's targets. Tanner's senior year saw him with perfect standings to enter the biology and ecology studies departments of a dozen major universities.

Most students took a grav train home from school, unless they had their own vehicles or could hitch a ride from a friend. Whenever Tanner could not manage the latter, he walked. It saved money, and Geronimo hardly ever got past 48 degrees Celsius, anyway. His residential district had a community pool to help beat the heat when he got home.

Walking home the evening before the Test, Tanner had thought more about that pool than about what faced him in the morning. He had run out of decent practice test materials weeks ago, anyway; the only worthwhile form of studying he could find at this point was in tutoring others. There just wasn't any point in stressing about it anymore.

Then Tanner walked into his small, humble home to find his stepmother packing up her art, her books, and other belongings.

She hardly even noticed him when the door opened, focused as she was on wrapping up her prized sculpture. It looked to Tanner like a three-dimensional inkblot. For a moment, his heart jumped—was she leaving his father? They didn't seem like they were having problems.

"What's . . . Sharon? What's going on?" Tanner asked.

"Hm? Oh, hi, sweetie! You know, I wish you wouldn't call me Sharon," she said in that gentle but slightly distant "teacher voice" she always used with him. She talked often of how she wanted him to think of her as family, but she still felt more like an extension of his school environment inserted into his home life.

Her voice bore no distress, so that settled the worry of divorce. He felt relieved for Dad's sake, at least, but that meant Tanner still had to live with her. Sharon would remain as a blight on his life. The wedding of Mr. Stephen Malone to Ms. Sharon Hayden, teacher of modern literature and art at NorthStar Educational 722, was the (comedic) social event of Tanner's sophomore year. Half the school attended. Tanner stood as a reluctant, wide-eyed groomsman in his father's second wedding in front of dozens of gawking classmates. Most of his peers had mustered the decency not to giggle at him. Most.

Tanner looked back at her awkwardly and repeated, as non-confrontationally as he could, "What's going on, Sharon?"

She sighed. "Your father and I are doing some preliminary packing."

"Preliminary packing for what?"

Her face glowed. She looked like she was about to burst. "He got the promotion and we're moving to Arcadia in a week!"

"Dad!" Tanner shouted. He didn't mirror Sharon's excitement.

His father hustled down the stairs to meet him. Like Sharon, he still bore the youth and vitality of a man half his actual age thanks to gene therapy treatments. Though not an athletic man, he was trim enough, his hair cut short and his clothing just the sort of casual chic that Sharon preferred.

"Hey, Tanner, I . . . oh . . . I can see your mother already told you . . ." Stephen's voice trailed off.

Tanner gritted his teeth. "She's not my mom."

Sharon stiffened, took in a sharp breath, and walked into the next room.

Stephen's pained expression was lost on her as she left. "Tanner, you know how much it would mean to her if—"

"Moving off-planet in a week? A whole nother system?"

"Yeah." Stephen sighed. "Yeah, I wanted to tell you myself. I guess Sharon just . . . couldn't contain the excitement."

"Jesus, Dad! I'm happy for you, too, but you know where I am right now! I've got graduation before the end of the week and I've got my lab internship coming up," Tanner said. "Did you remember that? The reason I put off university applications?"

"Yes! Of course I remembered that. And the internship. We already knew you didn't want to move to Arcadia when this came up on the horizon, though, didn't we?"

Tanner rolled his eyes, reading the worst implications into the question. Arcadia was the sort of planet where the wealthy went on vacation. Promotion or not, it was an expensive place to live. More so when one had dependents. Stephen's raise would just barely meet the cost of living there. Sharon had no guarantees of a job of her own. "So what's the plan?" he asked. "Can I stay here for a while after you're gone? I can't, can I?"

"Well, no, we had to notify the residence manager so we wouldn't end up paying for another full month. But I'm sure we could make some sort of arrangements. Maybe you could stay with one of your friends?"

"My friends who are all going away to universities?"

"All of them? Right, right, sorry." Stephen took a deep breath and straightened up. "Well, Tanner, it's just something we'll have to figure out right away."

Tanner blinked. "Dad, do you even know what tomorrow is?"

"Sure," Stephen said, "and that's tomorrow's problem. Deal with that, get through that test—do good—and then worry about living arrangements. In the worst case, I'm sure your internship can qualify you for some sort of student loan program.

"Look," he added, somewhat lamely, "I'm sure we'll think of something."

Tanner sank into the couch and put his face in his hands. He knew his father was focused on pleasing Sharon. That wasn't anything new, and, ultimately, Tanner couldn't hold it against him. His mother's death had crushed son and father alike. Sharon lifted Stephen's spirits when Tanner thought nothing would. They were good for one another, and genuinely happy together. As embarrassing as it was to have his father fall in love with and then marry one of his teachers, Tanner endured it all for the sake of putting Dad back together again.

Yet Sharon fit every stereotype of flighty artists as if it were a conscious goal. She also seemed to see Tanner as a constant reminder of her predecessor . . . who had always been the real source of strength in the family. Stephen's late first wife was also a much more sensible and practical person.

Tanner's hands fell away from his face. He stared off at the opposite wall. Stephen sat beside him. Having gone through gene therapy at twenty-five, Stephen could easily have been taken for Tanner's older brother rather than his father. "I've got to do this, Tanner," he said. "I know you think it's about Sharon, but it's not just that. The company won't wait on me."

"I know," Tanner said glumly. "I just . . . you could've timed it better in telling me."

"A lot of things could've been timed better."

• • •

"We begin with basic astronomy," the computerized voice of the Test explained. The spoken words also flashed across the screen in text.

"Okay." Tanner sighed gratefully. He was good with astronomy. At least he could start off with one of his strengths.

"Using the palette provided, illustrate and label your star system. Please remember to consider proper scale, distances, and orbits."

Tanner's jaw dropped. "Wait, what?" The instructions repeated, but he paid them little heed. The scope of the question stunned him. It would be one thing to label a picture or provide an answer in text, but to draw one from scratch? And to create a proper scale all on his own?

The palette program offered by the computer wasn't like anything he'd ever used, either. Struggling with its counterintuitive interface, Tanner created images of the star of Archangel and its planets. "Ambrose, Michael, Raphael, Jerome, Gabriel, Uriel, Ophanim, Gregoria, Augustine," he murmured to the tune of the nursery song. The rhyme scheme never really fit. Nor did the rhythm. *This is what happens when you let popes name planets*, he thought with a grumble.

Shit. Do I need to do moons, too? Asteroid belts? Inhabited stations? Do I need to work out their orbits, too? He scribbled out answers, adjusting as best he could. Tanner noticed the clock ticking down and realized what a time sink this project could be. He wrapped it up as quickly as he could and moved on. *Hopefully they'll ask some actual astronomy questions*, he mused.

"Using the palette provided, illustrate and label the solar system."

"Holy shit, really?" he interrupted.

"Please remember that you are in an academic setting and choose your language carefully. Using the palette provided . . ."

An hour into the Test, Tanner knew he was in real trouble. Normally calm and competent at math, Tanner now found himself making simple arithmetic errors. He caught and corrected some before submission as final answers, but not all of them, and he knew it.

He thought, repeatedly, that he should've forced himself to eat something before leaving the house. He could have consciously controlled that much, at least. Forcing himself to sleep wasn't possible, so he'd lain awake all night—which, with the planet Michael's nineteen-hour rotational period, was somewhat subjective. Tanner had stared at the ceiling all night, thinking about where he could possibly stay during his internship, how much rent and food and all the rest would cost, and what he would do if all the stress made him blow the Test so badly that it affected his loan standings. He thought about how much his internship meant to his plans to become a planetary survey specialist. He'd always dreamt of exploring new habitable and near-habitable worlds, of being the guy who got to make the real discoveries and slap whatever names he wanted on every new fungus or bug or whatever turned up.

Now he could only think of his dismal chances of attaining his dream job if he blew everything.

"Remember," the computer noted at the beginning of each section, "this portion of the evaluation is timed."

"No shit," he mumbled. "It's all timed." He let the time tick away. Better to be a little late than completely wrong.

He found no periodic table of the elements for reference in the chemistry section. Several of the questions were misleading. Others lacked critical details. The clock kept ticking away.

Life sciences, encompassing some of his greatest academic strengths, turned out to be considerably shorter than he expected. His hopes of making up for lost time and points soon evaporated. The questions were either of dry, rote knowledge or of interdisciplinary matters that required some pondering.

Before long, Tanner had the response pad in his lap. He gave up on answering orally when his mouth felt too dry and he stuttered so much the testing program kept displaying errors in his answers that required correction. He stared, blankly, at the extended-response question on the paper-thin pad.

"Discuss in detail the unique role producer organisms on Raphael played in enabling early settlement and terraforming projects in the Archangel system," the pad read.

Tanner knew this. He had practically written this answer two years ago in another exam, one without such dramatically high stakes. Early surveys of Raphael revealed an oxygen-rich atmosphere without nearly enough plants to explain it. Eventually, scientists discovered that metabolic processes in a large swath of its smaller animals closely mimicked photosynthesis. Tanner knew all about it. He knew who the discoverers were, could reconstruct several pertinent DNA sequences of Raphael's prairie rats from memory . . . except now he stared at the black response pad, drawing a complete blank. He didn't know where to start.

"Remember," the pad flashed helpfully, "this portion of the evaluation is timed."

• • •

Three hours and four essays of thinly disguised bullshit later, Tanner staggered out of his testing cube and squinted at the comparatively bright lights of the testing center. Someone promptly punched him in the arm.

"I have kicked ass all morning and, oh my God, Tanner, are you okay?" Madelyn's voice shifted from pride to surprise as Tanner turned his head. His classmate grabbed his wrist. Ordinarily, Tanner would've been all too happy to have Madelyn grab him. Maybe this was what he'd done wrong all along? Maybe he should've played more pathetic with her?

"Hi," he croaked. "Um . . . I'm kind of stressed. How much time do we get for lunch?"

"We've got forty-five minutes. What's wrong?" Concern wasn't one of her normal expressions. It didn't mesh with her normal looks of "competitive," "driven," "amused," or "heart-wrenchingly beautiful."

"All my plans for life after school died in a fire last night. I've barely slept and haven't eaten." He frowned. "There's a cafeteria here, right?"

"Screw that. Let's go get some real food. I'm buying."

"You don't have to do that." Tanner knew she meant well, but he also knew they wouldn't be alone long. Madelyn would inevitably pick up several hangers-on before they got out of the building without even intending it. Such things just happened to her.

"Well, I was going to tell you you're buying, but that's before I realized you just pulled your face out of a black hole. Come on. Mush."

"Hey, Madelyn, where are you going for lunch?" asked someone behind her. Tanner sighed. She had made it three whole sentences before a friend appeared.

"Uh, wherever Tanner takes me," she replied. "We've got to go talk. I'll see you later." Surprised but grateful, Tanner let Madelyn direct him into the blazing, sunny streets outside.

"Wow." She stopped to stretch stiff limbs. "I can't wait to get off this rock."

"You know where you're going yet?"

"It's the Sol system for me. On my way to Annapolis."

Tanner blinked. "Annapolis? You mean the Academy?"

Madelyn grinned. "Yeah. I'm accepted, soon as I graduate."

"I didn't think you were the military type."

"Are you kidding? I spent every recess period playing space marines in school."

"When, before puberty?"

"Don't go all sexist on me, jerk!" she said with a laugh. "There's a whole galaxy of ass out there to kick, and I've got just the feet for it."

Tanner shook his head. "You're more man than I'll ever be and more woman than I'll ever be with. When are you leaving?"

"Couple days after graduation." Madelyn shrugged. "It's kind of sad. Not so many graduation parties for me. Anyway, what's going on with you?"

"I crashed this whole test already," Tanner answered, rubbing his eyes.

"What? You? No way. I thought this thing was written just for you. God, that biology section was huge, and the astronomy stuff . . . crap, I sat there thinking, 'Can't I just draw this out?' I'm better with visuals!"

Tanner stopped in his tracks. "You're serious."

"Well, yeah. What?"

His eyes narrowed. "Those sons of bitches," he growled. "The computer probably tailors the Test to hit you in all your weak points and to avoid your strengths!"

"Oh, whatever, people say that every year," Madelyn countered with a roll of her eyes. "Don't buy into every conspiracy theory you hear. You know better. Anyway, something bigger than that is going on with you. Spill."

He swallowed his anger. He had no way to prove his suspicions, anyway. "I got home last night and found Sharon packing. Dad got a lead designer spot on Arcadia, only he has to leave in about a week, and that leaves me out in the dust. I just found it all out about twelve hours ago."

Madelyn whistled appreciatively. "What are you going to do?"

"Hell if I know. But I'm already in trouble. I didn't think I'd have this many problems on the Test. All my plans counted on having to pay for only half a year of school at the absolute worst. If I come out with twenty K or worse in debt, a bunch of my financial support floats away. I looked for hours for a loan for situations like mine and came up with nothing. I just can't stop thinking about what the hell I'm supposed to do now, and it's only making it worse in there," he finished, jerking his thumb at the evaluation center.

"You can't do anything about all that today. You'll just have to focus past it."

"I know, I know," he groaned. "But I just . . . can't. I need a plan."

"Well, the astroecology thing was part of what made your university applications look so good, right? So it's still worth doing even if you rack up more debt. You've got friends. Lots of friends. I'm sure you can crash at someone's house."

"I don't have friends who are in any position to take me on as a burden, even if I were willing to do that to them. Almost all my friends are leaving for universities, anyway."

"Okay . . . stay with my family. You can have my room while you do your internship, at least until you come up with a better plan."

"I can't do that."

"You can. My parents always liked you better than all my other guy friends."

"They did?"

"You're the only one who wasn't obviously trying to get me naked."

"What, they respected my subtlety?"

"Yes. Shut up. Okay, you're right, that won't work . . ." She thought for a long moment. "Fine. Do what I'm doing. Join the military."

"What? Are you kidding?"

She threw him an indignant look. "What's wrong with that? Your mother was a veteran!"

He blinked, surprised she would remember personal trivia about him like that. "There's nothing wrong with it, I just . . . Can you honestly see me running around with a gun? I've never been in a fight in my life! I'm the guy who got Professor Jenkins fired over how he treated the lab animals!"

"You don't have to go infantry or marines. There are more noncombat roles than you can count."

"Besides, where would I even begin? It's too late to get into any of the academies for this year. Applying for admission for next year doesn't do me any good for the situation I'm in this year. It's still the same problem."

Madelyn shook her head again. "You couldn't get into an academy, anyway. No team sports. I told you to go out for some teams. Might've taught you to keep your eye on the ball at a time like this," she said, nudging him gently. "Maybe some time in uniform would do you good. Anyway, there's no academy option you could swing at this point. I'm saying you should enlist."

He looked at her like she had two heads. "You seriously think I'm the military type?"

"I think you can do anything you put your mind to. You're smart."

He thought about it as they walked. "Join the fleet?"

"No. Not the fleet. The Union fleet stinks for enlisteds. I've done my research. Only good way to go into the Union military is as an officer, like I'm doing. And don't join a corporate security force; they're just debt traps. You'll never get out again. But you could sign up with the Archangel Navy. It's actually got some pretty good options."

"I don't know. I thought about doing a reserve term for the educational benefits, but Dad hated the idea. Said it'd screw up all my plans. I looked into it and it turned out he was right."

"No, don't go reserves. I looked at that, too. Even the regular Archangel Navy treats those guys like a joke. No, you'll have to go full-term. It's only five years."

"Five years? Everyone else will be done with university by then!"

"Life's not a race. This isn't about everyone else. It's about you. And don't act like it's a waste of time. You know it's not."

Tanner scowled. "You really think enlisting is a good idea?"

"It's not as good as the options you had yesterday," Madelyn answered honestly, "but you're running out of those, right? And you said that you need to feel like you've got a plan to get through the Test today. So, there's today's plan. If you really do crash, you'll go see a recruiter."

"I guess I could . . ."

"You know you could. I'm surprised you didn't think of this on your own."

"I just . . . didn't really consider it. Dad would go into convulsions."

"No, Mrs. Hayden-Malone will go into convulsions 'cause it'll remind her of your mom." Madelyn smirked. "But she'll be convulsing on Arcadia, so screw her. We should all be so lucky."

They walked together silently. He hadn't expected Madelyn to remember so much about his family situation. To his thinking, they had never been close despite his efforts to the contrary. Finally Madelyn prodded him with an elbow.

"Fine! Fine. I'll do it. If I crash the Test, I'll join the Archangel Navy."

"Good," she said. She fell quiet for a moment and grinned again. "So you should know, there's a rule about fraternization between enlisteds and officers."

"Huh?" Tanner blinked.

"If you enlist, you can't see me naked," she taunted with a wink.

Tanner moaned and looked at the ground at his feet. "What about before then?"

"Shut up and buy me lunch."

• • •

"In less than fifteen hundred words, compare and contrast the themes found in the major works of pre-Expansion literature with the common themes of post-Expansion literature."

That question couldn't be serious. Tanner read it over and over again, even tracing it with his finger and reading it aloud to make sure he didn't miss something as a result of fatigue. Nothing this broad or vague appeared in practice tests. Pre-Expansion literature? All of it? Going all the way back to, what, *The Epic of Gilgamesh*? Or just Anglophile literature? Did the scorers intend for respondents to focus on their own systems and cultures?

Frowning, Tanner reached for the "Help" menu at the bottom right of his screen to summon a test proctor. While he waited, he continued to ponder the essay prompt. What counted as a major work? Did he have to justify the "majorness" of his selections in his answer? Did they expect him to limit himself to works studied in NorthStar classes? The curriculum changed almost annually. Variations existed between schools.

An older man in the bland, business-casual clothes that everyone seemed to wear here entered Tanner's testing space. "Hello. Did you summon help?"

"Yeah, thanks for coming so fast." Tanner gestured back to the question. "Is that all there is to this question? It seems awfully broad."

The proctor read it aloud. "It seems pretty straightforward to me."

"But there are no qualifiers or context at all," Tanner said. "Not everything written after Expansion began is actually about the Expansion era. The only accurate similarity is that they all have to do with the 'human condition' or something really broad on that line. And am I supposed to just pick examples out of thin air? This is open to hundreds of thousands of books. I have no way of knowing who's going to read my essay and whether or not they have any familiarity with the texts I choose."

"Ah," the proctor said with a reassuring tone, "don't fret over that. Certified scorers grade only a random sampling of tests. The vast majority of responses go through the scoring AI, and that's loaded up with every work you could name. I wouldn't worry about it lacking familiarity with anything you cite."

Tanner's eyes practically shot out of his head. "An AI?"

"Yes." The proctor smiled. "It just came online last year."

"What, for checking grammar and mechanics? That's not a true AI."

"Oh, it'll do that, too, but it also evaluates the content of your essays."

"My *literary analysis* is going to be judged by a fucking computer?"

"Son, you need to watch your language," said the proctor.

Nothing about this appeared in any of the published updates on the Test. Tanner had dutifully read them for the last three years. "You're telling me that NorthStar has come up with a computer that can accurately judge the validity of compelling arguments about a potentially limitless range of entirely subjective issues?"

The older man's eyes fluttered with worry for a moment. He wasn't used to these sorts of arguments coming from teenagers. "Er, yes," he said when he finally caught up to the question.

"Bullshit. 'Artificial intelligence' is just an advertising term to sell expensive programs to ignorant consumers. Do you even know what you're talking about?"

"Young man," the stiffening proctor growled, "apart from not knowing how to address your elders respectfully, you seem like a bright boy. I'm sure you'll come up with something adequate."

Tanner's eyes flared. So did his suspicions. "Do students in the Society of Scholars program get graded by real people or by this alleged artificial intelligence?" The proctor inhaled sharply. He opened his mouth to speak, but Tanner cut him off. "I'm right, aren't I? We've got to pay thousands of extra credits just to have our tests graded by live human beings!"

"Son, the longer you whine about this, the less time you have on the Test. Just do the best you can." With that, he walked out.

"There's no such thing as an AI!" Tanner shouted at his back.

• • •

Pure rage probably wasn't the best emotional state for writing a comparative literary analysis, but Tanner pushed through it. The literature portion of the Test was the shortest, reflecting NorthStar's view of the worth of the subject. Aside from the essay, there were a mere twenty vaguely worded multiple-choice questions.

From there, his test shifted to social studies, another of his usual strong points. The Test strongly emphasized rote memorization of names and dates. As with so much of the rest of the Test, Tanner found many of the questions entirely arguable.

The timer ticked down. Three short-answer questions to go. Ten minutes.

"Briefly describe the primary points laid out in the Articles of the Union of Humanity. What did it do? What didn't it do?"

Tanner expected this. It was easy enough. Then, as he began to write, he stopped. *What determines "primary"?* he wondered. *Is my answer supposed to be exhaustive? Shit. This is another goddamn trick question.*

He answered as best he could: "The Articles established a confederation of human worlds (a semantic irony cherished by historians). They established and limited the office of the president and general assembly; bound member worlds to mutual defense and unified diplomacy with regard to nonhuman powers; commissioned the Union fleet and set funding quotas for said fleet; and set up basic regulations to astrogation.

"They pointedly did not ban war between member states, establish basic human rights, create a universal currency, or codify extradition standards."

Seven minutes, sixteen seconds.

Next prompt: "Illustrate the difficulties encountered in forging stable, mutually supportive alliances between the Union and its starfaring nonhuman neighbors."

Oh God. He knew NorthStar's scorers wanted to hear that aliens were just jerks who didn't understand economics. Seven minutes wasn't long enough to come up with bullshit that would please a corporate scoring machine. There was only time to tell it like it was.

"Human self-interest and the fractiousness of our governmental and corporate entities have been the primary obstacles for the influential Krokinthian and Nyuyinaro states. Krokinthian negotiators walked out on treaty discussions to officially end the Expansion War within the first two minutes of talks. They later cited an expectation of bad faith negotiation on the part of the Solar Coalition. The Krokinthian viewpoint can be supported by one hundred fifty years of broken treaties on the part of the Coalition and the Union as its successor state."

Wrapping that up with a few more points of support took another minute. Tanner winced as he submitted his answer. His social studies teachers had been far from corporate loyalists. While they had broadened his worldview as a person, they didn't exactly train him to give responses palatable to people—and computer programs, probably—who graded with a pro-corporate bias.

Three minutes, twenty seconds.

Dammit! Standard weights and measures! How could he forget that for the Articles? Son of a bitch! Tanner looked for a way back to the previous question to enter corrections, but found none.

"Provide a brief narrative of your system's foundation and social development. What government or corporate entity was the system's primary sponsor in colonization? How is your planet's population still similar to its founders? How has the population changed?"

"Who the fuck wrote this test?" Tanner screamed in aggravation. This was insane. How open-ended and vague could this get? How could Tanner even be certain his Test would be scored with the right system and planet on the rubric?

Three minutes, seven seconds. Tanner got ahold of himself. Once more, he had no time to come up with anything fancy.

"The primary colonizing sponsor in the development of the Archangel system was neither corporate nor governmental, but rather the Catholic Church. During and after the Expansion War, the Church saw interstellar colonization as a way to spread the faith and ensure its own survival. The Church leveraged its considerable resources to finance Archangel's initial terraforming and colonial development. The majority of early colonists were expected to be religious conservatives.

"However, many applicants, particularly those from North America and Western Europe, either deliberately deceived the Church's selection process for colonists or later reconsidered their positions upon arrival. Regardless, many colonists still harbored a great attachment for the concept of a separation of church and state. Political struggles such as those over birth control and the immigration of non-Catholics broke the Church's hold on political power within the Archangel system."

Tanner didn't like any of his answers, but then, he didn't have much time left to come up with anything better. On an ordinary school test, he would've been among the first finished. He usually had a lot of time to kill on exam days. The fifty-plus minutes he lost by being late hurt him badly.

• • •

"This completes the Union Academic Investment Evaluation," said the warm, feminine, soulless voice of the testing cubicle. "Please wait."

Tanner's shoulders slumped. He remained jittery after lunch, but he at least felt a bit better after talking with Madelyn and coming up with a backup plan for the next few years. Still, he thought, he might not need that plan. He could potentially come up with another option. And, really, perhaps he'd simply read too much into the questions on the exam. Maybe he was more upset with his performance than he needed to be.

Trying to release stress, Tanner stretched his arms and legs out where he sat. He wondered how long it would take to get his final results back. Then the screen flashed again.

"Your financial obligation for your compulsory educational benefits is 67,879 credits."

TWO

Theater

"We talk a lot about hope and aspirations this time of year. We talk about awakening potential and reaching for the stars. We talk about achievement. About the long, hard road through twelve years of primary education. About how 'mandatory' education is only the beginning of what is truly mandatory to succeed in today's economy. We tell success stories.

"What we only briefly acknowledge, however, is the fact that on this day, on the day of the Test, hundreds of thousands of Archangel's young people and, indeed, many millions throughout the Union are hit with their first major financial debts. While we highlight our most successful students, while we encourage every student to reach for the stars, the vast majority have lead weights attached to their feet."

The holographic image of President Gabriel Aguirre shrank away as if the viewer floated back in the air into the audience. Seated in the foreground and now pivoting in her chair to face the viewer was one of the news program's main anchors. She sat in an auditorium seat dressed in a sharp, flattering suit, but anyone watching the broadcast knew that most of this was computer imaging done after the president's speech. It looked as if he continued to speak in the background, but in reality the anchor's presentation had been put together during and after the speech. The anchor most likely spoke once the seats around her were completely empty—or, just as likely, the anchor had never physically been at the speech at all.

"Speaking at the prestigious Michelangelo Academy, President Aguirre has chosen the day of the Union Academic Investment Evaluation to attack not only the corporations that run our schools, but indeed the very essence of student financial accountability. While President Aguirre called on all of Archangel to remember the passengers and crew of the *Aphrodite*, he noted that information was still coming in and chose to push on with his speech."

Once more, the news presentation shifted to an up close holographic view of the president. His salt-and-pepper hair and the mild signs of aging in his face gave him an air of maturity, but like any man of means, he was quite a bit older than he looked. The spontaneity and energy in his speech were as much a matter of long-polished skill as they were a matter of natural passion.

"This system evolved out of pressure to ensure that students took responsibility for their own education. The Union required, and still requires, an educated populace for its own survival and prosperity. But who should foot the bill? Society? Not everyone has a child. Parents? That would create a daunting economic barrier for many would-be mothers and fathers interested in having a child, all while the Union and most of its member worlds so strongly encouraged raising families.

"The answer our forefathers came to was simple: the student should pay for it. Naturally, a parent could choose to help, but the final legal obligation should land on the student, who at graduation is expected by society to be a responsible young adult. And that answer," Aguirre said, pausing and shaking his finger just subtly enough that the right cameras would catch him innocently pointing toward the NorthStar builder's seal on one wall of the auditorium, "came from the very corporations who brought humanity to the stars—and the very corporations who run the highly profitable business of education today."

"Tanner, are you seriously watching the news?" broke in a live voice. Swaying somewhat on her feet, the young woman moved into the broad kitchen with an empty glass in her hand and an amused look on her face. She wore an adorable party dress and heels much too high for her obvious level of inebriation.

He looked up guiltily. Despite treating his sunburns earlier, his face remained quite red from his run to the test site that morning. A shower and nicer clothes made him look like less of a disaster. The presence of friends and a shift from panic to resignation had at least settled his nerves. "I was just gonna be in here for a few minutes," he said.

Music and loud, happy voices drifted in from the various exits. Nathan Spencer's kitchen was bigger than the whole bottom floor of Tanner's home.

The presidential hologram kept speaking. "Scoring systems and academic expectations have crept, inexorably and constantly, toward ever-higher requirements. Now mere proficiency isn't enough. It's not enough if your essay simply answers the test question and gives evidence. It isn't enough anymore to communicate effectively, to understand day-to-day math and science. Now it's only the very top scorers who eliminate their educational debts."

Heather Verde pointed at the image of the president as she walked in on wobbling feet. "Turn him down or turn him off," she ordered. "This is my moment of triumph, and he's making me sad, and I didn't vote for that guy."

"Our system now puts the expectation on every student to be well above average," Aguirre said, again flashing his knowing grin. "I look out in this auditorium here and I see an awful lot of people who know exactly what you get when you claim that everyone is above average."

The anchor replaced the president once more. "The president's speech is already being portrayed by his advisers and leaders of his party as a shot across the bow for NorthStar, the Lai Wa Corporation, and other education providers. We have reaction from opposition party leaders and from corporate—"

"You weren't old enough to vote for him," noted Tanner as he cut the projection.

"Well, I won't when he runs again and I am old enough," she said. "He's a terrible Catholic."

"*You're* a terrible Catholic," teased Tanner.

She gasped dramatically. "Don't say that!" Then she looked down at her glass. "Oh, I am a terrible Catholic. And I'm drunk. I'm still not supposed to drink yet. My mom's gonna kill me."

Tanner started to laugh, but then he saw Heather's face screw up into a prelude to wailing tears. He immediately came around the island counter full of *hors d'oeurves* and put his arm around Heather's shoulder. "You're not, I was kidding. You are a fine Catholic."

"No, I'm not!" she argued. "You don't even know! I've had my earbuds in so I could study during mass every time my family went to church for the last three months! And then I didn't tell the priest at confession!"

Again, Tanner had to control his laughter. It was a simple fact of life in the Archangel system: one never knew who was a genuine believer and who was simply a cultural Catholic like himself.

"Hey, don't be upset," Tanner said. "You walked out of there not owing a goddamn credit, right?"

Heather sniffled hard and nodded. She also hit him on the shoulder. "Don't say that," she mumbled. "*You're* a terrible Catholic."

"Well, yeah."

Heather nudged his shoulder again in disapproval. "Anyway . . . you were saying? I did good on the Test, so . . . ?"

"And you can go confess tomorrow or this weekend or whenever and everything will be okay, right?"

She sniffed again. "Yeah."

"So it was all worth it."

"M'kay," she mumbled. "How did you do? Did you wind up owing anything?"

He held his tongue. "A bit," he said.

"That's too bad," Heather replied, making her sympathetic face. It turned to her quizzical face. "Why did I come in here looking for you? Oh!" She nudged him again. "You're not mad at me being valedictorian, are you?"

"Why would I be mad?"

"Because you're not and you maybe could've been. I didn't do it to beat you, y'know. I was just doing my best."

"Heather, it's fine. I wasn't even number two or three. I was number five."

"Because I didn't want to make people feel bad."

"Right, I know."

"It's nothing personal."

Christ, he thought, *she's really drunk. Or maybe she's never been drunk before.*

"So you're not changing your plans? Nathan said he offered you a ride home from the Test and you had him take you to a recruiting station for the system navy."

"Yeah. I did."

She looked shocked. "Tanner, you can't join the navy! You've never been in a fight in your life!"

"That's . . . one of the things my stepmother said about it, yeah," he winced, scratching his head.

"Why don't you want to go to university? It's not because of me, is it? Because even if I did better in school than you, that doesn't mean you're not smart! You're sooo smart, Tanner! You figured out things in school before I did sometimes!"

"Did Nathan tell you I was in here?" he asked suspiciously.

Heather's eyes widened. "He did," she said, "because he thought you might be avoiding me!"

"Uh-huh."

She looked over her shoulder at the closed kitchen door and then turned to Tanner to whisper, "I think Nathan likes me. He said he might visit me at Oxford. That's on Earth, y'know."

"Yeah, I know where it is. What the hell, is everyone going to school on Earth? When did Nathan get accepted to someplace there?"

"No, no, he's taking a gap year," Heather corrected, slurring mildly. "That's when you take a year off between graduation and university so you can travel. Only his may be a little longer than a year. I guess his grandparents promised it to him if he kept his debts low on the Test."

Again, he held his tongue. He knew what a gap year was. "Well, if you want to make sure he comes to see you on Earth, you should maybe leave a serious impression on him while you're both still here, right?" Tanner suggested. "Like maybe tonight?" He saw her eyes light up in agreement. "Let's go find him."

He ushered Heather out of the kitchen through the dining room and its lush spread of food to rejoin the party. More than half their school and a portion of several others were in attendance. It made for a bigger party than anything Tanner had seen before at the huge house.

Few knew of his plight. Many had their own debt issues now but had resigned themselves to such months and even years ago. As the president said, burdensome educational debts were an accepted fact of life for the young.

They found Nathan on a couch, surrounded by his peers. Whatever topic they had before Tanner arrived with Heather died as the valedictorian immediately leapt into Nathan's lap. He feigned happiness at her arrival until she looked away, and then he shot Tanner a frustrated glare.

Tanner merely smiled and waved back before disappearing into another hallway. Heather was a lovely girl; Nathan had nothing to complain about there . . . except for a little awkwardness and self-absorption.

Roaming through the house, Tanner found any number of friends but felt less inclined to talk to them. Nobody needed to hear of his woes on a night like tonight. Nor could anyone likely help him. He kept up a brave front, smiling, waving, and occasionally conversing, but largely just drifting through the party.

I may never see most of these people again.

Some would move to other spots on Michael. A few would relocate to other planets in the system, and some beyond. A good number would likely remain in the city of Geronimo.

Tanner hadn't planned on staying. He loved the desert and the heat, but he grew up feeling that adulthood meant moving away from home. Both of his parents had done that. Now he had no way to stay and only one way to leave.

"Hey! Tanner!" a voice shouted as he passed the open doors to the balcony. He turned to see Madelyn playfully pushing through a swarm of young men, clad in a form-hugging green silk dress that threatened to stop his heart. For all he knew, she had gone straight from the Test to a salon.

She threw her arms around him, hugging him tightly and then letting go to take a look at him. "Nice burn. Life any better?"

"I'm not really sure how to answer that," he admitted.

"C'mon." She gestured to a free portion of the wide balcony. "Let's talk."

"Hey, Madelyn!" called a voice. "Gymnastics team photo!"

"Five minutes," she answered back over her shoulder, waving them off but still flashing a grin. She tugged Tanner over to the balcony edge. "So what happened?"

"I got on my holocom and did some research after the Test while I waited for Nathan to finish. He thinks I'm crazy for even considering this," Tanner added. "But it's just like you said. System militia fleet is the better option for enlisting. I read up on the credit-matching payoff program they offer for educational debt. Seems like a worthwhile thing financially."

"How did things go with the recruiter?"

"I'm definitely qualified, at least. We talked, filled out the paperwork, he went over my records and his eyes lit up like it was Christmas bonus time or something. I get the feeling they reject a lot of applicants." Nothing in his tone conveyed excitement. "I didn't commit to anything. He said he'd hold a place for me that could have me ship out next week. Then I went home to think about it and talk to my parents."

"How'd that go?"

"Sharon flipped out, just like we both knew she would."

"Yeah. What about your dad?"

"He didn't know which way to go. Mom hardly ever had anything bad to say about her time in the service, but he kinda feels the same way as Sharon. Mostly I just think he doesn't see me as soldier material. But he didn't say a lot. Seemed like it only just then sank in how screwed up my situation is and he felt guilty about it.

"I dunno, thing is . . . Sharon wasn't wrong." Tanner frowned, looking out over the balcony as he spoke. "She said the military preys on people in bad financial situations like mine. Said they take advantage of the whole system. Said they'd work to change me and make me more callous and comfortable with hurting people. And she said that virtually all wars are just the young and poor like me dying for the lies of old rich people. And she's right."

Whatever Madelyn's first response might have been, she bit it back. "Yeah." She sighed. "Yeah, I can't entirely argue all that. Still. Sometimes the lies are all on one side."

"No, I get that. But it's a lot to think about. She asked me if I wanted to be a tool for someone else's political agenda, and . . . well, I don't."

"It's not always like that."

"You don't get much say in things when it *is*, though. I'm not worried about Archangel going on some imperialist rampage or something, but it's still a lot to think about." He turned to face her. "I'm not trying to talk you out of anything."

"I've thought all this through for myself." Madelyn shrugged. "I've got faith in how all this works. I know how far I'll go and what I won't do. If you're gonna enlist, you have to have that in mind, too. You don't get to quit if you don't like the job." She looked at him thoughtfully. "You seem like she talked you out of it."

"I'm still thinking. There are reasons to go. There are reasons not to go. I don't exactly have a lot of great alternatives." He fought with whether or not to say the rest. "I don't want to do it to impress you. I know that's not even on your mind," he added when he saw her blink. "I'm just saying . . . y'know?"

She let out another sigh, gripping the top of the balcony rail with frustration. "Yeah, I know."

He glanced over his shoulder. "How many guys have given you last-minute heartfelt confessions?"

"In the last week? Three. Four, now."

"Oh, please, I don't count. You've known I've had a thing for you for a couple years now. I've asked you out plenty of times. Hey, I'm not bitter. We're fine." He smirked. "But I have to recognize that it could mess with my judgment."

Madelyn nodded. "You've put other people first as long as I've known you," she said, "including your parents and your friends—including me. This one is all about you, Tanner."

"I know." He gestured to the party behind them. "All this is over now, one way or the other. That's how I have to think about it."

"Maybe I *should've* spent more time with you. But yeah. All going away now. And I'm not going to do anything to make myself regret my decisions."

"That'll disappoint a lot of guys." Tanner grinned.

"Madelyn!" cried out a young woman behind them. "Come on! You can talk to him later!"

"I can't help being amazing," Madelyn deadpanned. "It's a burden." She put her hand on his back. "Don't leave the party without seeing me again. I head out for Earth in a couple days and I want to make sure we stay in touch."

She walked away, calling back happily to her other friends. He wondered if he would ever be able to shift emotional gears like that.

The party carried on. He had other people to talk to. For the moment, though, he felt better alone. He keyed the cheap holocom on his wrist again, calling up a much smaller holographic projection this time and returning to the media broadcast he had been watching before.

Icons at the bottom of the projection indicated that this was a live broadcast. With the distance between planets across the star system, that still meant a delay of a few minutes, but Tanner had hoped to catch this particular news conference as it went out. He was a faithful fan of the woman at its center.

Andrea Bennett stood amid a throng of reporters, apparently still somewhere at Michelangelo Academy given their surroundings. Little media gear was evident; journalists typically had their tiny cameras and microphones woven into their clothes. With the audio off, a viewer could have taken the president's press secretary for a tour guide showing off the Academy's artwork collection. Instead, she conveyed grim, tragic news.

"Seven hours ago, elements of the Archangel Navy located three Argent Mark VI Lifeboats containing over six hundred survivors of the luxury liner *Aphrodite* not far outside the legal Faster Than Light line near Augustine. Responding units have also discovered the bodies of many others drifting in space. The liner itself is believed to have left the system.

"Again, we don't have an accurate listing of names of survivors yet. What I can tell you is that the survivors were largely made up of the ship's crew. Recovery is still underway, so I don't have an accurate number for the deceased, but I am told it is in the hundreds."

"Are you saying these people were just spaced?" blurted one journalist.

Andrea swallowed as she nodded. Though she was calm and collected, no one would mistake her demeanor for indifference. "Many were clearly assaulted or killed beforehand, but it appears that most died from exposure to the void.

"Details currently indicate that *Aphrodite* was the victim of open piracy. Investigations are still ongoing and that conclusion is not final. Unfortunately, I have no details on the suspects or their vessel or vessels at this time. Once we've cared for the survivors and interviewed them, we'll share as much detail as possible."

"Do you know when you will have that information?" asked one reporter.

"What about reports that there were children among the dead?" called another. Andrea blinked, but let that one go.

"Is there any explanation of how a liner could be tracked and taken in open space?"

"Which units of the Archangel Navy are on-site? Why weren't they present in time to intervene?"

"The navy corvette *St. Jude* was the first on scene, and was joined within hours by the corvette *St. Patrick* and later the destroyer *Resolute.* The Archangel Independent Shipping Guild has three freighters en route, something that the Guild volunteered of its own initiative and for which they have the thanks of the administration and the people of Archangel.

"All this adds up to diminished safety for our people and visitors," she continued. "The efforts of our men and women in uniform under these circumstances are exemplary, but all of this clearly underscores the need for an expanded home defense capability."

"What about the Union fleet?" asked Herman Deng of the always-hostile Uriel Media Service. "Corporate security forces?"

"That would be a great question to ask the Union fleet and our friends in corporate security, Herman"—Andrea frowned—"because I seem to recall a significant portion of our defense budget going to contracts for NorthStar and CDC patrols. Yet they're nowhere to be found on this one. As this appears to be standard operating procedure for our alleged partners—"

"Andrea," interrupted Deng, "the president just wrapped up a speech attacking Archangel's corporate partners for their performance in the educational field. Now you're calling them out for their security measures, too?"

Though she never lost her composure, Tanner noticed the brief flare of her eyes. "Yes, Herman," she said, "that's exactly what I'm doing. They can answer for themselves all they want, but once again I imagine it'll just be empty rhetoric. Words are cheap, so we'll undoubtedly get plenty of them."

"Does the president believe an expanded Archangel militia will be effective in solving this problem?" asked another journalist.

"We're talking about hardened criminals and mass murderers," Andrea replied. "They aren't going to give up piracy if someone asks them nicely."

With that, the press conference came to an end. Tanner turned off his holocom, leaning backward on the balcony railing. He looked up into the dark skies above and thought about what lay out there.

• • •

Predictably, Andrea heard a cacophony of shouted questions as she turned away. Her stride and poise held firm until she turned a corner. Then her shoulders sagged, her eyes looked skyward, and a long sigh escaped her throat.

She found the president's chief of staff waiting for her. Victor Hickman stood amid passing staffers and bureaucrats looking at his holocom's media screens. A pair of "aides" accompanied him, both with serious, off-putting scowls on their faces and eyes constantly scanning their surroundings.

"You handled that well," he said.

"I just want to go hide in a closet or under a blanket somewhere."

Victor nodded in understanding. "I know what you mean. You did good, though. Nice jab at the end, too," he observed. "You're good when you improvise."

Andrea huffed. "Sincerity sells. Victor, there were children?"

"Yes. At least twenty-three, maybe more. They're still collecting."

"Oh my God."

"I know." The older man shrugged. "So, what are we going to say when we're inevitably accused of trying to score political points from this?"

Ghoulish though it seemed, Andrea knew she could ward off tears by keeping her head in the game. She took a deep breath. "We say there's no place for politics in the middle of an atrocity like this. Then we point out that if the Union and our corporate 'partners' were holding up their end of our security bargains, our people in uniform would be able to do more than pick up innocent children floating in space." Anger crept into her voice as she spoke.

"Sounds like politics."

"So what? Sometimes politics is also the right thing. We've got the political *and* moral high ground and we'll have the public behind us, and probably support from other systems, too. This story will definitely go interstellar if it hasn't already."

Victor gave a nod. "I agree. So does the president."

"Good," Andrea said. She folded her arms and looked down the hallway for a moment. "They just spaced a bunch of kids? Why would they do that?"

"People like this aren't interested in sorting out child care arrangements."

"They couldn't spare another lifeboat?"

"Those are worth money."

"But they put the crew in lifeboats. That just seems bizarre."

"What's the baseline for normalcy with people like this?" He frowned for a moment, then touched his tiny, transparent earbud and looked back to Andrea. "What do you have on your plate right now?"

"Before this blew up I expected to spend my day following up on the education speech. Now I'm in a holding pattern just like the media out there. It'd help if I could get details as they come in so I can pass them along. Better than leaving everyone to speculate."

"I know," Victor said. "Come with me."

"Where are we going?"

"System security briefing in the president's transport on our way out of here. You just got cleared to be present."

"Really?"

"Senior staff." Victor grinned at her. His thinly disguised bodyguards accompanied them as they walked. "I'll grant you look more 'freshman' than 'senior,' but you've still got the security clearance."

Andrea swatted his arm. "I wasn't sure you could remember that, gramps."

"Well, don't let me catch you playing ball with the other kids on my lawn or anything. My wife already thinks we spend too much time together as it is."

"Yours and everyone else's," she grumbled.

"I know. Beauty's a curse. I get it all the time. Oh, wait, were we talking about you?"

"Where's the president right now?"

"Private meeting with some university chancellor types. Should be out soon. I heard you wrote most of this speech."

"It's fluff. I'd feel better if it pushed concrete initiatives," Andrea admitted. "Right now we're just trying to deepen the wedge."

"It's a good wedge. We keep the pressure up like this, the bastards will have to make further concessions."

"Or not," Andrea said. "It's been tried before." She turned to thank the marine opening the door to the bright, sunny day outside as they continued on. The president's transport sat right outside the auditorium along with several escort flyers. It was noticeably larger than most atmospheric transports, mostly to account for extra armor and flight capacity.

"Yeah, well. If they don't want to play ball, we've got a plan for that, too."

"That sounds ominous." His lack of a reply seemed even more foreboding. "Victor, what aren't you telling me?"

"All that stuff I'm not supposed to tell you yet."

The interior of the president's transport played to the expectations of taxpayers. Its décor and furnishings, comfortable yet conservative, were more suited to a small lounge than an aerial transport. Internal gravity generators and inertial wells kept everything stable and safe in flight.

Holo projections lined the walls depicting star charts, communications links, and ships' statistics. The *Aphrodite* featured prominently on more than a few of them. Andrea surmised that the other ships were those involved in rescue and recovery. She wasn't used to seeing this many active displays in the president's cabin. Nor was she used to seeing more than one or two military types present.

"Admiral Yeoh." Andrea blinked. "I didn't know you were here."

The head of Archangel's navy offered a quick, tight smile. "Hello, Andrea. Naval Academy graduation was just yesterday, so I was in the neighborhood." The thin, endlessly calm woman turned back to the holo screens and the somber mood she'd carried all morning. "Just as easy to be here with the president or at headquarters at a time like this. Or just as hard."

"What do you mean?" Andrea asked. "Is there anything you need?"

Yeoh shook her head. "What I really want right now is my own ship again. My own ship and some sort of a trail on these bastards. But it looks like I won't get either one today."

Andrea nodded. She felt silly for having asked. "We weren't sure whether to follow through on the education speech today," she said, feeling somewhat apologetic. "We received word just before the event began. Couldn't decide if we should have canceled in light of this."

"I've got twins," Yeoh noted. "They get to take that stupid test in a couple years, too. Pirates don't make all that go away."

"No. No, I guess they don't."

The admiral's eyes stayed fixed on the holo screens. "I owed fourteen thousand when I took mine and counted myself lucky. It ate up almost my whole salary during my first couple years at the Academy. Life there was so regimented I didn't exactly have much else to spend money on, but even so I could only imagine what it'd be like if my situation were different." She changed several holo displays with a gesture. "How about you?"

Andrea pursed her lips and looked away. "I, uh"—she faltered—"I didn't actually owe anything when I was finished."

Yeoh's tight-lipped smile returned. "Of course." The older woman chuckled. One of her officers caught her eye with a small wave. "You'll have to excuse me, Andrea."

"No, don't let me keep you," Andrea urged, stepping back quickly. She bumped into another officer, turned, and found an empty chair next to Victor.

The holocom on his wrist beeped before either said anything. He eyed Andrea knowingly. "I've been waiting on this call." He keyed an open channel on his holocom and pointedly didn't enable video display. "Frank, how are—"

"You sent him out there to call us out after everything we've done for you people?" broke in the bitter voice of Frank Andrews, NorthStar Corporation's "adviser" to President Aguirre. "We boosted teacher benefits in Archangel because of you guys and we're still catching hell for it in a dozen other systems."

"Well," Victor tried to interrupt, "maybe you should take better care of your teachers in those other—"

Frank would not be deterred. "We doubled enrollment in the Society of Scholars for you guys. We did the credit-matching payoff deal for your little navy. Do you know what that does to our profits?"

"Oh bullshit, Frank!" Victor countered forcefully. "You guys did that to keep up with Lai Wa when they agreed to the same deal! And those aren't actual credits you're spending. It's all money you save because of capital expense breaks and tax loopholes we created for you. And by the way, thanks for the extra system patrols you agreed to provide. Fat lot of good they did for the people on the *Aphrodite*."

"Son of a—that was *our ship*! You want to know how many of our people were on board, asshole?"

From across the room, Admiral Yeoh caught Victor's eye and gave a soft shake of her head. It was too late to take the comment back, though. Best to redirect.

"Look, Frank, you want to talk real education reform or concrete changes in patrol coverage, I'm all ears," Victor said. "But if you're just calling to bitch at me because the president called a spade a spade, I've got bigger priorities." With that, he cut the line.

"Ought to be fun walking back from exchanges like that come election season." Andrea agreed with everything Victor said, but there was honesty and then there was pragmatism. One had far more value in politics than the other.

"Yeah, well." Victor sighed, smugly happy with himself. "We've got a plan for that, too."

"You going to handle Lai Wa and CDC's guys the same way?"

"Lai Wa's rep is nicer to me. She won't call for another hour at least until her bosses are done micromanaging her. And the CDC guy doesn't get aggressive."

"What's the CDC guy's name?"

"If I could remember that, I'd probably remember what his stupid company's initials stand for."

The entry hatch to the transport opened. President Aguirre walked in with several other staffers and cabinet members. The day's original plans had been ruined by the incident with *Aphrodite*; several officials who had been along for the president's "education day" trips were now mostly superfluous. Others had to be called in. Aguirre's intelligence minister and foreign minister weren't normally a big part of domestic policy events, yet here they were, right beside the minister of finance.

Everyone rose as the president entered. "How are we doing?" he asked. He was already removing his jacket before he sat down in his customary chair.

"If I could have just a moment more, Mr. President?" Admiral Yeoh asked, conferring with another officer in one corner.

"Sure, sure." Aguirre accepted the glass of water handed to him by an aide as he looked to Andrea. "You handled the press conference during the speech?"

"Immediately after, sir," Andrea confirmed. "I gave as much detail as we had to give."

"She might've thrown some punches at the same people you slapped today while she was at it," added Victor.

"Excellent. What about you?"

"Already got the earful from Frank Andrews," Victor replied. "I told him to go to hell without, you know, actually saying, 'Go to hell.'"

"You'd better not. If anyone gets to tell that man to go to hell, it had better be me."

"Due respect, sir, you've talked to him three times at most."

"Yes, but he's symbolic of NorthStar and I'm the symbolic head of state." The engines of the president's transport gave their first soft rumble. The cabin shook only slightly and only for a moment, but enough to demonstrate that they were airborne. Aguirre saw Admiral Yeoh waiting with a patient expression on her face. "Please, admiral, whenever you're ready."

"We have 641 survivors," she began, "all of them crew. Not a single passenger among them. Apparently, the pirates separated them out for a recruitment pitch. About a dozen took the pirates up on the offer. The rest were shoved into the lifeboats."

"That many? In three lifeboats?" asked David Kiribati, head of Archangel's Intelligence Ministry.

Admiral Yeoh nodded. "The pirates had the crew tear out most of the seats and then packed everyone in, standing room only. Someone took the priciest bits from the engines and nav systems on the lifeboats before setting them adrift, too. They waited for hours before they were found. Two of the crew didn't survive the ordeal.

"Most senior officers are still missing. A number of junior officers witnessed the captain's murder. We don't have the first officer, the chief engineer, or the ship's doctor. The chief navigator may not survive his severe injuries.

"We know that *Aphrodite* didn't put up a fight," she continued, calling up a three-dimensional image of the ship in front of her. "We believe she had armament and armor enough to have made that a genuine option, but the captain didn't take it."

"You think it was an inside job?" Aguirre frowned suspiciously.

"I wouldn't go that far, sir," Yeoh replied. "The decision to resist or surrender was entirely the captain's call. Civilian captains have to quickly weigh the prospects of resistance to pirate attacks. Failed resistance generally leads to much greater violence toward a captured crew and passengers than they face if they surrender quickly. From the sound of things, the captain didn't think he could fight off the pirates."

"But you said that his ship was well armed?"

"As you know, we suspect NorthStar skirts Union arms limits with many of their ships. It's in your intelligence briefings. We believe *Aphrodite* is one that could be converted to military use with relative ease, but we don't have proof. As it stands, her weapons are more of a deterrent than anything else. The ship might hold up in a serious fight, but the crew would've been another matter. I suspect that was on the captain's mind when he decided to surrender."

"I see. Why would they go to that effort to spare the crew?" Aguirre asked.

"I'm merely speculating," mused Kiribati, "but as the admiral said, these pirates made a recruiting pitch. It's been done before. A lot of pirate organizations pride themselves on an ideology of personal freedom. You're not exactly making a free choice if the recruiting pitch is 'join or die,' so . . . they may have simply wanted to avoid being seen as hypocrites."

Aguirre snorted derisively. "That's lovely. I'm sorry, admiral. Please go on."

"*Aphrodite* had a passenger listing of 2,744 passengers. As of our last count from the *Resolute*, we have found 896 bodies floating in space. That leaves us looking for 1,848 more."

"Jesus Christ." Aguirre blinked. "We've got everyone we can spare out there looking right now, don't we?"

"Yes, sir, we're already doing that," Yeoh confirmed. "There's more, sir. A significant number of the passengers are highly placed medical professionals, most if not all under contract with NorthStar. They were on their way to a vacation/conference on Michael. We believe they were kept as hostages."

"NorthStar will pay the ransom," Kiribati warned with a deep scowl. "I'll be able to confirm that in a day or two through some sources, but they're probably negotiating it right now."

"Already? We're still sorting out what the hell happened out there, and NorthStar is already talking to these bastards?"

"So much for not negotiating with hostage-takers," Victor put in.

Kiribati just shrugged. "NorthStar has a whole insurance wing for this. It's cost effective."

"I imagine they'll find a way to pass the costs onto us," Victor mused.

"Probably," put in Abdul Shadid, Aguirre's finance minister. "They'll likely scale back their exposure on this end of space, nudge up interest rates and fees on everything here to make up for the losses, and claim that risk like this justifies it."

"And then they'll leave those price hikes in place even after the expenses are covered," Aguirre fumed.

"No real surprises there, sir." Shadid shrugged. "If they do it quickly enough, we can use it to our advantage to obfuscate a little bit more of our own budget shifts," he added, glancing meaningfully at Andrea, "but that's a short-term disguise. In the long term it will obviously be a squeeze."

"The clock's about to run out on that game soon," Aguirre grumbled ominously. He looked up at Yeoh again. "How did they nab the liner, anyway?"

"Most of the freighters and the like that are hit by pirates simply don't see them coming in time and can't run away fast enough once they do," Yeoh explained. "In this case, though, the pirates apparently put up a good disguise as a derelict ship. Legally, *Aphrodite* was obligated to go investigate. By the time she recognized the danger it was too late. She couldn't get away.

"From what the survivors and the lifeboat sensors gathered before the pirates jumped away, this was done with a single ship. She's most likely a second-generation Centurion-class destroyer, which makes her old but easily upgraded. The construction fundamentals on those ships were excellent. She could be a hundred years old and would still stand up well to the destroyers we have today."

"How do pirates get a ship like that?"

Yeoh shrugged. "I could come up with plausible explanations all day long. She could have been part of any number of system navies or corporate security forces. She could've been purchased as surplus last year or maybe her crew mutinied decades ago. But someone has put in enough money to modernize her."

"So what are our prospects for running these bastards down?"

"At the moment, not good," Yeoh admitted. "They could be operating out of the other side of Union space, or even the far side of Krokinthian territory for all we know."

Aguirre turned his attention to Kiribati, wordlessly repeating his question. The spymaster also shrugged. "We'll try to follow up on the ransom transaction and hostage handover, but I don't know how far that'll get us. NorthStar will play it very tight because they won't want to jeopardize their ability to cut such deals in the future. If *Aphrodite* turns up on the surplus market, we'll have a lead, but that could be months down the road. Our best bet is to keep our eyes and ears open and hope that one or more of the crew does something stupid with his share of the loot or gets too drunk and brags too much in the right place."

"Aren't you the one who's saying that the galaxy is too big to watch everywhere at once?" Aguirre snorted. He tapped the table lightly. "Is that it for the bad news?" Yeoh and Kiribati glanced at one another. Aguirre groaned again. "What?"

"The Kingdom of Hashem—" Kiribati began.

"Oh Christ . . ."

"—has lodged demands through diplomatic and military channels that Archangel enhance security facing the Hashemite frontier. They asked whether or not we plan to provide compensation for their subjects lost amid the passengers of the *Aphrodite*, which, given that her point of origin was in Hashemite space, made up a considerable portion of those missing and dead."

"Are they serious?" Aguirre fumed. It was a rhetorical question, of course—the Kingdom was always serious—but his exasperation was sincere. "Their 'frontier' is twice the size of ours and their navy outmatches us four to one."

"Three point five, sir," Admiral Yeoh corrected quietly.

"Still. This is ridiculous. If anyone should be responsible for preventing violence on the Kingdom's frontier, it should be them, not us."

"They have stated that they intend to shift their fleet's strength toward us, but that we should not see this as an act of war."

"Is this what you were handling while I was giving that speech just now? Why didn't anyone tell me this before?" Aguirre tapped his fingers on the table. "That's just what we need. The Hashemites deciding it's time for our once-every-century shooting wars again. Is that everything?"

"At the moment, yes, sir," Yeoh said. Kiribati concurred with a nod.

Aguirre looked around at the other ministers and advisers present. "I want to talk about the long term. Does anyone have anything else they need covered before we can move on?"

Andrea sat up straighter. "Admiral, I got a question at the media briefing about children among the dead. Do you have anything on that?"

Yeoh scowled. "I would appreciate it if you could tamp down on that for now, but between us I can confirm it. At least twenty-six of various ages, maybe more."

"Do you know how that got out?"

"It came from the skipper of *St. Jude*," Yeoh answered, and her scowl only deepened. "That was a violation of protocol. It'll be dealt with. Again, if you could minimize that for now as best you can, it would be better all around. I don't want the media to smell an accurate leak and start trying to encourage more."

"No, I understand and agree," Andrea assured her.

"Anything else you need to know, Andrea?" the president asked.

"Well, you wanted to talk about the long term. Anything I can offer up as concrete steps to deal with piracy will certainly help." She shrugged. "Numbers and action play better than rhetoric."

Aguirre glanced from Kiribati to Yeoh, receiving nods from both. "The defense minister should really be the one to brief you," he said, "but Admiral Yeoh certainly knows what's going on. Admiral, tell her the solid stuff. We'll leave out the maybes for another time."

Andrea sat up in her seat, ready to take more mental notes. Military expansion had been quietly discussed for some time. So far, it had been mostly theoretical. There had been nothing to tell the public. She suspected that planning had pushed beyond theory without her knowing, but she wasn't sure. Yeoh didn't care for leaks.

"We've recently finalized the purchase of three destroyers and contracted domestic shipyards to produce sixteen more corvettes," Yeoh said evenly. The admiral was neither surprised nor distracted by the way Andrea's eyes bulged. "The destroyers come from different sources. A few of the corvettes will be put into service within the next few months. I've already spoken with the defense minister about accelerating delivery of the rest. We should see them in the yards within the week. We're also in negotiations for a cruiser, and things look promising."

Still trying to decide which of her multitude of questions should get out first, Andrea found herself stammering. "But when . . . I'm . . . how did we pay for that?"

Most of the men seated around her grunted uncomfortably. Yeoh waited serenely for someone else to answer. "We're going to be a bit late on a couple of interest payments to our corporate creditors," Shadid said, shifting in his seat. "And maybe our Union dues."

"And our security contract payments after today," grunted Aguirre.

"How late?" Andrea asked.

"We can go over the numbers later," Shadid answered. "Nothing catastrophic, but we'll catch some heat for it outside the system."

"Outside the system? What about domestically?"

"Well, it wasn't exactly hard to get approval from some of the opposition leaders in the senate," Victor explained. "I might have, um, promised we'd all attend church a lot more along the way, though."

"You have fun with that." Shadid snorted.

"The point is," Aguirre broke in, "we'll get support from enough of the conservative opposition parties that nobody will want to make a real fight over this."

"And our own party?" Andrea pressed.

"Our own party wants to be reelected next year and knows they'd better play along with us on this," Aguirre answered. "We'll lose a few on principle. I'll talk about how I respect their principles. They'll win or they'll lose and we'll be okay either way."

"You really think Lambert and his people will hold their fire over this?"

"I do."

"They aren't just going to give up on the next election."

"No, they aren't," Aguirre conceded, "but they want the military expansion *and* they want to see me fall down on my ass trying to pay for it so they can claim that I'm incompetent."

"And how are we going to fight that?"

"By not letting me fall down on my ass trying to pay for all this. That's why I have all you smart people around me."

Unsatisfied but not wanting to get into an argument, Andrea bit her lip and turned back to the admiral. Yeoh simply remained where she stood, watching passively. "This is a huge increase in fleet strength, isn't it?" Andrea asked.

"It is. Fifty percent more destroyers, almost as much in light patrol craft with the corvettes. There are a few support craft, too. I'll have one of my aides brief you on the ship purchases."

"Isn't this going to require a big increase in manpower?"

"Significant, yes, but we've done well with recruiting since the school payoff-matching deal. We have several retention incentives lined up for our more experienced personnel that we'll be implementing over the coming months.

"We're also effectively doubling the time and intensity of enlisted recruit training," Yeoh added. "The pilot program begins next week."

Once more, Andrea was taken aback. She wasn't familiar with the intricacies of the military's budget, but doubling anything had to mean increasing its expense. "What does that mean?" she asked. "Are their funds for that? Isn't that a massive change?"

"The training reforms aren't entirely a matter of financial logistics," Yeoh said. "I've been involved in planning for all of this personally. Many of our current instructors at our training centers are rather creative people. They can get a lot done once we let them think outside the box."

Sitting back to consider all this, Andrea found that she didn't know whether to be frustrated at Victor or herself. "None of this sounds like it should've been any big secret up until now."

"The measures themselves, no," Aguirre told her. "What we didn't want was a public discussion on how to pay for it all. We didn't want blowback from NorthStar or Lai Wa or the Union assembly."

"The new ship purchases bring us right to our militia limits per Union treaty," Yeoh put in. "We're taking advantage of some loopholes in the treaty's language with the corvettes as it is."

"Better to apologize later than ask permission in advance," Victor said with a grin.

"Exactly," Aguirre agreed. "Andrea, we planned to bring these changes out to the public slowly, but at this point, I say the hell with it. We need to get ahead of this. Hell, we can show that we've *been* ahead of this and that *Aphrodite* is the sort of thing we worried about all along. We've already gotten buy in from Lambert and Waikowski and most of our other opposition heads, too. We can play the multipartisan card."

Pondering her options for a moment, Andrea finally nodded. "I think that'll work. We don't want to call it a buildup, though. Something less aggressive. Enhancements."

Aguirre pointed to Yeoh. "Anyone asks you, we're enhancing, not building."

"Yes, sir," Yeoh acknowledged.

"We'll definitely get blowback from the big three about this," Shadid reminded Andrea. "That's our real battle."

Andrea scowled. "Last I checked, the big three didn't have ships out there picking bodies out of space."

"Good. Use that. If there are no other questions," Aguirre went on, "I need to get up to speed on some operational matters going forward. Unfortunately, that means we're going to have to clear the room of everyone who isn't actually involved in defense."

THREE

Oscar

One hundred seventy-seven recruits stood silently at attention among neatly arranged rectangular tables in Squad Bay Zero. It was the only squad bay with a numeric designation, as it served solely to house recruits for their first few days at Fort Stalwart, Archangel Navy's integrated training facility on Raphael.

They were young and healthy, though not all in good shape. Every head, male and female alike, bore only freshly shaven stubble. The recruits wore simple gray vac suits with no markings beyond a name tag. Some came as navy enlistees, others as marines. Thus far, such distinctions mattered little. Nobody beyond the other recruits themselves seemed to care what they wanted to be.

On the table before each recruit sat a simple gray canvas bag, a neatly folded dress uniform, several more vac suits, and an assortment of very plain, cheap toiletries. As with much of their surroundings, a good deal of their new gear went beyond simple to the point of being archaic.

Up until now, an odd assortment of unfriendly marines and navy ratings shepherded the recruits through rudimentary orientations, calisthenics, and very basic marching and outfitting. Few of their keepers had been around long enough for names to matter. They provided a cursory instruction to military courtesy and traditions, some of them centuries old. Mostly it centered on how to stand at attention properly, whom to address as "sir" or "ma'am," when to salute, and how to read the various rank insignia.

The recruits were told once, in a single hour-long class, the proper naval parlance for a thousand ordinary terms that they had used all their lives and would now have to shed. Walls became bulkheads. Ropes became lines. Left and right were now port and starboard, except when they weren't, and no one offered a consistent explanation for which was used or when.

Of an initial pool of two hundred recruits from Archangel's four inhabited worlds, moon colonies, and space stations, twenty-three had been rejected by the end of the four-day "processing" phase. Several failed medical at Fort Stalwart, where the health staff was much more diligent than the civilian contractors attached to local recruitment depots. Two different "couples" caught "fraternizing" in the showers after lights-out were promptly expelled. Three recruits were arrested and hauled away for criminal charges back home. Amazingly, six different recruits failed even the most basic educational testing. Three more were caught with recreational drugs. One young woman had even been cut for religious intolerance when she refused to eat at a table with non-Catholics.

Tanner stood straight and silent in front of his table like everyone else. He found the empty table spaces unsettling. The medical discharges were one thing; those poor souls had received a green light from their recruiters, only to be cut for unexpected issues beyond their control. But as far as he was concerned, the rest of them had been thrown out because they were just *stupid*. He felt no sympathy for them, but he didn't feel any sense of superiority, either. Instead, he wondered what kind of system would let such morons in to begin with, and how much of a screwup he must be to have landed here with them.

The company began at twice the number Tanner had expected. He gathered that the other recruit companies on base were larger than normal, too, and wondered if the other recruit training centers saw similar increases. Nobody who actually knew anything showed the slightest interest in discussing the matter with recruits.

Two minutes ago, some electrician's mate signed off on the last of the recruit inventory checklists and called the squad bay to attention. Then he walked away without another word. Like many of the recruits, Tanner expected this was some sort of test. Some, though, were too curious to stay still. Rather than looking straight ahead like they were supposed to, they turned their heads this way and that. Tanner winced, hoping they wouldn't get the whole group into trouble.

He needn't have worried. They had plenty of warning. Everyone heard the steady click click click of approaching footsteps from down the hallway behind Tanner. It was a distinct sound, as if someone had put strips of metal on the bottom of his shoes.

Before Tanner knew it, a tall woman with dark-brown skin and the deep-blue uniform of Archangel's marines walked into the squad bay. She strode silently to the front of the room, turned around, and scowled. A similarly tall, lightly tanned man with broad shoulders and a completely shaved head followed her. He wore a gray navy uniform and was obviously the one with the clicking heels. The man joined his companion near the front with a more relaxed but still entirely unwelcoming expression on his face.

"I am Chief Boatswain's Mate Everett," the navy man said with a loud, perfectly calm voice. "You are Oscar Company, and I am now your company commander. This," he said, nodding only slightly to his left, "is Gunnery Sergeant Janeka. She is the assistant company commander. There is no difference in our authority or purpose as far as you are concerned.

"Today many of you will be assigned positions of responsibility within the company. Gunnery Sergeant Janeka and I will assign these positions based on our estimation of your abilities. We will remove you from these positions should you fail in your duties."

His gaze swept the room. "That's the pep talk."

No one spoke. No one had permission.

"Ordinarily," Everett began anew, "we'd head to your squad bay right now. There has been a delay in getting it ready for habitation. However, the navy's time is not to be wasted lightly. Company! Burpees, by the ten count! Begin!"

Tanner and roughly half the company got right to it: a squat with hands on the ground, then kicking their legs straight back into a push-up position, then two push-ups, then back into the squat, and finally jumping straight up into the air, all of it counted out just fast enough to make it stressful. Others simply blinked. "Right here?" one recruit asked.

The recruit paled as Janeka approached him, her eyes promising death. "Th-the tables are too close!" he protested lamely. All that stood between the two of them was the table and his gear upon it. Janeka promptly swept the gear to the floor, where much of it clobbered the next recruit over.

The sergeant pointed at the table. "Stand on it, Gomez," Janeka snarled, reading his name tag. "Now." Gulping, the recruit did as he was told. "This table is two meters across," she said. "You aren't quite two meters tall. It should be perfect for you."

"But I—"

"Are you saying you aren't ready to deal with tables?" she roared. "Are they too complicated for you? You have an order, recruit! Get to it!" The recruit started cranking out hesitant burpees, doing his best not to fall off the table. "Recruit, you will keep pace with the rest of the company. This table is perfectly adequate for your task. If you fall off, I will know that tables are too complicated for you and you will eat your meals standing up until I tell you otherwise!"

Cowed, the recruit picked up his pace before she finished yelling at him. So did everyone else. The tables were indeed too close for such exercise to be done safely. One recruit after another slammed his head against the table in front of him or hit the table behind him with the small of his back. Others, kicking their feet backward under the table behind them, managed to strike a fellow recruit in the shoulder or the skull.

Everett and Janeka allowed no pause or adjustment. They moved from table to table, barking insults all the while. Virtually every individual they addressed had his or her gear knocked from the tables. "You're gonna have to move tighter than that on a ship!" Everett demanded. "Quit strikin' your shipmate! He didn't do anything to you! Don't move, I didn't tell you to move out of your spot! I didn't tell you to stop, either!"

As Tanner dropped into a squat, the foot of the woman in front of him came down on his right hand. He yelped and kicked his legs back, only to thrust his foot into the face of the guy behind him. Janeka stood over Tanner and watched with open disgust.

"Didn't either of your parents qualify for prenatal defect treatments?" Everett demanded of a smaller female recruit. "Christ, every one of you has a brain deficiency that should've been corrected before birth!"

A resounding crash interrupted his rant. Recruits yelped and grunted. Janeka looked back at the mess. "No tables anymore, Gomez!" she yelled. "I see you sitting at a table at chow, I will cripple you for life!"

Tanner kept performing as ordered. The one thing he knew for sure was that he didn't want any extra attention from either of these two. He thought morbidly that it would be interesting to measure their voices for kinetic energy and compare it to, say, getting pelted by rocks. Everyone knew that recruit training for any military service, be it a system militia or corporate forces, involved a lot of physical exercise, verbal abuse, and stress. Yet knowing that from secondhand sources and experiencing it were very different things.

It couldn't have been more than a few minutes, though, before Tanner realized that neither trainer was yelling anymore. He didn't see either one out of the corners of his eyes. He kept going, though, as did most everyone else. The stomps, grunts, and heavy breath of the recruits filled the room.

Whimpers and wheezes from other recruits reminded Tanner of his own weariness and fading endurance. Tanner resolved not to add to such noises. Clearly, passing out would be preferable to getting caught making a half-assed effort. He saw absolutely no chance that Everett or Janeka would call the company to a halt because someone showed pain, discomfort, or fatigue.

He squatted, kicked out, did his push-ups, tucked in his knees, and jumped up. He did it again, and again, and again. He didn't even count out. He just kept going and hoped he could at least keep up with the company average, whatever that was.

Then he spotted one recruit, off to his left and toward the front of the room, who wasn't keeping up at all. The young man had a dark complexion and close-cropped hair, with the upper edges of a tattoo across his back reaching just up over the collar of his vac suit. He waited in a half squat, looking around the room suspiciously.

"They're gone," he said almost too quietly for Tanner to hear.

"So?" huffed the guy next to him. "Keep going, fool."

"No, come on," scowled the first. "It's a game. They're fucking with us. Just wait and watch. Only suckers keep this up."

"Gonna catch you and take it out on everyone," someone else grunted.

The slacker tossed a quick sneer over his shoulder to his new critic. "You guys are idiots," he said. "This is all just a mind game."

Tanner wanted to yell something out, but that was only more likely to draw attention. He couldn't stop glancing at the slacking recruit as he continued doing burpees. He saw a couple of others also stop.

"Shit." The slacker shrugged. "Hey, Matuskey! Keep lookout on the hallway!"

"What?" huffed a tall, stocky man close to the door, behind Tanner.

"Shut up!" Tanner warned.

"Man, fuck you," the slacker scowled, waving Tanner off. "Matuskey, keep watch! You don't have to keep jumping!"

"Matuskey, don't listen to him!" Tanner hissed. He caught the slacker's eye as he jumped up and then squatted down again. The slacker glared at him intently, but Tanner went back to paying attention to what he was doing.

"Matuskey!" the slacker whispered. "Come on!"

Matuskey thought about it, caught the eye of a couple of other recruits—all of them still doing the exercise—and shook his head before dropping into another push-up.

The slacker growled in frustration. Then his eyes suddenly went wide and he got back to business with the rest of the company, but it was far too late. Gunnery Sergeant Janeka was already half-way across the squad bay, having appeared from out of nowhere. "Stand up! You stand up, slick! What is your name?"

His name tag clearly read "Eickenberry," but Janeka ignored it. "Eicken-um," the slacker stammered.

"Ein-what? Einstein? Are you Albert Einstein? You must be, if you're smarter than everyone else! Are you done here, Einstein? Did you get done before everyone else? You must have, 'cause everyone else is still moving and yet you're done! You must have known that I was coming in to call everyone to a halt before I even thought of it! That's some genius thinking you've done there!"

"Einstein" remained at attention and failed miserably at staring straight ahead.

"Everyone here is still working, Einstein," she shouted. "But not you. You're all set, right? Are you all done? Ready to go hit the showers?"

"Yes, Sergeant Janeka!" Einstein replied.

"That's good. You just stand right there until everyone else is done." She walked to the back of the squad bay. "Not you guys! You morons aren't done yet! Einstein's the only one finished!"

The company carried on. There was no unity of movement, but at least the accidents diminished. Janeka fell silent and eventually headed for the door.

"Pff," Einstein snorted quietly. "Suckers."

On her way out, Janeka slapped the emergency response panel next to the doorway. Jets of blue, freezing cold foam erupted from slots imbedded in the ceiling and floor.

Laughter erupted from several of the recruits who thought that this was some final punch line to the whole big joke of the introduction of their company commanders. Most, though, realized they hadn't been told to stop. They pressed on despite the drastic change in their environment. Slips and falls abounded, yet it was only a minute or two—seemingly endless though those minutes were—before the laughter died and everyone was back to business.

Everyone except Einstein, who found the whole thing hilarious. As the foam jets exhausted their payloads, his giggles became easier for everyone to hear. "C'mon, hurry up and get done, guys," he quipped. "I wanna go dry off."

Burpees continued. So did the glares.

"Attention in the squad bay!" roared Everett's voice from the doorway. Everyone, even Einstein, popped to attention. "Do we all understand now that we will obey orders?"

"Yes, Chief Everett!" the company shouted back.

"Stow your gear in your backpacks and get down below and out on the deck outside," he said. "You are responsible for all your gear. Leave nothing behind. You have ninety seconds to form up."

Chaos followed. Many recruits had seen their belongings tossed aside by their new oppressors; others knew it had happened, but had no idea where their gear had landed. To make things worse, everything was now wet.

Tanner luckily found his gear close by. He snatched up toiletries, towels, and underwear, frantically shoving it all in the backpack. Small stuff on the bottom, he thought quickly, since it wouldn't take up much room and he could just shove the bigger uniform items in after it.

Then he realized how much water his dress uniform had taken on. It simply wouldn't fit in with his vac suits, socks, underwear, and towels. He glanced around, looking hurriedly for someone with a good idea he could copy, but found that either nobody else had the same problem or they had already resolved it. "How do we—" he asked the recruit to his left, who promptly ran his fingers over the static seals of his bag and rushed away. Tanner turned to his right, wanting to ask the same thing, but found himself alone.

He tried again. His bag simply wouldn't seal. There was too much stuff and no time to wring it out. "Fuck it," he fumed. Tanner yanked the towels free, unzipped his vac suit and stuffed the freezing cold towels inside.

Tanner was among the last out. Someone roughly shoved past him along the way, sending him stumbling to the floor under the weight of his backpack just before he got to the stairs.

"Dammit," Tanner grunted. He got to his hands and knees, wincing from the pain in his left elbow, and then quickly found himself scooped up off the floor by a pair of recruits. Their name tags, Tanner noted, read "Ravenell" and "Gomez."

"Thanks," Tanner huffed.

"In this together," said the tall, dark-skinned recruit on his left. Gomez was already headed down the stairs; Ravenell stayed long enough to give Tanner a tug in the right direction. "Just keep moving. You okay?"

Tanner wanted to make some quip about the relativity of a concept like "okay" in a place like this, but he was far too out of breath to be funny.

• • •

If the antique liquid fire suppression system in Squad Bay Zero was an unpleasant surprise to Oscar Company, their arrival at their new living facility was much worse.

The company failed to muster in time for Everett's deadline. Ten more agonizing minutes of soaking wet burpees on rough pavement followed before they formed up again. The company found it difficult to form up into columns despite having learned to do so on its first day. They found it even more difficult to manage the punitive calisthenics that resulted from their failures. Along the way several overstuffed backpacks burst and had to be cleaned up while other recruits performed push-ups and ran in place so as to not waste the navy's time. Everett demanded further torturous calisthenics under the premise of educating the company of the differences between left, right, forward, back, up, and down.

Squad Bay Oscar turned out to be an ancient underground emergency shelter well apart from the main buildings of the base itself. A grassy, overgrown hill with plenty of trees covered most of the structure. The exposed walls were all titanium alloy and reinforced concrete, with large, heavy doors built to withstand heavy weapons.

"The government of Archangel has seen fit to expand our militia's numbers, starting with increased recruiting incentives and reservist training," Chief Everett announced to the assembled company outside their new home. "I'm sure more than a few of you probably missed out on what will be some good deals for those who will soon follow you. Tragic, I know. On the other hand, you will benefit from sharply increased recruit training standards and curriculum. For one thing, you'll be pleased to know that we'll all be together for twice as long as the ordinary basic training sequence."

Eyes widened, jaws dropped, and no small amount of shocked profanity fell from the mouths of the recruits. The most common refrain was only three words: "Six fucking *months*?"

"Drop!" Janeka and Everett snapped simultaneously. The company quickly and collectively fell on its face in the dirty road. Janeka kept yelling. "Fifty! Begin now! You weren't given permission to speak!"

Satisfied that the interruptions were quashed, Everett continued. "You are the first to go through this experimental new curriculum, designed in no small part by Gunny Janeka and myself. These changes provide Fort Stalwart with unique logistical challenges. One of these has been the question of recruit housing.

"You will find that the navy requires frequent improvisation. As a case in point, Gunny Janeka and I volunteered Oscar Company for nonstandard housing arrangements for the good of the service.

"The navy thanks you for your sacrifice," Everett finished. His face bore no smile, but his voice carried an audible grin. Everett turned and pushed open the door. He ordered them to their feet when they hit fifty push-ups—a serious trial for most by now—and then directed them to file inside.

The entrance involved three sets of thick, armored doors. Inside, recruits found rows of single-mattress bunk beds, old-fashioned standing plastic storage units, and an unpleasant, musty stench. There were absolutely no windows. Toward the rear, they saw signs of staircases and lifts, but many of the lights were out. The shelter seemed like it hadn't been cleaned in years . . . which became Oscar Company's first mission.

Janeka doled out tasks as if she read them from an invisible checklist. Mops, brooms, rags, buckets, and soap waited in the entrance passageways, apparently left by some unseen welcoming committee before the company arrived. Young men and women used to automated room sweepers, sonic cleansing wands, and computerized dust filtration systems took up the old-fashioned tools with trepidation and distaste.

"Ahmed, Gonzalez, Huang, Ravenell," Janeka called out, "you get the vents. Get up there and start cleaning. Take off the grills and reach inside. Don't let me catch you just wiping off the faceplates. Start with the ventilation terminals and access ports on this floor tonight. You'll get a chance to crawl all the way into the atmospheric recycling tanks down below before the week is out. If you're claustrophobic, congratulations. You're about to get over it.

"Espinoza, Perelli, Whittier, Gomez, and *other* Gomez," Janeka said with a roll of her eyes, "you're on inventory duty. Sweep through this entire floor and mark down literally every piece of equipment, every tool, every rag, everything that is not mounted or bolted down into a bulkhead, the overhead, or the deck. That means walls, ceiling, or floor for those of you who never bothered to read your orientation manuals. Record everything and bring your manifests to me. You will also *collect* everything that *might* be garbage of some sort into a central point. There hasn't been an internal inventory on this facility in years, so we will double-check every previous record immediately.

"Ramos, Matuskey, Malone, and Einstein," she continued, "you chatterboxes get to clean the head."

Silence followed. It wasn't the first time the trainers at Fort Stalwart used some odd word for something completely mundane. They had heard this one before, but nobody remembered it. Tanner bit his lip, wanting to translate in the painfully awkward silence, but he worried he'd be speaking out of turn again. Finally, Ramos spoke up. "Sergeant Janeka!" he called out. "What is the 'head'?"

Janeka just snorted. "The head is what you kiddies used to call the potty. From now on, you call it the head. You get to scrub out the toilets and the showers. There should be hand tools and chemicals in the cleaning closet inside. Don't put any of it in your mouths."

Chemicals? Tanner thought with surprise. *Who the hell even* makes *chemical cleaning agents anymore?*

Matuskey blanched. "Uh, Sergeant Janeka?" he asked. "Are there protective gloves?"

"It's *Gunny* Janeka if you're trying to be friendly, and there's nothing in that head that can't be cured," Janeka asserted. "You already got your basic inoculations. There'll be more comprehensive immunizations later if you don't wash out of basic training, but those cost money. We don't want to invest too much in you 'til you've earned it. Now stop sandbagging! Fall out!"

The four recruits stepped out of line and headed for the back of the squad bay. What they found shocked them. The shelter was designed to accommodate two hundred people for an extended period, with sanitary facilities to match. Not one of the recruits had ever seen such a foul mess. Even in the most impoverished, multifamily dwellings of Archangel, bathrooms were built with the ability to self-disinfect and eliminate foul odors in mere seconds.

After countless dissections and other less pleasant tasks in his advanced biology classes, Tanner could endure rather nasty smells. Even so, the head disgusted him. "Jesus," he muttered, "how's a bathroom still stink when nobody's used it in years?"

Einstein slapped him on the back hard enough to push him forward a step. "You get the toilets," he said. Tanner looked up to find a challenging glare. Galling as it was, he saw nothing to be gained in arguing. Someone had to do it, and Janeka or Everett could turn up at any minute. Tanner scowled and turned to the stalls.

"Oh my God," Ramos said, covering his mouth and nose. "I think I'm gonna be sick."

"Did they purposely mess this place up for us?" Matuskey wondered.

Einstein walked to a sink, stopped it up with his rag and ran the water. "Might as well get to it," he said. "You guys get the showers, I've got the sinks."

"Who put you in charge?" asked Ramos.

"Oh, what, you got a better plan?"

At that, Ramos and Matuskey just looked at one another, frowned, and got to work.

It became obvious after half an hour that Einstein worked the slowest and grumbled the most. He complained of stains in the sinks that just wouldn't scrub out. He took frequent breaks to stretch and look around and talked to every fellow recruit who came in to use the facilities.

"This is bullshit," Einstein declared. "There have to be rules against this. It must be cheaper to buy automated cleaners than to have us clean by hand. And those two assholes? They don't have to lay it on this thick. How does any of this make us good crewmen? Bullshit. We're all citizens. Who the hell do they think they are?"

"Combat veterans," answered Tanner. He didn't bother looking up from scrubbing his toilet.

"What?" Einstein sneered.

"You saw the red stripe down the side of their pants, didn't you?"

"What's that got to do with anything?"

"Those are blood stripes. It means they're both combat veterans. Archangel's been at peace for thirty years, and the Union hasn't been to war in sixty, but somehow both of them wound up in actual battles."

"So? Are you saying they're mentally damaged or something?"

"No, I'm saying they might actually know a thing or two, and . . . forget it." Tanner sighed, shaking his head.

"Yeah, that's what I thought," Einstein huffed.

"Malone!" called a recruit from outside the head. "Everett wants to see you in his office outside the squad bay." The cleaning crew all looked at one another blankly for a moment before Tanner answered the summons.

"Hey," said one recruit as he passed other cleaning crews. She was a petite girl whose name tag read "Wong." "When you go up there, slap the bulkhead once, stand at attention next to the doorway—but not in it—and say, 'Recruit Malone reporting as ordered.'"

Tanner blinked. "How did you know that?"

She smirked. "I just saw two other guys get fifty push-ups for getting it wrong."

"Gotcha. Thanks."

"No problem. Good luck."

Outside the squad bay, Tanner found an office with Everett and Janeka's names outside the doorway. He caught a glimpse of decent, modern desks and carpeting, and while the construction was still the same concrete as the rest of the squad bay it was at least painted. He wasn't sure if anyone was inside, though. Tanner slapped the wall and stood at attention. "Recruit Malone reporting as ordered!"

Silence. He waited and heard nothing. Eventually, he called out again, "Recruit Malone, rep—"

"I heard you the first time," Everett shouted from inside. "Get on your face! Fifty push-ups! Count 'em out!"

Wincing, Tanner obeyed immediately. Exhausted as he was already, the task took him a while, but Everett didn't complain or criticize. When Tanner finally got to his fiftieth push-up, he stayed down on his face and waited. It turned out to be the right move.

"Recover," Everett called out. "Step inside."

Tanner came to attention as best he could. His whole upper body trembled from all the calisthenics he'd performed today. It took effort to keep his eyes focused on the wall directly across from him, a difficult trick to master even when well rested.

Everett sat at his desk with a pair of holo screens open before him. "Who told you how to report properly?"

"Recruit Wong, Chief Everett."

"Glad to see some of you looking out for one another. You owe her one for trying," Everett murmured. "Not her fault you fucked it up." He looked up from the holo screen. "Recruit Malone, are you an honest man?"

Tanner blinked. "Yes, Chief Everett."

"What in the hell are you doing here?"

"I'm sorry, Chief Everett?"

"I didn't ask you if you were a sorry person. I assume that much of every recruit. I asked you what the hell you're doing here."

"Er . . . Recruit Jun told me to report to you, Chief Everett."

"Stupid! I mean, what are you doing joining the Archangel Navy?"

"I want to serve and protect the Archangel system, Chief Everett!"

"See, now you're not being honest with me, Malone. That's the bullshit answer from the recruit manual, which nobody else even bothers to read before they get here. And that's just my point. I've got your enlistment records and transcripts right here. I could've bet a month's salary that you read the manual. You did, didn't you?"

"Yes, Chief Everett."

"How many times?"

"I lost count, Chief Everett."

"And how many other books about basic training did you read?"

"Only eight, Chief Everett." The chief let out some sort of noise between a snort and a choke. Tanner added in a slightly apologetic tone, "I only had a couple of weeks between deciding to join and shipping out, and I had a lot to tie up before I left home."

The chief openly laughed. "Why in the hell aren't you partying it up for the next two months before going off to some university?"

Tanner didn't answer immediately. He wondered if this was some test of his zeal. Neither Everett nor Janeka seemed like the type to appreciate being told enlisting was anyone's second choice. He tried not to frown.

"I crashed on the Test," Tanner answered. "That kind of screwed up my original plans. The navy seemed like an excellent way to recover. Maybe grow up some more."

Everett grinned. "Well, that's just goddamn tactful." He turned his attention back to one holo screen and dragged his finger down its length to change the display, then whistled appreciatively. "Holy shit. You sure did crash. Debt like that doesn't match with grades like yours. What the hell happened? Did you pass out?"

Tanner felt himself turn red with embarrassment. "Family stuff happened the night before the test. Screwed up all my plans. Couldn't sleep at all the night before, couldn't concentrate . . . I couldn't get my mind off it."

That earned him a grunt of acknowledgment. "Most of your fellow recruits probably owe at least as much. A lot of kids your age would just suck it up and take out more loans. Why didn't you?"

"The more I thought about it, the more I thought this could be good for me. My mother served a term in the Union fleet at my age and always spoke well of her experience. And like I said, it seemed like a good way to pay down some of that debt. Serve the state. All that stuff."

Everett thought about it and nodded. "Fair enough. But back to you crashing that test. You can't worry about personal stuff when you're on duty. This isn't like working in retail where you can bitch and moan and gossip with your friends. People like to think that the Archangel Navy just sits around on its ass and writes safety citations on freighters, but this stuff is for real. Can you learn to handle that?"

"Yes, Chief Everett."

"All right. Well, only a handful of people in this company can read and write worth a damn. I've already got Wong and Sinclair assigned to other jobs, so . . . You know what a yeoman is, Malone?"

"A yeoman was a farmer in medieval Europe, Chief Everett."

The older man laughed. "Jesus, you are a bookworm. Malone, in the navy, a yeoman is a clerical specialist. Like a secretary. Oscar Company needs a yeoman. There's a lot of paperwork that goes with recruit training. A lot of that's gonna be your job. Gunny Janeka and I will assign tasks as necessary. Ordinarily a yeoman has a desk of his own, but I've found that separating the yeoman out from the company to do his work just makes him look like he gets some sort of privileges. I figure just giving you a holocom and having you do your work in the squad bay might leave you better off."

"Thank you, Chief Everett."

"Don't thank me, recruit. I'm not doing you any favors. I need this job filled and you look like the most qualified, but I could be mistaken. You still have to keep up with the rest of your training just like everyone else. If you fuck up, you're fired. Understand?"

"Yes, Chief Everett."

"Here it is," the Chief said, holding out the holocom. This model was a small silver rod that could easily fit in a pocket. Tanner accepted it and resumed the position of attention. "Keep it with you at all times. Come up with your own password—I recommend doing the retinal scan—and take care of that thing, because it's your ass if you lose it. Any questions?"

"No, Chief—yes. I mean, yes, Chief Everett. Why did you ask me if I'm an honest man? Wouldn't you expect that of everyone?"

"Recruit, I just gave you access to the records of every recruit in the company. You're going to track everything from disciplinary infractions to testing scores to payroll. That's a lot to check up on. A lot for Gunny Janeka and I to double-check.

"You can mug a man or pick his pocket and anyone would call you a thief, but there are a million ways to cheat a man on paper and just call it a clerical error."

Tanner nodded. "Understood, Chief Everett."

The chief looked at him for a long moment. Tanner remained at attention, thinking this was some sort of test to see if he could just hold a straight face or keep from speaking until he was spoken to. It seemed like an eternity.

"Eight books and the recruit manual, huh?"

"Yes, Chief Everett."

"So you probably already know all about what we're doing here, right? I expect these weren't children's books."

"I wouldn't presume I know everything just because I've read a lot, chief." He remained at attention, unsure as to how casual his voice should be. "Most of it might have been thrown out the window already, anyway, given what you've said and where we're setting up living quarters."

Everett grunted. "Good. Now tell Recruit Baljashanpreet to get in here. I'm not done assigning section leaders."

• • •

Tanner awoke with the sensation of falling, followed by a pair of painful crashes. His thin mattress offered no significant protection from the impact of the concrete floor beneath him. There was even less protection from the weight of Gomez, his thin mattress, and the framework holding it all in place as it crashed down on top of him.

His head felt like it had imploded, to say nothing of the not-exactly-cushioned elbow that drove into his side upon impact. Tanner all but panicked. He didn't know what could be happening, only that he awoke hurt and confused. He wasn't even sure where he was in those first few moments; he thought of home, and his family, and possibly an earthquake or perhaps a vehicle hitting his building.

"Up!" someone snarled over the clatter, the groans and the protests. "Get up! Get on your feet, recruits!"

Scrambling out from under the bedding, Tanner jabbed his knee in the metal framework of his rack, inadvertently shoved a neighbor to the floor, and found himself immediately disoriented in the darkness. He was in the squad bay. He remembered that much. Moreover, he recognized the voice of Gunnery Sergeant Janeka. It seemed her every word foretold some painful punishment, yet the penalty for sluggish obedience was doubtlessly worse.

His head started to clear. There was a flow to the wreckage; the line of collapsed bunks stretched from his end of the squad bay into the shadows beyond, where further crashes still pierced his ears. Tanner realized then what was happening. The furnishings were designed to be easily compacted for storage. All Janeka had to do was pull on a single safety rod and turn a small lever to collapse a bunk.

"Line up!" Janeka barked. "Line up in front of your bunks! Line up at attention and sound off!"

They assembled as instructed beside their wrecked bunks and sounded off by number. They failed to synch up with one another immediately, leading to the first of the morning's calisthenics.

"The sound you will hear before you awaken for the foreseeable future is this one," Janeka announced sharply. A sudden alarm rang through the squad bay in a rapid, piercing tone. "That is the sound of an impending impact upon a ship. It's the sound you'll hear right before a collision. You will learn to brace for it, night or day, awake or asleep. You will get used to it. You will learn to wake up fast. And when you're asleep in your bunks on your ship and something hits you, you'll react appropriately, saving yourselves from injury, panic, and death."

Janeka stalked the rows of recruits with an almost palpable aura of irritation. "You're welcome," she added.

"Thank you, Gunnery Sergeant Janeka!" the company bellowed in unison.

"Yesterday we had to learn to do as we're told and how to tell our left from our right. That took two hours that ate up chow time and, apparently, didn't quite get through to everyone. I can tell that today we'll have to learn to count, too."

She found a spot at the center of the assembled recruits and got even louder. She had amazing control for someone speaking at such a volume. "Does anyone know what 'Oscar' means in naval parlance?"

Silence. She sighed. "Does anyone know what 'parlance' means?"

"Parlance is a particular manner of speaking, Gunny Janeka!" Tanner called out.

"I did not ask what it meant! I asked if anyone knew what it meant! Fifty push-ups, Recruit Malone, right now!" As he dropped, she looked around the squad bay for signs of amusement. "Einstein! You, too! Drop!" The recruit grunted in frustration, but he obeyed.

Janeka continued. "Oscar is the letter *O* in the military alphabet and has been so for centuries. Way back in ancient history, sailors on ships used color-coded flags to signal messages to other ships. Each letter had a distinctive flag. Each flag also had a specific meaning apart from that letter. The 'Oscar' flag meant 'man overboard,' meaning someone had fallen into the water and was in danger of drowning.

"If you fall off a ship at sea, you may be able to tread water for a time, or maybe hold on to something that floats. If you are lucky, you may be in water warm enough that you won't just die of hypothermia regardless of your ability to stay afloat. You may survive a few hours.

"You have not signed on for a seagoing navy. The Archangel Navy works in space, boys and girls. They may not have explained this to you before you got onto the wrong shuttle on your way to moron summer camp.

"A human exposed to the vacuum of space will survive unprotected for roughly thirty seconds if he is exceptionally lucky. A human in a vacuum suit can survive for upward of a few hours if his suit functions properly and if he has an oxygen tank. But if you are wearing a vacuum suit and you are accidentally dumped from your ship, the chances that your suit has also taken some damage are high.

"Thus, we still have drills for 'man overboard,' even in space, and they must be carried out with all possible speed," she said, stressing the point. "That *shipmate* out there does not have long to live without your immediate aid. He won't give up on you. You must not give up on him. *You will not give up on yourself.*"

She paused until both Tanner and Einstein completed their push-ups. "Recover," she said. They both resumed the position of attention. Janeka pressed home her point: "You people move awfully slow for a company with a name like Oscar. This is intolerable. You will all learn to move with deliberate haste and accuracy. You will run faster and more often than any other company. You will learn to jump out of those bunks or out of your chairs like someone's life is at stake *whenever* you are called. Do you understand me?"

"Yes, Gunny Janeka!" came the responding chorus.

"Morning chow is in fifteen minutes and the galley is clear on the other side of the base from here, so we've got a jog ahead of us. I will recommend only once that you avoid any sort of stimulants like caffeine. Learn to cope without them, ladies and gentlemen.

"Also, Recruit Gomez, don't forget: you do not sit down at a table to eat. Fall out onto the street, people."

FOUR

The Education of Darren Mills

Darren expected more screaming, or crying, or some pleas for mercy. He figured they'd beg to be spared or something. That's how it always went in the movies. Instead, the passengers mostly remained silent as they were shaken down one by one by his new shipmates for jewelry, pricy personal effects, and cash. He imagined hours of wild, opportunistic looting, but everything was put into a single hoard to be shared out in an orderly manner later.

Darren also hoped to get a gun right away, but, in hindsight, that was naive. All he'd done was step over the make-believe line in the carpet when Casey had called for recruits from Aphrodite's *crew. It wasn't like he'd earned his wings yet. Or his pirate eye patch. Or whatever pirates used to separate men from boys.*

He helped with crowd control in the passageway, preventing anyone from running off, and generally keeping an eye out. Beside him stood Marcos, one of the passenger attendants. Darren didn't know much about him other than the name on his uniform. Machinist's mates didn't often associate with attendants.

Marcos seemed to enjoy all the manhandling and slapping people around. It probably came from years of having to kiss ass to these people. Darren did as he was asked, but Marcos clearly got a kick out of this. Then, almost abruptly, he stopped spewing insults. He went quiet and just pushed passengers along like Darren did.

"Marcos? You okay?"

Marcos nodded, not looking up.

"Is something in your mouth?" Darren asked.

Things changed. There weren't any more passengers, just Marcos being held down while two pirates roughly searched him. Darren had blood on his hands. It was from Marcos's mouth, which bled while Darren held him down.

"A necklace," yelled Murray, an angry pirate with long red hair and a scar running halfway down the left side of his face. "You stupid fuck, this was all over a fucking diamond necklace."

Marcos coughed out an apology, or maybe a plea. Darren couldn't make it out, because the guy's teeth were ruined. He kept trying to speak as Murray, Yuan, and Darren all pushed Marcos into an engineering access airlock. Marcos stumbled to the floor as he was pushed in, and then Murray—no, Darren—reached up, hit the controls, and sealed the internal hatch.

Then Marcos pounded on the hatch, and screamed, sounding just like the door chime in one of the passenger suites.

• • •

"We don't want anyone sneaking up here and trying to take the ship while most of the crew is down dirtside living it up," Casey explained. "The crew has a serious decision to make about this ship. We're looking at five or six hundred million for it if we decide to sell, but we can't hold a vote on that while everyone's stir crazy. People need to let off some steam first. In the meantime, we can't have our prize float away."

"Okay." Darren sat on the edge of the bed in his appropriated passenger suite, clad only in his underwear and sweat. He hoped he didn't seem shaken up by his nightmares in front of Captain Casey and Wilson, the pirates' chief engineer.

"It's happened before with other ships," Casey said. "But not to us."

"Isn't that why we're leaving a watch section on board?"

"Sure." Casey smirked. "And in general, I trust my crew . . . but this is an awfully tempting prize, isn't it? Might make a few men a little crazy."

"I could do this myself, but you're a native bilge rat on this ship," Wilson said with a strange accent and a black, creepy stare. "So you're gonna do it, and you're going to send us a specific list of what you've done."

Darren's skills and knowledge quickly won his shipmates' appreciation. He had been only a junior machinist's mate, but that meant that he actually did work as opposed to sitting around on his ass and "supervising." Darren single-handedly cut in half the time it took the pirates to get *Aphrodite* moving again after the raid. He knew where all the spare parts were kept and the real performance numbers of the engines, as opposed to what was listed in the manuals. His expertise also meant that when *Vengeance* and *Aphrodite* docked on the repair platform orbiting Paradise, he was a natural pick to stay on board the prize vessel with the first watch rotation.

"And then you don't say shit about it to anyone," Casey said. "All anybody needs to know is you're doing safety shutdown stuff."

"Okay," Darren acknowledged, nodding frequently through the instructions.

"Crawl into the sublights and the FTL and change out a few things, but don't make it *look* like you've done anything," Wilson explained. "Switch out some fittings with the wrong resistances. Pick a couple power tubes and push them out of tolerance, but just a little. You know, the delicate stuff. Use your imagination." His eyebrows floated up as if he said something profound. Really, it just made the engineer look a little bent. "We want the ship to look ready to go, but anyone who tries ought'a have a terrible time finding out why she won't move. It should give us a chance to intervene."

"Got it," Darren replied.

"I'll be up to check on your work in a day or so," said Wilson.

"Any questions?" Casey asked.

"Just one. I'm the new guy, right? Why would you trust me with this?"

The captain and engineer looked at one another with a smirk. "Darren," Casey said, "anyone who'd turn his back on two different ship's crews in less than a week is either a master schemer or a complete moron. Either way, he isn't fit for anything but a swim out the airlock soon as he's outlived his usefulness. Anyone who'd try to steal this ship would know that. And so would you."

Casey lingered a moment as Wilson left. "You all right, son?" he asked.

"Yeah, just . . . nightmares."

"Marcos. That idiot with the earrings, right? You did the right thing."

Darren looked away and just shrugged a bit.

"Listen," Casey continued. "First couple times things get rough like that will always shake you up. But you made the right call. We're your family now, right? You don't hold out on family." Darren nodded a bit. The captain put his hand on Darren's shoulder. "What happened out there was just natural selection, and that isn't often pretty."

• • •

Twenty disappointed men and women remained aboard *Aphrodite* for its first twenty-four hours in orbit over Paradise. They observed few duties beyond a fire watch and presenting an obvious deterrent to anyone who'd steal the ship. Most amused themselves in the liner's spacious casino, staying well fed and at least slightly inebriated. Much of the ship's fine food and alcohol had already either been consumed by her captors or transferred to *Vengeance*, but *Aphrodite* could accommodate over two thousand of the Union's economically privileged. Even after days of plunder by a few hundred pirates, she had provisions to spare.

Darren found he enjoyed the company. For a band of cutthroats and deviants, many were remarkably sociable among their own.

Eventually, Darren walked off a shuttle from *Aphrodite* with a full belly, a good night's sleep, and a mild alcoholic buzz. He stepped into warm morning sunlight tempered by a cool ocean breeze.

The pirates called the planet Paradise. Paradise City, the only town of significant size, sat on the coastline of a pleasant spot in the planet's subtropical zone. A handful of settlements elsewhere on the planet were dedicated to providing a few staple agricultural products, but all the real action was here.

Darren fumbled around for his sunglasses. All of his shipmates had photoreactive contact lenses or implants over their eyes. He decided he'd have to get set up with those himself.

Tents, cargo containers, trucks, shuttles, and a few small starships sprawled out before them in an otherwise open field. The most permanent things he could spot were a couple of prefabricated shelters, and even those could be folded up and removed with little effort. Tall grass surrounded the bazaar, but within the area's perimeter the greenery had been long trampled into the dirt.

Bedraggled, tired, and hungover pirates from *Vengeance* waited for the shuttle. One of them was hauled along unconscious by two of his mates. The other half of the incoming watch section had already boarded *Aphrodite*. These were the last, and they were fewer in number than those coming off.

Along with them stood Lauren Williams, the quartermaster from *Vengeance*. She wore a blue-and-white sundress that would have given her a bright, innocent look, were it not for her choice of accessories. The machete and heavy pistol hanging from her hips seemed to clash with her outfit, but Lauren was a pirate's pirate. She could wear whatever the hell she wanted.

"Boys," she said cordially.

Joey Chang, the off-going watch section's chief, waved but scowled. "Hey, where the hell's the rest of the watch?" he asked.

"Wally and Hangnail got in the ring last night and fucked themselves up pretty bad," explained Lauren. "Nobody's seen Yuan since we got here."

"Assholes," Chang grumbled. Though a scruffy, long-haired pirate like the rest, Chang was a former Union fleet corpsman. That effectively made him the ship's surgeon, and also one of the few to take watchstanding very seriously. Darren didn't envy the missing men when he thought about what Chang would do when he caught up to them.

As the groups passed through one another, Darren caught the eye of Crewman Hong—now just Sheng Hong to everyone—and waved. "How are you doing?" Darren asked.

Hong blinked at him with bleary eyes and smiled. He wobbled more than walked. Expensive silk clothes and genuine leather boots replaced his uniform. He wore glittering necklaces, a golden cuff on his ear, and other bits of jewelry. Matching laser pistols hung from holsters on each hip of his shiny new gun belt.

"This town's the greatest fuckin' planet in the universe," Hong slurred at Darren after clapping him on the shoulder—or, perhaps, steadying himself upon it. Hong giggled and wobbled on up the shuttle ramp.

Darren marveled at the transformation. Hong had always been reserved, humble, and self-controlled as a crewman on *Aphrodite*. Darren couldn't even remember the guy drinking. He mostly spent his off-hours in his bunk reading or watching movies.

"So, before you go off, I brought you all something." Lauren smiled, holding up a stylish, expensive-looking purse. "We've already got the bulk of the loot fenced and shares allocated. Anyone feel like being paid?"

"Hell, yes," said Jerry, the husky, older pirate who'd taken Darren under his wing. He pushed forward in the crowd. Lauren sorted through the cards in her purse, found Jerry's, and handed it off. Jerry activated the card's holographic data screen to check its balance and hooted with delight as Lauren moved on to the next happy recipient.

Being last only heightened Darren's anticipation. He would get only half the shares of a regular pirate like Jerry, whereas pirates with positions of particular responsibilities like Chang and Lauren received two or more. Even so, the liquid cash taken from *Aphrodite*'s passengers and crew, shared out before they made port, put a nineteen thousand credit card in Darren's pocket before they even got to Paradise. That nearly beat his annual salary.

"Hey, new guy." Lauren smiled at him. "These assholes treating you all right? Showing you the ropes?"

"Yeah, pretty much," Darren answered.

She handed off his card with a grin. "There you go. Forty-nine thousand."

Darren almost choked. He checked the screen and could only blink.

"Money from repatriating our 'guests' is still coming, of course, along with the ship itself . . . but no telling how long all that'll take, so don't spend it all in one place, 'kay?"

"Wow," Darren breathed. She had to be joking. How could he spend that much that fast?

"Hey, Jerry, Chang, you guys wanna get Darren here set with a gun before you go off to drinkin' and whorin'?"

"First thing, Lauren," Chang assured her.

Jerry grabbed Darren by the back of his shirt to push him along. Lauren swatted his butt playfully with her purse as he left, but Jerry hustled him along before he could respond. "Let's get geared up," the older pirate said.

Darren followed Jerry and Chang through the bazaar. The makeshift lanes weren't crowded, nor were they as deserted as Darren expected from everyone's stories. At this hour, he'd figured most of the pirates in town would still be passed out, and he'd wondered if any of the merchants would even be open for business. It dawned on him, however, that the pirates were much like *Aphrodite*'s passengers. They were people with lots of money to burn and few scheduled obligations. It was up to the merchants to keep up.

Salesmen hawked and beckoned to passersby like a scene out of movies about Old Earth. Pretty women and more than a few men, all scantily clad, did their best to tempt and entice, casting hungry glances and calling out to anyone who didn't look like they were here working.

A couple of women noticed Darren's appraising looks and approached, but Chang waved them off. "They can't tell you're a pirate yet," he warned. "Wait for it."

"What, we all wear signs or something?" Darren asked. "Can't assume every person with a gun here is a pirate. Look at the merchants, half of them are armed, too."

"You noticed most of us have pretty long hair?"

Darren blinked. "Huh? Yeah, I guess I did, but . . . is that a sign?"

"Long hair and a gun is pretty much the uniform," said the admittedly bald Jerry. "It's not like we keep grooming standards. As long as you don't stink, nobody gives a damn."

"It's not a grooming standard," Darren said, shaking his head. "The hair gets in the way of putting on the helmet in a vac suit. It's a safety standard."

"Right," Jerry said dryly. "Darren, we're not a navy boat. You see anyone from *Vengeance* wearing a vac suit? Hell, how many people on *Aphrodite* wore theirs besides the guys on the shuttle deck?"

"Well, no, that'd freak out the passengers. But a ship like *Aphrodite* isn't normally going into battle. I figured you guys changed into suits before a raid."

"Did you see anyone in a vac suit when we boarded?" Chang asked. "Ship-to-ship fights are pretty rare. *Aphrodite* was a fluke. We've hit ships, yes, but most of them are hardly armed. If someone who can really give us trouble shows up, we're gone. Just because *Vengeance* is a destroyer doesn't mean we're out to pick serious fights. Mostly we hit small settlements and mining camps. Dirtside work."

"Huh. Guess I hadn't thought about that yet."

"Look, if you want to buy a vac suit, go ahead." Chang shrugged. "We've got a few dozen on board. They're useful. If you want to wear one around all the time while on board, though, that's your choice . . . but you'll look like an asshole."

The three drifted to the eastern end of the bazaar, where between the tents and vehicles they could see the open fields beyond. Jerry led them to a pair of rectangular cargo units sitting underneath the boxy bow of a light freight hauler. Outside the opened doors of the conjoined cargo units sat a shirtless man of Asian descent lounging in the rising sun. A woman dressed mostly in scarves rubbed and washed his bare feet. The merchant's chest bore a tattoo of a serpentlike dragon encircling a star. In his lap sat a gun that Darren didn't recognize, something like a rifle with each end chopped off.

"Morning, Jerry." The merchant was all smiles. "Have you brought me another baby pirate? Seems like a lot of them coming through this week." He didn't get up. Given the man's sunglasses, Darren wasn't even sure he had opened his eyes. The woman at his feet continued her work.

"Sure have. Say hello to Tenzing, Darren."

"Baby?" Darren asked with a raised brow.

Tenzing waved his hand dismissively. "Think nothing of it," he said. He had a voice and diction suitable for hosting a sports broadcast. "Congratulations on your newfound freedom, Darren." Tenzing offered his hand, which Darren shook. "I'd get up, but then my girl here would have to start all over again. Feel free to look around. Ask away if you've got any questions."

As if that were her cue, a lithe young woman stepped up to Darren and the other pirates with a tray of drinks. Darren hesitated, only taking one after he saw his compatriots claim theirs without a second thought.

Racks of firearms of every practical size lined the containers. Darren spotted a couple of guys seated at the ends of the racks with guns in hand. It seemed perfectly reasonable. He'd never shopped anyplace with armed attendants before.

In fact, he'd never shopped for guns at all. He only knew guns from popular entertainment, which wasn't to be trusted. Yet just like in a movie, he stood amid row upon row of laser pistols, laser rifles, pulse weapons, solid projectile guns of every sort, air bursters, and even plasma guns. Grenades sat in boxes in the corners. He found a whole shelf of beam weapons disguised to look like common tools and toys. Another rack held the sort of heavy stuff used against armored units and aerial bombardments. Two racks bore rifles with intricate etchings depicting dragons and snakes.

Darren was more than a little overawed. He picked up a few different things, checking out their weight and feel. "What should I look for?" he asked.

"Mainly what you want right now is something big, scary, and solid that could blow a giant hole in a car," Chang told him.

"Really?" asked Darren. "I mean, it sounds good, but shouldn't I start out with something more controlled?"

Chang shook his head. "You're not looking for precision. You're looking to scare the piss out of folks who don't shoot people for a living. Accuracy counts, but intimidation counts for more. I'd be happy if the whole crew practiced more often, but we're not going up against a fleet marine force anytime soon.

"You'll want to buy a second weapon eventually," Chang continued. "You want something accurate and steady for groundside raids. Something with a full optical suite . . . these might be good," he said, gesturing to the rifles. "You need a good assault weapon that'll do some of the work for you. You can put that off for the moment, but definitely buy something on those lines before you sign on for a cruise. And don't skimp on corrective gear; sometimes the locals put up a fight and sometimes they know what they're doing. You need the edge of having a smarter gun than they've got. But right now, all you need is a big, obviously powerful sidearm."

Darren considered the advice as his eyes continued to roam. He spotted three mannequins in a corner, each wearing slick, imposing combat jackets. "What about body armor?" he asked.

"Oh, forget that shit," Chang scoffed.

"It's a good idea!" called out Tenzing. "State-of-the-art stuff there!"

"It'll blow most of your cash," Chang countered. "That stuff will protect you from a lot of trouble, but not everything. Hardly any of us wear it. Focus on the guns."

"This would be good," Jerry suggested. He hefted a black monster of a gun, not quite a rifle but too big to call a pistol. The barrel, hidden under a blocky dorsal housing, was a good five centimeters in diameter.

Darren's eyes went wide. "Is that a plasma gun? How's that good for self-defense? I mean, if I get jumped, that's going to be kind of slow to draw, isn't it?"

After a moment's quizzical looks between the two older pirates, Chang groaned in realization. "Oh, no, no," he said with a bit of a laugh. "Don't worry about self-defense. I mean, sure, that's good to think about, too, but nobody here is likely to fuck with you. They don't want that kind of heat. Ain't that right, Tenzing?"

"Don't fuck with a pirate in Pirate Town," Tenzing sang out from his lawn chair.

Darren frowned. "That sounds a little too good to be true."

"No, seriously. That's how it is here. The other pirate crews are generally pretty friendly. Sure, you've got to look out for the belligerent drunks, and they're out there. Don't be dumb and don't be shy about asking for help on the holocom if you get into trouble, but by and large you don't need to sweat it. Any brawls between more than two guys just aren't okay, and everyone pitches in to break up a fight that goes too far. Real disputes get settled in a ring."

"We've got all the same sympathies," Jerry concurred. "Sometimes pirates jump from ship to ship while in port. Whoever's going out puts out a call and if a brother's looking for fresh loot, it's not like he has to give his employer twenty days' notice. More than a few other ships come through here. Some of those tramp ships and yachts you saw in orbit are pirate ships, too."

Chang nodded. "Talk to Lauren sometime. She's cruised with half a dozen different ships. If anyone can teach you all about the life, it's her."

After considering it, Darren took the plasma carbine from Jerry, felt its weight in his hand, and pointed it in a couple of directions to test the balance.

Tenzing joined them without interrupting. The gun dealer smiled confidently as he watched the new pirate check out the weapon. "So normally I'd let you shoot up some boxes outside to test that out," he began, "but my magic sense of commerce tells me I might be able to make a sale with a little more effort. Bring that around back to the shooting range," he said, gesturing for the others to follow. He snapped his fingers to one of the armed attendants in the back of the container, who grabbed a small metal tube out of a box before catching up.

The merchant showed them around to a spot underneath his ship. Discarded crates and packaging materials lay scattered around in the freighter's shadow. Beyond them sat the remains of several other crates, peppered with holes and some partially slagged from various demonstrations.

"I got hold of a couple of these things that fell out of the back of a freighter on Korbin III," Tenzing explained as he brought them to a collection of standing crates. "I was hoping to sell them for a good price, but then we tried to do the maintenance and the security programs kicked in. Slagged all the circuitry inside, so now they're just hunks of metal. But they're good for a demonstration." He opened one crate. Inside stood a full set of NorthStar security powered armor.

Chang whistled. "That's a hell of a find. Can't do anything with it now?"

"Nah," Tenzing said. "It'd still stop civilian-legal firearms and most regular infantry stuff. But it's heavy as shit, and even in zero g, it wouldn't move right. The joints are all slagged. Proprietary security systems are pretty hot these days. Now it's only good for target practice." He looked to Darren with a twinkle in his eye. "So I can let you fire off a couple blasts at the grass or the rocks for free, or you can kick in a hundred creds and see what that gun will do against the real thing."

"A hundred credits?" Darren blurted.

"I got it," Jerry offered. The older pirate's sudden generosity surprised Darren.

"Phuong, stand this thing up out there," Tenzing directed. The attendant handed Tenzing the tube he'd brought along and then pulled the armored suit out on a simple hand truck. As he wheeled it out into the field beyond, Tenzing loaded the tube into the plasma carbine, showing Darren how simple it was to operate. "Never fired a gun before?" he asked Darren.

"Never," Darren answered, trying not to grin like a little boy.

"Well, then let's start you off right," he said with infectious enthusiasm. "Use both hands like so. Flip off the safety here, and let's use the target acquisition suite. All you gotta do is point toward the target and make a quick pull of the trigger. Second pull shoots. Long as your aim is fairly close, she'll help correct on her own. If you can hit the broad side of a barn, you can hit a man with this. She's got a bit of a kick, so be ready."

Tenzing put the gun in Darren's hand. His assistant propped up the armor twenty meters out, then cleared away quickly with his hand truck. When Tenzing clicked the charger button, Darren heard the gun whine quietly. It almost hummed in his hand. He looked across the field, aimed, and confirmed the target as instructed. After another moment's pause, he took a breath and then fired.

A glowing neon-green ball of plasma erupted from the gun with a shudder, expanding several more centimeters after it left the barrel. It was slower than a bullet, but far more grandiose. When the ball of plasma hit its target, the suit all but exploded.

Laughter burst from the observers. Tenzing took the gun back from Darren to power it down again before they walked out to survey the damage. They found the armor laying in a heap, its chest plate completely gone and several holes burned through the back plating. The intense heat of the blast had severed numerous limb joints.

Tenzing said something about the gun only being good to about such a range, with the power and effectiveness of its blasts dying off rapidly past thirty meters. Darren didn't really hear it. From the moment he joined the crew of *Vengeance*, he felt like he was free for the first time in his twenty-five years of life. Now Darren felt powerful.

"How much?" was all he asked.

Chang and Jerry talked Tenzing down to sixteen thousand, plus another two grand for ammunition. Had they not spoken up, Darren would gladly have paid the full twenty.

• • •

Darren spent the rest of the afternoon tooling around the bazaar on his own, a bottle in hand the entire time. The cute and willing women for hire along the lanes continued to tempt him, but he was still a bit wary of Paradise's alleged hospitality. Darren appreciated the flirtation and teasing, but, for the most part, he was happy to just shop.

Each individual article of the new outfit he bought would have eaten up most of his former monthly pay. He bought a duffel bag and filled it with more clothes. His new boots were stylish, thermal-insulated works of hand craftsmanship with internally controlled gel pads that massaged his feet. Something about forking over a full grand just for boots thrilled him.

He walked a few dozen paces out from the edge of the bazaar, hurled away the bag holding his old crewman's jumpsuit and boots, and blew it to hell with his brand-new plasma carbine just because he could.

In the open cargo bay of a grounded shuttle, he got fitted for photoreactive contact lenses. He bought the latest and greatest earring-mounted personal holocom off the back of a hovertruck. His pockets soon bulged with new toys.

On occasion, he considered that he might be spending too much too fast. Yet there was still more to come. He still had his half share coming from the hostages and the ship itself. That could realistically go as high as a half million.

With that in mind as the sun set, he headed away from the bazaar toward the permanent structures of Paradise City. Few of the buildings rose higher than three or four stories. The roads were paved primitively, sometimes with plant life breaking through, but for a couple of kilometers in each direction he found all the amenities of civilization . . . except, of course, for serious law enforcement.

It wasn't hard to spot either of the high-class places recommended to him by his new shipmates. The Palace and the Harem stood within eyesight of one another. Unlike several other "hotels," neither building had any of its workers lounging around outside beckoning to passersby.

More or less at random, Darren picked the Palace. He strode up the steps to the hotel's main entrance, looking on appreciatively at how clean and well maintained the building was in comparison to its surroundings. Though the lovely young hostess in the tiny black dress politely asked for his name and ship as he entered, neither she nor anyone else objected to his gun or demanded to see his credit balance. She merely offered a drink, a place to check his duffel bag, and a bath.

"A bath?" Darren asked, curious.

The pert blonde's lips twitched in a bit of controlled amusement. "Forgive me if this is a bit forward, but are you one of the new crewmen of the *Vengeance*?"

"Yeah," he answered, and his chest puffed out a bit.

She nodded, checked a holo screen to her left, and then looked back to him. "Would you like me to show you?" she asked with a friendly smile. The hostess took Darren's arm, waved for someone else to take over in the lobby, and brought him down a nearby flight of stairs. She led him through a hallway to a nondescript door, where she activated a chime. A moment later, the door opened.

Inside lay a spacious room dominated by a sunken square "bathtub" three meters across. There were towels, soaps, and a spread of finger foods and drinks, but Darren didn't notice them. His attention fixated on the pair of strikingly beautiful women lounging beside the tub. They seemed coolly pleased to see Darren . . . who at first could only stare in awe.

The hostess leaned in to whisper helpfully, "This bath is seven thousand an hour. If you need some time to consider . . . ?"

"No," Darren murmured, "this'll do fine."

• • •

Fourteen thousand credits later, Darren wandered up to the Palace's main lounge feeling fantastic. He looked over the many restaurant tables and the bar, wondering where to sit. He spotted the captain seated at a table and having a drink with Ms. Ramirez—no, not Miss anymore. Vanessa Ramirez, *Aphrodite*'s former junior astrogator.

He'd never spoken to Ramirez, and was genuinely shocked that any of the ship's officers would sign on with pirates. But he stopped reflecting on that when he noticed the displeased expression on Casey's face as Ramirez downed the last of her drink and stood. He didn't say anything, nor did he snarl, but he surely seemed put out.

Ramirez left with Casey looking on. She passed Darren with only a polite nod. The new recruit considered following her, but then Casey stood and called to him. The cloud over the captain's spirit seemed to pass.

Obediently, Darren headed over. "Evening, Casey," he said. It still felt odd to address a captain with such familiarity.

"Darren, how the hell are you? Let me buy you dinner. You look good," Casey observed. "And I recognize the scent. They got you downstairs already, eh?"

"Sure did." Darren smiled shamelessly. He jerked his thumb toward Ramirez's exit from the room. "I'm not stealing her seat, am I?"

"Nah, she's gone." Casey shrugged. "Even captains get shot down. I should really stick to paying for the company of women."

Darren's smile only widened. "It does seem to make things easier."

"So you're all hooked up now? Got yourself a hand cannon, I see."

"Yup. Chang and Jerry helped me out. I like it, but it still feels like it's a bit much. Can't say I've got any experience with guns. I'm from the New Dawn system. Civilians aren't even allowed to have guns there."

Casey nodded. "We use some spots here as shooting ranges. Spend the money on some ammo and go get used to the way she feels and the aim. You can buy practice programs for a holocom that'll tie in the targeting suite. And keep your eye out for messages from a guy named Flexner. Ex–Union marine, puts on some informal shooting classes every couple of weeks. He charges, but it's worth it."

They chatted for a while longer on the topic, with Casey dispensing sage wisdom on handling oneself while armed. They ordered dinner and soon found themselves joined by more crewmates. Darren heard stories about raiding colonies and wildcat mining operations, of squandering loot shockingly fast and of the crazy things they did to get by until the next cruise. As the food gave way to drinks and more drinks, they gave advice about places to go, of how to tell when a victim is holding out on something valuable, and how best to enjoy one's fortune.

"Look, prostitutes like the ones here? They're licensed professionals," explained Carl, the crew's designated know-it-all. "They could take off today and make just as much money on a couple dozen other planets, 'cept they'd have to pay taxes and fees there."

Darren nodded; his "bath" had certainly been unforgettable. "I was thinkin' about staying here for the night."

"Woah, slow down there, son," counseled Casey. "Don't go too crazy too fast. We're all for hard partying, but you're running on a half share. Stretch your money out a little at least until the next cruise is on the horizon."

"Oh, don't listen to him," Lauren said, kicking the captain's leg under the table. "Knock yourself out. If you like the baths, staying overnight will blow your mind."

"You should know," Jerry warned, "that Lauren here's co-owner of the Palace. She's a little biased."

The quartermaster shrugged and sat back in her chair. "I like pretty things," Lauren said.

Casey waved a hushing hand at her. "Listen, Darren, a lot of guys drop into town with far more money than you've got after a big score and they piss it away in two, three weeks. Then they're stuck waiting for another ship to go out on another raiding cruise, and that's if they can find a berth on it at all. It's nice enough here to go wander out and sleep under a tree, and we've all done it, but not because we wanted to."

"Killjoy." Lauren kicked the captain again with a smirk.

"There's nothing wrong with the cheaper hotels around here. Take your time."

Darren gave it some hazy thought, staring at his glass. "Guess you might be right. It's just nice to get laid again. It's not like you can maintain a relationship on board a ship."

Lauren shrugged. "It happens on a pirate crew sometimes. Not like there's management to frown on your workplace romance."

"Oh yeah, and the ladies on *Vengeance* are a pack of real sweethearts," Casey said with rolling eyes. "Stick with the girlfriends that charge up front, Darren. Don't get tangled up with the women on our ship. They're all crazy, bloodthirsty criminals."

• • •

In the end, Darren couldn't stay at the Palace after all. Casey bought one round of drinks after another long into the night, and then Darren discovered the Palace's talent would not work with staggering drunks. Apparently professionals had standards. Darren stumbled out into the street—then returned for his belongings and stumbled back out into the street again—and wandered through the still-active streets of Paradise.

He came to a three-story hotel made of concrete, probably dating back to the days when the planet had been minimally colonized for resource extraction. The sign over the front entrance labeled it the "Friendly Shores," which after a moment of contemplative swaying in the roadway seemed clever to Darren. It was, after all, built right on the seashore, and so far everyone had been friendly. He was sold.

The elderly Asian woman who watched over the lobby sent him upstairs after asking pointed questions about "trouble" and "wanting company." Darren found his room, entered, and gave it a look around. It wasn't nearly as posh as the passenger suite on *Aphrodite*, but it wasn't too much of a dive, either. Of course, he realized, that might have been the alcohol influencing his opinion.

Darren decided it was fine. The place didn't stink, the sheets and carpet were clean, and he couldn't hear his neighbors. He dropped his stuff and pulled off his shirt to go to bed. Then the doorbell rang.

Outside, Darren found a pretty, shapely woman leaning on the doorframe. She looked a bit younger than Darren, with short-cut black hair and smooth, golden features that defied ethnic classification. She wore shiny, skintight black pants and a shimmering silver bikini top. Her right hand held a bottle of wine.

"Hi." She smiled and looked down with obvious pleasure at Darren's bare chest. "You're not going to bed alone, are you?"

Darren blinked. "Thought about it," he admitted.

"Aw, that'd be a waste."

"Who are you?"

"Call me Gina." Her hand roamed up and down his chest. "I've got this whole bottle of wine here and I'm looking for someone to share it with."

"You mean pay for it?"

"Aw, don't be mean." Gina pouted. "Wine's on me. Won't find many girls who'll share."

"Piss off, whore," said a new voice. Darren and Gina found another woman walking up to Darren's door. She was dressed in considerably less than Gina, and what little she wore was practically transparent. "This is my fare. Nobody sent you up here." She pushed Gina aside and immediately assumed exactly the same stance. "Hello," she cooed sweetly, touching Darren's chest.

"You know," said Darren, feeling brave, "you could both—"

Without a word, Gina smashed her wine bottle over the other woman's head. Darren gasped as the nameless girl went down in a heap, and then stared at her nearly unconscious form as she groaned on the floor.

"Jesus." Darren blinked at Gina.

Gina looked up at Darren with starry eyes. "Sorry." She giggled. "I guess I dropped my wine." Seeing Darren's shock and indecision, she slid her fingers down his chest and then under the top of his trousers. "You can handle a clumsy girl like me, can't you?"

• • •

The next day's watch section on *Aphrodite* was even thinner than the last. With only fourteen men and women, they needed just a single shuttle. A couple of them were new recruits from *Aphrodite* herself. Ramirez, the junior astrogator, had to reintroduce herself to the watch leader, a short, grouchy drunkard named Jiang. She had to reintroduce one of the other recruits, too, a pretty, ethnically mixed passenger's attendant with golden skin named Carla.

Jiang had a hell of a hangover. He only barely remembered Ramirez, but everyone vouched for her. He didn't even remember Carla at all and could've sworn Ramirez was the only woman recruited from *Aphrodite*. Haywood and Butler spoke up for her, though. That seemed good enough.

Once on board, Jiang doled out a couple of chores. He took the first watch on the bridge. Haywood volunteered to go with him. Jiang assigned Ramirez and Carla to split off and do visual rounds of the ship, teaming them with Ismail and . . . hell, Butler. Butler looked like he was volunteering to go with Carla.

Jiang shrugged it off. Maybe Butler was banging her. "Go ahead. Rest of you, do whatever. Just keep your holocoms on and don't get so shitfaced you can't tell an emergency alarm from the casino toys."

He headed to the bridge with Haywood, who asked, "Figure Butler's fucking her?"

"Probably," Jiang said. "Your first job is to find a security camera wherever they go so we can record it."

Haywood chuckled. Once they got to the bridge he found the security control station and got to work. Jiang sat in the captain's chair and checked in with the *Vengeance*'s bridge watch and port control.

"Sloppy shit, this mess," Jiang grumbled over his shoulder to Haywood. "Someone should've stayed on the bridge at least until we got here."

"No kidding," Haywood agreed. He easily located everyone with the security station's controls. Haywood did a quick sweep of the ship via its internal surveillance equipment. Fourteen people, all accounted for. He then tapped twice on the holocom hidden in his pocket.

On one video screen, he saw Ramirez walk through the corridors of the main promenade with Ismail. She calmly tapped twice on her earring holocom in response. Casually falling a pace behind her partner, she drew the long dagger from its sheath on her leg. Ismail hadn't a clue; one moment he was walking, and in the next he had a blade through his throat.

She took off running. On another screen, Butler and "Carla" made a beeline for engineering. Haywood checked the screen showing the casino floor again, ensuring the rest of the watch was there.

Jiang kept grumbling. "I mean, fuck, if we're going to go to the trouble of setting up watch sections, you'd think the people on watch would at least be serious about it." He called up a holo screen from the captain's communications suite and started scanning channels for something good to watch.

Consequently, Jiang never saw Haywood draw his pistol and point it to the back of his head. The first bullet shattered Jiang's skull; the second was unnecessary and was fired mainly out of habit.

Less than two minutes later, Ramirez crouched beside the open entryway to the casino. Screens projected by her holocom displayed the feed from the chamber's security cameras, routed to her from the bridge. She took the time to count and re-count the pirates. Her luck held; they were all gathered around the same large poker table.

Ramirez slipped inside, staying low and using every bit of cover to her advantage. The pirates remained wrapped up in conversations about rates at the Harem and how long it might take to ransom the hostages. Slinking carefully under tables and chairs, pausing to choose cover carefully, Ramirez closed in.

She pulled the thermal grenade out from her jacket, set its blast radius, double-checked her sight lines, and then stood and threw. Exposing herself even for a moment seemed like a bad idea, but accuracy was vital. Better to commit and get them all at once than botch things and have to face survivors.

Just the same, she ducked beneath the roulette table. Even under solid cover, she could feel the intense heat. Debris flew, much of it igniting instantly. Ramirez rose again with her pistol in hand to finish off anyone who survived. Water rained down on her from the flame-suppression system as she fired into the sole twitching body.

"Nice job, Ramirez," Haywood said over the holocom.

"Are we all set?" asked Butler.

"We are," Ramirez confirmed, already headed for the exit. "How's engineering?"

"So far it's just like the notes said," Butler answered. His voice took on a patronizing tone as he added, "Carla's already being a real help passing me tools and finding parts."

Ramirez ignored it, hoping Gina would as well. The last thing she wanted was a feud between the two. Whore or not, Gina—not Carla, though the men didn't need to know that—had proven herself amazingly resourceful. Ramirez couldn't help but develop high hopes for the younger woman. Butler and Haywood, on the other hand, were typical greedy, treacherous lowlifes. If technicians weren't so vital for this caper, Ramirez would just as soon have shot both of them already.

She would likely have to eliminate them before too long, anyway. They represented too much risk. Neither one would be pleased to learn who "Ramirez" really was, or why she had posed as a junior astrogator on a cruise liner.

Nor would they be happy to know why the former "junior astrogator" refused to let a ship like this remain in the hands of this bunch of pirates—or any other.

"Stick to the plan. Haywood, head down to engineering. I can handle the bridge on my own as long as you and Butler can get us moving."

"It's still like I said," Butler warned, "we're not going to be able to warm up enough to get very far right away."

"We don't need to," Ramirez answered. "We just need one FTL jump to get us to the middle of nowhere. I'll take it from there."

• • •

Darren woke to the sight of Lauren and several other pirates glaring at him with guns drawn. They ordered him to shut up, called for Casey, and waited.

Nobody even let Darren up to use the bathroom. The friendliness vanished. *Come to think of it*, Darren realized, *that whore from last night is gone, too.* He could've sworn she'd fallen asleep with him.

Casey came in, took one look at Darren and the room, and sighed. "Darren, did you talk to anyone about the job Wilson and I had you do on the ship?"

"Ugh," Darren mumbled. "What job? Ship?"

"The fucking starliner!" Casey exploded. "*Aphrodite*! Your goddamn ship! Did you say anything to anyone?"

"What? No!"

"Want me to ask him?" Lauren offered grimly. Casey only shook his head in response, his eyes still on Darren.

The younger man, for his part, could easily guess what Lauren meant. "What's going on? Casey, who was I going to say anything to? What the hell?"

Lauren and Casey exchanged glances. She shrugged. "He'd have to be an unbelievable idiot to help and not go with them," she noted.

"Sure," Casey agreed. "My question is if he was dumb enough to help without knowing it?"

"What the fuck happened?" Darren repeated desperately.

"*Aphrodite*'s gone, Darren," Casey fumed. "Took off out of here twenty minutes ago, not an hour after the watch changeover. She powered up all of a sudden and fired off her guns at the dock and *Vengeance* and everything around her, then broke off the docking rings and shot off too suddenly for anyone to pursue. She jumped into FTL before anyone caught up to her. Whoever took her knew exactly what to fix in engineering."

Darren's jaw dropped. He looked at the angry faces around him and wondered if he'd even live out the day. How many of them would believe he had nothing to do with it? How many would care regardless? Darren buried his face in his hands . . . and then realized that something was missing.

The earring with his new holocom, along with all its personal files, was gone. "Oh no," he groaned and then looked around the room in a rising panic.

"What?" Casey demanded.

"Last night—there was a girl here with me, she . . . God, I think I remember her wanting to get paid before we did it again, so I opened up my holocom in front of her and . . . oh my God," Darren breathed.

Plainly fighting to control her rage, Lauren stepped away. "Told you he should've stayed at the Palace last night," she said bitterly.

"Yeah, well," Casey grumbled, "looks like he's not going to be able to afford to be in there again for a while."

FIVE

Hit Me

"Tanner, you're supposed to hit me!"

"Unh. Wha?"

"Shit, are you okay?" Wong sounded somewhere between annoyed and worried. Tanner wasn't exactly sure where she was. All he could really make out from his vantage point on the mat were the squad bay's overhead lights and a few silhouettes towering over him.

"Nother win for Recruit Wong," Janeka said with an audible frown. "Mark that down on your tally sheet whenever you get up off your back, Malone."

Pain throbbed in Tanner's jaw. He propped himself into an upright sitting position as he grunted out an "Aye, aye." Strong hands helped him off the floor. Ravenell and Sinclair stood by him, making sure he could stand on his own before letting go.

"I'm all right," Tanner mumbled. "I'm all right."

Then Janeka was in his face. "Look at me, recruit," she demanded. "Now look that way. And that way." She watched his eyes track her finger and nodded. "How do you feel?" she asked without sympathy.

"Fine, Gunny Janeka," Tanner said.

"What?"

"Fine, Gunnery Sergeant Janeka!"

"Good. No concussion. No excuse to slack off." Janeka turned to the recruit behind her. "Wong, I catch you goin' easy on Malone or anyone else again, you'll have to learn to do push-ups in your sleep." With that, Janeka strode away to survey other sparring matches.

The sergeant's "dojo" was only a temporary configuration of the squad bay. Every afternoon, the company collapsed their bunks and stacked them along the walls. They rolled out large foam mats and erected sparring dummies and other gear from two floors below. At the end of each session, they put everything back the way it was until the next afternoon. Only those on light duty due to minor injuries got out of sparring, and even they had to help out however possible.

Tanner sighed as Janeka left. Alicia Wong promptly took up the gunny's vacated spot. "I left myself wide open three times," she complained.

"I'm pretty sure I swung at you three times," Tanner replied. "Or kicked. Or whatever I did."

"My great-grandmother could've blocked those."

"You're only nineteen and you're already a badass. I don't want to know how many black belts your great-grandmother—"

"Swear to God," Wong threatened, "if you make an 'all Asians know kung fu' crack—"

"Woah! Just sayin'. You're a scary badass. I'm willing to bet it's a family trait."

"I'm serious. You should be doing better than this. Your forms are fine, but you lose almost every sparring match."

"I've won a few. I even beat Ravenell once."

"I sneezed that time," the taller recruit noted.

"Hey, don't diminish my glory."

"Einstein, stop!" someone behind Tanner yelled. "He tapped! He tapped!"

Tanner and the others turned to the growing commotion. Einstein had his sparring partner on the ground, one arm wrapped around the recruit's throat, while he punched with the other again and again at his opponent's kidney area.

Janeka moved across the room in a heartbeat. "Stop!" she ordered. "Einstein, stop!" She grabbed Einstein's punching arm, twisted it, and pulled him off and away. She shoved Einstein back while other recruits attended to their beaten comrade.

For a brief second, Einstein looked as if he would take Janeka on. Then he hesitated. Tanner wished he had gone for it. A dumb move like that would've solved a big problem for the whole company.

"Your observers said he tapped," Janeka said coldly.

"I didn't see."

"You didn't see *what*?"

"I didn't see him tap, gunny."

"That's why you've got observers, jackass." She looked to the other recruit without stepping away from Einstein. "Rivera, who is that? Is he okay?" Normally, she could identify any recruit at a mere glance, but all the blood from the fallen man's nose made it a little difficult.

Oscar Company's unofficial "recruit corpsman" shook his head. Rivera was older than most of the recruits, having gone on a religious charity mission between graduation and enlisting. He had a little more worldliness than the rest and much more first aid training. "It's Andrews, sergeant," Rivera said. "He doesn't look too good."

Janeka stepped away from Einstein to look Andrews over. Then Einstein giggled—quietly, but she heard it. It was the first time they'd ever seen Janeka's anger run hot rather than cold. "Who's laughing?" she demanded. "Which asshole thinks this is funny? You've got a shipmate down and you laugh? On your faces! Everybody but Rivera, on your faces now!"

The entire company dropped into push-up position wherever they stood. "Down!" Janeka ordered. Everyone lowered themselves to a held position six inches from the floor. They did not, however, rise up. Janeka hadn't ordered it.

Tanner now realized just how forcefully Wong had kicked him under his left arm. His jaw didn't feel too great, either. Everything began to throb with pain.

"How are you doing, Andrews?" Janeka asked. "Can you hear me?"

Andrews grunted weakly.

"Your nose looks bad. How's your back feel?"

"Bad, gunny," Andrews stammered. "I think something might be wrong."

Most everyone near him heard just fine. The only other sounds in the squad bay were the occasional grunts and gasps of one hundred sixty-five young men and women still only halfway through a push-up.

"Just relax, Andrews." Janeka activated the holocom on her wrist. "Medical to Squad Bay Oscar. Potential internal trauma."

As the last words left her mouth, every light in the bay went to a distinct bright red. A siren wailed. Everyone snapped out of their push-up positions and scrambled for their bunks. Many were well across the room from where they needed to be, leading to some chaos. Several recruits stumbled. Headed in opposite directions, Einstein and Tanner barely avoided a collision. Even with the crash avoided, though, Einstein shoved Tanner as he passed.

Tanner got to his collapsed bunk, scooped his helmet off the floor, and shoved it over his head. With its firm, metal faceplate and snug padding, putting the thing on quickly was always unpleasant. At least it was broken in well enough that both lenses lined up with his eyes now instead of riding too high. As the smart-fabric seals wrapped around his neck and tightened against his vac suit, Tanner reached for a brightly lit green panel on the nearby bulkhead. He tore the panel off, pulled out the small compressed oxygen cartridge mounted in the recess behind the panel, and slammed it into the receiving slot in the back of his helmet.

The ready lights of Tanner's helmet blinked green a half second before the squad bay lighting dropped completely. Through the lenses of his helmet, Tanner saw other tiny green indicator lights scattered throughout the darkness. He also saw numerous reds.

The regulation goal was to have the helmet on and sealed in fifteen seconds or less. It already held one preloaded oxygen cartridge, which would last at least thirty minutes. Immediately loading up a fresh cartridge was standard procedure, however, because there was always the chance of a leak or diminished capacity in the preloaded cartridge. Any of a dozen things could go wrong. Oscar Company held to the standard of having the secondary supply loaded and ready within that same fifteen seconds.

"I say again," Janeka repeated in the silent darkness, "medical to Squad Bay Oscar. Potential internal trauma."

"Acknowledged," replied a voice from her holocom.

Silence held for a moment more. "Recover," Janeka finally ordered. The lights returned. The members of Oscar Company stood up wherever they were. Only a couple of the recruits were missing their helmets. Poor Rivera was still looking for his helmet where it had fallen on the mat. Given the circumstances, it was a much better performance than Tanner expected. But it still wasn't flawless.

"So that's seventeen of you dead," Janeka announced, "along with Andrews and Rivera here, whom nobody came to help." The fallen recruit remained sprawled out on his back next to Janeka in a bloody mess with Rivera still kneeling beside him. "Nice job, Oscar Company."

Tanner winced. Standard operating procedure held that every crewman saw to himself first and then his shipmates. Loyalty and selflessness aside, a dead crewman couldn't rescue his buddies. At the same time, however, there was no excuse for Andrews and Rivera "dying" in the drill. Nobody had even moved toward Andrews . . . including Tanner.

"Now then," Janeka went on, "there's still the matter of some sick shithead among you who's amused to see one of his shipmates in pain. Down."

Again, everyone assumed the push-up position. "Down. Stay down," Janeka ordered calmly. "Maybe those helmets will keep me from hearing any of you giggle at your shipmates' pain. We're all supposed to be able to rely on one another out there, but I'd hate to have my life in *your* hands."

• • •

Not one of them had seen sun or stars in thirty-six days.

Rehabilitation of Squad Bay Oscar became the company's first order of business. For over a week, each day held an hour of organized physical training (PT), followed by marching drills for the remainder of the morning (punctuated, constantly, by PT), and then work crew details inside the shelter (also punctuated by frequent PT) right up to lights-out. They knew of the other recruit companies because they saw them at chow in the base galley, but socializing was out of the question.

According to Tanner's reading, there should have been more in the way of formal orientation to military customs, courtesies, and traditions. There should have been endless inspections and care for uniforms. Instead, most of the formal clothing issued to the recruits stayed in their canvas bags, which remained in each recruit's small storage unit beside each bunk. Rather than learning military etiquette, Tanner learned an awful lot about plumbing, ventilation, and atmospheric recycling systems.

As Tanner had suspected, much of the standard training practice lay dead on the parade field.

The company cleaned and inspected every inch of the extensive shelter. Below the squad bay was a small assortment of necessary facilities: an infirmary, a kitchen, and refrigeration rooms. Below that lay engineering spaces to provide constantly recycled air and water, along with power generators so finely tuned to the shelter's low, efficient needs that their fuel would last for years. Still below that was a large, open water tank bigger than any public pool in Tanner's hometown. Under Everett's direction, recruits who'd never maintained such equipment before brought it all to working order.

Even with all the repairs the company did in that first week, some systems and machinery broke down frequently. The shelter hadn't been maintained in decades. Base personnel had clearly made a habit of raiding it for spare parts. Aside from the marching and PT, Oscar Company worked on the shelter day and night for a week.

On that first Sunday, immediately after various religious services concluded, Chief Everett called the company to attention in the squad bay. "You will write to your families, friends, whomever. I expect each of you to write to *someone*. The message you will write is short and sweet. Tell them that they will not hear from you for an extended period, nor will you hear from them. All communications are to be routed to me. I will attach information on how to reach that point of contact to your letter.

"Do not use ambiguous terms. Do not tell them they 'might' hear from you, or that I 'may' be pulling your leg, for I am most certainly not. There is a time frame involved. I will tell the recipient of your letter what that time frame is. I will *not* tell you.

"Tell them that no news is good news. Whatever heartfelt messages or cries for help you want to include are your own business, but you *will* relay these details to your families and loved ones. People care about you. Don't leave 'em wondering. Anyone who fails to follow my instructions will be dealt with harshly."

His lean face was hard as stone. "You have fifteen minutes. Get it done."

That Sunday was the last time they went outside the shelter.

• • •

"This repair and maintenance bullshit is bullshit," Einstein fumed. His face loomed over Tanner's, looking down at him through seven feet of machinery and tubing.

"Did you just say bullshit is bullshit?" Tanner asked. He lay on his back, twisted uncomfortably to get at the guts of the secondary oxygen recycler. There were two smaller recruits in the work party better suited for this work, but it was his turn.

It was also Einstein's turn. "Fuck you," the bigger recruit answered. He did little actual work; his only real role was to feed rigid tubing down to Tanner until it could be firmly secured. That, and to drip sweat from his face down onto Tanner's. "Nobody needs to hear your schoolboy grammar bullshit. It's not gonna get this fixed any faster."

"Neither are your circular statements." Tanner grunted repeatedly as he tried to force the wrench in his hands around another ninety degrees. It stopped moving after the first twenty. "Sonofabitch!"

"Whatsamatter, you too weak?"

"Shut up, Einstein," Tanner heard Baljashanpreet say from outside the recycler. "Tanner, what's wrong?"

"I can't get this stupid nut to turn." He pushed yet again, achieving no more success than he'd met over the last minute.

Ventilation and circulation systems repair wasn't the sort of work Tanner expected when he enlisted. Nor did the company receive much in the way of training other than several lessons on the fundamentals of equipment and repair safety. Past that, all they had to work with were technical manuals, tools so scarce that repair parties frequently had to borrow from one another, and the endless impatience of their instructors.

It hadn't been on any recruit-training syllabus Tanner had seen. It wasn't part of training for Union fleet recruits, nor for NorthStar Security Forces, nor for Sol System Defense, or any of the other system militia training programs Tanner researched before coming to Fort Stalwart.

On-the-job training brought valuable lessons. Tanner learned that despite the numerous technological advances of the last few centuries, some jobs—like providing an enclosed, perpetual supply of oxygen—could only be accomplished with big, clunky machinery. He learned that engineers designed equipment with the belief that it would never need to be fixed, and thus ease of access was never an issue. He learned, therefore, that he hated design engineers.

He learned that he really, truly loved trees.

"You need me to get in there?" Alicia Wong's voice carried through the crevices of the recycler.

"No." Tanner grunted yet again. "No, I'm gonna get this . . . stupid!" he growled, slamming his hand on the stuck wrench. "Fucking! Nut! Gah! There." He sighed. "Now it's moving. Dammit."

"Finally. Can I let go now?" Einstein complained.

"Yeah, let go," Tanner said. "Just lower the last few bits." He shifted to work on the next nut and bolt. It would have been easier had Einstein remained to keep the tubing firmly in place, but Tanner didn't want him staring down at him and complaining anymore. He expected Einstein to at least pass the last few parts down to him by rope, though, rather than dropping the bits carelessly down on and around his head. “Hey!” he shouted. “What the hell?”

“Bruning,” Einstein called as he pulled away, “come patch this thing up.”

“I’m not done yet,” Tanner protested, then sighed as the light from above was covered up. “Fuck it,” he decided, activating the holo screen for the tech manual program in the holocom on his wrist. He didn’t need the schematics so much as he needed the light.

“Aren’t you finished with this yet?” he heard Everett ask. Tanner let out another rueful breath as he picked up the pace of his work.

“Almost finished, Chief Everett,” Wong answered. She and Baljashanpreet were both squad leaders. Having the better performance scores of the two, Wong was in charge of the twelve-person work detail. Tanner would have preferred to work with his own squad, or Wong’s. Everett, however, seemed to feel that learning to work with assholes like Einstein was a high priority, and so he continually mixed up work detail rosters.

“What’re we waiting on?”

“Recruit Malone is still fastening the last few relay tubes, chief,” Wong said.

“Malone!” Everett yelled. “When are you gonna be done with that?”

“Just two more minutes, chief!” Tanner answered, turning nuts and bolts quicker still.

“You’ve got one! You’d better move!”

“Aye, aye, chief!”

“Is this thing gonna break again?” Everett asked. “We’re running on only one recycler. We’re supposed to have two.”

“I think we’ve got it licked now, chief,” explained Wong.

“You think? You thought so before. Why’d it break again?”

“We—the last set of tubes weren’t fastened properly and the casings melted, chief.”

"Melted? Who fucked that up?" Everett's irritation doubled. Tanner kept working.

"I take full responsibility, chief," Wong answered.

"I didn't ask that! I know you're responsible! I want to know who actually did it. Tell me who had his hands on the tools and the tubes before it melted. Don't even think about trying to take one for your team, Wong. Tell me."

"Recruit Einstein, chief," Wong confessed.

"Goddammit, Einstein, I knew she'd say that. What's your excuse this time? Who are you gonna blame for this one?"

"Recruit Malone, chief!" answered Einstein without hesitation.

"What the hell did Malone do?"

"He gave me the wrong fittings, chief!"

"Malone!" Everett barked again. "Did you give him the wrong fittings?"

"No, chief!"

"Are you calling Einstein a liar?"

Tanner blinked. There clearly wasn't a right answer here. "No, chief!"

"Well, you should! I've caught him lying before! Einstein's a lying slack-ass! But what the hell is *your* problem?"

"No excuse, chief! I got confused on the fittings—"

"How could you get confused?"

"Again, no excuse, chief! I was tired and got confused while giving Einstein the fittings while he was down here but I—"

"Malone, you are boring me already. Did you give Einstein the right fittings or not, yes or no?"

He paused again. The right fittings were, in fact, lying next to Tanner right now. He had passed Einstein the wrong fittings, but then realized his mistake before the job was finished. Rather than correcting the error, Einstein just left the incorrect ones in place and called it good, leading to the problem Tanner now fixed.

"Yes, chief!" Tanner finally admitted.

"So Einstein is lying to me!"

"Sort of, chief!"

"Malone, you were confused on the fittings and now you're confused on whether or not you're calling Einstein a liar! What the hell's going on with you?"

"I thought that—"

"Don't think so much! Just patch that up and get your ass out here right now!"

Tanner grimaced, knowing further punitive PT awaited him. He put the last fitting in place as quickly as he could, then gathered the ones he'd had to strip loose to correct Einstein's work.

Along the way, he heard a further grilling. "So you're not payin' attention to what you're doing, is that it, Einstein?"

"No, chief!"

"No, what? No, you're not paying attention, or no, I'm wrong?"

". . . I'm not a life support tech, chief!"

"You are if I say you are."

"I'm a marine recruit, chief!" Einstein pushed. "This is navy crew work. They're the ones that fix ship systems, not marines."

"On your face, Einstein! Everyone, on your faces! Malone, you get out here and get on your face, too, right now!"

"Aye, aye, chief!" Tanner replied, hustling to squirm out of the recycler. He rushed to join the others as he was ordered.

"Don't leave the job undone," Everett snapped at him. "Get over there and button that thing up, then get down on your face."

Tanner scrambled back to the recycler to replace the access panel that he'd just crawled from. "Aye, aye, chief!" he huffed.

"As for you assholes, your job is what I say it is!" Everett roared. "You got me?"

"Yes, Chief Everett!" the work detail shouted in unison—except for Einstein.

"Einstein, what are you gonna do on a ship if the life support systems take a hit?"

"Get the engineers to fix it, chief!"

"What're you gonna do when the engineers get killed in that same hit, dumb-ass? Have you considered that?"

Einstein didn't answer. Tanner rushed over, taking up a position next to Einstein on the floor.

"Nothing? You've got nothing to say? Is that what you're gonna do in combat, Einstein? Nothing? That's not much of a plan. Down! Up! Down again! Hold still there."

Everett walked over to the recycler, gave it a quick inspection, and activated it. The machine hummed to life perfectly. "Good thing this works," Everett said, "otherwise I'd be unhappy. Is it gonna keep working now, Wong?"

"Yes, chief!" grunted Wong.

"Is she right, Malone?"

"Think so, chief!" He winced as soon as he said it. Sometimes it was hard to keep up with what passed for acceptable conversation with his instructors.

"You think? That's not much of an answer. Is Oscar Company gonna have enough oxygen to survive, Malone?"

"Yes, Chief Everett!"

"Why'd it take you so long to get this done?"

"No excuse, chief!"

"I didn't ask for an excuse. I asked why it took you so long to get this done."

"Not much experience with machinery, Chief Everett," Tanner answered. His arms trembled. He'd been up all night, along with the rest of the work detail. "Just a steep learning curve for me, chief."

"So you're great in a classroom, but not much else?"

Tanner winced as if punched in the gut. That one hurt. Yet before he could respond, the lights flashed red and the decompression alarm sang out. Tanner, Wong, Einstein, and the rest leapt for their helmets, which were now never more than a couple meters away. Tanner heard the seals on his helmet working even as he reached for the oxygen cartridge panel on the closest wall. At least he was getting quicker at this.

As he inserted his spare cartridge in his helmet, though, he spotted the red indicator lights of the helmet on the recruit beside him. The helmet's tank was either depleted or jammed; the spare was apparently just as useless. There were no other spares in the wall recesses nearby.

Tanner promptly grabbed her shoulder before she could scramble away and threw the switch on the back of her helmet to eject one of her tanks. "Hold on!" he shouted, then reached back to pop one of his own cartridges out of his helmet. It spewed out oxygen under fierce pressure, but he held on tightly. The recruit tried to turn around; he had to fight with her to maintain his hold at first, but then she realized what he was doing. She held still while he inserted the cartridge into her helmet.

When the lights in the squad bay went out entirely, Alicia had one green light and one red light. So did Tanner. Her faceplate covered up everything but her eyes, which looked back at him through the helmet's lenses with obvious surprise.

"Recover!" Everett barked. The lights went back on. Three of the work detail's recruits already had their helmets off. With no air to breathe in either tank, they had to unseal and remove the helmets before they suffocated.

"Smalls, Mohamed, Quinto," the chief called out, "you all just died from asphyxiation. Point to the nearest person to you. Whoever's closest, I don't give a shit who it is. That's right. Now, you people they're pointing at, you're the ones who could've saved your shipmates if you hadn't just stood there with your thumbs in your asses when you saw they had two red lights on their readouts.

"You are all proficient enough at saving your own butts. That's step one. Next step is to start lookin' out for one another. I didn't say put your fingers down!" Everett snapped. "Keep 'em pointing!

There. Now if you're pointing at someone or you've got someone pointing at you, that means you get to stand a double shift on fire watch tonight.

"Recover. No, wait," he said, stopping himself. "Leave 'em on."

The work detail watched in confusion as Everett walked over to a sealed compartment against one bulkhead. He input a numeric code on the nearby keypad, unsealing the hatch. Standing in front of the compartment, he reached inside where the work detail couldn't see.

"Like I was sayin' to Einstein," Everett said, "there are times when you don't have the right people on hand, but the job's gotta be done. Maybe your engineers die. Maybe they asphyxiate 'cause their helmets don't work and nobody looks out for them.

"Everybody down. Now."

Without hesitation, the work detail hit the deck once more. They expected more push-ups. They didn't expect Everett to produce a large, bulky rifle from the compartment.

Tanner blinked. "Holy shit."

Smiling, Everett threw the power safety switch on the pulse rifle, pointed it toward the recycler, and fired. Bright-blue flashes of light lit up the recycler room. The rifle itself was quiet; the damaged recycler was anything but. Sparks and smoke flew as the machine screamed to a halt. Burned and slagged metal caved in upon itself.

"Recover," Everett said. He watched as the work detail got to its feet. "Looks like your oxygen recycler took a hit. Better get to work fixing it. Oh, and you'd better go find some spare oxygen for your helmets, too, 'cause you aren't taking them off until the recycler's running again."

As he passed through the stunned work detail, the chief paused in front of Tanner and Alicia. Everett slung the rifle over his shoulder. "Might want to consider that you perform a lot better when you don't sit around thinkin' too much, Malone."

• • •

Chow was monotonous. The company had essentially five warm dishes to choose from, with each choice determined by the day's mess detail. There were many scrambled eggs. There was a lot of toast. There was a lot of chili barely worthy of the name. Sinclair's squad managed to at least do simple things, like turning toast into garlic bread. Baljashanpreet's squad tended to inflict at least a few random cases of indigestion.

"Better than it being burned again," Tanner mumbled as he shoveled more food into his mouth. He sat on his plastic locker with his tray in his lap. Several other recruits sat with him. Chow was one of the few opportunities for anything close to socializing.

"I can't believe you actually ate that stuff," Alicia said, making a sour face at him. She sat on a locker pulled over from the next row. Her bunk was clear across the squad bay, but she preferred the company on Tanner's end.

"I'm a growing boy," he answered with a shrug.

"Growing?" asked Other Gomez, whose real first name seemed long forgotten. "Fuck, I've lost ten pounds since I got here. How are you putting on weight?"

Tanner chuckled. "I think it's all my bruises."

"So when are you gonna tell us our standings, Malone?" spoke up Ravenell. He sat on Tanner's bunk, for which he had never asked permission yet never heard objections. "You're the one with the grade book."

"I don't really look."

"Seriously?"

"I don't have the names sorted like that on the records sheets." Tanner shrugged. "They're all alphabetical. Makes it easier to get stuff done."

"So what would it take for you to sort 'em by performance average and just take a look? Just see who's in the top ten?"

Tanner frowned. "It'd take pressing two buttons," he admitted.

"So why don't you?"

"Because then I'd know, and then I'd be vulnerable to your peer pressure." Tanner smirked. "Anyway, why do you want to know?"

"It affects billeting priorities for when we get out of here," Alicia said. "You know that."

"We're never getting out of here." Tanner's voice took on a sarcastically morbid tone. "You know that."

Alicia threw her crumpled napkin at him. Tanner chuckled, then stopped as Alicia pointed at his chest. "Aw man," he grumbled, noticing the stain from her napkin. He grabbed for his own napkin to clean it off. Everett and Janeka considered food stains inexcusable.

"Sinclair!" Everett's voice boomed through the squad bay. "Einstein! Baljashanpreet! Malone! Get your asses outside my office!"

Alicia and Tanner shared a wide-eyed glance. "Just go," Ravenell urged him. "We'll clean up your junk here, don't worry about it. Just go."

Seconds later, Tanner and the others were lined up outside the instructors' office at attention. Sinclair hissed, "Tanner, that stain—" But there wasn't time to deal with it. Everett stalked out, his face set in cold rage. He immediately saw the offending red stain on Tanner's chest. "Malone, get on your face!" he snarled.

Tanner dropped. "Down!" Everett snapped. Tanner executed half a push-up and remained in the down position. He wondered how long he would be there. It should have become easier over all this time, and in fact it had, but he hadn't noticed it.

He heard Everett's heels click around the group. "Recruit Macias will not return to the company," he said. Tanner winced inwardly; Macias was a good guy. He worked like hell and helped his shipmates. He was also a member of Sinclair's squad, and therefore Tanner's.

Sinclair couldn't hold back his concern. "Is he—"

"Drop, Sinclair!" Everett barked. "You didn't have permission to speak!" Obediently, Sinclair took up a spot on the floor beside Tanner. He couldn't be sure, but Tanner thought he heard a snort from Einstein. He wondered if Everett caught it, too.

"Dr. Sanchez tells me that Recruit Macias suffered mild brain damage from oxygen deprivation as a result of the incident in the pool," Everett went on. "He will recover, but only after significant therapy. Obviously this means he won't complete the training cycle with Oscar Company, if he remains in the navy at all. Sinclair, you will see to the collection of his gear. Malone, you will adjust the records accordingly."

"Aye, aye, Chief Everett!" they both shouted.

Tanner had nothing to go on but sound and his peripheral vision. All else was just concrete. Everett's feet came to a halt in front of Einstein's. "Recruit Macias would still be here if you followed directions, Einstein."

"I did follow directions, chief!"

"Bullshit! Macias was your swim buddy! You were supposed to look out for him, not drag him down! If it hadn't been for Vega and Wong, Macias would be dead right now because of you!"

"He was a weak swimmer, chief!"

Tanner's eyes flared. Growing up in Geronimo, Tanner spent part of practically every day in a pool. He knew a strong swimmer when he saw one. Macias was fine. He wanted to object, but he knew better.

"You don't make that call! Gunny Janeka and I make that call! Is that understood?"

"Yes, Chief Everett!"

"This is the second goddamn recruit you've injured, asshole, and your own scores aren't getting any better. Recruit Baljashanpreet, I am hereby transferring Einstein to your squad. You will help him get his act together. Is that understood?"

"Yes, Chief Everett!" answered Baljashanpreet.

"No more fucking 'accidents,' Einstein," Everett seethed. He turned and walked back into his office. "You two are dismissed," he added over his shoulder.

That left Sinclair and Malone on the floor. Baljashanpreet immediately turned to leave. Einstein was slower. Tanner was sure he heard him laugh.

He never wanted to hit anyone so much in his life.

• • •

"Slow. Again."

Tanner's leg shot out in an arc toward Ravenell's head. The taller recruit blocked.

"You're still slow, Malone." Janeka sighed. "Do it again." Tanner kicked once more, making his instructor no happier. She had a talent for conveying annoyance. "He knows it's coming. Don't worry about hurting him. Kick like you mean it."

Tanner gave it all he could. He was faster this time, tighter and with better extension. Ravenell blocked, as advertised, but a grin played at his face. It had the shine of approval.

The sense of triumph was short-lived. "Malone, at attention!" Tanner stood straight, looking ahead at nothing as Janeka came into his line of vision. "What the hell is your problem?"

"I don't understand, Gunnery Sergeant," Tanner responded.

Grunts and shouts, slaps of hands and feet on mats and on human bodies, filled the squad bay. Janeka could easily project her voice over all of it. Now she spoke quietly, loud enough for Tanner to hear but no louder. She was even scarier when she was quiet.

"I see you on the practice dummies and the holo programs," Janeka growled. Her nose was no more than an inch from his. "You're fine on those. Better than fine. You even look like you're becoming proficient. And then the second you're up against a live opponent you flop around like every fight's your first. You know all the forms but you can't apply 'em for shit. So what the hell is your problem?"

"My problem with what, Gunnery Sergeant?" Tanner asked levelly. There were more polite ways to ask, but all of those ways were incorrect with Janeka. You asked her straight or you didn't ask at all.

"How many sparring matches are on your tally sheet?"

"One hundred eighty-six, Gunnery Sergeant." He knew exactly where she was going.

"And how many of those did you win?"

"Seventeen, Gunnery Sergeant."

"Less than ten percent!" Janeka snapped. "You're not a cripple! You aren't sick! *Dead people* could win more than ten percent of their fights!" She waited for him to respond, but hearing nothing, she shoved him. "I think your problem is you're a pussy."

Pushed off his balance, Tanner blinked but quickly recovered. He returned to attention. Janeka advanced into his spot. "I think you're afraid to fight."

"I am not afraid, Gunnery Sergeant!"

"Yes you are," Janeka said, shoving him once more. "You're afraid to *fight*." She pushed him back yet again. Recruits turned to watch. "That's what it is, isn't it? Don't fight back so hard, you don't get hurt so bad, huh?"

Tanner stopped trying to stand at attention. "I've been hurt every day since we got here, Gunnery Sergeant!" he shot back. "I haven't quit yet!"

"Oooh, that's a good act, recruit," Janeka said, shoving him again. "You win the 'most inspirational' award in school? You get straight As for effort?"

She shoved him again. Tanner didn't know what would make her happy or when she'd make her point. He didn't know what to say.

"I need *fighters* in my navy, Malone," she continued, shoving him yet again. "You grin and bear it and put on your act, but you don't fight. What're you gonna do when you're out there, huh?" Another shove. Two recruits behind him now got out of the way. Janeka had pushed him into their sparring circle. "What're you gonna do when you're faced with some smuggler? Some Hashemite raider? You gonna face down a Krokinthian warrior with all that *heart* and just hope he gets tired of hurting you before you die?"

Tanner blinked. "Those are different—"

"Don't bullshit me, Malone!" Janeka said, slapping him hard across the face. She slapped him again. "Fight, goddammit!" Again, her hand came back. "Fight!"

Tanner forcefully blocked her third slap. His eyes flared. Janeka's lip curled back. "Somebody start a clock!"

"Aw shit," Tanner mumbled, but then it was on. He blocked, dodged, and gave ground, taking a few shots that he just wasn't fast enough to avoid. Janeka wasn't just better trained or more experienced; she was frightening. The left cross and right crescent kick both came so hard and fast that even though he blocked them she still knocked him around.

Janeka didn't let up. She threw out swings and strikes and advanced into his space as he backed away. He took a hook to the jaw, then a snap kick to the hip that sent him tumbling to the ground, and barely rolled out of the way of the stomp that came in to follow it up. Janeka swung another foot up into his side as he scrambled to his feet. He grabbed at it, twisted, and pulled, yanking the sergeant off her feet. She landed on her hands, spun, and practically flew back up; by the time Tanner was standing again, he had her foot coming up for his face. He slapped the foot down in time, but couldn't block the fist that came straight at his nose, knocking him back with a resounding crunch.

The blackness behind his eyelids erupted with flashes of color. Most of the flashes were red. Something struck his stomach and something else hit his hip, but they didn't hurt nearly as bad. Tanner's eyes opened again. His anger and training blended. He caught her on the cheek with a solid, forceful right cross.

He followed up, but she was ready for it. Janeka caught his left arm, twisting him around and sending him spinning past. Tanner lost his footing, stumbled, but immediately recovered.

Janeka smirked. "You starting to fight back, or having an epileptic seizure?"

Blood flowed freely from Tanner's nose down across his mouth. He hardly noticed. "Can you even spell that?" he shot back.

Janeka's lip curled back. She came at Tanner again. He countered with his own advance rather than backpedaling as he had before. Tanner came out worse in the exchange but held his ground, attacking more often than he defended. No observer would have claimed he was winning, but the fight was no longer one-sided.

Anger gave way to determination. She was faster, stronger, and in every way better, but Tanner would be damned if he gave up. Fists and feet kept flying, but eventually Tanner took a risk. Janeka used speed and extension; he thought, in less than a heartbeat and without real consideration, that perhaps she wasn't as good close in. Hooks and uppercuts led to tangled arms. Tanner pulled in and went for the head butt.

Janeka did exactly the same thing at exactly the same time. Foreheads slammed together. The two staggered away from one another.

A roar that could have been a crowd or just the death cries of millions of brain cells filled Tanner's head. He found himself on his hands and knees with no memory of how he'd gotten to the floor. Something inside told him he desperately needed to get up. He shoved himself to his feet, dizzy and more than a little lost. Tanner saw Janeka pushing herself up off the floor just a few feet away.

Janeka. That's what was so important. He was fighting Janeka for some reason. She had hurt him. Tanner swept in with his foot coming up at her head as if kicking a football.

She caught his ankle, twisted, and flung him face-first onto the floor. He felt her foot land straight onto the small of his back. Pain shot from that one spot all through his body, overwhelming even the terrible feeling in his face.

"Rivera," he heard Janeka grunt, "look him over."

"Nnngh," Tanner managed. He shoved himself to his feet, found Janeka turning to look at him in surprise, and promptly slammed a right hook into her chest. He meant to hit her jaw, but he was a touch disoriented.

She caught his arm, fully extended it, and punched him repeatedly in the side with that third arm he never knew she had until now. Locked into that position, he couldn't stagger back or get away; she had his arm, to which his popping ribs were connected, until there was another pop in his shoulder and he got perhaps another inch farther away from her, even though she still had hold of his wrist.

Hitting her meant everything. He remembered that. He held the thought, and when she let him go, he spun around with his left hand out and slapped her across the face.

The sergeant was shocked. He registered that. A boot came up into his jaw then, slamming him backward. The floor hit him, too, on the back of the head and more or less everywhere else on him all at once.

Someone shouted. He couldn't really understand it. Janeka loomed over him, stepping close with a surprised look on her face. She was even more surprised when his legs swept up around hers and pulled her down in one of the few ground-fighting moves Tanner had been taught. Tanner pivoted upright, cocking back his right arm to throw another blow at her only to discover that it didn't work right anymore.

He glanced toward Janeka, but saw only the sole of her boot coming at his face.

• • •

Nothing in particular woke him. It was a strange thing, waking up naturally and not at the instigation of outside stimuli. Something warned him to jump to his feet before his bunk collapsed, but that order seemed to come from a long way off. It was like he was yelling at himself from down a long, dark hall. Moreover, there was no bunk above his. There was just the ceiling. The only light came from the small monitor off on one corner.

He was in a hospital room.

"Good evening," said exactly the sort of voice that was usually used by machines. "Please rest. A nurse has been summoned."

Yup. Hospital. He tried to sit up but found it very difficult to move. Thin, barely flexible blue plastic encased his shoulder, as well as his elbow and his hand. He realized his ankle was similarly wrapped.

It was the sort of stuff one put on broken bones.

"Glad to see you awake," said the man who entered. He had a middle-aged look about him, Tanner thought. "I'm Dr. Hsu. I imagine you're pretty out of it right now, though. Can you understand me, recruit?"

"Did I wash out?" Tanner mumbled.

"I'm sorry?"

"My company," he said. "Did I wash out?"

"No, no." The doctor chuckled. "Though you got a day off that I imagine nobody in your company envies. I haven't seen anyone this beat up in years. Not without filing a criminal incident report," he added somewhat darkly. "How are you feeling?"

"Numb. Can I have a new body now? I think I broke this one."

"Corrective surgery doesn't go quite that far," the doctor said with a kind smile. "At any rate, you didn't break that on your own. Do you remember how you got here?"

"Had a match with Gunny Janeka," Tanner said.

"You didn't have a match," the doctor corrected. "You had a fight. Matches don't get this rough. Look, you're a little too groggy from the painkillers we used. We'll put you on subtler stuff now, but the concussion you suffered limited our initial options."

"So I didn't wash out?"

"No." The doctor shook his head. "You've only been out a day. You'll be here tomorrow, on light duty with your company the day after that, and fit for full duty in another two at the worst."

Thinking clearer now, Tanner read the display on the monitor across the room. It showed a shifting display of his body systems, first skeletal, then muscular, then cardiovascular, and finally vital organs. He had focused in biological studies in school, and Everett provided excellent first aid training. Tanner knew what the body on the display was supposed to look like. What he found instead was ugly.

Medical care for the Archangel Navy was certainly of high quality, but only rich people could afford the kind of care that would bounce them back from this sort of condition within days. "Isn't this expensive?" he asked.

"You let us worry about that," said the doctor with a comforting smile. He patted part of Tanner's arm that wasn't covered by isolation plastic. "In the meantime, you need to relax and then let the cobwebs clear so you can talk to Lieutenant Alvarez."

"Hmh?" Tanner blinked. Alvarez was the only officer on base whom the recruits knew by name; ultimately, all the company commanders reported to him. He was low-ranking in terms of officer ranks, but as far as recruits were concerned, he might as well have been God.

"You suffered a severe beating," he said. "I sent out the notifications as soon as we had you at rest. You need to give a statement, and then there will likely be an investigation."

"Why?"

"Sparring matches don't break that many bones or cause internal bleeding at multiple points, son," the doctor said. "We're bare-knuckles here because we can afford it and because the instructors feel it's more realistic, but that's no excuse to take things to this extreme. You have rights, and that includes the right to not be beaten to a pulp."

Tanner quietly shook his head. "No. I could've stayed down. Tapped out. I didn't."

"She could've stopped," the other man said gently. "She didn't."

"I'm not gonna toss the gunny down a garbage chute 'cause I lost a match."

"Did you have designated observers for this 'match'?" Hsu asked. "I can't say we trained in hand-to-hand like this when I went through training. This is new stuff here. But I know the rules and regulations. Did any of them call the match finished?"

Tanner didn't answer.

"Well"—the doctor shrugged—"it's not your call how to handle this. It's the lieutenant's. But let the painkillers settle so you can think clearly before you decide how you feel about it, okay? You're spending the night here, anyway." His holocom beeped. The doctor gave it a flick, calling up a display that he read with a scowl.

"I'm thinking clearly already. No investigation. Not 'cause of me."

The doctor's eyes went from his holo display to meet Tanner's. "She just requested to see you, actually. Your company commanders asked to be notified as soon as you were conscious."

Tanner blinked. Janeka went from an abstract concept to something real. He wasn't sure he could stand at attention right now, and he definitely didn't want to be yelled at. He had never known anyone so intimidating . . .

And yet he hit her. Repeatedly. She put him down, repeatedly, but he had struck back. She was flesh and blood.

"I can send her away. I outrank her by quite a bit," he added comfortingly.

"No, sir." Tanner shook his head, realizing now whom he was talking to. Doctors were officers. "Please don't. It's okay if she wants to see me, sir."

"Do you want anyone in here with you?"

"No, sir." Tanner shook his head again. "Thank you, sir."

The doctor nodded. He glanced down at his display again, calling up a new set of graphics and then explaining things about the healing process, but Tanner only half paid attention. He should have been fascinated. Tanner had no real interest in becoming a doctor, but it was all still biological science. Once upon a time, he was supposed to intern for a research center. Instead, he was spending his summer in an emergency shelter, cleaning out ventilation shafts by hand, absorbing verbal abuse, and having his ass kicked.

"Anything you need?" the doctor asked.

"Sir," Tanner mumbled, looking to the curtains. "Is that a window?"

"Yes," he said, walking over to the door without a second thought. "Here you go." He pressed a button on the wall.

"Oh, no, sir, I don't think I'm supposed . . ." Tanner tried to object, but the doctor was already gone. The curtains slid open. The hospital building was one of the taller structures in Fort Stalwart. Other floors had mostly neighboring buildings filling up their windows. Tanner's window had stars.

He looked out at them for a long time. Everyone he loved was out there somewhere. Not one of his school classmates was on this planet. The ones he loved most didn't even orbit the same star anymore. His father and Sharon lived in a whole different system. Madelyn was all the way out on Earth.

Feeling very much alone, Tanner tried to blink away the tears that came to his eyes. They blurred his view of the stars.

"Recruit Malone," broke in a harsh, familiar voice. Tanner looked over to see Janeka in the doorway, sporting a black eye. "Permission to enter?"

"You need permission from me for anything?"

"You're in a hospital bed. There's a proper etiquette."

Tanner blinked in surprise. She seemed to completely ignore the tear tracks. At least the tears had stopped before she arrived. "Permission granted?" he said.

Janeka nodded, then stepped forward to stand next to his bed. "The doctor says you'll be back tomorrow."

"Yes, gunny," Tanner replied. "I'm kind of surprised. That looks . . ." He gestured at the display. "I didn't think the navy would go to this sort of trouble for training injuries."

"That's not for you to worry about, recruit." She spoke without anger or derision. Either she didn't want to get sidetracked or the Archangel Navy's medical capabilities were some great big secret. "You did better than I expected yesterday."

"I did?"

"I'm not here to blow sunshine up your ass." Janeka frowned. "This isn't praise. Now I know you haven't been giving it your all. I don't tolerate sandbaggers."

"I'm not a sandbagger, gunny," Tanner protested quietly.

"Then what the fuck have you been doing all this time?" Her voice was controlled. Clearly, the gunny had a broad range of tones, volumes, and expressions with which to communicate her endless disapproval.

Tanner hesitated. For the first time, Janeka didn't admonish him for failing to answer promptly. "I don't want to hurt anyone, gunny."

"You plan on hugging the enemy into submission?"

"No, gunny, I just . . . they're not the enemy." Tanner shrugged with his uninjured shoulder. "The enemy isn't in the company. You're not the enemy, either."

"Not until yesterday?"

"Not until you were beating me up, no," Tanner admitted.

Janeka stepped closer. She called up a display on her holocom, projected it, then turned it around for Tanner. "I thought you might need to see this."

It was a flat projection, showing only one camera angle of Janeka and Tanner facing off. He saw himself block her snap kick, then take the cartilage-crunching blow to his nose, then more shots as he was left reeling. He saw himself surge back with the first punch he ever landed on Janeka, knocking her away. The screen froze.

"What did you do there?" Janeka asked.

"Right cross," he said.

"A *perfect* right cross, Malone," Janeka corrected. "Perfect form, especially right in the middle of a fight when nothing's perfect or rehearsed. Excellent extension, good follow-through. Were you even thinking about that?"

"I just wanted to hit you." Tanner half shrugged again. It was an odd thing to say, but once more, Tanner remembered that Janeka didn't care for pleasantries or tactful eloquence. She demanded straight talk.

"Your training took over," she said. "You were stressed. Maybe frightened, maybe not, but you knew you had to act, and so you acted as you were trained.

"That's the point to all this, Malone. You need to learn to *fight*. With your hands, with your equipment, whatever. *Things will go wrong out there*. You will be scared and tired and hurt and things will go wrong, and you need to be ready to fight in spite of all that. We aren't putting you through all this hand-to-hand combat because we expect you to get into fistfights. It's not about throwing punches and kicks. It's about facing pain and adversity and fear without giving up. You did that. You could've done it better.

"If you'd been trained to handle real stress by your school or your parents, you wouldn't have crashed the Test, and you wouldn't be here now, would you?" she asked.

Tanner looked up at her, searching for a dig or an insult but couldn't read her poker face. "Chief Everett told you about that?"

"We share the same brain," Janeka said. "Didn't you know?"

The recruit grunted. It was, in fact, something that the company generally suspected. The only topic of debate was whether their brains were unified by some cybernetic relay or if they had a telepathic link.

"You'd never been in a fight before yesterday, have you, Malone?"

"No, gunny."

"Why not?"

"I've usually been able to think my way out of trouble, gunny."

"That's good, but you need to move beyond that now. You're in a uniform. It's a dangerous world out there. You can think or talk your way out of a fight when you're dealing with someone else who also has a functioning brain, but there are an awful lot of people out there who don't. Or they're following the orders of people who don't. That uniform means that if there's gotta be a fight, you want it to come to you and not to someone else. You ready for that, recruit?"

"Yes, gunny."

"I don't think you are," Janeka said. He found himself staring into her eyes again. "I think you've got the guts, but you've got to start taking all this more seriously. You've got to start doing all this for real."

"I am, gunny."

"You're not." She let it hang there for a moment before she said, "My first fleet duty was on the *Resolute.* We picked up a distress call from a freighter getting attacked by pirates halfway out to hell and gone from Augustine. All we found were bodies floating in the void. We found one guy alive, an engineer who'd been lucky enough to have his vac suit on and was able to slip away, and he had his holocom recording the whole time.

"His ship tried to resist, but in the end the captain surrendered. They spaced the whole crew. Thirteen passengers, too. Civilians. We picked up thirty-seven bodies, and not all of 'em died from being spaced, and not all of 'em died quick. Thirty-seven bodies and one bloody teddy bear."

She stared at him to make sure it sank in. "Malone, when you get in a fight, you gotta do it for real and give it everything you've got, and I don't care if it's dirty and I don't care if it's ugly. There's no such thing as a fair fight. You fight for real and you fight to win and to hell with anything else, because *you do not know what's gonna happen if you lose.*"

She fell silent.

"Aye, aye, gunny," Tanner said.

Janeka called something else up on the display. He saw the two of them tangle, followed by their synchronized head butt. "What were you trying to do there?" she asked.

"I thought . . . I thought you were keeping your distance from me," Tanner said, "and that maybe getting in close would put you at a disadvantage."

"How'd that work out for you?"

"Not so good."

"No. I am trained at grappling and fighting close," Janeka explained, "and I'm stronger than you. That wouldn't have worked out for you at all. It's only dumb luck that it didn't turn out worse than this. But you were thinking, Malone. For one little moment in all of that, you were thinking.

"Untrained, inexperienced people are all rage and panic when they fight. You get someone trained up, they can think while they fight. That's where we've got to take you, Malone. You and everyone else in the company, and they can't get there if you give them the bullshit half-assed matches you've been putting on so far. You got me?"

"Yes, gunny."

"I hope so," Janeka said. "You've got a lot of heart, but you don't have a lot of mean in you. You better find a way to build some up real quick, or you don't belong in a uniform fighting for anybody."

Tanner swallowed. "Yes, gunny."

Janeka nodded. She pulled the silver rod that was his yeoman's computer from one pocket and handed it to him. "Catch up on your files. Do something useful with your time while you get fixed," she said. The gunny turned to leave, then turned back. "One more thing." She pointed to her bruised eye. "Do you know what this is, recruit?"

"It's a black eye, gunny," Tanner answered. He had a sudden, somewhat disappointing realization. "That's not something I gave you, is it, gunny?"

"No. This came from Recruit Wong about two minutes after you were carried out of my squad bay. She requested a match right then and there." Janeka stared, almost daring Tanner to laugh, but he did not.

"Did she win, gunny?"

"No. She did a whole lot better than you did and her ass isn't in the infirmary like yours is, but that isn't my point. Recruit, if I find out about anything going on between you and Wong at all—you lay a finger on her outside of a sparring match, you so much as draw a smiley face on something that she's meant to see—I will personally beat both of you beyond the ability of modern medicine to correct, do you understand me?"

Tanner's eyes were wide. "Yes, gunny."

"Do whatever you want come graduation, but until then there will be no fraternization in my company."

His initial appraisal of her had been correct all along. Janeka was insane. "Yes, gunny."

"I'll send the doctor back in," Janeka said with a masterful scowl before she left. "Can't be healthy for your face to be that red."

• • •

"Malone," Everett called out from his office, "you all caught up on performance scores for this week?"

"Yes, chief," Tanner replied. He sat at a small table just outside the company command office with several screens displayed in the air around him. Most of his work could be done in the squad bay, but some matters had to be kept confidential. He glanced at the screen showing the individual performance scores of each member of the company just as Everett logged in and shifted its organization from an alphabetical sort to a top-down sort by scores.

Alicia was at the top of the list, but that was no surprise. He turned away without reading the others. Tanner busied himself with double-checking payroll routing instructions against individual recruit requests. Everyone's entire first pay deposit had gone toward covering personal uniform and supply costs; only now would anyone get money they could call their own. Tanner didn't want to screw anything up.

"Malone," Everett called again. Nothing followed.

Closing his eyes as he accepted the inevitable, Tanner killed the screens, stood, and came to attention in the doorway to the office.

The chief sat at his desk behind a pair of data screens. "Go get Kalodner, Michaels, Waikowski, and Palmotti."

"Aye, aye, chief," Tanner said with all the energy he could muster—which wasn't much. He'd done this before with others. He did a left face, stepped out of the doorway again, and headed into the squad bay.

Oscar Company's weekly field day of the squad bay looked nearly complete as he walked in. Tanner wished he could just scrub or mop with everyone else rather than doing yeoman chores. Tasks like this one left him feeling far apart from the rest of the company.

He found Janeka standing over a pair of recruits as they performed push-ups for whatever screwup she must have discovered. "Gunny Janeka," Tanner said, coming to attention beside her. "By your leave, I have instructions to direct four from the company to the command office."

"Go ahead, yeoman," Janeka said without looking at him.

Tanner turned away to find the squad bay unsettlingly quiet. Everyone understood. He swallowed hard before he called out, "Kalodner, Michaels, Waikowski, Palmotti. Fall in outside the command office."

Heads turned. Palmotti was the only woman among those called; she and the others headed for the door. Several of their fellow recruits offered quick handshakes or pats on the back as they passed.

"Oscar Company!" Janeka called out. "Secure from cleaning detail. Configure the squad bay for unarmed combat training."

Tanner took a deep breath as he marched out of the squad bay, not wanting to look at anyone as he passed. He told himself that this was all out of his hands, yet he felt responsible, anyway, simply for having been the messenger.

Outside Everett's office, Tanner waited for the four recruits to silently form up. Kalodner had to be reminded about where he was supposed to stand. It was, ultimately, the sort of thing that got him called out in the first place.

Tanner slapped the side of the doorway to the command office. "Recruits assembled as ordered, chief."

"Carry on, yeoman," Everett said as he rose from his seat. Tanner winced as he turned away. Had he been dismissed, he could've returned to the squad bay. Instead, he had to sit through this. He returned to his small chair just outside the office, pulling up his data screens once more.

Somehow the familiar click of Everett's heels had lost none of its intimidation value since the first time the company heard the sound. Everett emerged from his office to stand in front of the recruits.

"I have reviewed the current performance scores for the company," Everett explained calmly. "The four of you have not met with the minimum standards to move on with your training. I am therefore reverting you to a junior company further back in the training schedule. Your files have been forwarded to the commander of Papa Company. His company yeoman is on the way here to direct you to Squad Bay Papa.

"This is not personal. Recruit Palmotti, Recruit Michaels, I have informed your new company commander of your effort. It is clear to Gunny Janeka and I that you have not slacked off in your training.

"The four of you will collect your gear and return here immediately. Dismissed."

Of the four recruits, only Kalodner made a sound. He seemed to choke somewhat, looking up at Everett as if to speak, but then he turned and followed the others back into the squad bay with his head hung low. He wouldn't be the first recruit to weep in the squad bay. It was the one thing neither Everett nor Janeka ever mocked.

"Something to say, Malone?" Everett asked.

"No, chief," he answered, keeping his eyes on his data screens. He felt Everett's gaze on him. Hoping to get rid of it, he finally said, "Glad it wasn't more names, chief."

Everett grunted. "Right. Names. Tell Baljashanpreet and Einstein to get up here."

Tanner blinked. His spirits soared. Baljashanpreet was one of the most successful recruits; there was no way he would be reverted to a junior company, but he had been directed to help Einstein get his act together. That hadn't come to pass. Could they all possibly be that lucky? "Aye, aye, chief," he said, killing his data screens again before heading back into the squad bay.

"Gunny Janeka," he called out as he entered.

"Just do it, yeoman," Janeka cut him off tersely from the other end of the chamber.

"Recruit Baljashanpreet! Recruit Eickenberry! Report to the command office!" Fighting a grin, Tanner made an about-face and exited before anyone could catch his eye. He promptly returned to his seat, having no trouble maintaining his posture or energy now. He called up whatever the hell data screens were most recent in his work queue and failed utterly at looking disinterested in what was about to happen.

Finding Everett still standing outside his office, the two recruits immediately came to attention before him. "Reporting as ordered, chief," announced Baljashanpreet, with Einstein echoing him half a beat behind.

"Einstein, you're a complete fuckup," Everett said flatly.

Tanner bit his lip.

"You slack off, you mouth off, your test scores are consistently just barely above failing, and what really pisses me off is that you show no regard for the safety or well-being of your fellow recruits." He stared at Einstein, apparently to let his words sink in. Tanner didn't hold out much hope for that. "Certain hard-and-fast technicalities within training regulations prevent me from reverting you to another company, otherwise you'd be gone today. Do you understand all this, recruit?"

"Yes, Chief Everett," Einstein shouted with an undertone of defiant pride.

"Recruit Baljashanpreet," Everett continued, "I directed you to help Einstein here improve his performance. Have you worked with him?"

"Yes, Chief Everett." Tanner could attest to that. Baljashanpreet tried hard with Einstein. It was Einstein who could not say the same.

"And have you seen improvements?"

"Yes, Chief Everett."

"I haven't. Has this been too much of a task for you?"

"No, Chief Everett. No excuse, Chief Everett."

"I think it has been too much of a task for you, recruit. I don't think I've been fair to you. Recruit Baljashanpreet, I am hereby transferring Einstein out of your squad. He is no longer your concern any more than any other shipmate within the company."

"Understood, Chief Everett."

"Einstein, I would give you to Recruit Wong, but she's already babysitting several other struggling recruits. I'm transferring you to Sinclair's squad."

Tanner's eyes went wide with horror. Sinclair's squad. His squad.

"Sinclair's squad currently has the highest performance average in the company. Maybe they'll all be able to work as a team to help you get your act together. Go tell him that I said it's his squad's job to help you stop being a fuckup."

"Aye, aye, Chief Everett," Einstein replied.

"You're both dismissed."

Everett didn't see Einstein's grin or his swagger as he left. Tanner saw both.

Silence reigned outside the command office. Just around the corner the company busily set up for unarmed combat training, but somehow Tanner didn't hear a thing. He stared at the numbers and letters floating in the air in front of him without reading.

"Make sure you note the transfer in the personnel files," Everett reminded him.

"Aye, aye, chief." Tanner swallowed his frustration. He heard Everett turn to go back into his office. "Chief Everett?"

"Hm?"

"Permission to join the company, chief?"

"You just came off light duty yesterday," Everett noted. "Didn't the doctor say you should lay off sparring for another day to be safe?"

"He did, but I felt fine at morning PT, chief," Tanner said, still looking straight ahead.

"It's up to you. Sure you're up to it?"

"I think I'd really like to hit something right now, chief."

"Ah. Dismissed."

Tanner killed his data screens and entered the squad bay. He heard the click of Everett's heels not far behind him as he reported to Janeka. The gunny already had the company separated out into individual exercises.

"Malone, you joining us?" she asked. "Head over to Wong's group."

"Aye, aye, gunny," Tanner replied, turning and walking over to the sparring circle. Beyond it, he could see Michaels, who'd busted his ass at pretty much everything and just couldn't handle the more academic matters, clearing his gear out of his locker.

Michaels was leaving. So was Palmotti. But not Einstein. He'd just moved into Tanner's squad.

Alicia looked up at Tanner and smiled. "You with us? Ready to spar?"

"Yeah."

"Good, 'cause it's my turn." She stepped into the circle and gestured for him to face her.

Tanner sighed. Naturally, with all his pent-up frustration, he got stuck sparring with the last person he wanted to hit *and* the best fighter in the company. Resigned to another loss, Tanner stepped forward and faced off against Alicia.

"Ready?" asked Ravenell, serving as observer.

"Ready," Alicia confirmed.

"Ready." Tanner scowled.

"Winner fights Einstein!" Everett barked from out of nowhere.

Heads turned, conversations stopped, and sparring matches ground to a halt all across the squad bay. Tanner's jaw silently clenched. Alicia didn't bother to fight her grin. "Sorry, Tanner," she said, assuming a ready stance.

"Fight!" Ravenell barked.

Alicia's head rocked back from the sudden force of Tanner's punch. Nearly knocked from her feet, Alicia staggered back, her eyes wide with shock. Blood trickled from her nose.

"Wong?" Ravenell asked.

Oscar Company's undisputed champ blinked again. Her legs wobbled. Alicia's gaze didn't seem to track with either her opponent or the match's referee. Ravenell and Other Gomez came to her side, helping her settle back onto the mat. "Wong, are you okay?" Ravenell asked again. "Can you go on?"

"Whurr," Alicia replied.

"I'm . . ." Ravenell blinked, looking up at Tanner and then at the others forming the ring around them. The words that came from his mouth surprised him: "I'm calling this one for Malone."

"Very well," Everett said, fighting a grin. "Einstein! You're up!"

Tanner, too, had trouble registering the moment. His fist had just launched out at Alicia's nose without any conscious thought. Yet there she was, sitting there just shy of a concussion. Then Einstein stepped in front of him, taking on both a ready stance and a disdainful, cocky grin, and it all made sense.

Tanner bowed, but only a little. Einstein just nodded. Like everything else, he did this wrong, too.

Taller than the rest of the company and quicker than most, Einstein usually employed his speed and reach to soften up an opponent. He played to his advantages. He did that much right. He was stronger than most, so there was that, too, but ultimately Einstein relied heavily on his superior reach.

It wasn't normally the sort of thing Tanner thought about, but it was at the forefront of his mind as Ravenell asked, "Ready?"

"Sure," Einstein answered with a shrug.

"Ready," Tanner grunted.

"Fight!"

Einstein led with a high kick to Tanner's head. Tanner moved in, seized Einstein's ankle with one hand, and pushed it upward, while his other hand came in with an uppercut right into Einstein's groin.

Lifted an inch or two off his other foot from the force of the blow, Einstein quickly crumpled and fell to his knees with his hands between his legs. Tanner knocked him over with a merciless sweeping kick across the face.

"Hold!" Ravenell yelled out. He jumped between the two of them, amazed but not so shocked as to lose track of his responsibilities. "Einstein, are you okay?" The fallen recruit groaned.

"*Get up,*" someone growled at Einstein. It wasn't until Ravenell's eyes turned to Tanner in shock that Tanner realized the growling voice was his own.

"Fucking kill you for that," Einstein huffed.

Ravenell turned back to him. "Can you go on?"

Again, Einstein nodded. Ravenell gestured for Tanner to step back. "Give him a sec," Ravenell said.

Einstein winced as he got to his feet. "Lucky shot. Won't get one again."

Having nothing to say to Einstein, Tanner returned to his starting point. He hardly noticed what a crowd the match had drawn. As soon as both opponents assumed a ready stance, Ravenell gave the order to continue.

Einstein came in lower this time, leading with fists instead of feet. Tanner accepted the first hit across his shoulder in order to close in. Now inside Einstein's superior reach, Tanner unloaded rapid shots to the taller recruit's midsection. Tanner's fists quickly outpaced his legs; Einstein was shoved back faster than Tanner moved in.

He missed a swing, then a second. Einstein caught his arm and twisted it, pulling his opponent to the floor with him. They quickly wound up in a tangle. Memories of Einstein holding Andrews down and pounding him in the back flashed through Tanner's mind. Rather than fear, Tanner felt nothing but hate. He hated Einstein too much to let that happen.

Tanner's left arm was twisted behind his back. Einstein's other arm wrapped around Tanner's throat. Before Einstein could solidify his grip, Tanner swept back and down with his free hand to grab savagely at Einstein's crotch.

Einstein roared in pain. He shoved Tanner away again. Quicker to recover, Tanner spun around on the floor, cupping both of his hands to slam them simultaneously onto Einstein's ears. Einstein threw out another punch; Tanner caught it, twisted it at the wrist, and pulled, then drove his other hand down into Einstein's shoulder from behind. There was an audible pop. Einstein shrieked.

Tanner didn't stop. He twisted harder, bringing his free elbow down on Einstein's. He heard another crack. Rather than survey the damage, he kept at it, grabbing Einstein's head and slamming it back down onto the mat.

The mat. The mat offered protection. Slamming Einstein's head into that wouldn't hurt him enough. They had to go beyond the mat. Gripping Einstein's head firmly, Tanner wrenched himself and his opponent to their feet. The fact that Einstein was too battered and weakened to effectively resist didn't even register. Tanner shoved a pair of onlookers aside as he hauled Einstein out of the ring. They kept going until Tanner found the stack of collapsed bunks against the wall. He threw Einstein against them, casting him forward with all his rage.

Disoriented and wounded, Einstein couldn't do much to save himself. He fell stomach first against the frame of one rack, his body pivoting on it to slam his face down on the concrete floor below.

"Get up!" Tanner roared. He became only dimly aware of shouting all around him. Tanner saw Einstein laying against the rack, fucking around like he always did, once again feigning incompetence or confusion whenever his bluster didn't work out. "Get up, motherfucker!"

Tanner snatched up one of Einstein's feet, intending to drag him out for more punishment. Then something knocked him away from behind. He turned, spun, and soon found himself on the floor underneath Janeka in a tangled hold.

"At ease, Malone!" she barked in his ear. "Settle down! That's an order! Quit struggling with me!" Her hold was firm and unrelenting. It forced him to take a moment to breathe and consider how to get out of it. Then another. Then Tanner blinked and realized that he was fighting Janeka now, not Einstein.

He relaxed. "Aye, aye, gunny," he huffed.

"Are you done, recruit?"

"Yes, Gunny Janeka."

She didn't let go. He heard Everett calling for medical. There were boots around him, hushed commentary, and shadows blocking out the light.

Eventually, Janeka let him up. "Walk it off, recruit," she ordered.

Tanner looked up at her, then at Einstein, who was lying on his back with blood all over his face.

"Walk it off," Janeka repeated. Tanner glanced at her, nodded, and half-walked, half-staggered away.

Scowling, Janeka stepped over to where Everett stood watching Rivera as the recruit tried in vain to get a response out of Einstein. "Yeah." Everett sighed casually. "That's gonna be a day or two in the infirmary. He's barely scraping by as it is, too. Might have to revert 'im to another company. Blood on your uniform there, Michelle."

Janeka glanced down at herself. She spotted Tanner as he sat against a collapsed bunk across the squad bay. He wasn't bleeding. She looked back to Einstein, then at her colleague.

"You're an evil man, Bill," she said quietly.

"What? Me? No idea what you're talking about."

"You're a scheming, manipulative, evil man."

"No, I'm not. I just help people find motivation."

SIX

The Only Constant

Hey, Tanner,

Got your message. That's incredible that they won't let you communicate with anyone for twelve weeks. Wait, I take it back; that's not incredible, that's insane. Our communications rules here are restrictive, but they aren't nearly that bad. If we can find time to write, nobody stops us. They figure that's important here.

It's probably not a shock that I don't have much time to write. If I'm not in a class, I'm outside marching, doing PT, or getting yelled at. I could swear I sleep occasionally, but that's probably just me hallucinating. I imagine you know how that is, right?

Crazy as it sounds, I'm having a blast. It's pretty hilarious to hear people complain about the heat here. It's barely forty and you'd think half my cohort is going to die.

I hope I don't seem like a bitch for this, but I'm probably not going to write again until I hear from you first. They're fierce on time management here and it seems like kind of a waste to send what will be weeks of old news by the time you get it, you know? So write to me when you can, and I'll start responding. Hang in there!

Yours,
Midship(wo!)man Madelyn Carter

He read it three times, slower with each repetition. He didn't doubt her for a second; she was probably doing fine. Madelyn thrived on competition. Having all those other cadets to measure herself against was all the motivation she needed.

After sending his "you won't hear from me for a while" message, Tanner wondered if he'd get anything from Madelyn at all. As he had been on the day of the Test, he was surprised to have her attention. On the other hand, though, he was probably the only one of her friends who could empathize with her current situation. The rest of her social circle from school all enjoyed a summer vacation before starting at civilian universities.

His father took a very different approach from Madelyn's. She'd only sent the one message. His father had sent dozens.

Swallowing hard, Tanner checked the time on the holo screen. Lights-out approached swiftly. He sat in his chair outside the command office, right where he had been when Everett went into the squad bay and announced the release of the accumulated mail. Tanner was free to head back to his bunk to read his messages, but moving seemed like a silly waste of time. Had he been in the shower when Everett had made that announcement, he'd probably have read his mail in there, too.

He paused to pop to attention as Everett passed by, moving from the squad bay to the office. "They're gonna be a pain in the ass tomorrow," he heard Janeka say. "Like little kids the day after Halloween."

"Nah. Shouldn't be too much trouble to kick 'em back into line," Everett replied.

Tanner sighed. They were bound to find a reason to jerk the leash. It was a worry for tomorrow, though, not tonight. Right now, he had mail to read from his father. His stepmother, too. A few friends. Dad took priority. Rather than read from the beginning, Tanner skipped to the most recent message.

Dear Tanner,

If I've read the message receipts right, this may be the most recent letter you get when they let you have mail again. I don't know if you'll read this first or last, but I figured I'd keep writing to you either way just in case. Your mother told me once that mail meant the world to her when she was in basic training. I can't believe they're restricting yours like this.

Sharon and I talk about you every day. We're both so very sorry it all came to this. We should have thought more about you and we should have worked harder to have a plan if . . . well, if what happened with my job happened. We're both sorry about how we reacted, too. Sharon didn't mean half the things she said. She's felt like a complete heel ever since you left.

On the bright side, things are great here. There are details in the other messages, but Sharon swung a teaching position for this school year, so we won't be dependent on my income alone. She'll probably be working by the time you get this. Our neighbors are nice and this is a great place to live. We're talking about getting a cat.

At any rate: We will both support you, no matter what happens. If you decide to stay in the military, we'll support you. We both hope you're doing well. But if you're not—if you aren't making it or if you decide you want to get out, I'm sure there are ways to make that happen. We can take care of you, Tanner. You can live with us until we figure out what to do next. It's okay. We know this wasn't your first choice.

Tanner killed the holo screen. He swallowed hard as if it would reduce the lump in his throat.

Twelve weeks. He hadn't heard from anyone in twelve very long weeks, and in that time he'd been exhausted and exasperated with hardly a break. He hung on and endured. Now the first word from his family offered an escape hatch.

He stared across the room at the bulkhead. He called it that now. It was a bulkhead, not a wall. He'd adopted the lingo. He'd changed.

"Malone!" Everett barked from his office. "You still out there?"

"Yes, chief!" Tanner answered, standing at attention.

"Lights-out in two minutes. Handle it."

"Aye, aye, chief," Tanner replied. He spared another moment to breathe in deep, trying to put aside his thoughts of home—abstract as "home" was now that Dad and Sharon lived on a planet Tanner had never even visited.

"Bill, you ought to go home to your man," he heard Janeka say. "I can handle things for the night." It stopped Tanner cold as he reached to pick his helmet up off the floor. They clearly thought he was out of earshot already.

"Why don't *you* go home to *your* man?" Everett replied. "You're the one with a kid."

"My man knew what he was getting into when he married me. Yours never wore a uniform."

"You think we haven't talked this stuff out over the last twenty years? Anyway, isolation was my idea, Michelle," Everett said. "I'm not gonna slip out on it now."

Tanner forced himself to walk away. Inside the squad bay, most of Oscar Company was already in their bunks—or, more typically, on top of them. Sleeping under one's sheets meant making the bed again in the morning, and that consumed time. Better to simply sleep on top and smooth it out upon reveille. Tanner checked the time. "Lights-out in thirty seconds!"

He heard no response. Tanner walked to his bunk. He stowed his helmet, unzipped the top of his vac suit, and lay down. He would sleep in the same sweaty vac suit he'd worn all day long, then shower and change into a fresh vac suit in the morning.

The lights winked out. Tanner closed his eyes, still plagued by the jumble of thoughts and emotions created by his father's letter. Quit? Really? If that was even possible—and Tanner wasn't sure it was—did Tanner want that? Could he live with himself? Could he admit to others that he'd dropped out of basic training? Would he lie about it?

Thirteen weeks. Bad food, no privacy, endless shifts between crushing monotony and near panic. Decompression drills at any given moment; certainly there would be one tonight, maybe two. Some nights had as many as three. Half the time he woke up to his rack collapsing upon him. He spent two days a week, from sunrise to sunrise, wearing an oxygenated helmet. His muscles ached from constant PT.

A month ago, one of his instructors had put him in the hospital. Several days after that, Tanner had put someone in the hospital himself. It was the end of Einstein, and the company ran far better as a result. Tanner also performed much better in sparring after that. He felt more confident and self-assured . . .

. . . and, just like Sharon said, he was learning how to hurt people. He got better at it all the time. Was that all he had to show for all this?

He took another long, deep breath. He'd have to respond to that letter. He wasn't sure what to say. But he couldn't do it tonight.

Tanner then noticed the shaky, shuddering breath of someone nearby. He frowned, listening intently. It was Other Gomez on the rack above his.

Turning his head to the left, he found Ravenell still awake on the next bunk over. Tanner gestured up at Other Gomez with a quizzical look on his face.

"Got a message from his girlfriend," Ravenell answered quietly. "You ever hear of a 'Dear John letter'?"

Wincing, Tanner put his head back on his pillow. "Aw hell," he whispered in sympathy. "I'm sorry, Gomez."

He heard no response.

Other recruits cried that night. Tanner heard them. Unable to do anything about it then, or about his father's letter, he went to sleep.

• • •

He was awake when the collision alarm went off. It certainly seemed like he'd awoken just before it, anyway. In the very first second of its high-pitched wail, Tanner rolled out of his bunk and hit the deck. His bunk collapsed in the following second. Other Gomez was ready for it, too. For him, the drill was different; he simply grabbed for the rail and hung on, bracing himself to minimize the impact. Both recruits immediately scrambled for their helmets, slamming them down on their heads while rushing to the nearest wall to grab backup oxygen canisters.

Oscar Company handled dead oxygen canisters without confusion or complaint. Every helmet light read green within fifteen seconds of the alarm. Recruits calmly lined up along the collapsed bunks at attention. The squad bay fell silent.

"Helmets off, stay at attention," ordered Janeka. Seconds later, every member of Oscar Company stood tall and straight, helmets tucked under the left arm.

"You will secure from drill and get cleaned up," Janeka said. "Morning mess detail is canceled. Fall in here in columns in time for morning PT as usual. Move."

Oscar Company obeyed. Those who could not keep up had already been reverted to junior training companies. Einstein was the last to go.

Hushed questions circulated about Sinclair's squad being relieved from mess duty that morning. All anyone could guess, given that they had received the mercy of mail from home just the night before, was that they would go without breakfast to balance the scales. Fifteen minutes later, Janeka stalked through the center of the squad bay, surveying the recruits. Everyone stood at attention with helmets in hand.

"Some of you may get the mistaken impression that today is Christmas," she said, the familiar tone of menace returning to her voice. "I assure you it is not. You have only proven that you are ready for the next phase of your training. You have not proven yourselves actual crewmen and marines in my military. Do not let your progress go to your head. Do not fuck up. Am I understood?"

"Yes, Gunnery Sergeant!" responded Oscar Company.

"Morning PT will take place on the parade ground this morning." Janeka vigilantly scanned for any break in the company's stance. She saw widened eyes and sharp breaths, but nothing to pounce on. "This will be followed by close-order drill. We have not performed close-order drill for quite some time. I understand refreshers will be necessary. Do not test my patience.

"If, and only if, you measure up to my expectations, we will have a late morning chow in the base galley. If you blow it, we'll just have to skip breakfast in favor of extra PT."

"Gunnery Sergeant Janeka!" a voice called.

"Yes, Recruit Gomez?"

"May I eat at a table with the rest of the company, gunny?" Gomez asked in as dignified a manner as he could muster. It had been quite some time since anyone had eaten at a table; typically the company simply ate over their bunks.

Janeka paused. "Why, yes, Recruit Gomez. I think you've earned it."

"Thank you, gunny!"

"In fact," Janeka said with a savagely sweet grin, "you can sit next to me."

It was too horrifying for anyone not to laugh. "Drop! On your faces!" Janeka barked at the snickering crew. "You think that's funny? You see something wrong with that? Would you *fine* ladies and gentlemen be embarrassed to sit next to me at breakfast?"

"No, gunny!" Oscar Company shouted in unison to the floor now mere inches from their faces. Most still grinned. Some of them still struggled to contain their laughter.

"Burpees! Now! Count 'em out!" She stalked through the aisles, listening to numbers shouted out in unison by the company. They had gotten better at this, too. The only real challenge came from the gunny's commentary.

"I think some of you have a problem with me," she scowled. "I think some of you are picturing me sitting at the dinner table with you at home right now. I think you're afraid to have me over for dinner to meet your mothers. Or maybe your girlfriends. Sinclair, you've got a girlfriend, don't you? Aren't you planning on marrying her someday? Am I gonna be invited to the wedding? Why is that funny, Sinclair?"

One hundred fifty burpees later, Oscar Company regained its collective composure. The recruits marched out in two columns, up the steps to the main doors of their shelter, then into the gray, rainy, glorious morning outside.

Over the entrance was posted a sign in plain blue letters. It read, "Time Passes."

• • •

"Recruits, my name is Lieutenant Miguel Duran. I am the captain of ANS *St. George*. The officer beside me is Lieutenant Lynette Kelly, captain of ANS *Joan of Arc*." Speaking in a loud, clear voice with just enough scratch in it to give the man some extra panache, the handsome lieutenant stood proudly before the front ranks of Oscar Company. He and the redheaded woman beside him wore much the same vac suits as the navy recruits, though theirs bore rank and unit insignia. Both also wore a utility belt around the waist, life support regulator pad attached to one hip, and other emergency gear strapped to their suits. It was all the gear necessary and required by regulation while underway in space.

The two white craft looming above and behind them silently explained why they dressed that way while on a planet's surface. The ships were shaped much like daggers, only the afterburners gave a more rectangular end. Both ran fifty meters from end to end, with swept-back wings thick enough at the center for a man to stand in, tapering to much thinner ends roughly ten meters from the hull.

Duran pointed at random to a recruit in the front rank. "What's your name?"

"Ravenell, sir," came the answer. Tanner breathed a sigh of relief. He was afraid that the lieutenant had been pointing at him.

"What class of ship are *St. George* and *Joan of Arc*?"

"They're Vigilant-class corvettes, sir."

"What's their armament?" asked Lieutenant Kelly.

"Ma'am, each has a forward-mounted laser cannon, twin light laser turrets mounted on her wings, one ventral laser turret in the center, and twin missile tubes mounted within each wing, ma'am!"

"Crew compliment?"

"Sir, standard crew compliment of sixteen, sir!"

"Excellent. You, directly behind Ravenell," Kelly said. "What's your name?"

"Ma'am, Matuskey, ma'am!"

"What's their primary manufacture?"

"Ma'am, domestic manufacture, ma'am! Raphael shipyards, ma'am!"

"Outstanding." Duran smiled. "Sounds like you've had some excellent instructors."

"Sir, yes, sir!" answered the company.

"It is our understanding that you recruits have been cooped up in your squad bay, and today is your first breath of fresh air. Is that correct?"

"Sir, yes, sir!"

"How long has it been?"

"Sir, twelve weeks, sir!" replied one hundred fourteen voices in unison.

The lieutenant blinked. He didn't lose his composure, but there was a moment of pause and a curious half grin thrown to Chief Everett, who stood at ease beside the company. Duran turned his attention back to the company. "So would you folks be interested in cutting your time in the sun a bit short to go for a ride?"

Tanner felt his heart leap into his throat. He wasn't alone. Trained though they were to respond with snap and confidence to such questioning, Oscar Company didn't expect something like this to follow their first civilized meal in three months. Some recovered quicker than others, calling back, "Sir, yes, sir!"

Duran couldn't help but grin. "I'm sorry, what's the verdict there?"

"Sir, yes, sir!" repeated a much more unified Oscar Company.

"Chief Everett?" he asked.

The chief came to attention. "Oscar Company would be honored, sir."

"Excellent. It'll be a bit crammed, but between our two ships we should make it work. It'll be a short trip. We think you'll like where you're going today. You'll need to be equipped. Chief Cavalli?"

St. George's head engineer stepped up from behind the lieutenant, gesturing for five other men behind him to follow with several carts. All of them, like Duran and Kelly, wore gray navy vac suits fitted out for space. Chief Cavalli launched into a brief recitation of what would be issued to each recruit. The company had trained with everything already, but no one expected to have use for it today. Nor did they expect to be told, as Chief Cavalli explained, that the utility belts, regulator pads, survival knives, and the rest were permanent additions to their standard individual kits. It was all for keeps.

Tanner could barely track it all. He listened with as much focus as he could spare, but in the end, that wasn't much. Every thought of family and friends fell away. The notion of quitting vanished from his mind. He wasn't sore. He wasn't tired.

A junior engineer from the *St. George* stepped up to issue his gear—his vacuum-ready, military-rated, state-of-the-art survival gear. It was a far cry from the courteous, reassuring safety briefing before getting on a passenger liner.

This wasn't a tourist cruise. He was no longer at some brutal, demented summer camp. Tanner accepted his gear, checked it to ensure proper operation, and strapped it on.

Everyone received instructions on where to sit on their respective ships. Fifty-eight passengers, counting recruits and instructors, was no small load for a corvette. *St. George* was soon crammed, with every possible seat taken. Much of the company took up spots in the cargo bay. Others sat in the small galley, the tiny crew berths, even a few spots in the bridge.

Tanner was one of the lucky ones. A crewman strapped him into the starboard dorsal laser turret. He could actually see where they were going.

St. George was clean and neat, but she wasn't a showpiece. She bore small dents in the bulkheads and scuffs on the deck from any number of heavy jobs. Signs of patch jobs and jury-rigged equipment showed up here and there. Everett had told the recruits many times of how often military space travel was a game of improvisation and ingenuity. Popular media and fiction in Tanner's day tended to portray military activity as a matter of precision and smooth, seamless expertise. Reality hardly matched the image.

Excitement rose as the *St. George*'s antigrav drives kicked in, putting a low but discernible vibration through the bulkheads, the decks, and everything attached to them. Tanner felt a slight moment of nausea as the vibration died out and the antigrav steadied itself. He chalked it up to nerves. Commercial space travel hadn't made him sick since he was a little boy.

The ship floated up from the ground, at first with just a lurch of a few inches but then a steady rise. Again, Tanner felt butterflies in his stomach and lightheadedness, but it all quickly vanished. The skyline fell away, soon leaving only sky. *St. George*'s main engines engaged with a rumble and shudder felt throughout the ship.

Seconds later, they were through the clouds, then high above them. The blue sky swiftly grew dark, then black, and shortly thereafter Tanner had an unfiltered view of thousands of stars.

He didn't have long to take it all in. The ship banked to starboard and tilted ninety degrees. Tanner looked up at the planet he'd been on only seconds ago.

Something beeped next to him. Tanner turned to a control panel next to the turret controls. A green indicator light came on as the intercom spoke. "So as long as you guys are sitting in the turrets, there's no reason not to put on the targeting displays," said a female voice. "We'll control them from the bridge. Don't touch anything. We wouldn't want a friendly fire incident."

It was nice to hear a friendly voice out of someone other than a fellow recruit for a change. Tanner watched as the display activated all on its own. It showed the ship's position relative to other objects in orbit, their ranges, transponder signatures, and more.

"As you may have been taught," the woman on the intercom continued, taking on a pleasant, lecturing tone, "corvettes form a considerable portion of the Archangel Navy. We're big on versatility. We handle everything from system security and customs patrols to search and rescue to courier duty. Smaller crews mean greater responsibilities for lower-ranking crewmen than on most other ships. The crewman driving the ship right now is only six months out of basic herself."

Tanner grinned. That had all been part of the company's "book learning" curriculum while imprisoned in the squad bay. Now that he was on such a ship, it all fell into place for him. It all became real.

It became something he actually wanted.

The ship turned again, wheeling on its axis. Tanner saw on the targeting display that they were headed for a specific contact. The nameless crewman on the bridge remotely controlling the targeting displays paged through a couple of different readouts before settling on one that offered a clear, detailed image. Half a minute later, Tanner could make it out with his naked eye through the turret canopy.

The last few weeks had caused him to reflect constantly on how far he had come from his old life in such a short time, all as a result of his own choices. The thought hit him again as he stared at the massive, gleaming white Archangel Navy cruiser up ahead.

• • •

Andrea Bennett had been on larger ships, but those were civilian transports designed for luxury. She had been on military craft, as well, but nothing like this one. CDC Shipyards Cruiser NN-1221, still officially unnamed, outweighed and outgunned all the other cruisers of the Archangel Navy . . . and it was still, formally at least, an "it." NN-1221 would not become a "she" for another three days.

Given the historic nature and PR value of the occasion, the choreography of that ceremony fell in her hands. It was a significant if lighthearted responsibility.

"Don't get me wrong, commander"—Andrea grinned as she walked through the passageways with the ship's executive officer—"the First Lady would probably be thrilled to walk out onto the bow of the ship in a vacuum suit to crack open the bottle."

"We can make that happen, ma'am." Commander Sutton seemed just as amused by the image. He was tall, muscular, and handsome, wrapped up in a dress uniform bristling with ribbons and insignia. Andrea found him charming enough, and wondered how often women swooned for that smile.

"Still. I think she's better off doing it on the bridge," Andrea chuckled.

"She'd be perfectly safe," the commander offered.

She'd probably throw up in her helmet, Andrea thought, but couldn't make that comment out loud. They had a silent companion. Walter Lowney from the *Raphael Chronicle* tagged along with her to work up a "behind the scenes" piece. If all went well, it would offer a brief revival of the story once the initial media attention passed.

On one hand, it demonstrated President Aguirre's commitment to transparency and media access. On the other, it meant that someone from the media followed Andrea's every step and heard her every word. It also left her continually dodging questions of how the government planned to cover this new ship and the others it procured in its budget.

The ceremony still lay several days away. Work crews performed their tasks with vigor. Technicians installed secondary backup cables and wiring along the bulkheads. Specialists replaced the original computer terminals with systems preferred by the Archangel Navy. Smaller touches were put in place as well, like name placards, warning signs, and color-coded paint jobs.

There was also cleaning. An endless amount of cleaning, Andrea figured, but the ship's executive officer—or XO, as everyone seemed to call him—and the captain both vowed to have the whole enormous ship ready. The confidence of the ship's command officers impressed her.

"So, commander," she said, turning her head curiously at a cleaning detail of young personnel in plain gray and blue vac suits, "I thought you didn't have your full crew compliment yet?"

"Not entirely, no, ma'am," replied Sutton. "As you can see, a number of civilian specialists are at work here alongside the ship's crew. We've also borrowed more than a few technicians from other ships and planet-side installations. Quite a lot of temporary duty in place here."

"And the cleaning crews?" she asked. "Those are non-rated uniforms I'm seeing, aren't they? Navy crew and marines?"

"Oh. Them." Sutton smiled again. "Those are loaners, too. We got 'em from Fort Stalwart. Everyone in those unmarked vac suits is still in recruit training. They'll be here doing practical hands-on training soon. It's part of the new program for enlisteds. Right now, though, it's all about scraping, scrubbing, and painting. Not so different from the life of a non-rate to begin with, to be honest. Much of this recruit company will probably be assigned to this ship after they graduate."

"What's the new program like?" piped up a voice from behind them. Sutton and Andrea looked over their shoulders at Walter Lowney. She kept almost forgetting him.

"Fort Stalwart is training them longer and harder than ever now," explained Sutton, "at significantly less cost to the taxpayers than one would expect, I should add," he offered, tossing Andrea a knowing look.

Andrea pursed her lips. She suspected he was trying to be flirty before, but now that he was trying to offer up political support on the sly, she was sure of it.

"Could we talk to some of them?" Lowney asked. Noticing the wary glance shared between Sutton and Andrea, he added, "You said before that a lot of them would be assigned here when they completed their training. It might be a nice angle."

"I can't think of any reason to object," replied Andrea.

"You understand that these guys are still in the middle of basic training, right?" Sutton warned. "They might not be all that talkative. Hell, at this stage a lot of them are still trying to rediscover which way is up."

"I'll keep it simple."

Sutton considered it, then finally nodded. "How about these guys?" he suggested, gesturing through an open hatch to his left. He strode inside with hardly a pause. Andrea and Lowney followed.

"Attention in the—attention!" blurted out one recruit. Everyone in the compartment came to a ramrod straight stance, dropping their cleaning gear to look straight ahead with their arms glued to their sides. All five recruits looked young, fit, trim, and openly nervous.

"You were about to say 'attention in the squad bay,' weren't you . . . Malone?" asked Sutton.

"Sir, yes, sir!" answered the red-faced recruit.

"Only you should have said something different, right?" he asked. His gentle demeanor didn't seem to make the recruit feel any better.

"'Attention on deck,' sir?"

"Correct." Sutton's eyes swept the compartment. "Who's in charge here?"

"Sir?" Another blinked. "We're all recruits, sir."

"No squad leader?"

"That'd be me, sir," said a third. "Recruit Sinclair, sir."

"Ah. Good." The commander turned to Lowney. "Fire away."

Lowney stepped forward, clearly not expecting this degree of formality. "Yeah, but . . . can they relax at all?" he asked. "I feel like they're just going to shout out lines from a training manual."

"The rote answers sound much better when they're shouted." Sutton smiled. "Especially by five guys at once."

Andrea glanced from one recruit to the next. Despite their stance, they were plainly terrified. “Commander,” she spoke up, “I think he might have a point. We wouldn’t want to impede the media.”

“No, of course not.” Sutton nodded. “At ease, recruits. Mr. Lowney here is a civilian journalist. He’d like to ask you a few questions. Just speak your minds.”

The group of recruits relaxed . . . marginally. Palpable tension remained.

“What’s your name again?” Lowney asked. “Sinclair?”

“Yes, sir,” confirmed the nominal squad leader.

“Where are you from?”

“Raphael, sir. New Venice.”

“What are you guys doing in here?”

“Cleaning detail, sir,” Sinclair answered with a shrug.

“And what is this room?”

“It’s, uh . . . auxiliary port fire control, sir.”

“You think you’d like to be assigned here when you finish recruit training?”

“Yes, sir! Of course, sir!”

Andrea noticed a proud grin on the XO’s face at Sinclair’s response. Lowney asked much the same questions of the other recruits. True to his word, he kept things light. Andrea had almost begun to tune things out before he got to the last of them. It was the red-faced young man who’d called the group to attention when Sutton walked in.

“Why did you join?” Lowney asked.

“I’m sorry, sir?” The recruit blinked.

“Why’d you join?”

The recruit blinked again. He didn’t answer right away. Sutton tilted his head curiously. “It’s a simple question, recruit,” he said. “I’m sure you’ve answered it before.”

“It’s not a simple answer, sir.”

"Try me," Lowney said before Sutton or Andrea could stop him.

"My life fell apart the night before the Test. All my future plans evaporated," Malone answered. "The navy had a lot of good options, but militaries get misused. I don't want to die in a war started over some rich man's lies. My family was against it. I was pretty torn on the idea."

Andrea's eyes went wide. Suddenly she wanted nothing but rote answers from a manual. She glanced at Sutton, hoping to think of a way to get the XO to cut this off gracefully, but the XO wasn't looking her way. To make things worse, Malone kept talking.

"Then I heard about the *Aphrodite*. The lady next to you pointed out that pirates don't quit because somebody asks nicely. So I joined up. Sir."

Lowney was as stunned as everyone else. "That's . . . quite an answer, Malone."

"I think we should probably be going now," Sutton said.

"Recruit Malone," Lowney asked, ignoring the XO, "have you had any regrets?"

"No, sir."

"Why not?"

"Because I'm with good people, sir. Because I've learned how to do things I could never do before. I wanted to go to a good university," he said, his lips cracking with just the hint of a grin, "but instead I got to go on a spaceship and meet one of the president's chief deputies. Seems like I did pretty well." He risked a glance at Andrea. "It's an honor to meet you, ma'am. I'm a big fan of your writing."

Andrea blinked. "Thank you."

Sutton picked his jaw up from the floor. He couldn't call this inappropriate, couldn't articulate what was so wrong . . . but it clearly was. "We'll be going now. Carry on, recruits."

"Sir, yes, sir," the five young men in the compartment answered in unison as Sutton ushered his companions out. Unfortunately, the first turn he took put him and his guests right past an open ventilation shaft on the other side of the compartment.

"Tanner, how'd you know who she was?" they heard a recruit hiss.

"What're you, blind? I never missed a press conference before I enlisted!"

Sutton coughed loudly as he passed. The recruits didn't get the hint. Before the visitors were out of earshot, they clearly heard one of the recruits warn, "You're gonna do burpees until you *die* for that one, Tanner."

"What? He said to speak our minds."

"Yeah, but he didn't fucking mean it!"

"His mistake."

Lowney chuckled, flashing through a couple of notes on his holocom. "Not sure if I'll be able to use that boy's story. Falls out of pace with my other quotes."

"That's too bad," Andrea thought aloud.

"Hm? I would think that's a bit more controversial than the president would like."

"The president appreciates honest dissent," Andrea said tactfully, "and all the more so when it's from someone stepping up to serve his people despite sincere misgivings." She paused. "The president would call that patriotism."

Lowney smiled, perhaps a bit cynically, as he continued his notes. Seeing that their company was a bit distracted, Andrea said to Sutton, "I thought that poor guy was going to have a heart attack when you talked to him."

"Hm?" Sutton murmured. "Oh. I thought so, too, at first. But now I don't think I was the one who had him flustered at all."

"You don't?"

"No." Sutton shook his head. "I may be a big, important officer, but I'm pretty sure the only person in that compartment that mattered to him was you."

• • •

"Fuller: *Los Angeles*, engineering department. Garrison: *Joan of Arc*, engineering. Gomez: *Los Angeles*, deck department. Other Gomez . . ." Janeka stopped herself. For once, she allowed a slight grin. "Someone in the billeting office has a sense of humor. Other Gomez: *Los Angeles*, deck department."

Both Gomezes groaned. The other recruits got a good laugh. They sat together, collected on the floor of Squad Bay Oscar, hearing the first duty stations of the company's navy recruits. The marine recruits were there, too, though they had at least another four weeks of combat training after graduation before they would learn where they'd be assigned. Until graduation, though, they were all simply recruits, regardless of service branch.

They had trained like that from the beginning and maintained that cohesion until the end. They had the same PT requirements, the same customs and courtesies, and the same lengthy training with small arms that ate up much of their final two months of training. Only during the company's three-week "apprenticeship" phase on board *Los Angeles* did the marines and navy recruits separate. Oscar's navy recruits learned basic helm, navigation, and procedures for common ships' tasks. Marine recruits trained in guard duties and weapons maintenance, and received a surprising amount of sit-down classroom work on etiquette and regulations over the use of force.

Yet they all learned damage control. They all learned to fight fires and plug holes in the hull. They all conducted mock boarding actions, over and over, of *Los Angeles* and of other ships linked up to the cruiser. Their apprenticeship phase was the most grueling portion of Oscar Company's training, but, in hindsight, it had also been the most enjoyable.

"Huang: *Resolute*, deck department. That's a good ship. Congratulations," Janeka said. Her voice was as low on cheer as always, but Oscar Company had learned to detect nuance. Many felt sure that Janeka would show signs of humanity after graduation. Others bet significant money against it.

Tanner sat toward the middle of the company, all but holding his breath. The hopes and dreams of individual recruits were ultimately the least influential factor in where they would be billeted, but everyone at least got to put in their wish lists. Tanner never got over that first ride on *St. George*. He wasn't particular about which Vigilant-class ship he might be assigned to, but he knew what names he wanted to hear.

"Jun: Fort Stalwart, clerical department, Raphael," Janeka read, making a sour face. "Jun, did you ask for this? Do you actually like it here?"

"No, gunny!"

"Are you lying to me? Were you afraid you'd miss me?"

"Uh . . ."

"Are you not sure what answer will displease me more?" she pressed. Jun blinked. Janeka grunted. "Better work on that." She read more names. Recruits patted Jun on the back as if he'd been sentenced to prison.

"Madison: *Belfast*, deck department. Malone: *St. Jude*, deck department. McAlister: *Rio de Janeiro*, deck department . . ."

Tanner hardly listened to the rest. He restrained himself from cheering. *St. Jude* was based out of Augustine, the planet on the farthest orbit from Archangel. Augustine was a cold, inhospitable rock, yet one with a pair of universities, several corporate research labs, and no small number of tourist traps. Its spaceport had entered a boom period five years ago as Augustine came around in its long orbit to face Hashemite space, and would remain a place of constant activity for several years to come.

By the time Tanner got ahold of his feelings and scrambling thoughts, Janeka finished the list. He glanced around, caught Alicia's eye, and shared a grin. She knew he had been hoping for a corvette assignment. Alicia had her fingers crossed for a spot on *Los Angeles*, but it would be some time before those orders came through.

"People, we're gonna get back to our field day of the squad bay," said Everett, bringing the moment to a close. "We don't want to spend the last days of training on a cleaning binge, so let's get it done and make sure we don't make a mess later." He glanced at a note on his holocom screen. "Baljashanpreet, Matuskey, Espinoza, Huang, Jun, Malone. My office."

The recruits summoned to meet with Everett formed up outside his office without worry. This was unlikely to be another ass chewing. Performances held to expectations, and often exceeded them. There had been no major screwups for weeks.

Everett came out to meet them with his holocom screen still up, floating next to him as he moved. "At ease," he said, allowing the recruits to relax as they stood. "Gunny Janeka and I received your orders last night. We've had time to do some math and send out a few messages. Espinoza, Malone: your ships won't be in port again for at least five weeks. Matuskey, Jun, and Huang: you're going to shore billets where you aren't urgently needed. Baljashanpreet . . . well, you're going to the *St. George*, so you could be aboard a couple hours after graduation concludes, but I've got a pretty solid relationship with Lieutenant Duran. He's willing to put off having you aboard for a while if you're interested in taking up an opportunity.

"The fleet is serious about cross-training our marines and navy crews. The higher-ups like the versatility. Recruits, given the details of your orders, you have a choice after graduation. Four of you can ship out immediately while the other two cool your heels here at Fort Stalwart and do whatever bullshit jobs they come up with until it's time to go . . . or you can join Oscar Company's marine recruits for weapons and tactics school. It won't be as easy or as relaxing as temporary duty here on base, but it will certainly be more interesting and you'll get to blow up lots of shit," Everett finished nonchalantly. "Questions?"

"Chief, will this be like an extension of basic?" asked Matuskey.

"Yes and no. They don't treat you like you're still just recruits, but that means they'll expect you to act like regular personnel. You'll be in a nicer barracks than this one. You'll have liberty after sunset and you can get off base on occasion. WTS doesn't start up for several days after graduation, too, so you'll be on temporary duty here until then regardless. Or you can burn some leave time if you want. I'd recommend it. You need to get out of here and remember that you're human beings."

The recruits chuckled. Everett's expression grew serious. "People, we've been training you for the real thing because that's our job, but I think the real thing is coming. I see changes in procedure and expectations in the fleet. I see a buildup of ships and arms. I can't tell you what our civilian leadership plans or expects will happen, but all this trouble can't be for nothing. Nor does command view this company and the ones following it as just some fuck-off experiment in military pedagogy."

Matuskey frowned. "Uh, chief . . . ?"

Everett sighed. "Malone."

"Pedagogy is the art or science of teaching," Tanner said.

"Oh." Matuskey nodded.

"Think it over. Dismissed."

As the other recruits headed back into the squad bay, Tanner lingered. "Chief?" he asked. "I don't need to think it over. I'll stay for WTS."

Everett looked at him thoughtfully. "I'm glad to hear it. Only reason they can afford to send you guys is because we lost some projected recruits along the way. People like Einstein," he added with a grin. "Back to work, Malone."

"Aye, aye, chief." Tanner returned to the squad bay to find the company working at a more relaxed pace than was normally allowed. His eyes scanned the room until he found Alicia wiping down the lockers against the walls. "Need any help?"

Alicia smirked as she handed him a second towel. "What was that about?"

"Turns out you're not rid of me yet. They gave us the option to go to WTS with you guys."

"Huh. All six of you?"

"Well, I don't know if they're going for it. I already said yes."

Alicia nodded. She didn't seem especially impressed or excited. "Good."

Tanner smiled.

"I'll get to punch you in the face a bunch more," she mused.

"You're never gonna let me live that down, are you?"

"Nope." She kept cleaning. He'd faced Alicia in many sparring matches since that day, and despite his best efforts, he'd lost every time. "So what're you gonna do between graduation and WTS?" Alicia asked in an offhanded tone. "Stay on base? Burn some leave time?"

"I dunno. I was thinking of staying here." Tanner frowned. "No sense burning leave time or travel cash until I can go see my parents."

"Or until you can go all the way to Earth to see your *girlfriend, Madelyn*," Alicia teased with a snotty, singsong tone.

Tanner sighed. "It's not like that. Okay, I've had a crush on her for a couple years, but seriously? She's a good friend, but it's just that. I'm not on hold for her."

Alicia moved around Tanner to wipe down the next locker. She sprayed it down, then handed Tanner the bottle. "You mean that?" she asked skeptically.

"Yeah."

"You really have control of your emotions like that?"

Tanner snorted. "I know better than to develop a bunch of unrealistic expectations."

Alicia was quiet for a moment. "You should use some of your leave time before WTS."

"You think?"

"Yeah. You know, relax, decompress. You don't have to go far. There are a couple cool cities on this planet. It'd give you a chance to be who you are out of that uniform. Besides, hotel beds won't be so expensive if you split 'em with me."

Tanner dropped his bottle of spray cleaner. It burst open at his feet, covering his boots and the floor with fluid. Smiling as if nothing was wrong at all, Alicia turned away. "Hey, I'm gonna check my squad. I'll be back in a few."

Stunned and speechless, Tanner watched Alicia go.

SEVEN

Predators

"We used to argue about this shit constantly," Lauren explained, gesturing to the mob of pirates gathered around the fires. "Secret ballot or public vote? Chits? Show of hands? What do we vote on first, captains or targets? Officer elections or ships' rules?"

She took a pull off her bottle of whiskey, then flashed a grin at the new pirates surrounding her. "Hell, we're still arguing. Direct democracy's a pain in the ass."

"Beats the alternatives, though, right?" asked Sheng Hong. He held a plate of simple fare in his hands, most of it just meat roasted over an open flame. His beer sat at his feet.

"Pretty much. Y'know, you see those movies where the pirate captains are always these high-and-mighty assholes who shoot everyone who displeases 'em. What the fuck sense does that make? Pirate ships are full of career criminals. Why would they put up with that?"

Darren Mills shrugged in agreement. He was admittedly surprised to still be breathing himself. After the theft of *Aphrodite*, Darren found the camaraderie of his fellow pirates more than a little strained. Insults and threats flew, some of them veiled, others open. The warmth of his welcome into the crew went cold overnight.

Only the influence of Casey, Lauren, and Jerry prevented things from getting violent. They prevented brawls, and talk of worse, through tactful words and offers of drinks or dinner. Darren learned quickly that even the most respected of pirates had only minimal real authority while in port. Their opinions carried great weight, but in the end, they couldn't order anyone to do much of anything.

Nothing made that plainer than what Darren witnessed tonight. Word went out that *Vengeance* and several other ships intended a voyage. The call had been anticipated for days; people were already running low on cash. A great many pirates from *Vengeance* had been so sure of a huge payday from *Aphrodite* that they quickly squandered their initial shares of the loot. The money from ransoming their captives hardly assuaged the disappointment of losing the ship. Many pirates consoled themselves by spending their cash even faster.

As Darren learned, the initial sign-on was only an agreement to journey to the other side of the planet under complete communications silence. *Vengeance* and four smaller vessels landed in the desert, arranged in a ring. Bonfires and grills soon appeared, along with kegs and racks of alcohol. Most of it was fairly cheap stuff, either donated by the wealthier pirates or scrounged up from ships' stores. Serious matters had to be hashed out—namely where the ships were going and who would be in charge—but that was no reason not to make a party out of it.

"Hey, Lauren," said Chang, striding up with a mug in his hand, "we gonna get this show on the road?"

"Yeah, yeah." Lauren urged Jerry out of his simple collapsible chair. She stood on it, hoisted a pistol into the air, and fired off a pair of rounds. "Hear ye, hear ye, assholes!" she called. Tiny speakers sewn into the shoulder pads of her vest for just such an occasion boosted her voice. "Mates and crew of *Vengeance*, gather 'round so we can hash out all our shit!"

Conversations ceased. Music dropped. The men and the few women who had signed on to the ship—and there had been hundreds, enough that some had to be turned away back at Paradise City—drew close in a crowd around Lauren and her impromptu pedestal. Farther away, similar clusters gathered for the crews of the *Guillotine*, the *Yaomo*, and the *Liberty Rose*. The crew of the fifth ship, the *Monkeywrench*, would get around to it when they felt like it, as was their way.

"As most recent quartermaster, it falls to me to kick this off," Lauren explained for the first-timers, new recruits, and those drunk enough to need the recap. "The first order of business is the election of a new quartermaster to run the rest of the meeting. Are there any candidates?"

"I nominate that scary-assed Lauren!" called out Chang.

"Scary-assed Lauren accepts!" She smiled. "Are there any other candidates?" Her gaze swept the crowd. "Come on, don't be shy. You all know I won't take it personally. Seriously? Am I running unopposed again?"

"Nobody's an ugly enough bitch to beat you!" Jerry shouted.

"Oh, sure you are, Jerry!" Lauren shot back, and then waited for the laughter to pass. "All in favor?" she asked, then nodded as she heard a roaring "Aye!" in response. "All opposed?" Silence. "So be it. I accept the post of quartermaster for this voyage!"

A cheer went through the rowdy assembly. Lauren bowed sloppily. "Our second order of business is the election of a captain."

"Casey!" several men shouted out.

"Is Casey even here?" Lauren asked. "I figured he's passed out somewhere . . . aw, there he is," she said as her longtime comrade worked his way through the crowd. "Casey, do you accept the nomination?"

"I suppose," he replied with feigned reluctance.

"Other candidates?" Lauren asked. Again, silence. "Don't feel shy about speaking up. One pirate, one vote. No one is on a power trip here." Finally, she shrugged. "Casey runs unopposed. All in favor?" She waited for the resounding "Ayes" and cheers. She was then cut off before she could call for nays.

"Hey! What the *fuck*?" someone yelled nearby. Lauren spotted a burly man with bared arms and a bald head pushing through to the open space in the center. He pointed an angry finger at Darren, who stood near the inner ring of the crowd. "Why is that fucker voting? Why's he even here?"

"He signed on like anyone else, Parker," Lauren answered. "He votes just like anyone else."

"That's bullshit!" Parker growled, throwing a bottle down on the ground. "We'd all still be swimming in cash if it wasn't for this fucking moron!"

"Wasn't his fault, Parker," said Casey in a calm, firm voice.

"Casey, why are you protecting this asshole?" demanded the bigger pirate. He practically frothed at the mouth with rage.

"Hey, I'm not protecting anyone," he said, holding his hands up. "I'm just another pirate right now. I'm just saying it isn't right to hold what happened against him. I'm not telling you what to do."

Parker needed a moment to process that. Darren tensed, figuring he'd get jumped any second. He had no ground to give. The crowd was too thick for that. If he pulled his gun or a knife now, there'd be a fight for sure. Yet if he didn't do it now, he'd probably never get it out in time. Darren had survived a few brawls, but this guy was half again his size and looked like bare-handed murder was his favorite debate tactic.

Parker's gaze turned on him. He moved in and swung his meaty fist. Darren ducked under it, rushing forward to get behind his attacker. Parker spun and threw a left hook that caught Darren in the side. His follow-up punch landed right in the jaw.

Darren staggered back, saw Parker closing in on him, and swung. He caught Parker in the nose. The bigger pirate cocked back one fist to pound Darren's face—and then found his arm suddenly tangled up in Lauren's.

Hardly anyone saw Lauren move around him. She was considerably smaller than Parker—her head came up only to his shoulder—but she got behind him, driving her elbow up into his armpit with an audible crack.

Parker roared in pain. Lauren slipped around in front of him. Her fist shot straight into his jaw. Staggered by the blow, Parker didn't even register the leg that slipped in around his until Lauren shoved him back. He hit the ground hard.

"Casey's not in charge here!" Lauren barked loudly enough to silence all the cheers and commentary. "I am! I am the quartermaster of this voyage and I run this meeting! We will *not* attack our shipmates! We will *not* break faith!"

Her challenging gaze swept the crowd. No one took her up on it. "We were in the middle of a vote on Casey," Lauren huffed. "Any opposed? No? Fine. Casey wins." With that, she stomped back to her chair.

The silence held as Casey stepped forward. He passed the fallen Parker, leaving him to cough up blood where he lay. Casey held out his hand to help Darren up.

"Darren followed my instructions as captain to the letter," Casey announced to the crew. "Yes, he got rolled. Yes, he was conned. Maybe we all got screwed 'cause Darren slipped up, but it was his first night here and he was alone. Maybe it's my fault for not looking out for him. Maybe it's the fault of all of us for not looking out for one another."

He turned to look Darren in the eye. "Are you going to follow the ship's rules we set down here?" he asked. "Are you gonna follow orders in battle? Look out for your mates? Fight like hell when the time comes?"

Darren almost answered with "yes, sir," but then he remembered where he was. "Yeah." He wiped the blood from his nose. "Yeah, I will."

"Then I've got no problem with you." He turned back to Lauren. "The floor is yours," he said with a bow and a flourish.

"Somebody get that asshole out of my sight," Lauren said, gesturing to Parker. "He's lucky he pulled that before we hashed out our rules, or he'd be in much deeper shit right now." She waited for a couple of other pirates to heft Parker up. The crowd parted as the men hauled Parker away, but they didn't go far. They simply dumped Parker back to the ground just a few meters away from the edge of the crowd.

"On that note," Lauren continued, "the code. We work from the code of the last voyage." She held up her holocom in the air, projecting a large image for all to see. It displayed a bullet-point list in bright letters. She set the flat projection to rotate slowly.

"One: One pirate, one vote, in all matters of the ship. We set course on a vote. We attack on a vote. We go home on a vote. All in favor?" The unanimous vote of approval, though a foregone conclusion, always boosted morale.

"Two: In combat or shipboard emergency, we follow the orders of the captain and officers without dispute. Every shipmate backs the officers in time of emergency. Every officer is just another shipmate at any other time. All in favor?" Again, consent was unanimous.

"Three: No mate shall strike another, nor steal from another. Disputes are brought to the quartermaster and settled under direction. All in favor?"

The measure met with loud approval. In many ways, the quartermaster wielded more power on the ship than the captain. She meted out justice. She maintained a semblance of order. Without a battle to fight or a disaster to manage, the captain was just another shipmate—surely the most influential, but still just a popular individual among equals.

"Four: Every mate shall stand watch with care. Every mate shall maintain weapons with care. Every mate shall answer to his mates for failure in either of these charges." Again the crowd roared its approval.

It was all very simple, Darren considered, but that wasn't much of a surprise. Nobody became a pirate without first becoming fed up with the restrictions and expectations of society at large. Religion or lack thereof, ethnicity, planet of origin, personal habits—outside of harmless banter, nobody gave a damn.

The final matter had to be handled with some slight delicacy. Lauren cut the power to her holocom projection. "So on to our last item. One pirate, one share. I'm sure we all agree to that. Let's talk bonus shares and compensation for injuries."

A new projection appeared. It listed the captain as getting three shares, the quartermaster two, and several other officers—all still to be elected—receiving extra shares as well. That would all be debated, as well as compensatory cash for anyone seriously injured. Several shares would be set aside to make up a bonus fund for acts of bravery or ingenuity. All that, Darren knew, would meet with some difference of opinion.

Surprisingly, the first man to speak called for another share for their captain.

• • •

"Hamilton VI?"

"No."

"New Corsica? Lotta wildcat mining ops in the asteroid belt. Easy to hit, easy to hide, easy to fence the loot."

"Hnh. We oughta think bigger."

"Casey's right. Not worth our time."

"Tarawal?"

"Probably too big."

"Izumoto's Star?"

"Seriously? Jesus fuck, Wei, you want to get us all killed? Fuck no." Casey spat a bit of bone from his meat into the fire. "Military budget's huge."

"What's wrong with Hamilton VI?" asked Krietmeyer. He was lean and eager, with hungry eyes peering out at the others from under a ragged mop of brown hair. Of the five captains present, he was the only one serving his first term.

"The whole Hamilton system is NorthStar territory, K," Casey answered. His patience implied a lot in a moment like this. These were all rough men and women. The fact that someone of Casey's standing spoke to him as a peer lent him legitimacy with the other three captains. "NorthStar lost a bundle on the *Aphrodite* raid. If we hit them too hard and too often, it becomes cost-effective to hunt us all down. If we spread out the pain, though, make others share the burden . . . then we're just part of the cost of doing business."

"*Aphrodite* was your windfall," Krietmeyer pointed out. "Not ours."

Casey shrugged. "NorthStar Security isn't gonna differentiate, K," he said. "When they finally get their dander up, we're all gonna look alike to them."

Conversation faltered. Most of the captains stared into the fire, considering targets for their raid. In the distance, the party continued. There would be an open vote to ratify the choices their captains offered; until then, cheap drinks and cheap laughs kept everyone amused.

"So I guess that leaves out anything in Archangel space and the Hashemites, right?" asked Wei. The bald, heavily tattooed captain of the *Monkeywrench* had just won his fourth term as captain an hour ago. He was perhaps a bit more daring than the captain of

Vengeance and allegedly loved combat more than the payoff at the end, but he'd been around too long for his survival to be a matter of pure luck.

Hannah Black, captain of the *Guillotine*, grunted in confirmation. "Archangel stepped up their patrols after the *Aphrodite* hit. And they've bitched up enough of a storm to get Union and corporate ships out there to share the load. We nearly got caught smuggling goodies out of the system. Had to bribe the hell out of the crew that boarded us."

She heard a whistle from Ming, the perennial captain of the *Yaomo*. "How much does it cost to buy off a boarding crew from Archangel?"

"Hell if I know." Hannah shrugged. "We got boarded by NorthStar people. The captain of the patrol ship would've gotten a big bonus for catching us, but the boarding team? Not so much. They were happy to be bought. Still," she said, swilling more of her drink, "cost us half the advance we were paid for the job."

Krietmeyer nodded. "Probably the same all over Hashem, then," he said. "*Aphrodite* made port there a lot. Hashemite media made a big stink out of it."

"Well, wait a second," Casey said, scratching his chin. "Hashemite space is too big to cover all their bases at once. They have a big fleet, but it's old and that's a lot of territory. Either they stretch too thin or leave some spots weak. And given what just happened, they probably shifted a lot of their muscle over to face Archangel . . . what's on the other side of Hashem from Archangel?"

Hannah pulled up a projection from her holocom and browsed through an astrocartography program. It was simple stuff, meant for secondary school or low-level university classes, but it did the job. Soon, Hannah had a three-dimensional projection of Hashemite space for everyone to see. It was, like most multisystem states, something of a free-floating blob. Star systems suited for terraforming, let alone naturally habitable ones, rarely appeared in neat clusters.

"Krok space," Wei spat. "Fuck that. Stick to hitting humans."

"Fair," Casey conceded. "What about the other directions?"

"Ras-al-Khaimah," Hannah noted, pointing to the topmost system. The image expanded, revealing a star orbited by seven planets. Labels and simple information appeared beside each planet. Two were inhabited, and according to the display, they currently lay on nearly opposite sides of their star. "Huh. Prime is probably out. Fifty million people there. They'll have invested in planetary defense by now."

"What's that other one?" Casey asked, leaning in with interest. He pointed to the icon for the less-populated planet. "Qal'at Khalil? Does that mean something?"

Hannah input a query. "Qal'at is Persian for 'fortress.' That doesn't bode well."

"Yeah, but I've never heard of it," Casey murmured. He poked his finger into the projection, calling up further information. "Khalil . . . okay, so Khalil's the third son in line for the crown. Must've named the place for him. The family probably stuffed him there to give him something to do out of the way from the actual government. See, look? Mining, some tech manufacturing. It's small, but it's not nothin'."

"Six million people is still way too much for us," noted Ming.

"No, look how they're distributed. The capital city's in this nice subtropical spot, but it's less than half a million people. All the working stiffs must be in this belt here in this mountain region. The loot's here, but all the people are over there, where we could lock 'em down from orbit. And that's if they feel like putting up a fight at all. How many of them wanna stick their necks out for Prince Khalil and his fat-ass royal buddies?"

"You never know," Wei warned. "Might stick up for him just out of pride."

"Figure it's a coin toss."

"Civilian gun ownership is illegal in Hashem," Hannah put in. "The royal family doesn't want the scrubs getting uppity. They'll have security forces to keep the locals in line and to put up a good show, but I doubt it'll be anything serious. The threat will be from whatever's ready to go on Ras-al-Khaimah Prime or patrolling the system at large. And like Casey said, that's a lot of space to cover."

Casey glanced around at the others. "Nobody's been here before, huh?"

"I've got a few Hashemites in my crew," offered Wei. "Don't know if they've been to this particular planet—probably not—but they'll know a thing or three regardless."

"Okay," Casey mused, "let's think of a couple other possibilities before we get excited, but we'll ask around. Maybe someone'll know a little more."

"You think we can sell this?" Krietmeyer asked.

"Well, we ain't done talking," conceded Casey. "We may come up with something better. Gotta pass this through the crews regardless. And we can't go in at all without taking a good look first. But yeah"—he nodded—"I got a hunch this will work out."

He let the topic drop after that. It wouldn't do to push too hard too soon.

• • •

"Can't believe they bought all that bullshit. *Twice*," huffed Ranjan as he stared out of the *Guillotine*'s bridge canopy screens. The ship had been on the ground at Khalil City's spaceport for over an hour, feigning the same atmospheric systems malfunction that brought them in for their first groundside look a day before. That touchdown had been the last of a week's worth of soft, tentative reconnaissance missions. This visit was the opening of something quite different.

"Hey, we're a luxury yacht, Ranjan." Hannah Black had her boots kicked up onto her control panel at the center of *Guillotine*'s bridge. There were only four crew posts in the compartment, but as shipboard operating stations went, they were all fairly comfortable. "They wouldn't want to offend any corporate bigwigs by inspecting us as thoroughly as the common rabble. And anyway, we got inspected. Sort of."

The *Guillotine*—under a different name, of course—spent a few hours on the surface yesterday doing repairs, took off, and then returned an hour ago claiming the same problem had resurfaced. A professional crew would have been embarrassed by such a fiasco. Port personnel naturally dropped a few smart-ass remarks.

Those same port workers might have held their tongues had they known what had happened to the *Guillotine*'s wealthy original owner, her family, and her personal staff.

"Two guys walking up to the edge of the entry ramp to poke their heads inside is my kind of inspection," Ranjan conceded. He was new to the crew, having signed on only two months before. He, too, might've been disturbed to know the details of the mutiny.

As Hannah considered telling him the grisly story, Ranjan spotted a blinking light that appeared on the flat screen of his status panel. He quickly accessed and read the message. "That's the warning signal. They're firing up. Sticking with Casey's plan. *Yaomo*'s in the lead."

"Casey's plan," Hannah snorted, slipping her boots off the control panel. "More like *my* plan. He just shuffled the ships around a little. Okay, I guess we're done with our 'repairs.' Call in the boys from outside. Tell 'em they can ditch the uniforms. Then get us in line to take off."

A moment later, the ship's indicator lights showed that all hatches were sealed. Hannah keyed the shipboard comm system. "Engineering," she said, "get us revved up. Everyone else, battle stations. I say again, battle stations."

An alarm announced takeoff, but not one to warn of impending combat. Normally, a crew took a final vote before making an attack; in this case, they voted before returning to Qal'at Khalil. Within moments, lights across the ship's battle stations display indicated full readiness. The ship's engines came online with a shudder that ran the length and breadth of the *Guillotine*.

Hannah's eyes darted between split projections on her status board. One side offered takeoff time and instructions. As expected, the port of Khalil City was quite accommodating; they offered a wide launch window and a polite farewell. The other projection displayed traffic outside the atmosphere as seen by orbiting satellites. Planetary scanning systems wouldn't spot the pirate ships until they decelerated below light speed—right on top of the planet.

Local military systems might see better than what was offered to private traffic, but nothing could see faster than light traveled. Given the lax security the *Guillotine* encountered, Hannah wasn't even convinced the local military had warning systems independent of the civilian infrastructure.

Hannah's compatriots would attack without much warning, but just how sharp their edge of surprise would be depended largely on her timing.

She noted nervous expressions on the three other faces on her bridge. Hannah felt the same way, but she didn't advertise it. She made herself breathe steadily, sitting calmly in her chair until the traffic display picked up a new inbound freighter contact. As it arrived, Hannah called up a clock beside it, counting down rather than up.

"Take us up slowly," she instructed, her eyes still glued to the display. The freighter—which had better be *Yaomo*, or things would get awkward quickly—was already in the atmosphere. Its approach vector toward Dammar, the larger city two thousand kilometers away, held more or less to the original plan. Certainly its speed had someone in traffic control alarmed by now.

Hannah threw the battle stations comms switch on and left it there. "Helm, come to zero-four-four. You know what we're looking for. Everyone else, you've got your targets. Wait for my command." She looked over the display screens that winked to life across her control panel. They gave the captain a view of each targeting system on the *Guillotine*. Luxury yachts commonly carried significant armament; they were, after all, prime targets for pirates and terrorists, or so their wealthy owners argued to the people who wrote shipbuilding standards. The *Guillotine* was no exception. Her original owners greatly exceeded Union limits.

"Ranjan," she asked, "do you mind?"

The shipmate to her right let out a little sigh. "No," he said, surrendering control of the ship's rocketry systems to her. "Go ahead."

"Thank you." Hannah smiled. With the target already locked in, it was really only a matter of tapping a light on her display screen. Hannah wanted to be the one to press it, anyway. Her fingers lingered for only a second before coming down on the trigger key.

Four missiles shot from within the wings of the *Guillotine*, bursting out of highly illegal concealed launchers that had been part of her original custom design. Each flew to a preprogrammed target. Two missiles demolished the spaceport's control building in a fiery explosion. One veered left, destroying the system patrol ship that *Guillotine* had spotted sitting in its hangar bay on arrival. The fourth soared halfway across the city, honing in on the undisguised anti–space/air turret system near the royal palace.

Guillotine's two turrets opened up on the spaceport as her missiles flew. The ship hovered in the air and rotated, allowing her gunners a moment to lay waste to targets of opportunity. Then she moved off on a strafing run over the city's police headquarters and the palace.

Hannah glanced at the screen displaying the planet's orbital traffic network. It showed only static. Her grin widened a little more; her timing had been excellent.

• • •

Yaomo plummeted out of the sky as if it would crash headlong into the peaceful streets of Dammar directly below. Her captain screamed the whole way down.

Ming held direct control of the helm. The five other people on the bridge of the freighter all looked more at one another than at their individual control stations. Ming had let out a yell when they hit the atmosphere at a less than gentle speed, which wasn't entirely inappropriate. What they were about to do was crazy. Exciting. Audacious. Ballsy. Something for the history books.

As the ship began to tremble with the stress of blazing through the atmosphere, trailing smoke across the sky, Ming ran out of breath. His war cry died off. Then he inhaled and screamed again, and that was when the bridge crew looked his way. They saw wild eyes, a wide-open mouth, and veins bulging in his forehead and his neck.

Yaomo was built with little regard for aesthetics. She was one hundred fifty meters long and mostly rectangular, with a bulbous bridge section and twin main thrusters. In between ran her primary cargo bay. The long, cylindrical cargo bays on her sides and top were attachments, not integral construction. The crew had long since forgotten the distinction; many of them made their living quarters in the cargo bays. *Yaomo* relied on deception and a strong, ruthless crew much more than on her arms and armor.

For this particular raid, a good number of her crew had to move their personal effects out of the ship's center cargo bay.

Yaomo fell to less than eight kilometers from the surface before her stabilizers fired. The move quickly halted her descent and aligned the freighter parallel to the ground. Her center cargo bay doors snapped open. An enormous bundle of large cylindrical fuel cells dropped out of the bay, along with numerous scrambler units and chaff flares to prevent it from being tracked and destroyed by anyone on the ground.

Barely three seconds later, *Yaomo*'s thrusters fired. Were it not for her internal gravity system, the wrenching force of the move would have pulped everyone aboard. Even so, the ship groaned and numerous systems sounded alarms.

In her wake, the fuel cells detonated a few hundred meters in the air above Dammar's spaceport. The shock wave reached well beyond the spaceport itself, followed by lethal heat. Witnesses would forever call it a nuke regardless of technicalities.

Virtually all of those witnesses were at least two kilometers away from the spaceport. Hardly anyone closer than that lived to tell about it.

• • •

"I just want to point out," Casey said, turning the volume of the *Yaomo*'s transmissions almost all the way down, "that as much as Ming wants everyone to think he's crazy, it was the guys on *Monkeywrench* who came up with that bomb in the first place." He glanced around the bridge. Graffiti, knickknacks, and slovenly pirate living had *Vengeance* looking somewhat less than military, but all the buttons, switches, and electronics still worked as originally designed. "Those guys sit around making great big bombs. Think about that."

"Ship full of engineers gone bad," agreed Jerry. "That'd keep me up at night if I didn't drink myself to sleep. Speaking of. She's alongside us now, ready to drop."

Casey glanced over to the three-dimensional display projected by the command and control table. Though coordination of a real fleet typically lay with battleships, destroyers still had to be built with the same command capacity. *Vengeance* was old, but she'd been built to last. Few expenses were ever spared when it came to upgrades.

Her image on the holographic tactical projection was still one of a proper military ship: sleek, lean, and bristling with weapons. Unlike smaller craft, she bore no wings or anything evoking imagery of flight. She was shaped much like a long shark, though instead of a tail she had large thrusters. Her armored hull ran in gently curving lines, with gaps cut here and there for gun emplacements, access hatches, and other necessities.

Beside her, *Monkeywrench* looked like a steam-era ship turned inside out in a mad attempt to imitate a psychiatrist's inkblot. Service and maintenance ships were usually ugly things, and *Monkeywrench* was no exception. Her original mutineers still made up much of her crew. The former Lai Wa Corporation employees had played merrily with all her tools and machinery ever since. *Monkeywrench* had originally been built for salvage missions, deep-space ship repair, and other assorted industrial chores. Now, in addition to her magnetic clamps, old-fashioned cranes, and tractor beams, she boasted ablative armor and a hodgepodge of weaponry.

Casey looked over to his display of the action on the surface. *Guillotine* continued her strafing runs while *Yaomo* sped out to rendezvous. *Yaomo* was packed with pirates ready to disembark and run through the city's streets, including many drawn from *Vengeance. Monkeywrench* would join her with an even larger share of manpower.

The problem came when *Liberty Rose*, a smaller, more maneuverable freighter than *Yaomo*, decided to cut in front of *Monkeywrench* to head for the surface. "Krietmeyer," Casey said after keying the comm channel, "what're you doing? You need to let Wei move in first."

"The hell difference does it make?" Krietmeyer's voice came back over the channel. "We're all going in the same direction, anyway!"

Casey watched *Liberty Rose* hit the atmosphere and snarled, "The difference is if there are antiair defenses Hannah hasn't hit yet, *Monkeywrench* has a better chance of surviving—"

"Then why haven't they shot at Hannah yet?" Krietmeyer interrupted. "Look, I'm not going in last and letting my guys miss all the best action."

"You stupid asshole, it's not about that! They aren't shooting at Hannah because she's too low and fast for—"

"Cannon emplacement!" announced Jerry. Casey's head snapped toward Jerry's display screen, which presented a computer-generated tactical view of Khalil City and its surroundings. Much of it already showed red from the havoc wreaked by *Guillotine*. Five kilometers away from the city, though, a hillside revealed the bright-red color of an intense heat signature. Then a wide, brilliant-green beam shot from the hillside through the *Liberty Rose* and into the sky beyond. The plasma blast continued on well out of the atmosphere before it dissipated.

Liberty Rose was all but cut in half. She immediately began tumbling in free fall.

"Jerry, we got that thing?" Casey asked.

He needn't have spoken. Jerry lit up the cannon emplacement with two of *Vengeance*'s laser batteries. Sharp red beams of light flashed through the atmosphere to cut through the hillside. At least one of the lasers struck something explosive, destroying the cannon emplacement in a ball of fire.

"Anyone else wanna ask again why this ship has to stay up above the atmosphere?" Casey grumbled, looking around again at his bridge crew. No one bothered to respond.

"Looks like we got 'em," Jerry said.

"Carl?" Casey asked, turning his attention to the man on his left.

The large pirate tracked several screens depicting the city five hundred kilometers below. He split off a new screen to follow the *Liberty Rose* to the ground. Carl shook his head. "Nobody's walking away from that."

Casey grimaced. "Well, if we were gonna lose a ship, I suppose it's best that it's the smallest one with the fewest guys on it."

"*We're* the ship with the fewest guys, Casey," Jerry reminded him.

"Well, right now, yeah, but I mean, I'd rather lose the smallest ship with the fewest guys on it that *isn't us.* Let's just make sure they don't have any more surprises like that."

"I've got a fix on the barracks and police stations," Carl said. "Or at least, you know . . . what we *think* are those."

"The fuck you waitin' for?" The captain shrugged. "Light 'em up."

• • •

It was easily the craziest, goddamn dumbest thing Darren had ever been part of in his life. It was dumber than signing on with *Vengeance*; he'd done that when he had nothing to lose and everything to gain. It was dumber than taking that whore to bed; he was drunk and alone and had a half dozen other mitigating factors in his defense there. But he'd known the assault on Qal'at Khalil was stupid when it was first suggested, and he was only surer of that as he heard out the "intelligence"—which amounted to the word of three Hashemite expat pirates and some articles found in an out-of-date encyclopedia. It was stupid, he knew it was stupid . . . and when the time came to vote on it, he didn't have the balls to vote no.

He was entitled to his vote. Some of the other pirates had voted no; Darren just didn't see any of them when it came time for the show of hands. He'd been surrounded by drunken fools, and he didn't have the guts to publicly disagree with them. The target met with overwhelming approval in the vote, and that was that. There was no turning back. Everyone was in it together, including those who had voted no.

And so it was that Darren found himself in a shooting gallery. He didn't have the expertise to keep himself aboard *Vengeance* instead of joining the ground crew. He was a machinist by training. He belonged on a ship rather than running through the streets shooting a gun. But he wasn't as familiar with *Vengeance* as a lot of other pirates were. Instead of serving in main engineering, he crouched under the windowsill of a restaurant as bullets, lasers, and who knew what else flew through the air.

Most of the fire came from Khalil City's palace, directly across a wide, open plaza. The steps to the palace itself rose up over a hundred meters away across open ground. Only pavement, low bushes, and open, empty space lay between the steps and the increasingly shattered buildings sheltering the pirates. Chang called the empty space a "kill zone."

Chang crouched beside him, keeping low as bullets flew through the thoroughly destroyed windows. Darren had stuck to Chang like glue from the moment they'd all loaded into the *Yaomo*. Chang was an ex–Union marine, so he knew how to fight. He was also a medic. Darren considered those very important details.

At the moment, though, Chang didn't seem to know what to do any better than Darren. Nor did the other three pirates in the café. Nor did the previous inhabitants, but then, the dead rarely offered useful advice. Darren, Chang, and the rest had mowed down everyone inside the restaurant as soon as they'd arrived.

"This is pretty goddamn accurate fire for bush leaguers," Chang growled.

"Yeah?" Darren huffed, doing his best not to panic. "How accurate is it if we aren't dead?" He resolved, not for the first or last time, to buy the best body armor he could afford the second he was back on Paradise, and fuck anyone who mocked him for it.

"Nah, it's not like that," grunted Chang. "They think we're in here, but they aren't sure. Don't wanna go wasting the whole neighborhood on unconfirmed targets. They're just trying to goad us into returning fire."

"What happens then?"

"Well . . . then they get serious. They'll use heavier bullets to rip through these walls. Or rockets. I'd go with rockets if I was them."

Darren blanched. It hadn't occurred to him that the shooting was somehow less than serious. Another burst of fire struck their building. The wall behind Darren shook with the impact of several bullets; other rounds sailed through the shattered window.

The plan for dealing with the palace perimeter had crashed and burned with the *Liberty Rose*. "Well," asked Darren, "what the hell are we still doing in here, then?"

Frowning, Chang pressed a key on the holocom on his wrist and pulled up an overhead image of the neighborhood. "Look, this whole area is designed as a kill zone around the palace," he explained. "Whoever's in charge of the security forces here probably decides who gets to set up shop closest to the palace. That's why they've got a hundred meters of open streets and plazas and shit all around it. My bet is they know exactly which building is at what range and how much punishment it can take.

"They've gotta have at least a couple hundred armed guys in that palace. Probably some powered security or infantry armor with 'em. We already took out the spaceport, the barracks, and the police stations, so that palace is the biggest concentration of resistance left in the city. They probably built that place to withstand a revolt or a peasant uprising or whatever sort of bullshit keeps royalty awake at night, so they've got no reason to come out and fight us.

"By now they know we've only got a few ships. If they've got more antiair, they'll keep it hidden until they've got a sure shot. Chances are they've still got at least a little, so we can't really call in any air support."

"Then why the hell are we coming to them?" Darren pressed. He tried to keep from sounding shrill. "If they're gonna stay there, then fuck 'em, right? Let 'em stay. Let's loot the rest of the city and bail! Or just blow the hell out of it from orbit!"

Chang scowled. "Are you crazy? That's where all the good cash and loot is gonna be."

"What're you talking about? This city is full of nice houses! There's good loot all around!"

"Not this good," Chang scoffed. "Prince Khalil or whoever's in charge has gotta be worth some serious ransom. Place is probably filthy with cash and artwork and all kinds of bullshit to keep him happy while he's stuck out here in the boonies. Nah, man. We gotta take the palace."

Chang risked a look up over the edge of the windowsill. "Yeah. They've got guys in powered security armor out there. Hundred meters of kill zone. I don't know how we're gonna get across that. There's no cover at all."

Darren lay almost fully on his back, with just his head and shoulders propped up under the windowsill. He stared at the holographic image of the neighborhood. This wasn't his place. He wasn't some army infantry guy. He was a machinist. A technician. He was supposed to fix things. Looking at the holo image, all he could think was that the city planners had created exactly what they'd wanted.

Then he frowned. "Chang," he said, "there are still cars and trucks all over this neighborhood."

"Nothin' that's gonna protect us against the kind of fire they're spitting out." Chang frowned, shaking his head. "Even in vehicles, we'd be slag before we covered the distance."

"No. Chang. You said we don't have any cover out there." He pointed to the empty space between the palace and its surroundings. "So let's create some."

Chang scowled. "Shit," he said, "you think they haven't thought of that already?"

"Did *you*?"

For a moment, Chang was at a loss for words. Then he said, "Look, if we can find some people who own cars, I guess we can take their keys, but that'll take hours—"

"Keys? Twenty-three hundred pirates and I'm the *only* one who knows how to hot-wire a car?" Darren blurted. "Fuck. Come on." He rolled over and began to crawl for the back door to the café. "I'll show you."

Chang and the other pirates exchanged dubious glances but followed. Soon they found themselves in the alley outside.

Darren ran down the block to a large, abandoned truck. Like many of the vehicles in the city, it was the sort that rode on wheels rather than a magnetic cushion. Its bubble-shaped driver's cab had been left tinted too dark to see through when it was parked. Darren aimed his plasma carbine at it and blew the top off the bubble. He waited only a moment for the remains of the frame to cool before climbing in.

Watching Darren work, Chang didn't even notice the first buzz from Lauren on his holocom. Finally, he answered. "Yeah. Chang."

"My side of the palace is the wrong end of one big target range," Lauren spat. "No way to get across without exposing everybody. How's it looking on your end?"

The truck's engine rumbled to life. Chang watched in surprise as Darren kicked the remnants of the front cab's door open. Inside, he saw the bottom of the dashboard cut open with wires and machinery exposed. "You can separate out the electronic security from the engine," Darren explained. "Then you just need to open the original starter circuit and stick something else with a charge in place to fool the engine into start-up. Something like a power pack from an energy weapon."

"Chang?" Lauren asked. "Chang, you there?"

"If it's that easy"—Chang blinked in awe—"why don't people steal that way all the time?"

"What?" Lauren asked.

Darren gestured to the vehicle's dashboard. "It fucks up the whole starter circuit. You can't turn it off and on again without major repairs."

Chang shook himself. "Lauren, I think we got an idea."

• • •

"Contact! Bogey dropped out of light—no, two bogeys now, both about one point five light-seconds out—"

"Helm, come about to face them and close at attack speed!" Casey demanded, stepping on the rest of the report. Adjustment or clarification would occur by the time Jerry finished speaking, anyway. Transmissions couldn't come or go faster than light; any data received through passive sensors took time to actually reach the sensor, and then another second or two to process. Active probing would require double that time to emit from *Vengeance*, hit the contacts, and bounce back.

Casey chose good, experienced, well-trained people for his bridge crew. He didn't have to order scans. That would be done as a matter of course. Immediately closing to attack made for a gamble, as the ships facing him could potentially equal or outmatch *Vengeance*.

"They're destroyers, Casey," Jerry grunted. The information on the tactical boards and the three-dimensional display revised automatically.

"Ops, let the ground party know fire support has pulled off," ordered Casey. "Carl, Jerry, the moment we're in range, you start pouring on the beam weapons fire. Focus fire on the one to port. Helm, as soon as you get within a hundred twenty K, go mild evasive but be ready to go full evasive on my order."

"Got it," replied Li from the helm.

"They're ordering to stand down, heave to, blah blah blah," called out Hakim from the ops station. Casey had borrowed Hakim from the *Monkeywrench* in case fluency in Arabic became important. The skinny, bearded pirate stood beside the ops station with a headset on, working with a projected holo screen instead of the normal ops hardware. "They're Hashemite Defense Force ships. *Asad* and *Fahd* mean 'lion' and 'panther' in—"

"Whatthefuckever," Casey grumbled with a dismissive wave. "Just name 'em on the board. Doesn't matter if you get it right on which is which. Cannons as soon as we're in range." Casey watched the display boards intently, in particular reading the distances between *Vengeance* and the two enemy ships. The newcomers split off, plainly hoping to force Casey to divide his attention and thereby leave a gap in his defenses. He watched the distance between *Vengeance* and *Fahd* tumble down closer to the 120,000 kilometers that marked the outermost effective range of *Vengeance*'s heavy laser cannons.

Range was likely in the pirates' favor, but only marginally so. Though *Vengeance* had excellent cannons, beam weapons could be inaccurate against spacecraft at such ranges. Anything capable of moving fast enough to make space travel practical was an inherently difficult target. Computerized evasion patterns coupled with the randomizing human factor made it even tougher. At such speeds and distances, even computers had a difficult job in timing a shot that would fly at the speed of light.

"We're not gonna get too fancy here, guys," Casey explained. His voice was loud and tense yet steady. "We're gonna shift targets fast. They'll expect a feint, so we're gonna commit a couple inches farther than we should before turning. Ready . . . hit 'em!"

Vengeance carried twin main laser cannons on recessed dorsal and ventral turrets midway toward the bow of the ship. The barrels of each glowed an angry red hue a split second before firing. Her first shot missed, as did her second and third. *Vengeance* closed as *Fahd*, running somewhat perpendicular to the pirate ship, focused more on evasion than attack.

Asad threatened *Vengeance* from behind, turning sideways to keep more guns trained on the pirates. *Asad*'s single main cannon and a broadside of smaller batteries fired, scoring only a few minor hits, which were deflected by *Vengeance*'s armor. A bolder attack by *Asad* would have delivered more significant damage, but the Hashemite captain hesitated. As Casey hoped, his enemy wanted to be sure of what he was dealing with before he committed.

Fahd had guns of her own; the pirate vessel had just come into range of those weapons, though, when *Vengeance* finally scored a hit. Hull plating all across *Fahd*'s starboard side blew apart as *Vengeance*'s powerful lasers cut an ugly scar through her.

"There!" Casey barked. "Secondary guns, fire at will. Helm, break off from *Fahd* and come about to intercept *Asad*. Jerry, fire off chaff missiles on *Fahd* and then be ready to hit *Asad*. Carl, main guns on *Asad*, now!"

More than one crewman on the bridge blinked at the seemingly contradictory orders, but obeyed. *Vengeance* wheeled sharply to starboard and up from her earlier plane. On the display boards, two small, fast-moving dots representing the chaff missiles moved from *Vengeance* toward *Fahd*.

The wounded destroyer's defensive batteries opened up immediately. They intercepted both missiles far enough out to prevent actual damage, but that was Casey's intent. The chaff missiles burst with an electromagnetic mess upon destruction. *Vengeance* now had a sensor-disrupting cloud between herself and the damaged destroyer behind her. *Fahd* would go around or through the chaff in seconds, but such seconds mattered.

Vengeance twisted as her main thrusters went into attack speed once more, narrowly avoiding a blast from *Asad*'s main guns. The ships fired away wildly at one another. Though they started out on nearly equal footing, *Vengeance*'s secondary guns added to the punishment as the range dropped.

Missiles shot out from *Asad*'s launchers too early. *Vengeance*'s defensive guns intercepted them as she fishtailed around to keep clear of the heavy bursts of the exploding missiles. The pirate ship shook, taking minor damage that would occupy her damage control crews, but few of the impacts went beyond what *Vengeance* was designed to take.

Keeping *Asad* bracketed between her main guns, *Vengeance* planted minor hits across the enemy's side with her secondary lasers. Two such hits proved critical, eliminating vital defensive guns. Casey spotted the damage on his display before anyone reported it. "Jerry! Missiles!"

Asad was only halfway through an emergency roll to present her undamaged dorsal side to *Vengeance* as the missiles closed in. Close defense guns had gotten increasingly better over recent decades, making direct hits rare; consequently, missiles were designed to blow with the largest possible blast radius. Modern missile fire was a game of getting in close enough to still count before interception. In this moment, though, only the trailing missile was shot down. The lead missile actually made it through to strike against *Asad*'s hull. Even a hundred kilometers out, the explosion would have crippled a destroyer. In this case, the missile blew its target apart entirely.

"Keep going!" Casey yelled over the cheers of his bridge crew. "Straight through the debris. Don't wheel about until we're through!"

Li couldn't help but grin as he plowed his ship through the hot wreckage. Loud thumps and cracks could be heard across *Vengeance* as she plowed through *Asad*'s remains. *Vengeance* cleared the wreck before she began to come about.

"Fire at will on that fucker," Casey commanded. "Anything but missiles. Things are expensive."

Across the ship, gunners at their stations likewise poured on fire at every opportunity. *Vengeance*'s evasive rolls and maneuvers occasionally interrupted her onslaught, bringing one gun up while turning another away, but it was all to be expected. Many of the gunners missed. More than a few of them hit.

Within moments, *Fahd* broke off from her intercept course. Her main thrusters went into full emergency FTL speed. The battered destroyer flashed away at her current heading, fleeing her tougher, unwounded opponent.

Cheers erupted across the bridge. Someone clapped Casey on the back, which he accepted with a grin. Pirates were predators in search of easy prey, not challenges. *Vengeance*'s crew might easily have failed this test.

"Li, bring us back to the planet and put us over Khalil City again," Casey said. "Ops, we need a damage report. And somebody get a shuttle ready. If we're not burning or bleeding, I'm heading down to the surface."

"You don't think we'll get more incoming?" Jerry asked.

"I think those were the only serious ships this system's defense force could spare," Casey explained, waving a dismissive hand. "Anything still orbiting Ras-al-Khaimah Prime is gonna stay there to protect it, especially now. Nearest system to this one is six light-years out. They have to send a messenger with an FTL drive just to raise the alarm. That's at *least* twelve hours to get there if they send some really hot shit starship. Any response will take at least that much time to get here, bare minimum, and that's presuming they're sitting around on ready alert.

"Plus, they just got their asses kicked by a destroyer. They'll probably figure we're military, so they'll presume we aren't alone. They won't come at us piecemeal. They'll want to get their shit together first. We've got at least a day and a half to fuck around here before we need to bug out. Should be plenty of time to take care of business."

• • •

Samir Majid Madani, captain of Prince Khalil's Royal Guard, had always been a good man. He was a good son, a good father, and a loving, loyal, respectful husband. His daughter, Fatima, was a doctor; her younger brother, Hamzah, was a schoolteacher.

They were far from their parents, but never far from their father's thoughts. He crouched under the cover of a palm tree planter near the western entrance to the palace thinking mostly of the tactical situation but also, in part, of his children. He found that odd. His children were out of danger.

His wife was not. She worked in the palace as a tutor to the prince's young children. It was not just his liege that Samir defended that day. He defended his wife, and friends, and innocent people.

He had always been a good soldier. He rose up from nothing to his position by merit and the grace of God. Samir remained at Prince Khalil's side when the last of the many courtly intrigues among the royal family erupted in bloodshed. More than once, Samir alone stood between Khalil and almost certain death. Naturally he was banished along with his prince to this backwater world by a king who felt the best way to keep the peace was to put distance between his potential heirs.

Samir found it all galling. Khalil never threatened anyone. He cared far more about astronomy and football than politics. Yet Khalil was third in line for the throne, and a decent, honorable man . . . and therefore a threat to his siblings.

He wondered if either of the other princes might be behind the attack. Nothing in the attackers' makeup or their tactics bore the hallmarks of either brother. Samir knew the attackers had at least one real warship. That much had been established when the main anti-space cannon, the only one that Prince Khalil could afford on this planet's pitiful defense "allowance," was demolished from space-based lasers. The clash in space only confirmed it. But everything else about the attack indicated that the enemy boasted a hodgepodge of weapons, craft, and ethnicities. They attacked with a collection of small arms, civilian spacecraft, and improvisation.

The last factor made it difficult to predict what the enemy would do. The fact that the palace hadn't been obliterated by that warship or the others in the air indicated that the attackers planned to take it intact, or mostly so. But they apparently had no armor with which to cross the kill zone.

He considered the implications of all this until he and his men began to see movement. First came a pair of heat signatures on his optic display, quickly recognized as ground vehicles. The two cars, floating on antigrav generators, burst from the city's alleys at high speed. "Open fire," Khalil ordered. A barrage of lasers and bullets promptly reduced the vehicles to smoking wreckage in the middle of the kill zone. It was no challenge.

Other vehicles followed, frequently in twos and threes. Some rolled on wheels. Others glided just above the ground. Khalil directed his men to keep up their fire over the comm network while destroying one vehicle after another. Chatter over the communications channels indicated similar activity at the other sides of the palace. The captain took a moment to play back his helmet's recording of the last few moments, looking carefully at the vehicles.

There were no drivers. He presumed as much; the enemy had to know what awaited them. Charging into a well-fortified position in civilian vehicles was suicidal. "This is Madani at the west side," he said into his comm channel. "I believe we face a diversionary attack here. Watch carefully for a breakout on your sides."

He switched back to live optics. The plaza quickly became a charnel pit of cars, trucks, and antigrav transports. Between the smoke, heat, and debris of earlier destruction and the speed of the oncoming vehicles, the shooting became tougher. Each vehicle was destroyed in turn, but they came closer and closer to the palace before elimination.

Over fifteen minutes, the steady trickle of wrecks built up to quite a mess. "North wall," Samir said, "are you seeing vehicular attacks?" He frowned when he received a negative response. It was the same for the other walls. Neither the south nor the east had much in the way of targets. They took fire from across the kill zone and fired back in response, but they saw no movement across the expanse.

He realized, too late, that the effort before him represented more than flash and distraction. Thermal imaging and straight optics were thoroughly disrupted by the smoke and flame, but radar was not so easily fooled. The cars kept coming, mostly antigravs now in order to get over the other wrecks, but smaller, slower movement followed behind. "West wall, we are about to face an infantry assault," Samir barked. Then the first blasts of heavy small arms fire erupted from the smoke and debris.

Bullets and small rockets struck all around Samir and his men. Red flashes of lasers and green pulses of plasma blasts hit the staircases, the overhanging concrete of the palace walls, and the decorative reinforced concrete planters all around them. Some fire came from the streets; the rest came from buildings out beyond the kill zone. Soldiers positioned above ground level in the palace were quickly pinned down. Samir heard one of his men call out for a medic. Then another, and another.

Samir joined in the battle with his plasma repeater, a weapon requiring such a large generator that only powered armor allowed it to be used in a man-portable fashion. An antigrav car finally got all the way to the staircase before exploding into a distracting mess of smoke and shattering plastic. Beyond it, Samir finally saw live targets. Enemy fighters ran from one wreck to the next, hiding behind the debris as they swarmed across the formerly open streets.

Their cover was imperfect. Samir cut down one fighter, then another, practically vaporizing them with each hit. Most attackers wore little in the way of protection; indeed, few had any body armor at all. His problem was not in the hardness of his targets, but in the lack of visibility. For every one he actually saw, a dozen more gunmen shot wildly through the smoke. Their fire was largely inaccurate, but it intensified with every moment. Numbers began to tell.

"Reserves to the west entrance!" Samir demanded. The planter he used for cover crumbled under machine gun fire. He shifted from it, feeling bullets bounce off his armor without doing serious damage. The captain kept low, moving over to grab the body of a fallen corporal and drag him back with one hand while firing his plasma repeater with the other. "Drop the barricades!" he said. "Drop them on my auth—"

She practically flew up from the stairs, moving straight for Samir with blades in her hands and murder in her eyes. The woman wasn't big. She wore only ordinary clothes. Given a moment to consider her, Samir would have dismissed the threat of her blades. Yet she rushed up at him, her thick blonde braid trailing in her wake, and before Samir knew it, one of those blades pierced through the vulnerable right armpit of his armor.

He yelled as much in rage as in pain, jerking involuntarily. The plasma repeater stayed in his hand more by the function of his armor than his muscles. Samir swung at her head with his other arm. The blow would have crushed her skull had she not ducked under it.

The woman swept under and around him. She targeted yet another of the suit's vulnerable points, this time behind the knee. The strong mesh fabric under the armor plating could withstand great heat and stress, but it wasn't proof against every attack. The blade came in as Samir stepped backward, stabbing through his leg in a bloody mess. Armored plates at the back of his calf and thigh pinched and snapped the blade in half as his leg bent.

The powered armor's automated gyroscopes prevented Samir from falling entirely. He staggered back into the entryway, bumping into a wall beside him. Samir struggled to spot his attacker and retaliate.

She had another blade, and now she had another shot. His helmet protected his head; his chest piece protected his shoulders and torso. Yet the suit had to allow for flexibility around the neck.

Nothing around Samir slowed or silenced as the blade punched into him. His whole body went numb. He suddenly couldn't think straight. Samir felt the metal that robbed him of movement and sensation as he fell. He heard himself hit the ground, realized his visual perspective had changed, and yet he couldn't do anything about it.

The blade came free from his neck with a jerk. He couldn't breathe. He felt like he was drowning. The blonde woman looked away from him, waved her blade in the air to gesture for others to follow, and then walked past.

Combat at the entrance quickly ended. Samir saw no more explosions, heard no more gunfire. Men and a few women rushed past his fallen form, all of them armed, all of them moving with purpose and determination.

A younger man in a smudged, dirty silk shirt and polarized lenses stopped over Samir. He looked down at Samir from over the barrel of his plasma carbine. His expression revealed his indecision. After a moment, the younger man swallowed and moved on.

"Jesus, Darren," someone said in the young man's wake. "You're just gonna let the fucker bleed out like that? Goddamn. And I thought I was cold-blooded."

A moment later, another man with a gun stood over Samir. This one did not hesitate before pulling the trigger.

• • •

"I am Prince Khalil," the holographic image said. "To whom am I speaking?" The prince wore hand-tailored slacks and a silk shirt, cutting an image of sophistication and affluence without the opulence normally displayed by the rest of his family. Though he stood tall and proud, signs of stress were plain. His breath came out heavily. It obviously required no small effort to remain calm. He felt fear, and also rage, but Khalil strove to master both.

Casey didn't hold it against him. The guy was completely fucked, just like all his people. "Afternoon, your highness," Casey said. He reached out to grab one of the five men kneeling before him with hands behind their heads, shoved the poor fellow down onto the ground, and casually put two bullets in his back. "*That's* who I am. Just so we understand one another. You can call me 'captain,' by the way. That's all you get."

Though horrified, Khalil reasserted his composure with a sharp, deep breath. He saw other pirates there in the palace conference room with Casey, along with four other trusted servants—men and women with families—right in their reach. "Please,"

Khalil said, maintaining his composure as best he could, "no further demonstrations are necessary." He swallowed hard, trying not to look at the body on the floor. "I am . . . told you wish to discuss demands."

"Yeah," Casey grunted. "A cease-fire, more or less. Not that many of your guys are left to shoot at us anymore. But I'm sure you've got a few in reserve in your little bolt-hole there." Casey took a cup offered to him by a comrade, sipped, grimaced, then tossed it aside.

"Ugh. Tea. Y'know, I had it in my head that I was gonna come down here and have this conversation over some good wine. I mean, I figured, hey, this guy's royalty, he's gotta have some good stuff, right? But then I got here and one of my guys reminded me that you Hashemites don't drink. And I knew that. Goddammit, I knew that. So now I don't know whether I'm more disappointed in you or in me."

Some of the conflict in the prince's eyes settled. He took in a deep breath, settling more on the side of contempt than fear. "What is the meaning of this attack?" he asked flatly.

"Thievery," Casey answered with a chuckle. "We're here for thievery. That's pretty much it." He paused a moment before elaborating. "Long as you want to cut right to the chase: We've got your palace. We've got your city, and we've pretty much got this whole planet by the balls. Help is a couple days away at least.

"We're gonna loot this place and leave. We're gonna take every valuable thing that ain't bolted down, and we'll probably pry up anything that is bolted if we like it enough. My men are running through your streets looking for cash and jewels and if they find any people they like, they'll take them, too. But I'm pretty sure that the single most valuable thing here is you."

Khalil took another deep breath. Someone outside the view of his cameras objected, but he held out a quieting hand. "If I turn myself over to you, will you end this attack?"

"Well. Agreeing to end the attack would imply that we aren't gonna loot anymore, and that's what we came for in the first place. But I can tell my guys to lay off with the violence, especially here in the palace. I can't say it'll stop completely, but we'll get it under control. I'm sure we've made our point by now, anyway. Mostly it'll just be up to your people not to get stupid."

"I find it hard to believe that all of this was done for the sake of simple thievery."

"Believe what you want." Casey shrugged. "Anyway. It's like this. You come out of that bunker, alone and unarmed, and we don't come in there and murder everybody we find."

"If you could do that, why haven't you already?"

"Mostly 'cause it's a pain in the ass. I'd lose guys. Also, I'll admit, it may be more trouble than it'd be worth. But we get sore when we don't get what we want. So yeah, maybe we won't break down the doors and kill everyone slow. Maybe we'll just bombard the palace from orbit until there's nothing but a crater a half-mile deep.

"Khalil," the pirate said, "I bet there's more down there with you than just bodyguards. You've got three kids. A wife. Probably some staff you care about. You turn yourself over and they'll all make it through this mess alive."

"You come here a thief and a murderer, and you expect me to believe you will hold to your word?" Khalil asked, his frown deepening into a scowl. "How do I know you won't kill or kidnap them once you have me? And what do you mean to do with me if no one pays for my freedom?"

"Oh, they'll pay. Don't sell yourself short, kid. Your dad kicked you out of the house to keep the peace with your brothers. It's really too bad for everyone you aren't the eldest, 'cause your brothers are shits. Anyway, I'm pretty sure you're the only one Daddy actually loves. He's a hard man and he's a realist, but everyone's got *something* they really care about.

"As for trusting me? I could say you can't. I could tell you that you really don't have any choice. All that cliché shit. But to be honest, you can trust me because I *have* to play this one fair if I want anyone to take me at my word after this. I need the credibility. Surely you're recording this whole conversation, or transmitting it, right? Gotta hope it'll provide some leads on how to track us all down when this is over. Sooner or later I'm gonna have to negotiate other things, either for profit or to save my own neck. Doesn't really help if I have a reputation as a double-dealer, does it?

"I don't want you dead, your highness. You're not worth any money to me dead. But if you don't come along after we've had this conversation? Well then, leaving you and yours alive is bad for my rep, too."

Silence fell between them. Casey waited as Khalil considered the offer. It was clear that others spoke to the prince, their voices shielded from the comm channel. Casey rather doubted that anyone encouraged the prince to put himself in the hands of vicious pirates. It surely wasn't something Casey would agree to do.

"If you leave now and bring no further harm to my people," Khalil ventured, "I will pay you right now."

"Oh, well, that depends. How much have you got?"

"I can give you forty million in bearer cards. I would offer you more, but much of my remaining cash on hand is marked corporate scrip or electronic transfer. It would be easily traced."

"That's considerate of you." Casey snorted. "But you're worth at least a whole nother digit on top of that. Anyway, now I want you and the cash. Shouldn't have brought it up."

Khalil's eyes grew ever colder with rage. "You were ready to gamble against my surrendering myself at all without the money. If I am to endure insult along with injury, I want something in exchange for this ransom."

"You aren't in much of a position to make counterdemands," Casey said. "You really want to watch your children die? It'll be slower than this asshole," he added, reminding him of the dead man at Casey's feet.

"No." Khalil shook his head. "Nor do I want to see my people suffer. I will bring the cash. In exchange, you will leave the hospitals unmolested."

Casey gave it a moment's thought. "Deal. Forty million and we leave the hospitals alone. Show up alone and unarmed."

"I will," Khalil agreed.

"Oh. And bring that wedding ring your wife's wearing. News said it's worth at least two million. You'll live with whatever insults I dish out, prince." With that, Casey cut the channel.

He waited for the other pirates in the room to finish chuckling. "Hey, when he shows up, make sure we keep some stunners handy. He's got some balls on him to bargain like that. We don't want him committing suicide by pirate or anything."

"Hospital loot's a lot to give up," Lauren noted soberly.

"Yeah, but it ain't forty million in portable cash," Casey countered. "Send the word. No looting the hospitals, no more shooting anyone just for the hell of it. Everything else is fair game, but we're out of here in eleven hours."

EIGHT

Boot

"Should I be doing something to help?" Tanner asked the flight deck chief. He stood behind the safety track lights on the flight line, waiting with the other navy crewmen under a cold, starry sky. This far from the star of Archangel, there was very little difference between night and day. Were it not for a carefully engineered greenhouse effect, Augustine would still be the frozen, lifeless rock it had been for billions of years.

The chief dismissed Tanner's offer. "Nah, we've got this. You don't want to get that uniform dirty. Chances are you'll put it right back in its storage bag in half an hour. Probably won't wear it again for months, anyway."

Tanner nodded. His service uniform wasn't quite as formal as his dress uniform, but it still felt out of place. The only people he ever saw in service uniforms worked behind desks. The occasion gave him the chance to wear his small, subtle but significant badges for marksmanship, close combat, and zero-g ops—not that he really wanted to invite more of the latter—but they made him self-conscious rather than proud. He was still a brand-new non-rate crewman apprentice about to have his first real day of work.

Waiting for twenty minutes now, Tanner shifted around the weight of his gear bag and the plastic folder carrying hard copies of his orders and personnel file. He watched the sky for any sign of his ship. The deck crew was less interested. They discussed other matters several feet away from him, all seeming to be in good cheer. Tanner appreciated seeing some social normalcy. He hoped to put the stiff formality and constant stress of Fort Stalwart behind him.

Several corvettes made their homes on Augustine, though their berths were little more than painted lines on the pavement beside service equipment. Two of the planet's five corvettes rested in port at the moment. One of them, *St. Martin*, had her main thrusters half-disassembled and strewn on the deck. The other, *St. Patrick*, looked ready to go. Tanner saw no sign of activity in or around either ship.

Cargo crates, pallet lifters, and service vehicles made up most of the scenery on the flight line. Out beyond them were larger berths for bigger ships, though they, too, were out at the moment. Beyond the flight line stood the permanent buildings that made up Augustine Harbor.

A signal on the deck chief's holocom caught Tanner's attention. The chief pointed to a moving dot of light in the sky. "That'll be your ride," he said. Other dots of light moved up in the black sky, all going this way and that. The one he indicated didn't seem to be coming for the base.

"How can you tell it from the others?" Tanner asked.

"Flight path. *St. Jude* always makes the regulation sweep around the base before landing."

"The other ships don't?"

The deck chief pursed his lips. His eyes hinted at something both regretful and amusing. "Corvette duty was at the top of your wish list, right?"

"Yes, chief," Tanner answered. There were only so many non-rate billets on corvettes to go around. Tanner needed endorsements from Everett and Janeka just to put in for corvette duty. Quite a few of Tanner's fellow recruits made the same request of their trainers. Not all of them received it.

It was therefore a little disconcerting when the deck chief smiled, shook his head, and said, "Well, like they say, you've gotta be careful what you wish for."

Tanner didn't press for details. Corvette duty didn't carry special prestige. Their crews were not elite. Such duty simply offered more involvement for junior personnel than one could find on a larger ship. On destroyers or cruisers, non-rates like Tanner performed mostly menial, low-skill tasks. Anything beyond that was subject to close supervision by personnel who had gone through specialist schools and had earned their "ratings" as operations specialists, gunner's mates, and such. It would be a year at the very least before Tanner could go to such a school. He accepted that there would be frequent grunt work in his first year regardless of his assignment, but placement on a corvette meant that grunt work wasn't all he could expect.

Minutes later, *St. Jude*'s white, dagger-shaped hull dropped out of the darkness and into the floodlights of the flight line. She floated down under the power of her antigrav engines, making horizontal corrections with small thrusters embedded along her length and breadth. The corvette settled with a rippling metallic thunk as each of her three landing struts came down. Tanner watched as the deck chief waved his handful of men and women in to connect hoses and cables to the ship.

Nobody told Tanner whether it was okay for him to move past the safety line. He considered calling out to ask but opted not to interrupt real work or embarrass himself. He walked over to stand parallel to the aft loading ramp.

After two seemingly endless minutes, the ramp dropped. The first person to appear was a man in a gray navy vac suit, who quickly turned off and walked to the side opposite Tanner. A second, younger crewman followed him a moment later. Tanner watched without comment.

A bell rang out from the ship's PA. Out walked a tall, bald, broad-shouldered man in a service uniform. He wore a lieutenant's rank insignia, but the bell clearly marked him as the ship's captain. The pale lieutenant strode toward Tanner with a preoccupied frown. Tanner popped to attention and saluted. The lieutenant did not return the salute. He passed by without a word. Tanner blinked, turning to watch him head off to the command building a hundred meters beyond. His stride was just short of a jog.

"Boot," someone grunted. Tanner turned back to find a large, muscular navy crewman before him. His black horseshoe mustache accentuated his frown. "You the new guy?"

"Yes, uh, Bo'sun Morales," Tanner said, quickly reading the insignia on the man's vac suit. "Crewman Apprentice Tanner Malone, reporting as—"

"Where's the rest of your gear?" the bo'sun cut him off. His voice was cool and devoid of anger, but also lacking in friendliness or patience. Something about his gaze conveyed a hint of disdain.

"I was told to report here with a vac suit and work coveralls," Tanner replied, blinking in surprise. He tucked his plastic folder under his left arm so he could shake hands with Morales, but the bigger man didn't react. "Uh, the other stuff is in my room in the barracks. Should I have—"

"You have the rest of your flight gear?" Morales asked. "Helmet? Thermal regulator? They give you all that shit already?"

"Yes, bo'sun." He dropped his hand.

"I guess you'd better be comfortable in that one vac suit for the next few days, then." The dismissive tone left no ambiguity as to his impression of Tanner's intelligence. He turned and yelled over his shoulder, "Stumpy!"

Two more crewmen had appeared from the loading ramp. Their amiable chatter ended when one answered the summons. He was short, stocky, and swarthy, appearing only a few years older than Tanner. His uniform marked him as an unrated crewman. "Yeah, boss?"

"New boot's here," Morales said, turning to Stumpy. "Take him aboard and tell him where to put his shit. Then take him to the XO to report in. Make it quick." Morales walked away without another word.

Stumpy turned back toward the ramp. "C'mon," he grunted. He either ignored or completely missed Tanner's outstretched hand.

Following quickly behind, Tanner found himself at a bit of a loss for words. Everyone seemed to be in a foul mood, but only the captain looked rushed. It wasn't like he expected hugs or fanfare, but this wasn't much of a welcome. He tried to break the ice with his fellow non-rate. "So, uh, does everyone call you Stumpy, or is that only for some people?"

"Stumpy's fine," came the grumble. They headed up a ladder to the upper deck and back, through a narrow passageway to the lower-ranked crew berth. The compartment spanned little more than four meters from end to end and less than that across. The bulkheads on Tanner's left and right each held three recessed bunk beds and three tall lockers. On the opposite side from the hatch was a very tiny head.

"Take either top bunk and put your shit on it," Stumpy told him, gesturing to the beds. "Doesn't matter which. You got a helmet and everything already?"

"Yeah." Tanner put his bag on the bunk to his left. Like the one on the top right, it had a thin mattress but no sheets. The other bunks were unmade. Articles of clothing and other personal belongings sat on them. Discarded food wrappers, empty cans, and even worn underwear littered the floor. The whole musty compartment needed to be wiped down.

"Does it work? You trained with it?"

"Oh yeah, it's all fine," Tanner answered. "Been doing decompression drills with this gear since the second week of basic."

"In basic?" Stumpy blinked. Once again he turned to walk away while speaking. "Oh yeah, you got that six-month deal. That must've sucked. Guess they gotta fill all those extra weeks with one sort of bullshit or another. C'mon, the XO's on the bridge. BM1 oughta be there, too. He's our department head, so he's our boss. You already met Morales. He's BM2, so he's also your boss. Basically everybody's your boss."

"Low man on the totem pole," Tanner acknowledged. His friendly tone was, once again, either missed completely or deliberately ignored.

They made their way down the passageway toward the front of the ship. *St. Jude* had only two decks, with the top being mostly crew quarters and the bridge. The ship's commissioned officers and its engineering chief had their own rooms. The rest shared two crew berths between them, one for the rated crewmen and the smaller one for the non-rates. Stumpy opened the hatch to the bridge and led the way through.

Tanner noted that the bridge, thankfully, was not at all in the same condition as the crew berth. There were only two chairs on the bridge, each of them mounted against opposite bulkheads and facing forward. Windows all around offered a view of the flight line.

Three men stood at the center of the bridge, facing a standing work desk that occupied much of the rear of the compartment. Over the desk floated a holographic star chart. Though the two older men addressed the third, who looked younger than both, as "sir," everyone spoke with casual familiarity.

"They'll probably run us on a patrol pattern through here, is my guess," the younger man said. He reached inside the projection to trace a finger from Augustine's icon out in a wide line and then back again. Tanner recognized the outer orbits of his home star system. He received just enough basic navigational training on *Los Angeles* during his apprenticeship phase to realize how complicated it was. This chart was much more detailed and technical than anything he'd trained with. It showed markers for buoys, outer-orbit satellites of Augustine, and frequent traffic routes, along with floating numbers to denote distances to and from many points of interest.

"Pretty wide path, sir," observed the oldest-looking of the three. Either he hadn't undergone longevity treatments until he was around fifty, or he was positively ancient. The grim weariness to his face seemed permanent.

The younger man, wearing junior lieutenant's bars, gave a shrug and a wry grin. Tanner took him for the XO. "I'm just throwing it out there, Bill. Not a clue where we're really going to be, but it'll still be a while before they shift more ships out here with us. *St. Martin* ain't going anywhere."

"Nah, they'd have to actually put in a day's work first, sir." The third man grinned. He looked to be in his midthirties—again, depending on his longevity treatments—with close-cut blond hair and a bit of a gut. Like the XO, he at least showed signs of cheer. He was also the most aware of Stumpy's presence, along with the newcomer. "This our new boot?" he asked.

"Yup." Stumpy moved aside as the XO stepped forward.

"Crewman Apprentice Tanner Malone, reporting as ordered, sir," Tanner said with a salute. The XO returned his salute, though with less crisp formality. To Tanner's relief, the XO offered a handshake.

"At ease. Welcome aboard, Apprentice Malone," the XO said. He released Tanner's hand to accept the plastic file from his new subordinate. “I’m Lieutenant Gagne. This is Bo’sun Freeman and Ops Specialist Reed.” Freeman stepped over to shake Tanner’s hand. Reed merely waved and mumbled something unintelligible and noncommittal as he turned back to the charts.

“Thank you, sir,” Tanner said.

“How long have you been waiting for us?” Gagne asked.

“Just since yesterday, sir. They set me up in the barracks and told me to be here waiting for you this morning, sir.”

“Well, it’s a good thing you were here on time. We’re going back out within the hour, or so’s the plan. Stumpy, you getting him squared away?”

“Yes, sir,” Stumpy confirmed. “He’s got flight gear already.”

“Good. Malone, get aft and change out of that service uniform. You’ll get caught up with us as you go.”

“Aye, aye, sir.” Tanner popped to attention and saluted once more. The XO gave a half smirk, saluted casually, and turned back to the charts.

“Hey, Stumpy, give his gear a once-over before you do anything else,” Freeman added.

“Okay. C’mon, boot,” said Stumpy, leading the way once more.

In the crew berth, Tanner opened up his flight bag and removed his vac suit and boots. He handed over the helmet and detachable emergency gear to Stumpy, who put each piece through its self-diagnostic tests as Tanner changed. “So what’s going on?” Tanner asked.

“A lotta hurry up and wait,” Stumpy said without looking up. His tone of disinterest remained. “They say we’re out of here in an hour, but it’ll be at least two. Probably three or four. We get ready in a rush and then sit here waiting for someone to get his thumb out of his ass and tell us to go. Every time.”

“Huh,” Tanner replied. “Do you know what we’ll be doing?” he tried again.

Stumpy shrugged. “Refugee pickup.”

"Refugees?" Tanner's mind raced. He'd always followed the news. There hadn't been stories about refugees, but he could guess where they came from. Archangel's closest and largest neighbor was on the verge of civil war. "Hashemites?"

"Yup. I guess some of 'em aren't waiting for the shooting to start. They're running away now." He tossed Tanner's thermal regulator onto his rack. "Your shit's fine. Finish suiting up and get outside. We've got a lot of supplies to load."

• • •

Focusing on the hull plating in front of him helped to fight off the usual dizziness. Magnetizing relays in the soles of Tanner's boots kept him steady on the hull, as did those in his vac suit's knees and elbows if necessary—and here, the knees certainly helped. In moments like this, though, floating off into space wasn't the real worry. The danger was that he'd vomit inside his helmet.

Ships ordinarily had no problem staying on whatever level plane they chose. Any corvette certainly could. *Abdullah-19*, a small civilian packet ship from Hashem, apparently had trouble maintaining such stability. Either its captain or *St. Jude*'s opted for a manual linkup rather than synching up their maneuvering jets via computer. Thus, *St. Jude* had to match *Abdullah-19*'s spin.

Tanner wanted to ask why this was necessary. He wanted to ask what was going on and what they would do once the ships were linked. After two or three hours aboard *St. Jude*, though, it became clear that most of the deck department felt that Tanner's every question was a stupid one. Tanner soon learned to restrict his queries to an absolute minimum.

Establishing the hard link would be the easy part. All they needed to do was put the magnetized foot of one of *Abdullah-19*'s landing struts against the underside of *St. Jude*'s hull where their airlocks would face one another. After that would come the erection of an improvised, sealed passage between the two very different hatches . . . but that couldn't be done until the ships settled together.

"How's that coming, Tanner?" asked Bo'sun Freeman. He stood nearby, watching the packet ship "above" him. Concepts like up and down became rather malleable at times like this. Tanner, Freeman, Morales, and Stumpy were all on the outside of their ship, looking at *Abdullah-19*'s dorsal section as her helmsman fought to slowly spin her 180 degrees for the linkup.

"Almost done," Tanner grunted. It was a simple job, or should've been. All he had to do was tape down some padding onto the hull where the landing strut would hit. The padding constantly folded up on him, though, clinging to itself because of excess static electricity. To make matters worse, the umbilical cord attached to his harness kept getting in the way.

"Need to pick up the pace, boot." Tanner didn't see the bo'sun's frown, but he heard it over the comm channel. It came right into his ear. He heard other chatter on Morales's second channel—the one tying him and Freeman in with the bridge's communications with *Abdullah-19*—but Tanner wasn't in on that one. He only heard snippets of it whenever Freeman or Morales spoke.

Tanner finally pinned down a smoothed-out section of padding with one magnetized kneepad. He ran electrostatic tape down that side of the mat. It should've been a simple job. Instead, it was frustrating as hell. "Sorry," Tanner said. "This thing's fighting with me."

"Just get it done, we don't have all day," grunted Morales. He waited out of sight on the starboard side with Stumpy. Only Tanner and Freeman were on *St. Jude*'s underside.

"He's almost got it," Freeman announced, sounding similarly annoyed. Freeman glanced up at the slowly spinning ship above him. The older man instinctively crouched lower against *St. Jude.*

"She's coming around slower this time. I think we'll be ready on the next rotation," the bo'sun declared.

As Freeman spoke, though, Tanner heard someone on the ship-to-ship channel say, "Execute landing strut linkup."

Tanner's eyes snapped wide. His head jerked up to see *Abdullah-19*'s landing strut extend and wheel toward him with alarming speed. Tanner threw himself away from his spot on the hull, abandoning the half-secured strip of padding as the magnetized foot swiftly came down onto it. Tanner didn't hear the controlled collision of ships or the ugly scrape of *Abdullah-19*'s foot against the area of hull left unprotected by the still bunched-up padding. One never heard much of anything in space. He did, however, hear the snap of his umbilical cord as it was caught between the hull and the landing strut. The vibrations from the break traveled along the cord to his harness and through his suit just fine.

"Tanner!" Freeman yelled a second too late. Tanner was already clear, saved by his own reflexes rather than his supervisor's sketchy vigilance. He floated away from the two ships as they slowly spun together in space, losing none of the initial momentum of his leap. He avoided being crushed, or maimed, or having his suit punctured or shredded.

Embarrassment sank in quickly. "I'm okay," Tanner announced, cutting the remnant of umbilical cord from his harness. Stars spun even more wildly now, making it hard for him to think. "I just need . . . I'm okay." He swallowed hard. His hands went to the controls of the emergency thrusters on his vac harness. They wouldn't get him far, but the compressed nitrogen capsules would maneuver him back to his ship.

"What the hell just happened out there?" the captain demanded. Tanner swallowed hard. He didn't realize the captain was listening.

"Close call, skipper," Freeman answered. "We're okay. Think the boot didn't have the padding all rigged up in time, though."

“Sounded like we got a scrape on the hull.”

“Uh, probably, sir. The boot was just getting the padding in place and I think the link snuck up on him, skipper.”

Flying back to the hull, Tanner didn’t stop to parse Freeman’s evaluation. It never occurred to him to reflect on his supervisor’s explanation or how the whole procedure was coordinated. He didn’t wonder whose fault it was.

His first day aboard *St. Jude* had already been one blunder after another, from not bowing his head immediately when the captain called for a prelaunch prayer to stumbling and dropping crates in the cargo bay twice. Why would this be any less his fault than the rest of that?

Tanner looked over at Freeman as he took hold of the landing strut. The bo’sun gave a shrug. “Eddie, Stumpy, bring the cables over,” he said. Tanner wondered if this was all business as usual for the crew.

Morales and Stumpy both came up and over, close enough to see the landing strut and the hull beneath. Tanner glanced down, too. There was indeed an ugly scrape; it was probably worse under the strut itself, but just the few inches where it had slid against the hull before coming to rest looked ugly enough.

“Good job, boot,” Stumpy commented as he passed by.

• • •

“This is a huge part of your job,” Morales said as Tanner wiped the last of his lunch off the cargo bay deck. “We do space walks all the time. You’d better get used to it quick.”

“I will.” Tanner swallowed hard again and tried to ignore the foul taste in his mouth. He had been lucky to hold it together until he’d gotten back to the ship and into the cargo bay. For the second time, he mumbled out, “I’m sorry.”

"Maybe you should keep your faceplate down so nobody has to smell your breath," Morales added as he turned away. Standing next to him, *St. Jude*'s gunner's mate handed Morales a holstered laser pistol.

Rising up off his knees, Tanner noticed that Morales didn't take the gun out to check it. Everett and Janeka had drilled that into everyone. Weapons and tactics school also emphasized it. Stumpy didn't check his, either. Nor did Leone, the tall, lanky young machinist's mate who seemed content to just loom in the background rather than take part in conversation. Knowing better than to speak while he was in the doghouse, Tanner simply moved off to place his rag in a waste receptacle. Then he retrieved his helmet from off the deck.

"I think he should leave it off," opined Miller. "Might have better breath than the guys over there. He could pick up on a refugee hottie. Get some tight Hashemite pussy."

Tanner blinked, trying to mask his shock. Every instructor in basic would've skinned a recruit alive for saying something like that.

"How would you know, Miller?" Stumpy asked. "You ever fucked a Hashemite?"

"Probably." The gunner's mate shrugged. "I dunno."

"It's not like they wear name tags," Morales said.

"Yeah, but some of 'em wear veils. Or hoods or whatever. Right? Never fucked a woman wearing a hood before. Fucked a few who should've, though."

"It's called a hijab," Tanner corrected, trying to keep the irritation out of his voice.

Miller gestured to Tanner and said, "Yeah, one of those heejeebee thingies. How did you know that?" he asked.

The XO's arrival ended the conversation. "We all ready to go?" he asked.

"Yes, sir," Morales answered, shooting Miller a look. The gunner's mate quieted as he handed Gagne another holstered laser pistol.

To Tanner's partial relief, Gagne immediately checked the weapon's test lights and power settings before he clipped the holster to his side. The XO looked to Tanner and asked, "Anyone explain what we're doing yet?"

"No, sir," Tanner replied.

Gagne nodded. He was simultaneously more casual than the others and more professional. "The crew and passengers of the shuttle are requesting asylum. Ordinarily we'd escort the ship to an isolated berth on Augustine and process 'em there. After what happened on Qal'at Khalil, though, the government ordered physical inspections of every ship coming into Archangel space." He smirked a bit, glancing at the other members of the deck crew. "That's made for some real traffic jams out here in the last couple weeks and some sleepless nights for us. Command was getting things more organized so we could handle the increased load and spread the work around, but now we're getting refugees on top of normal traffic."

As he spoke, Morales brought to Tanner a black device a little larger than a shoe box with a carrying strap on it. He ran a sequence of commands on the device's control panel. "You know how to use a sniffer?"

"Yes." Tanner nodded. "I've trained with them." He could already hear the whirl of the sniffer's intake vents.

Whether Morales ignored his answer or simply didn't believe him wasn't clear. Either way, he explained, "Just let the sniffer do the work for you. It's set to ignore the signatures from our weapons. If it picks up any other weapons, it'll let you know. You get any warning signs on this thing, tell one of us but don't freak anyone else out."

Tanner blinked. "So I'm going aboard with you?"

"That's why you're down here, boot." Morales scowled. Again. He put the sniffer in Tanner's hands.

"What'd you expect?" Gagne smiled, seeming a bit more patient.

"I just thought . . . I don't know, sir. I thought maybe I was staying near the airlock in case you needed something."

"We throw you in right at the deep end around here, Malone," Gagne replied. "Anyway. Just follow our lead and let me do the talking."

"Yes, sir. I, uh . . . am I supposed to be issued a sidearm?"

Gagne threw a deferential look to Morales, who looked to Tanner like the younger man had just suggested that he be allowed to set his hair on fire. "You haven't been checked out for that yet, boot," Morales said. "We're not gonna give a gun to a brand-new boot and have him shoot himself in the foot. Or one of us."

"Don't sweat it, Malone," the XO added without contradicting the bo'sun. "Technically you're not qualified to be a boarding team member for the ship until you get signed off on it by the ship's team leaders. That rule would hold even if you'd come aboard with twenty years' experience on other ships. We're bending the rules here by bringing you at all because we need the extra manpower," he finished, seeming for the first time as if he might be a little uncomfortable with this himself. "Don't worry, these people aren't here to cause trouble."

"Yes, sir." Tanner gulped. He didn't expect any trouble from a ship full of refugees, either, but someone had decided no one should go over unarmed. No one except Tanner.

The XO unslung his helmet from its perch behind his left shoulder. "We're on channel four, guys," he mentioned just before slipping it over his head. The others donned their helmets as the XO announced, "Bridge, this is the XO. We're ready to go over."

"Acknowledged," they heard Reed mutter in response. "Open the airlock up at your end when you're ready."

Gagne nodded to Leone, who knelt down to the circular hatch and keyed in commands. They heard the sucking sound of air flowing from the cargo bay into the passage beyond. On the other side of the hatch was the white triple-layered plastic tunnel that Tanner and the other "deckies" had fixed in place between the bellies of the two ships. A moment later, the hatch at the other side opened. Two men looked down and waved at the men of *St. Jude* as they, in turn, looked down toward *Abdullah-19*.

As he climbed through the hatch, Stumpy glanced at Tanner to say, "Don't puke."

Tanner went over last, following after Miller. He moved from an environment of artificial gravity to the zero-g tube beneath, and then floated across it to the ship beyond. Tanner had to push hard to get through the invisible "floor" created by the gravity projectors in the decks of each ship. *Abdullah-19*'s floor was slightly easier to deal with than *St. Jude*'s, but it still required significant effort.

Heaving himself through the hatch, Tanner found his crewmates in the center of the packet ship's cargo bay surrounded by people. Most of the ship's several dozen passengers sat on the deck, though many others stood to give the boarding team room. There were slightly more women than men, along with a number of children. Some looked worried; others put up a better front. All of them seemed exhausted.

Gagne and the others pushed the faceplates of their helmets up. Tanner did the same, allowing him to hear better as the XO spoke with a representative from the packet ship.

"You're actually from Qal'at Khalil?" the XO asked a bearded man in a tan vac suit. Tanner noted that virtually everyone else dressed in common street clothes. Some of the women wore hijabs while others did not.

"Yes, sir," the man said in thickly accented English. "Some of us lived in Khalil City. Others are family. Many of us were there for the attack. We thought when the pirates left that the nightmare was over, but . . ." The man shrugged.

"I understand, captain," said Gagne.

"We seek asylum," the man continued. "Please, call me Rasim. I am no captain."

"We've have to check several things before we allow your ship to move on to Augustine. I have to send some of my men to do a safety inspection on your engine room and I have to see your manifest."

"Yes. Please, send your men. I have two people back there now. As for a manifest . . . this was not exactly a scheduled departure," he noted awkwardly.

"Sure. We'll need to get a visual head count of passengers and crew, and we need to inspect the ship. Leone, Miller, Malone, you'll go to the engine room. Morales and Stumpy, come to the bridge with me."

"Usman will show you the way," Rasim said to Leone and Miller. "His English is very limited. My engineers, too. But I think they can manage." He turned to another man in a vac suit and exchanged a few words in Arabic.

"Let's do it," Gagne said. "Keep your com channels open."

"Aye, aye, sir," Tanner replied, then realized he was the only one to do so. He fell in behind his crewmates as they followed Usman into the packet ship's narrow passageways.

"You speak English, Usman?" Leone asked.

"Yes. Tiny. Tiny bit," Usman said, looking back to them with a helpful smile.

"You are the engineer on this ship?"

"I am engineer, yes. Ah. Little engineer. Ah . . . big engineer . . . higher engineer, you know? He stay on Qal'at Khalil. Not come . . . with."

"No wonder they can't fly straight," Miller muttered with a skeptical frown behind Leone's broad back. "Guy talks like a moron."

Tanner looked up from the sniffer's readout display. "English and Arabic don't even have the same alphabets," noted Tanner, carefully keeping his tone neutral. "English is hard to learn as a second language. Takes brains to pick up even a little. I get what he's saying."

"Yeah. Whatever. I just don't get why they're coming here."

"You don't follow the news?"

"It's usually just a bunch of eggheads talking about shit that doesn't affect me."

Tanner grimaced. This was the guy responsible for care and maintenance of all the weapons and ordnance on the ship. "You know about the pirate raid on Qal'at Khalil a month back, right?"

"Sure. Everyone does. I get that's why we're doing more boardings now. But it was a tiny colony out on the ass-end of Hashemite space. How's it turn into a mess like this?"

"Hashem's a monarchy. That means they have a hereditary king," he added, not wanting to take risks on Miller's vocabulary. "The king has three sons in line for the crown. Two of the sons are dirtbags. The decent one was taken hostage on Qal'at Khalil."

"Yeah, I heard about the hostage bit, but didn't they buy him back last week?"

"Yes. Nobody'll say how much it cost, but estimates are in the billions. Both of the other brothers argued that the king never should've paid. They say it'll encourage more kidnappings, but really they're just pissed to see that dad loves the third son enough to pay so much for him. That's got the other two worried about their chances of taking the throne when dad dies, so they're making power grabs."

"Yes. Yes." Usman nodded. "He is right. Prince Murtada, he take over Qal'at Khalil after the pirates go. He say we are cowards to not fight, but we have no guns! How can we fight? Murtada, he arrest many people. Take many things. Like pirates all over again. When Prince Khalil is free, Murtada say he cannot come back to Qal'at Khalil because he cannot defend."

"And now everyone expects a civil war, right?"

"Yes! Yes. War. We believe war come." Usman threw open the hatch to the engine room. "We take ship while she is being fixed. Security, they want to leave, too, so they bring families and we bring ours and we run."

Miller glanced at Tanner. "How do you know all this? Are you just really smart?"

Tanner considered and rejected a dozen wiseass responses. "No."

• • •

"Attention all hands, chow is served. Repeat, chow is served in the galley." Tanner turned from the ship's intercom as Storekeeper Second Class Flores pulled the last of the chicken from the oven. "That clear enough?" he asked brightly.

"Just like that," Flores said with disinterest. He slid the tray of baked chicken onto the counter and turned away. "Fill up the plates." With that, he turned around the corner of the cramped galley into the walk-in refrigerator.

Once more, Tanner swallowed his concern about the cold shoulder he seemed to get from the whole crew. At least in this case, he hadn't made any blunders. Mess duty wasn't terribly difficult. He wasn't surprised or annoyed to be stuck with it. Such was life as a non-rate. What he didn't expect was for the cook to hardly acknowledge him.

By the time he sorted out all the plates, several crewmen stood waiting around the two small tables in the galley's cramped dining area. The tables were arranged in a *T* shape, with four seats to a side on one table and only three seats at the other. Naturally, seats were arranged in pecking order by rank, reserving the three-seat table for the captain, the XO, and the chief engineer.

Freeman cheerfully talked with the XO about upcoming playoffs in one sport or another. Leone, still virtually silent, slipped into a space between the larger table and the bulkhead opposite Wells, a non-rate engineering crewman Tanner hadn't met yet. Chief O'Malley and another engineer came up from the lower deck. Tanner spotted a junior ops specialist named Harper and the deck department's other non-rate, a tall and muscular blond guy a couple years older than Tanner by the name of Heifer. Morales and Stumpy both trailed in shortly after them.

He quickly re-counted plates and matched them to seats. Sixteen crewmembers total, subtracting two on watch on the bridge, one on watch in engineering, himself, and Flores . . . and exactly eleven seats. He had plates ready. Yet everyone remained standing.

Freeman's eyes drifted toward the entrance to the galley. "Attention on deck," he said just loudly enough to be heard. Everyone came to attention as the captain entered. The tall, bald Lieutenant Stevens slipped around to the most accessible seat and turned to face the rest of the crew.

"Let us pray," Stevens said, just as he had before takeoff. Tanner watched as every head bowed in response. For all the trappings of Catholic tradition within the Archangel Navy, prayer and religious observance were by no means mandatory. Tanner was surprised to see ten out of ten heads bow in prayer at the word of their captain.

Then again, he considered, maybe they just didn't want to make an issue of it. Tanner knew he didn't.

"Bless us, O Lord, and these thy gifts which we are about to receive from thy bounty through Christ our Lord," the skipper said, ending with an "Amen" echoed quietly by the crew. The captain sat. No one followed suit until the captain said, "At ease."

Tanner knew that meals on ships underway tended to be informal. Certainly *Los Angeles*'s galley never saw such ceremony. Yet here sat a captain who opened up lunch with strict etiquette.

Hardly anyone checked a sidearm when handed to him. The non-rate crew berth was a sty. No one briefed the crew before or after launch. Brand-new, unarmed crewmen were sent on boardings. Poor coordination and communication had nearly gotten Tanner squashed against the hull . . . but the captain ran chow as a formal ceremony.

It was his first day. He was in no place to question anything or anyone. Tanner served the captain, XO, and Chief O'Malley first, as formal etiquette demanded.

"What's your name, boot?" the captain asked without looking up. Little emotion colored his question; it sounded neither friendly nor hostile.

Tanner stopped. "Malone, sir. Tanner Malone."

"Where are you from, Malone?"

"Michael, sir. City of Geronimo."

The captain's grunt didn't sound like one of approval. Stevens fell silent as he poked at his potatoes with a fork. Unsure as to whether he was supposed to wait or keep serving food, Tanner paused. After feeling awkward for a moment, he put down plates for the XO and the chief.

"Malone," the captain said.

Tanner froze. He turned back to the captain. "Yes, sir?"

"What happened out there during the linkup, Malone?" the captain asked evenly. He looked up from his plate at Tanner. He seemed perfectly calm, but not at all casual.

His mouth suddenly feeling very dry, Tanner glanced away from the captain for a brief moment. He saw Freeman and Morales both watching, the former's expression set in a firmly unreadable poker face while the latter frowned once more. "Sir. I was, um, having trouble getting the padding smoothed out because it kept, um, bunching and folding up on me, sir."

"And so you weren't watching what was going on around you when you were almost crushed flat?" the captain continued.

Tanner blinked. He was almost crushed because he couldn't hear communications between the bridges of the two ships. Someone had decided that was the proper way to handle the procedure. He only heard the order to execute more or less by accident. Tanner passed exacting training standards for zero-g ops and even earned the right to wear a coveted pin on his uniform marking him as fully qualified . . . but all he could think was that it was his first day on board. He was a barely nineteen-year-old non-rate fresh out of basic.

Freeman and Morales watched. Tanner didn't dare look up at them, but he felt their gaze. "Sir, I was—I thought I had been, sir. I guess I just didn't understand what was happening, sir."

Stevens gave a slow, sagely nod. "You see how important it is to stay on your toes?"

"Yes, sir."

The captain repeated his nod. He gave a small gesture as if to dismiss Tanner back to his mess duties. Rather than finding the move galling, Tanner felt relieved to be let off the hook. He went back to passing out plates. When he got to Freeman and Morales, neither looked at him. Freeman returned to talking about sports. Morales listened with partial interest.

"Malone," Stevens said before Tanner could slip back around the corner to return to Flores and his now comforting lack of conversation. "Turn on the view screen, would you?"

"Aye, aye, sir." He activated the flat screen against one wall of the galley. Any one of the crewmen present could've activated it from their seats with their personal holocoms. Instead, it fell to Tanner to press the right button. Given how the rest of his day went, he half-expected the view screen to fall off its mount or explode as soon as he touched it.

"Call up the most recent newscast. It should've been included in the last communications relay."

"You think we're already on the news again?" Chief O'Malley asked cheerfully, but then caught himself. "Ah. I mean. You think today's traffic is in the news, sir?"

Tanner could almost feel the captain bristle behind him. Something about O'Malley's question had clearly been a faux pas. He scrolled through options on the view screen as he heard the captain say, coldly, "I don't expect to see us so much as the situation out here, chief."

As soon as he had the news rolling, Tanner stepped out of the dining area and into the small kitchen space. Flores casually put together plates for himself, Tanner, and the current watch sections. Tanner glanced around for something to do. Finding nothing, he simply stood.

"You should go around the corner," Flores said without looking up. "Be there in case they run out of drinks or whatever."

It wasn't what Tanner wanted to hear, but he sucked it up and moved back into the dining area. He found a place to stand out of the way until called upon.

". . . continuing fallout after last month's unprecedented pirate raid on Qal'at Khalil in Hashemite space," said the news anchor on the view screen. "Violence has been reported on several Hashemite worlds and colonies, sending many citizens of the Kingdom fleeing. During today's daily press conference, Press Secretary Andrea Bennett reported on efforts by the Archangel Navy to address the growing crisis in our largest neighboring state."

"Shit," the captain grumbled. "This woman again."

The screen cut to the familiar scene of Bennett standing in a courtyard amid a semicircle of reporters. "As of noon today, system mean time, Archangel Navy units have intercepted eleven ships from Hashemite space with crews and passengers requesting asylum," Bennett announced. "These ships are often crammed, with those aboard requiring emergency resupply and sometimes medical attention. They have been brought to shelters on Augustine, where we will continue to provide aid."

"Andrea," asked one reporter, "does the administration intend to allow these refugees to settle in Archangel?"

"Andrea," cut in another, "we have reports of Prince Murtada and Prince Kaseem both denouncing these refugee flights, calling the people aboard thieves and traitors and demanding the return of stolen ships and of those aboard to stand trial. Has the administration responded to this?"

"Neither prince is head of state. The asylum requests are under review."

"Will the ships themselves be returned?"

"I don't have any information on that right now."

"Andrea," called out a third journalist, "given the increased traffic into the system, does the administration plan to scale back on its new policy of intense physical inspections of each ship entering the system?"

"Absolutely not," Bennett answered firmly. "Once again, the events on Qal'at Khalil have spelled out in graphic and horrifying detail the need to know who and what is coming here."

"Does the administration have any comment on complaints from business interests on the resulting slowdown of traffic in and out of the system?"

"Yes, Mike, I'm glad you asked. The president asks all the people of Archangel and all of our native companies to work together in ensuring that we keep our system safe and secure. As for the complaints lodged by NorthStar, CDC, and numerous other interstellar corporate interests, the president would like to remind everyone that Archangel's numerous security agreements with those corporations have so far failed to protect Archangel or her neighbors from pirate attacks and smuggling. If our security measures come at an inconvenience, our security partners would be well-advised to fulfill their agreed-upon duties."

"That woman loves being a snot," Stevens said, picking at his food with thinly masked irritation. "I like how she throws around statements like that as if she's ordering us around."

Tanner frowned thoughtfully, wondering what the captain's problem with Bennett might be as the broadcast continued.

The anchor's face returned. "In related news, numerous other Union systems have adopted similar measures of intensive ship inspections. Demand for increased security coverage by the Union fleet has increased dramatically, particularly in the outlying states.

"Orders for armed ships and planetary defense equipment have skyrocketed in the last few weeks, according to market observers. Major arms suppliers such as Lai Wa, NorthStar, and CDC have all justified price hikes by pointing to this sharply increased demand. Yet Defense Minister Robert Kilpatrick says that these price hikes will largely not affect Archangel's recent defense expansion."

The screen cut to the defense minister in his office, speaking from his desk to a single reporter. "Expense was certainly a primary consideration from the outset," he said, "and we took advantage of several cost-offsetting opportunities when we started. We locked in our deals at prices from six months to a year ago. If anything, we saved the system money by buying early."

"Yeah, like that was intentional." Stevens snorted. "They make out like they saw all this coming."

"Well, gotta score your political points wherever you can, sir," said Chief O'Malley.

"It's all a smokescreen, anyway," Stevens pressed, waving his hand at the screen. "They're paying for the expansion by blowing off interest payments on corporate debts. They'll have to make those debt payments later, anyway, and when they do, it'll be at a higher rate. We're not getting away with anything here."

"Boot," grunted Morales, pulling Tanner's attention away from the broadcast and the resultant conversation. "You're on the next bridge watch rotation with Freeman and Heifer in twenty minutes."

Tanner glanced at the clock on the wall. That hardly left time to clean up after everyone and have things set for the crewmen currently on watch, let alone get lunch for himself. As if Freeman read his mind, the bo'sun said, "Might wanna eat fast."

Not a seat remained open. Nobody looked like they would finish soon. Tanner ducked back into the kitchen area, picked up his plate, and found a place to stand where he'd be out of the way as he ate.

The food was good. Flores had skill. Tanner wished he didn't have to just shovel it down.

• • •

Watch relief, as Tanner learned it on *Los Angeles*, was something of a scripted affair. While no one exercised stiff military formality—it was a routine repeated several times a day, after all—regulations mandated a certain process. There was status info to pass along, orders to relay, and at the very least there was the need to confirm in a clear, unambiguous manner who was in charge on the bridge.

With that in mind, Tanner's jaw all but dropped when Freeman simply took Reed's seat on the port side of the bridge without a word about anything other than what Flores had cooked for lunch. Freeman barely glanced at the status boards before assuming a relaxed posture in his seat.

Reed's companion on the bridge watch was Miller. He sat with his feet kicked up on a console until Freeman and Heifer arrived with Tanner in tow. Heifer gestured for Tanner to stand with him at the operations console at the back of the bridge. Miller passed along no info; like Reed before him, he simply rolled out of his seat and headed for the hatch.

"First thing you do is check the ops table, boot," Heifer said, gesturing to the broad worktable. A three-dimensional display of space around *St. Jude* floated over the table. At the moment, no contacts appeared within the ship's immediate space. Floating at the edges of the display board were points and distance markers referencing other ships, space buoys, and natural bodies like Augustine and its moons, all of them beyond *St. Jude*'s two light-minute "bubble."

"But you see there's nothing going on." Heifer shrugged. "We make sure we have courses drawn up for home, for major space lanes, for wherever we might be going . . . and they're right here," he said, tapping a light on the table surface without even looking at the readings it displayed. "So that's good. You check the comms traffic, which says here that it's all been relayed to the OOD station and copied to the captain and XO's personal holocoms like always, and then you're set."

With that, Heifer left Tanner to stare at the operations table. The blond crewman nonchalantly took up the empty starboard seat. Tanner looked over his shoulder as Heifer opened up his personal holocom. Nothing on the projection in front of Heifer looked like it was military or ship's business. It was just a computer game.

Tanner turned back to the ops table and the bubble. He didn't know where to begin. Could Heifer really have understood and evaluated all the contacts on the sensors that quickly? How could he know the message traffic held nothing important without at least skimming it?

Minutes passed before anyone spoke. "So, Tanner, did they teach you anything about watchstanding in basic?" Freeman asked.

"Yeah." Tanner turned around to face him only to find that Freeman wasn't looking back. He apparently just stared off through the canopy at the stars. "Yeah, we had several weeks of an apprenticeship phase on *Los Angeles*. The ship was in orbit, so everything was simulated, but they had us rotate through bridge posts." Tanner had met the cruiser's standard qualifications for standing watch on each post. Most of Oscar Company did.

They had also been warned by Everett not to make too much of it when they got to their first assignments. He was proud, he'd told them, and their accomplishments had been real, but they shouldn't presume they were ready for prime time until their new commands said so. Weapons and tactics school repeated that advice: *Don't get cocky. Don't boast. Trained or not, you're still the new guy.*

Freeman snorted. "Yeah, well, on a cruiser like that, you've got a guy for every job, and assistants for half of 'em, right? And you had an officer at each position?"

"There were several officers on the bridge at all times, yes," Tanner said.

"Right. Well, we do more with less on a corvette. Right now Heifer's the helmsman and I'm the officer of the deck. Helmsman handles astrogation, takes care of the logs, monitors the message traffic and comms, maintains sensor lookout, and operates helm at my direction. Watches are four hours each."

"Okay," Tanner said. As Freeman noted, these were all individual jobs on a larger ship. Tanner had expected this, and had expected to be busy. He didn't expect to see the helmsman kick his feet up on the control console and play computer games.

"You're going to be the apprentice helmsman until you're signed off on all that. That means you'll stand a one-in-three watch rotation for a while. Once you're signed off, we'll put you in the helmsman rotation and then things'll be a little easier on you guys. You've got four weeks to get signed off. If it looks like you're falling behind or whatever, we put you on every other rotation."

"What do I need to do to get signed off?"

"Computer over there has all the manuals and the qual sheet. Download it to your personal holocom. We test you on each piece and sign you off, then give you a board examination on the whole thing."

"Okay." Tanner turned to the ops table's computer to retrieve the material. "When do I get tested?"

"When we think you're ready. Read up on everything and try to find answers in the manuals before you come to us—unless you're actually on watch and something comes up. If you're on watch and you've got a question, just ask. Better to ask than fuck anything up."

"Understood, BM1," Tanner said.

Heifer snorted. "He's still in boot camp mode, Ben."

"Ah, that's fine," Freeman said, waving one hand. "Tanner, you make sure you call the chief a chief and you say 'sir' to the officers and salute 'em the first time you see 'em on a given day. Do that and you're fine."

Tanner felt as much relief at what Freeman had to say as he received from getting an explanation of anything at all. He let out a breath. "That's really all there is to worry about?" he asked. "I kinda feel like I've been putting my foot in my mouth all day long. Like everyone's having a shitty day and I keep making it worse."

Glancing over his shoulder, Freeman gave another shrug. "I wouldn't worry too much about it. You're the boot. You're bound to get a lot of shit around here until you can pull your own weight. Plus we've been working like dogs for a long time and it's only getting worse."

Heifer laughed. "Yeah, we have. Ben, did you hear what the chief said about being on the news again? Can you believe that came out of his mouth?"

"Oh, he said that on purpose just to fuck with the skipper," Freeman replied. "O'Malley's a snarky bastard."

"Why was that a bad thing?" Tanner asked.

Freeman and Heifer shared a thoughtful look before the older man finally said, "Ah, you're gonna hear it, anyway. Everyone knows. You remember that luxury liner that got hit by pirates out here a few months back?"

"Sure," Tanner said. Of course he did. The news had hit on the worst day of his life since his mother had died. How could he forget?

"We were the first ship on scene. The pirates must've had pretty good jamming tech, because at first all we got was garbled transmissions. The captain decided to go check it out, but we were pretty far away at the time. We were still inside the system, so an FTL jump would've required emergency authorization, and the skipper didn't think the info met that threshold. Can't really blame him for that. Anyway, we got closer and then we picked up the beacon from the lifeboat.

"The whole scene was pretty bad," Freeman continued, choosing an obvious understatement rather than grisly detail. "We shot straight past the bodies before we even realized they were there, but then we wheeled back. Started looking at visuals."

Heifer shuddered. "That whole mess was so fucked up."

"Got that right," Freeman agreed. "Anyway, the captain called for aid on an open frequency, which is what he was supposed to do. Nothing wrong with that. No threats in the area and we obviously needed help.

"Thing is, while he was making that summons, we scanned over a few more of the bodies and started seeing kids among them, and the captain kind of freaked. I mean, he's got a wife and a little boy, right? So on the one hand, yeah, he screwed up, but on the other hand . . ." Freeman shrugged. "Well, it was a bad scene. Guy's only human. So he said, right there on the open channel, that there were kids in the void and we needed help right away."

"You're not supposed to say things like that?"

"No. No, it's in the manual under distress calls. There are reasons. Ultimately it made the captain look panicky. He created a . . . what was it they said? He 'created an unduly emotional atmosphere of crisis' and made us look 'less than professional.' Got reamed for it by command pretty good. Base CO on Augustine called him in and read him the riot act.

"Biggest part, though, was that Admiral Yeoh came through on an inspection thing or something, and I guess she bitched about how this came out in a press conference. Wanted to know why the president's press secretary asked her about it. Said it was an embarrassment to the service. Skipper's a religious conservative, so he doesn't really care for this president or his people to begin with. He kind of fixated on how unfair it was to catch flak for some politician's questions."

"And we've been in the doghouse ever since," Heifer put in.

Freeman nodded. "Yup. We're the hardest working ship in the fleet now. Command gives us every shit detail and extra patrol they can cough up, and the captain salutes and says 'yes, sir,' and does everything he can to make up for his goof. We've spent fifty percent more time underway over the last seven months than the next-busiest corvette in the fleet."

"We do all kinds of bullshit no other ship's crew does just so the skipper can impress command, too," Heifer concurred. "Wait 'til we're doin' PT out on the flight line under the ship. Or uniform inspections. And we spend a lot of time just cleaning the exterior of the ship. Hell, most of the time we scrub it down before we get to the atmosphere, and then again once we land. Seriously, we scrub the fucking hull while in space. That's our job, being deck crew," he added.

"All that for saying the wrong thing on an aid summons?" Tanner asked.

"All that for it getting into the media," Freeman said. "Shit rolls downhill. We're at the bottom. I won't say that's the only reason the skipper's in the doghouse with command, but it's the reason they harp on now. Listen, you want help, you get yourself qualified fast and you make sure you look sharp back at base."

The bridge fell silent. Tanner looked from Freeman to Heifer and back again as the two lounged in their seats. "So you guys will be training me a lot from here out, right?" he ventured.

"Gonna have to push yourself," Freeman answered as he folded his arms behind his head. "A lot of times it's too busy around here to hold anyone's hand, and when it's not, we're all pretty tired."

Neither of the two crewmembers on the bridge with Tanner saw his jaw drop. Each man looked to his own matters—not that those matters were ship's business. Even now, Tanner was reluctant to criticize, but his department head had just said in a single breath that it was vital that Tanner trained up and that he was too tired to train him.

Tanner stared at the ops table. He already knew much of this by the book. He needed to learn what *wasn't* in the standard manual, how this particular ship's captain and crew wanted those things applied . . . and no one learned that alone and overnight.

Taking a deep breath, Tanner opened up the ship's "book" on his holocom and began to page through its contents. He wasn't listed in the stations bill yet. That seemed understandable, except his orders had come through over a month ago. They'd had time to make changes. He looked at the names and ranks listed for battle stations, damage control, abandon ship . . . and consistently found the name of a crewman he'd yet to meet.

"Who is Crewman Herrera?"

"He's the guy you're here to replace," Heifer answered.

"Big shoes to fill there," Freeman added.

Tanner looked over the various station bills. "So I'm on Team Two for damage control?" he asked. "And I'm on the port laser turret?"

"Yeah," Freeman said, still not looking back. "We'll get you trained up on that eventually."

Tanner's eyes bugged out of his head. Eventually? Freeman was just talking about pirate attacks in this very corner of the system, and they'd get around to training him on the ship's guns *eventually*? Not starting maybe, oh, *tomorrow*? He didn't know whether to be worried or angry.

Tanner looked up at the projection of the ship's "bubble" a heartbeat before a new contact came into view. He read it aloud just as the soft notification tone sounded, going by the book just as he'd been taught. "Contact, three-three-four by three-one-one, just out of FTL at three point six light-minutes. Size rating 'massive.' Contact's bearing is—"

"Woah, woah, waitaminute," Freeman interrupted, climbing out of his chair. "You don't need to give me all that. This isn't a cruiser."

"I'm sorry, Ben," Tanner said with deftly feigned innocence. "How are we supposed to relay contacts on this ship? Could you show me?"

NINE

Good Enough for Government Work

"Two degrees starboard."

"Two degrees starboard, aye, aye, sir. Mark." Tanner kept his eyes on the screens embedded in the helm control panel. He glanced frequently at the belly of the long, sprawling hull of the vast and somewhat battered cruise liner below *St. Jude*. For all the computerized aid, manning the helm still required the naked eye and an instinctive sense of distance. All the manuals said so.

The manuals couldn't teach everything, though. Three months on board and he still wasn't qualified as a helmsman. He had mastered everything about the post—though no one cared to acknowledge it—except its actual namesake.

Tanner put it out of his head and listened for the captain's commands.

"We're horizontally aligned now," the captain said. Stevens sat in the port-side chair little more than arm's reach away. The captain seemed completely calm. His voice was firm. He wouldn't blow up at Tanner, but he didn't seem thrilled, either.

"Three meters forward," Stevens said.

Tanner swallowed. "Three meters, aye, aye, sir." Normally, such commands were keyed or spoken into the computer. Maneuvers this fine weren't ordinarily left to manual control. They were, however, part of the many tasks that Tanner needed signed off on his qualification sheet. Half his skill requirements on helm control remained unsigned; he couldn't finish those, many of which were much easier, until he executed this one.

Three meters. One for every time he'd screwed up this test. One for every dent he'd put in the ship. At least, the dents he'd put in while at the helm.

In his defense, they weren't big dents. *St. Jude* was a warship. She wasn't exactly made of paper. But a dent was a dent, and each one provided silent testimony to someone screwing up.

Tanner kept his grip on the yoke light, just as he'd been taught, and gave the acceleration grip in his right hand the gentlest twist he could. It was hardly even a twist, really. He just tightened the grip.

St. Jude crept forward ever so slightly along the bottom of the liner.

"Easy. Brake."

There weren't brakes as such on spaceships. *St. Jude* had a button on the left-hand control that fired maneuvering jets to counter minor forward movement. Luckily, computers handled that; Tanner didn't want to think about how tricky it would be to stop the ship manually. Tanner pressed the button and let it go, rather than leaving his thumb on it like he had on his second test. *St. Jude* came to a stop relative to the liner.

He waited for another command, or a criticism, or something. The captain didn't speak. Nor did Freeman, Reed, or even the XO. The bridge was crowded. Technically, Morales and Stumpy had the watch, but they stood out on the hull. Tanner was on watch now, too. After Tanner's second failed test at the helm, Freeman directed him to stand every other watch, rather than one watch out of three, in order to get more practice and more motivation.

He'd been plenty motivated all along. He learned every other aspect of watchstanding quickly. He could astrogate. He could run comms. He did both all the time. Helm vexed him, though, and the extra watches hardly brought more practice time.

Freeman claimed it wasn't a punishment. Tanner was pretty sure that Freeman almost believed that. At least, he was pretty sure that Freeman almost believed it had a point *besides* punishment.

"Okay," the captain said, "pull us away and do it again. You're on your own."

Again, Tanner gulped. "Aye, aye, sir," he managed, bringing *St. Jude* farther away from its targeted airlock-to-airlock linkup with the *Aurora*.

St. Jude didn't go far. That wasn't the point. Tanner only had to move the ship far enough away to wipe out the advantages of earlier expert guidance. He halted the corvette relative to *Aurora*'s motion, then took a deep breath and said over the comm channel shared with *Aurora*'s bridge, "Beginning linkup approach."

"Confirmed, *St. Jude*," said the liner's comm officer, whose voice carried far more good-natured patience than anyone on Tanner's crew.

"Okay, guys, keep your heads down now," Freeman warned over the ship's private channel.

Tanner tried to ignore the quip. Freeman's teasing didn't help. Ultimately, though, it didn't matter what Freeman said or thought here. It mattered if Tanner could slide his ship into place over *Aurora*'s airlock, which he did. It mattered if he could close the distance smoothly, which he did. It mattered if he could align the ship properly for linkup, which, after a couple of very minor adjustments, he did. And it mattered if he could connect gently . . .

. . . which, in this case, resulted in a ship-shaking thunk as *St. Jude* connected with the extended airlock passageway of the *Aurora*.

Tanner stared at his control panel. The instruments said he was fine. The video screens said he was fine. "Deckhands," he all but croaked, "check connection. Do we have a good linkup?"

The voice on *Aurora*'s end said he was fine. His ship's crew, given voice by Stumpy, said only, "Yup. You're a fuckup."

Tanner winced.

"What's wrong?" the captain asked, open annoyance coloring his tone.

"We've got some scratches, sir," Stumpy said. "Nother little dent here."

"We have a good seal, sir," corrected Morales. "It could've been cleaner. There are some cosmetic scuffs."

Stevens leaned in over Tanner's screens, as if his own weren't good enough, and then leaned back. "Are you satisfied, BM1?"

"Yes, sir," Freeman answered.

"Very well. Morales, Stumpy, come on back in and suit up for boarding." The captain sat back in his chair, tossing a look at the other men on the bridge.

"Hey, Tanner," Freeman spoke up, "head down below to the cargo bay and make sure everything's set for the boarding team."

Tanner accepted the obvious busywork. Everything was already set up after their first boarding that day, but it got him off the bridge. "On my way," Tanner said.

Outside the bridge, Tanner keyed the audio on the helmet slung over his shoulder. Experience had taught him how sloppy the crew could be with turning comm channels on and off. Today was no different.

". . . got to be the worst hand on the helm I've ever seen," he heard the captain say.

"I dunno, sir," Reed mumbled, "could be worse. Some people can't do it at all."

"He got the job done, sir," the XO pointed out.

"With more dents in my ship."

"Oh, I bet Stumpy's exaggerating, sir," Freeman said. "We'll clean it up."

"We can't fix the other dents. We're lucky they don't show too badly, but up close?" The captain shook his head. Tanner didn't need to see it to know.

"Sir . . ." Freeman ventured, clearly trying to keep well short of arguing with his CO, "he may be barely passing, but he did pass. Chances are he'll never have to do manual fine maneuver again. He can take off, he can land—"

"I'm surprised nobody lost a tooth last time he landed us," the captain snorted.

"—and he sucks at it, and we know that, and he knows it, sir. He's spent four hours on the simulator program every time he's been on watch in port, sir, and he comes in to practice on his own time, too. He qualified for in-port watch on time."

"I'm surprised you're sticking up for him. I thought you guys didn't like Malone?" broke in the captain. Tanner froze. It was one thing to know it through implication, another to hear it outright. "I know Morales doesn't."

"Sir, I don't have to like him. My point is, sir, we've got nine other qualified OODs and helmsmen on this ship. The only time Malone's ever gonna have to land the ship or execute a manual linkup is if the computer's fried and every other one of us is dead."

Tanner moved down the ladder toward the cargo bay imagining the captain's "pondering" expression. "And if we're ever at battle stations and he's all that's left on the helm?" Stevens asked.

"Sir, if we're ever at that point, we're fucked, anyway," Freeman said half-jokingly. Tanner couldn't disagree. In three months there hadn't been a single battle stations drill. Nor had they run a damage control or firefighting drill, or an abandon ship drill or anything else. One could argue that they were too busy with boardings and active patrols. Still, it bothered Tanner. *St. Jude* was a military ship. He hadn't once practiced what he was supposed to do in combat. He didn't relish the idea of going into a fight, but the prospects of not even knowing what he was supposed to do in such an event was downright disturbing.

"What's his battle station?" the captain asked.

Tanner winced. *Seriously? The captain doesn't know?* "Port laser turret," he muttered aloud. It was another breath before Freeman finally answered with the same thing.

Stevens gave another snort. "Can't imagine putting that kid on a gun."

Tanner stopped on the ladder. He gripped the rails tightly, trying not to be mad. "Okay," he heard the captain say, "call him back up."

A moment later, Tanner's holocom beeped with a summons to the bridge. Tanner gritted his teeth. He hadn't actually made it to the cargo bay. He turned off the comm channel for the bridge just before the XO and Freeman passed by. Neither man said anything.

The captain sat reading a data screen as Tanner arrived. Tanner looked around at Reed and Harper, but both of them were also pointedly busy with other things. Trying to make himself useful, Tanner turned to take another check at overall comm traffic.

"Malone," Stevens said. Tanner faced him. "Freeman's signing you off on fine maneuver linkups. You'll be landing us when we get back. If you do that right, you'll be signed off on that, too. Freeman says you're ready to be signed off on all the rest, so as soon as we're back on base and we're secure, you'll have your helmsman's board. Are you ready for that?"

"Yes, sir," Tanner answered firmly. He noted, silently, that the captain had been the one to direct this test, but he didn't want to put his initials down on Tanner's qual sheet. He simply deigned to allow someone else to do it.

"Okay. Back to work," the captain said, jerking his thumb over his shoulder at the worktable behind him.

• • •

"Ten months. Ten fuckin' months on this boat with nobody but you to talk to, and—no offense, right?—but that's a long goddamn time. I seriously thought I was gonna go crazy. Hell, maybe I actually did."

"You have no idea how grateful I am, Gina," Vanessa Ramirez assured her. "For everything. You've been wonderful." She stood with Gina at the airlock, waiting for the corvette's boarding crew to finish their preparations. The pair wore the simple crew vac suits of the *Aphrodite*, though the ship's emblems had been removed. It had been a long trip for her, too, but at least Vanessa knew what she was getting into from the beginning . . . and had done so with a sense of purpose. "I can't imagine what those assholes would've done with the money they'd have gotten from selling this ship, and the thought of them keeping it and using it for more piracy is just as bad. You saved a lot of lives by helping me with this. I couldn't have done it without you."

The younger woman looked sideways at her companion, smirking thoughtfully. "You know I thought for a while that you were gonna plug me, too, right? I mean, after you took care of Haywood and Butler?"

Vanessa shook her head. "I thought you were going to kill me when I realized the astrogation computers had been wiped." She chuckled. "But no. You're a hero. Not many people will ever know it, but you are."

Gina just laughed. "Hero. I like that. I never thought I was gonna be anything more than a plain old whore."

"You can be anything you want when we get this ship where it needs to go, Gina," Vanessa said. "We'll get you a new identity, get you in school, help you find a new job . . . whatever you want. And you'll be paid for all this time. I can promise you that."

The airlock seal indicators flashed and beeped. Vanessa reached for the controls.

"You ever gonna tell me who you work for?" Gina asked.

Vanessa smiled. "I more or less have to now," she said.

"Permission to come aboard?" someone called through the airlock.

"Permission granted," Vanessa called back.

Helmeted crewmen in Archangel Navy vac suits pushed one by one through the artificial gravity field at *Aphrodite*'s airlock. Each of them came armed, but made no sign of hostility. Vanessa and Gina waited until they saw the third, who wore a lieutenant's bars on his uniform.

"Hi," he said, flipping up his visor. "I'm Lieutenant Gagne. I'm the boarding team leader."

Vanessa's face went stone cold. She held up her holocom, which projected an intricate seal. "Lieutenant Gagne, my name is Vanessa Rios and I'm an officer of the Archangel Ministry of Intelligence. You, your boarding team, and your crew are now hereby informed that this boarding and everything you see and do here is top secret. You are not to discuss this matter with anyone, for any reason, unless instructed otherwise by the Ministry of Intelligence. If you're smart, you won't even discuss it among yourselves."

She let it sink in. Gagne blinked, looked to his shipmates, and then turned back to her. "I will need to speak with your captain to verify my identity," Vanessa told him. "And then you're going to send a secure message to Augustine Harbor for me and send me and this ship on our way."

• • •

"So is there anything you're actually good at?" Stumpy asked as the cruise liner floated off toward Augustine.

Tanner looked up from the manual projected by his holocom to Stumpy, who sat in the starboard-side seat on the bridge doing basically nothing. That was how it usually was on watch. Tanner did all the work, because he was the apprentice and ostensibly needed the practice. He was already proficient at everything but helm, though, and thus it was really just a matter of the other qualified helmsmen taking advantage of him.

He stood for the entirety of each four-hour watch. There were only two chairs.

"I thought I was good at astrogation and comms," Tanner replied evenly.

"No, I mean, outside of this," Stumpy said. "Like in school. You do any sports in school? Anything you were good at?"

"I got pretty good grades in school," Tanner replied. "But no sports, no."

"How good?" Morales asked. He sat in the port-side chair, scraping dirt out from under his fingernails with his feet up on the control panel.

Tanner didn't answer immediately. Much of the crew teased him about anything they could. With the exception of the captain—who could dish it out, but never had to take it—the crew gave one another shit all the time. As the newest body on the ship, Tanner got the largest share by far of such attention. His low rank sharply limited his options for retaliation.

Tanner spent little time with his shipmates when they were in port. He preferred to be alone. It wasn't like there were invitations, but then again, Tanner would have been torn on whether or not to take anyone up on it. Off-duty socializing might have presented a way to make things a little friendlier around the ship, but it could also just mean more time in the line of fire.

Such attention was always just a bit more venomous with Morales and Stumpy.

"Malone," Morales repeated, "how good is good? In school?"

This got into territory Tanner didn't want to discuss with the crew. Moreover, this was one of those conversations where people were "just talking" until they smelled blood in the water. Tanner looked for a safe response. "I wouldn't have had trouble getting admitted into a lot of universities."

"What, like St. Michael's?" Morales asked. "Uriel Academy? That school on Augustine?"

"Yeah," Tanner said, looking more at the deck than anything else. This stung more than they knew. "Yeah, I was above all their admission requirements." He had acceptance letters, too, but nobody needed to know that.

Stumpy snorted. "Think you could've gone to Harvard? On Earth?"

"Those big-name universities on Earth can get pretty political. Their admissions choices don't always have much to do with how good a student's application is." It was an honest answer; they didn't need to know that he had, in fact, met all the academic requirements for Harvard.

"I think it'd be cool to see Earth," Stumpy said.

"I've got a classmate going to Annapolis," Tanner muttered.

"Was he a better student than you?"

"She. And no, not really. I mean, she's good. She's smart, and I wouldn't say I'm smarter, but being a good student isn't always just about that. She had other things going for her. I didn't do any team sports. I swam a little, but not enough for it to matter."

"You said you could've gotten admitted," Morales said.

"Yeah."

"But you didn't apply?"

Tanner frowned. "No point."

"Why not?"

"Turns out universities are expensive."

"Yeah, but if you're smart enough to get in, there're ways to pay for it, right?"

"Sometimes," Tanner admitted, more to himself than to the other two men on the bridge. "I might've gotten a couple of scholarships to help things along. Maybe worked during school. I just didn't want to take out loans."

"Uh-huh." Morales grunted. "But you probably could've found a way. So why didn't you apply?"

Tanner's frown returned. He remembered whom he was dealing with. This wasn't idle conversation. This was a probe. "Because I wanted to do this."

"This was what you wanted to do coming out of school?" Stumpy sat up in his seat, looking at Tanner as if his answer was somehow odd.

"Yeah. Why's that weird?"

"Just doesn't seem to suit you. I mean, we all know you're some kinda nerd. Heifer says you watch fuckin' nature documentaries and shit. You wanted to be a navy crewman?"

"I can do the job," Tanner said. "I did fine in basic. I'm zero-g qualified—"

"You might be qualified, but you puke half the time soon as you get back on board," Stumpy countered. "Didn't you know you'd have trouble with that when you signed up?"

"Had no way to find that out beforehand."

"You get dizzy. You don't fit in. You really wanted this?"

He felt like he fit in fine during basic, socially and professionally, but he stepped on that argument. Tanner had no interest in discussing his initial motivations with these two. "Why's that so hard to believe? You think what we do isn't important?"

Stumpy just chuckled, settling back into his seat. Morales seemed to think it was funny, too.

Tanner figured the conversation was done. He turned back to plotting out courses just for something to do. Then Stumpy threw in his last comment: "Hey, Morales, you ever notice how book-smart people never ain't got no common sense?"

• • •

"And then she tells Miller, 'It doesn't matter how long I've been on this boat without a man, I wouldn't let you touch me even with your spacesuit and your helmet on.'" Heifer laughed. He faced the bathroom mirror, dutifully scanning his face for blemishes or stubble. Little more than his towel covered him. He performed the ritual each time *St. Jude* returned to Augustine Harbor and the crew was granted liberty: shower, primp, drink. "Seriously, two spy girls on a beat-up cruise liner, and Miller sees nothing wrong with makin' a play for either of 'em."

The other occupant of the barracks room sat on his bed, paging through ship's manuals on his holocom. He wore simple civilian clothes without shoes. He had no plans to go anywhere. "Pretty sure you're not supposed to tell me about this," Tanner said for the third time. "Just saying."

"Aw Christ, Tanner, are you really that worried about it?" Heifer groaned. "I mean, we're all on the same crew. We're all under the same information controls. It's not like we have to keep it a secret from each other. What're you worried about?"

Tanner genuinely worried about the loose lips of his fellow shipmates. He worried about being included among them when one of them slipped. He worried how much they would talk to impress girls in the bars once they'd gotten a few drinks in them. But he answered, "You're telling me Miller stories, Heifer. Why would I want to hear more Miller stories?"

Heifer snorted. He couldn't argue that. Satisfied with his grooming, Heifer crossed their barracks room to open his side of the tall lockers that stood between his bed and Tanner's. "So you just gonna sit there and read all night again?"

"Yup."

"Man, how come you never go out?"

"Never been invited," Tanner said, wondering how Heifer would take it.

Heifer paused. "No, I mean, you could go out on your own."

Tanner smirked. That was still more tactful than anything he expected. "I have no money to blow," he said.

"You make almost the same money I make," countered Heifer. "Where's it all going?"

"Education debt."

"Hah! I've got education debt, too. We all do. You don't see it breaking our backs, do you? Just pay the minimum on it. They can't go after you for more than that while you're in the militia."

"I don't plan on making a lifelong career of this," Tanner said. "I'd like to make some actual progress on it before my enlistment is up." In truth, he had to cough up at least five hundred credits a month just to keep up with the brutal interest rate, and more than that to make any progress. He had no intention of discussing those numbers with Heifer, though. His roommate might pass it on to someone else on the ship who could actually do math, and then Tanner would never hear the end of it. "Besides," Tanner said, "I go out."

"You go to the shooting range and the gym on base." Heifer snorted. "Meet a lot of women there?"

Tanner shrugged. "It's cheap entertainment." He walked over to the refrigerator to grab a drink.

The door chime interrupted their conversation. Heifer opened the door to greet Stumpy, Wells, and Miller. "You ready?" one of them asked.

"Time to get wild!" Heifer answered. Laughter and backslapping followed, along with talk of impending hangovers.

Not one of them acknowledged Tanner before they left, much less invited him along.

Tanner thought little of it. He didn't want to hang out with his shipmates, anyway, and it wasn't as if he had ever asked if he could go along . . . not that inviting himself seemed at all palatable.

Before he'd enlisted, he never had a Friday night to himself. There was always some party, some event, or even, more than a few times, a date. No such prospects ever turned up on Augustine. He refused to feel sorry for himself, but that made him no less lonely.

He stared at the manuals open on his bed. There was only so much studying he could do. Not for the first time, Tanner found himself alone and filled with the urge to hit or shoot something. The range was closed, but the base gym stayed open all night and had a full set of hand-to-hand combat drones.

Tanner opened his locker to grab his bag of gym clothes. Heifer wasn't the only creature of habit.

• • •

As it happened, Tanner's final board examination for helmsman didn't occur until *St. Jude* had been back in port for a full week.

He sat with his back to the wall at the center of the ship's larger galley table. Facing him were Gagne, Freeman, Reed, and Morales. Each held paper copies of the exam in front of them, trying not to look bored. Within the first ten minutes into the process, even Morales knew Tanner would pass.

"Which four alarms are on independent switches on the bridge?" Reed asked in his perpetual mutter.

"General quarters, engine critical, collision, and abandon ship," Tanner replied.

"Can you run those from anywhere else on the ship?" Morales all but yawned.

"They're also on the auxiliary helm control in engineering."

Then it was Gagne's turn. "What does 'bingo fuel' mean?"

"It means we have just enough fuel to return to base at cruising speed, sir," Tanner said. "Ordinarily that means here on Augustine. If we're in fleet ops or based out of another port, the helmsman recalculates accordingly, informs the OOD, and puts it in the log."

Gagne nodded. "Good." He turned to Freeman.

"Okay, you can take a moment to think this one through," Freeman advised before presenting the question. "If we're at seventy-five percent fuel and, for whatever reason, we have to do a maximum speed FTL run, how long will the fuel hold before it runs out? Don't include the reserve, just main fuel cells."

"If everything's working according to our standard efficiencies, we'd get a hundred-fifty-hour run," Tanner said, "which at max speed would at least cover the distance between any two systems in the Union."

Freeman's mouth twitched and he nodded, seeming a bit impressed that Tanner could comfortably put all that together. "Correct." He put his initials down on the space beside the question.

"But that's the ballpark. The question is posed to offer up simple numbers for the sake of illustrating normal fuel consumption. It would never be that neat and tidy in a real situation."

"Sure," Freeman said, glancing to Reed to move on to the next question.

Tanner decided he wasn't finished. "Given *St. Jude*'s current engine performance, we'd probably be looking at a hundred forty-one hours. I could crunch the numbers more accurately if I had a pen and paper or a holocom."

Freeman blinked. "Where'd you get that number?"

"I read the engineer's logs."

"Huh. Is that about right?" Gagne asked Reed.

The ops specialist shrugged. "We'd run a little less than what the original ship's books say, yes, sir. I'd have to ask one of the engineers, but that's probably about right."

"Well, okay, then." Freeman shrugged.

"We could stretch that out further by taking most of the ship's noncritical systems off-line and hooking the critical ones up to the power supply for the main cannon," Tanner said. "That'd take about twenty percent off the engine's power demands and would increase the flight range accordingly."

Freeman blinked. Gagne hid a grin. Morales finally stopped looking at the ceiling as Tanner continued. "We could also open up the magazines and pull the fuel cells from the missiles. It'd take some time to strip the cell casings, but once we did that, we could use the fuel cores to feed the ship's main engines. Every one of them would give about another five minutes of flight time at maximum speed."

"Who told you that?" Morales frowned skeptically.

"Nobody told me. I read the ship's ordnance manual. The fuel cores aren't any different from the ones powering the ship's engine. They're the same size and everything. They're just expected to burn out faster because missiles are meant to go really fast."

The four examiners glanced at one another quizzically. Gagne asked, "So you didn't ask any of the engineers if this would work?"

"No, sir," Tanner said, "but I'd be surprised if they haven't thought of it already, or wouldn't in the event it was necessary. They're engineers. It's their job."

Still controlling his grin, Gagne keyed up his holocom and waited for an answer. "Yes, sir?" the chief's voice piped up.

"Hey, chief, I've got a hypothetical for you. If we ran out of fuel for some reason, could we cannibalize the missile fuel cells and run the engines off them?"

"Sure, we could do that if we had to," came the answer. "It'd be a little messy and you'd only get so much power from each individual fuel core, but they'd fit in there just fine. Why?"

"Just had the question come up while we're giving Malone his board. And if you had to run all the ship's critical non-flight systems on the power supply for the main gun, how much of a load would that take off?"

The chief whistled for a moment, then fell silent, and finally said, "Oh, I'd say around twenty percent. I'm pretty sure that's in a book somewhere."

"And Malone didn't ask you about any of this?"

"No, sir. He asked Leone what manuals there were and asked for permission to download 'em, but that was weeks ago, sir."

"Thanks, chief. We're good." With that, Gagne cut the channel. "You hoping to become an engineer, Malone?" he asked, no longer trying to hide his grin.

"No, sir." Tanner shook his head. "I was hoping to go hospital corpsman or maybe research tech if there are spots open when the time comes."

"But you read the ship's engineer's logs."

"Yes, sir."

"And the ordnance manual."

"Yes, sir."

"In preparation for your helmsman's board, when the only thing you had to read was the helmsman's manual?"

"Yes, sir."

"I imagine you read the OOD manual and the astrogator's book, too?"

"Yes, sir, I did," Tanner answered innocently.

"Search and rescue manual? Rules of traffic flow? Court martial guidebook?"

"Haven't read that last one, sir. We've been really busy."

"Malone"—Freeman chuckled—"how many of the goddamn ship's books did you read?"

Tanner's mouth twitched. "All of them."

"And you understood 'em all?" Morales pressed, his skeptical scowl deepening.

"Yes, BM2, I did," Tanner said, his tone becoming ever so slightly firmer as he looked his supervisor in the eye. "I'm *book smart.*"

TEN

Things Will Go Wrong

Yaomo got screwed on the Qal'at Khalil loot.

The thought burned in her captain's mind day in and day out. He'd thought of it in the bars, he'd thought of it in bed, and he thought of it now, staring at the instruments and situation feeds on the bridge. Especially now. Had they not been screwed, they wouldn't be out here now.

Ming sat in the captain's chair with baleful eyes fixed on a holographic display of the CDC destroyer swinging in close to his ship. She'd just pulled off another freighter, moving into close scanning range while *Yaomo* crawled along.

His crew was tense. Ming couldn't blame them. If that destroyer got suspicious, *Yaomo* would have to bug out in a hurry. A boarding team *might* not find anything, and they *might* be bribed out of saying anything even if they did. There was an equal chance that *Yaomo*'s makeover wouldn't be good enough, that they'd be identified, and then it'd be a race to go FTL before *Yaomo* got splattered.

None of it would be necessary if Ming and his ship hadn't gotten screwed when the loot was shared out.

They divided the cash fairly. Ming couldn't complain there. Some of the material loot got split fairly, too, since that could be sorted out by sight and measurement. Each ship received an even split of fuel salvaged from Khalil City's spaceport. Guns were doled out equitably.

It was all the other random bullshit that just didn't work out right. Jewelry. Artwork. Pricy toys. Something about the offers put up by Paradise's fences didn't wash. Maybe it was the instant inflation that hit the planet as soon as the fleet returned. Maybe it was the smug looks on the faces of the Tong's guys, or the complaints the other fences made about the loot being too hot to be worth much.

Ming told the fences to take a hike. *Yaomo*'s crew voted to hold their share of the material loot, even while the bars raised their prices and Lauren said her prostitutes were overbooked and even the common whores started expecting *tips* for fuck's sake. None of the other ships' crews gave a shit. They were all too drunk or too stupid or both.

Hannah received extra shares for her ship because of their recon work. Casey and Lauren earned extras for their exploits. Hell, even that dumb fucker who'd let *Aphrodite* get stolen won an extra share out of the whole mess for suggesting they just throw cars at the palace, as if that was some form of rocket science.

After free-falling over the planet's largest city and dropping makeshift bombs, *Yaomo* needed a serious radiological scrub, an engine overhaul, and external modifications to change her appearance. A hundred different cameras had recorded her bombing run. Naturally her crew ran low on cash while all the other pirates from the raid still swam in booze and ass.

She had plenty of loot squirreled away in her holds. Ming just needed a serious buyer. Finding that buyer took months, and he damn sure wasn't going to Paradise for pickup.

"Understood, *Norfolk*," said Orion at the comms station. He coughed twice, then croaked, "We will hold this course and speed and"—he coughed again—"wait for further ins-instructions." The skinny pirate let out a wheeze. "*Sarah's Dream* out."

Ming grunted. "That's a good cough."

"Got out of school a lot with that cough," Orion joked.

"And look at you now." Ming looked from Orion to Kiyoshi at operations. "Status?"

"We've got two other ships in sensor range behind us," Kiyoshi murmured, staring at his screens. A grin appeared on his face. "One of 'em is a Lai Wa freighter."

"Right on time," Ming said. He stared at the approaching destroyer. "Take the bait, you stupid tools. Take the bait."

"Yup. *Norfolk*'s running an active scan," Kiyoshi announced.

A moment later, Orion turned back to his station to answer a hail. "This is *Sarah's Dream*," he hacked and gagged. "Go ahead, *Norfolk*."

"*Sarah's Dream*, we see significant radiation on your center hold," warned the voice on the other end of the channel. "You say you're carrying textiles?"

"Affirmative, *Norfolk*. Mostly silks. We know about that radiation. Gonna get a scrub at Apostles' Station soon as we get there." Orion clicked off the mic, then clicked it on, coughed, and clicked it off and on once more. "Radiation's not too bad. We've just been trying to get . . . grragh . . . get to a good . . . stopping point."

"And you guys are checking yourselves out over there, right?"

"Oh yeah. We're huuurrggghhhh fine heeechk. Fine here."

There was a long silence from *Norfolk*. "You're clear with a regulation scan and you'll get customs run-through at Apostles' Station. Just take care of yourselves. Continue on your original course. *Norfolk* out."

Ming tossed the others on the bridge a smug but relieved grin. "Told you we could wait on the radiological scrub."

• • •

So it finally happened, just like I was warned. Stevens had us all muster out on the flight line for PT. Apparently the last few times this happened, some of the crews of the other ships and ground support stopped working to watch and laugh. I think that's why Stevens had us muster before regular work hours.

Turns out, by the way, I'm still just as in shape as I was when I got out of weapons and tactics school. I've been worried, 'cause I'm tired and dizzy a lot while underway, but I'm surprisingly fit. Morales is a fitness monster and I guess Stumpy was a star athlete in school or something . . . but I almost wish we'd done something competitive.

Anyway. Our gunner's mate, Miller, showed up ten minutes late. He didn't talk to the captain, which was good, because we realized pretty quickly that he was still drunk from the night before. He hardly kept up with us and he fell out of formation constantly, but the XO and Freeman kept the captain distracted so he wouldn't notice. I always thought you'd be in deep shit for showing up drunk. Everyone seemed to find it hilarious.

Mostly I think it was just something else they could do to give the captain the finger without him knowing. That's basically how it is here. Everyone hates him because he works us so hard and so much of it is bullshit. He called everyone to the galley last week while we were in port, like there was some emergency or we were going to war or something, and then he stormed in and says, "There's a hard copy of an engineering certificate that's gone missing from my desk. Tear the ship apart and find it right now*!" Naturally, it was on his desk underneath some other papers.*

He freaks out over these things, he freaks out over how the ship looks coming into port, but then we haven't run a single general quarters drill since I've been here. Let that sink in: I've been here almost eight full months, and not once have I actually trained in my position for battle stations. Or boarding teams.

I can't say Stevens is all bad. He was good to the refugees. Every boarding we did during that mess, he made sure they had enough supplies and got medical attention, above and beyond our actual instructions. We had an informal all-hands formation on the base, and when they read off some of the metrics on the whole refugee flood, we were clear out on the top. Most hours underway, most ships inspected, all that. And then one of the base officers made some passive-aggressive comment about how "obviously nobody was trying to outdo anyone," and the other officers stood there chuckling about it. As if Stevens knew any of that would be reported. I really think he was just trying to live up to the whole Christian charity thing.

I wish I could say as much for the rest of the crew. Pretty much everybody with a rating is married, most of 'em with kids to boot, so it's not like they're good to hang out with when we're in port. The deckies haven't gotten any friendlier, especially Morales, who's still an ass. I tried going out with them a couple of times, but I just can't relate. I've got nothing in common with anyone except the job.

And that's the real problem out here. I've got no social life. Our schedule's always a jumble and the captain wants us to be ready to go within an hour of being called, even when we're in downtime status in port. I can't take any classes because I can't commit to a schedule. I go to the gym and the range and there's a dojo near the base, but that's about it.

Tanner leaned back from the screen of his holocom. He sat at a table in the galley, listening to music while he wrote his letter. A frown darkened his face as he read over the last paragraph. He'd be sending the letter out to several friends: Madelyn, Alicia, Ravenell, probably a couple of friends from Geronimo. On the one hand, he wanted to tell it like it was. On the other, there was no point in moping to his friends. They couldn't do anything about his situation, nor did he want to have a pity party.

Sighing, Tanner deleted the last two paragraphs.

At the moment, though, I can't complain much. We've been in port for a whole week and should be for two more. Stevens and Morales are away on leave for another week. Hell, with Morales gone, the other non-rates have lightened up on me some. I'm starting to think they give me shit mostly to buddy up to him.

The chime of the ship's comms system cut off his music. Tanner glanced over to the comms screen and noted that it was a local, civilian call, and audio only.

"*St. Jude*," he said, "Crewman Malone speaking."

"Hhhhey. Malone, 's Miller."

"What's going on, Miller?"

"I'm at my girlfriend's an' I wannda check in. Is anything going on there?"

Tanner's jaw dropped. Miller didn't have a girlfriend. Tanner couldn't even believe women would talk to him for more than five minutes if they had any choice. "Your girlfriend's?"

"Yeah! My girlfriend!" Miller's wobbly voice hit a defensive note before he hiccupped.

Tanner kept a friendly tone. He realized he was talking to a drunk. "Why aren't you calling me with your own holocom, Miller?"

"I kinda dropped it in a toilet at the bar."

Tanner buried his face in his hands. "Gotcha."

"So's anything goin' on?"

"No, I'm just sitting here on the midwatch."

"Hooookay, I'm gonna get laid an' maybe call you in a couple hours an' check in again."

"Miller, why don't you let me know how I can reach—hello?" The line was dead.

Tanner tapped the screen in search of contact info. Naturally, the call had been sent with privacy conditions. "Dumb-ass," he grumbled. Tanner turned his music back on. It was Miller's funeral if they got a call-up while he was out of touch.

Then the comms chime sounded again. Tanner smirked, figuring maybe Miller wasn't quite so drunk after all. "*St. Jude*," he said after touching the screen, "Crewman Malone speaking."

"*St. Jude*, this is Augustine Command."

Tanner's face went white. *Oh no . . .*

• • •

"I don't like this at all, XO," Reed muttered. The ship's resident old salt stared through the bridge canopy at the stars. "Hundred-fifty-meter independent freighter? There ain't no such animal. Not coming out here. Ship like that can't turn a profit on lanes this busy."

Lieutenant Gagne turned from the plot on the astrogation worktable. "You think she's a smuggler?"

"Hell, probably. If that CDC ship had boarded like they were supposed to, though, they prob'ly wouldn't have found anything. Those guys are sloppy and they don't care. I just can't imagine what legit cargo they could be carrying to make it worth coming out here. If it was a corporate ship, that'd make some sense, because they could maintain her cheaply. But if she's an independent? Profit margin's too narrow. I mean, it could be a lucky charter job, but it just seems unlikely."

Tanner listened from the starboard chair. Reed held immense experience and professional knowledge, but he hardly ever spoke. This was the most Tanner had ever heard Reed say at once. Even if the old ops specialist still mumbled and muttered it out while literally staring into space, this made him seem positively animated.

Everyone on the ship was groggy. Most had been woken from sleep by Tanner's summons. That led to grumpiness all around, and none more so than Freeman. "Hell, Reed, maybe they're just bad businessmen."

Reed gave a little shake of his head. "Maybe, but you can't get away with that for long, either. Sooner or later the math overtakes your stupidity."

"Malone," Gagne said, "you got anything on sensors yet?"

"No, sir," Tanner replied. "Still nothing out . . . wait. Yes, sir. Think I'm finally picking up a faint radiation trail. Yeah, right there, see? Right on the path she's supposed to be."

Reed leaned in to look over Tanner's shoulder. "Yeah. She's probably just another few minutes outside our bubble. Headed into Ophanim's gravity well. Boarding team's definitely gonna need serious anti-rads. You guys will be lucky if you don't come back sterile."

The XO leaned in and frowned. Soon, the ship's sensors came up with the freighter just outside the two light-minute sensor bubble as Reed had predicted. With *St. Jude* moving in pursuit speed, she would catch up in roughly fifteen minutes.

Tanner felt much more comfortable with Gagne than his other superiors. He decided to risk voicing a concern. "Sir," he said, "I don't want to sound paranoid and I'm sure there are a million of 'em . . . but from the description we got, she's the same class of freighter that dropped the fuel cell bombs on that city on Qal'at Khalil."

"Was that in the message?" asked Freeman with a frown.

"No, but they mentioned her freighter class," Tanner answered, "and I've read up a lot on the whole thing. It's probably a coincidence, but I thought I should mention it."

"All right, I want everyone on the same page," Gagne decided. He clicked on the ship's PA system. "All hands not on watch report to the galley. Repeat, all hands not on watch report to the galley for briefing. OP3 Harper to bridge to relieve helmsman." Turning the PA off, Gagne looked to Reed and said, "Hail them as soon as we're one light-minute away. Tell 'em to heave to and await inspection."

"Aye, aye, sir," Reed mumbled.

"Hey, Tanner," Freeman said, "I'm gonna need you to write out a statement about Miller before too long. You sure there's nothing you haven't told me yet?" It wasn't an accusation; for once, Tanner was clearly not the object of anyone's ire.

"Wish there was, but it's that simple." Tanner shrugged. "He only made the one call. Ship's holocom channel has it recorded."

"Yeah, I know." Freeman huffed. "Stupid asshole. Guess you're gonna get to see your first captain's mast. Anyway, here's Harper. C'mon, let's go. XO's probably gonna want you on the outside helping with the linkup."

In the galley, Tanner found a collection of tired, unhappy faces. Gagne stood behind the smaller table, looking over a screen from his holocom until everyone arrived. This represented a serious change of pace from the captain's usual leadership style. Stevens rarely held briefings, formal or otherwise.

"Sorry to drag you all out of bed," Gagne began with a wry grin. "So here's the deal. We've got an independent Ayrshire-class freighter headed for Apostles' Station, or so she says. A CDC destroyer let her pass with only a cursory scan. Command on Augustine decided that's not good enough. Nobody else was available, though, so they sent us, which is why we've been hauling ass since we lit out of port.

"She's a hundred-fifty meters long and she claims a crew of forty-two, but nobody's verified that. Our computer doesn't have any record of her coming through here before. She's showing radiation contamination on one of her containers, which is probably why the CDC boys skipped out on boarding her. That means everybody who goes over gets to take anti-rads beforehand and do a body system flush afterward." The XO let the groans pass before continuing.

"Obviously this may be no big deal, but here we are short three people and backup is a good ways away . . . and I want to point out that it was an Ayrshire freighter that nuked that city on Qal'at

Khalil," he said, glancing at Tanner. "She's one of thousands, but it's worth noting."

"The fuck does 'Ayrshire' mean, anyway?" grumbled Heifer.

"It's a kind of oxen," Tanner answered quietly.

Several pairs of eyes turned on Tanner. "Yeah, you would know that shit," Stumpy grumbled.

"Anyway," Gagne continued, "like I said. Three people down. With the captain gone, I can't leave the ship. That means Freeman leads the boarding team. We're also down Miller and Morales. Regulations say Flores can't go over if he's our only qualified medic unless there's a medical emergency. Chief, who can you spare?"

O'Malley winced. "Yeah, I knew you were gonna ask that, sir. I really don't know. We jumped from a cold start to takeoff and then pursuit speed. The engine's already cranky. I can spare a couple guys, but it'd be best if it was Wells and Leone. We need the rest on board here in case we have a problem. And technically Wells is supposed to be on light duty for another couple days to begin with."

"I'm sure I'm fine, sir," Wells piped up. "It was just a sprained ankle."

"Yeah, but it's a point." The XO shrugged.

"We've got me, Heifer, and Stumpy from the deck crew, sir," Freeman said. "We get Leone from engineering, that's four of us. Should be fine."

"Except that only leaves us Malone on the deck crew, and he's never even fired one of the turrets if we need someone there." Gagne didn't hammer on the ship's weak training schedule more than that; the point was now self-evident. "Obviously I can do it, but I'm supposed to be *calling* the shots from the bridge. Either Stumpy or Heifer has to stay here. I don't like the idea of you going over there with only two guys."

The galley fell silent. Tanner raised a hand. "Sir? I've gone over on boarding teams before."

"Those were different conditions." Gagne shook his head. "We should've gotten you boarding team qualified by now, and we're gonna make that a priority soon as we get back. At the moment, though, I'm not comfortable sending you over there. I'm taking this one seriously. Something might go down." The XO's gaze swept the table to ensure his warning sank in for everyone.

"Um. I don't mean to argue, sir," Tanner ventured further, "but I graduated third in my class in weapons and tactics school. That was a lot more rigorous than anything on the ship's qualifications sheet."

The XO blinked. He'd been about to say that reading books just wasn't good enough. "Weapons and tactics? I thought that was a marine thing."

"Yes, sir." Tanner nodded. "Me and a couple other navy recruits from my training cadre had the time before we had to show up at our first billets. Fort Stalwart's pretty serious about cross-training now."

"Bullshit," Stumpy muttered.

"You wanna see my training records?" Tanner offered without anger.

The XO already had them open. Stumpy looked over his shoulder at them and suddenly his eyes bulged. "Why didn't you tell us you could shoot like that before now?" he asked.

"Nobody asked. It didn't seem relevant."

"Shit, I'd tell every chick I ever met," grunted the shorter non-rate.

Tanner just frowned. "You meet a lot of women who are impressed by that?"

Gagne exchanged a thoughtful glance with Freeman. "Tanner," Freeman wondered, "how long's it been since you've been at a shooting range?"

"I usually go every couple days when we're in port."

The XO grinned. "That's what you do instead of going out drinking with everybody?"

"I ran out of nature documentaries, sir," Tanner deadpanned.

"You've read the boarding team manual, too, I imagine?"

Tanner nodded. "Couple times. And the training guide. I know the use of force regulations. Put the written test in front of me right now, sir, and I'll pass it."

"I don't know, XO." Freeman frowned. "It *is* against regs. I mean, I've got twenty-one years in and I've never pulled a firearm on a boarding, let alone fired it," he noted, glancing meaningfully at Tanner, "but if you're taking this seriously, regs are regs."

"Sir, I'm not in a hurry to do anything dangerous," Tanner offered respectfully, "and I'm sure as hell not looking forward to spending all day in a bathroom flushing out anti-rads. But we did boarding training in school. Hell, we did it in basic. Judgment shoot tests, too. Probably more than I'm gonna do to get signed off in the ship's books. We're shorthanded and I'll be less useless over there than I am over here."

"Okay," Gagne conceded, "but you follow the lead of your other team members, understood? This is a big exception to the regs, and I'll stand by it, but past that we do this one by the book. That means I want to see everyone carrying around helmets until we're back in port. All of us."

As the impromptu huddle broke up, Chief O'Malley chuckled. "Guess we ought'a stop teasing Tanner before he snaps and starts shooting people at random on the flight line."

"Don't worry, chief. I won't do it at random."

• • •

"God*damm*it," Ming growled as the blip came closer in on the bridge sensor bubble.

"Yup. They're hailing us. Archangel Navy, heave to, prepare for inspection, all that shit."

"Hold course for the moment. Kiyoshi?"

"Navy corvette," the ops boss said. He paused, reading the ship's data files. "She's up at her top speed right now according to the books, but there's no telling if she can put out more. We're not gonna out-accelerate her regardless. Even if we could, she's probably getting a good ID read on us now."

Ming fumed as he reviewed the info from the sensor bubble projection. If they could outrun the corvette in sublight, they still couldn't outrun communications without jumping to FTL. Even that wouldn't buy the many hours they needed to dock, locate their buyer, and offload, to say nothing of the illegality and genuine danger of jumping around in FTL within a star system. They'd have a lot of answering to do if they popped out of FTL right outside of Apostles' Station.

Swearing to himself, Ming hit his personal holocom to bring up *Yaomo*'s quartermaster. "Hari," he said, "we got us a major fuckin' problem and we're gonna have to put it to a vote right goddamn fast."

The muscular, golden-skinned quartermaster appeared on a holo screen. From his surroundings, Ming guessed that Hari was in the middle of a card game. He quickly relayed the situation.

Hari sat up and started inputting instructions to his own holocom while Ming spoke. "Putting out the all-hands notice now."

"Hey, Kiyoshi," Ming said, "what kind of crew does a corvette like that have?"

"Stats on file say it'd be around fifteen or sixteen."

Ming moved to Kiyoshi's station. He read over the other pirate's shoulder, reviewing the corvette's statistics. The public information might be inaccurate, but those inaccuracies could go either way.

"Ming," Hari said over the holocom, "we're ready."

The captain took a breath to calm himself before he spoke to the crew via the PA. "People, we're being pursued by a local navy corvette. She's got a good identification read on us and she's ordered us to heave to for inspection. We can try an emergency FTL jump, but we just entered the outer gravity well of a gas giant and it'd be pretty risky. I'd only give us a fifty-fifty shot in a straight ship-to-ship fight.

"We don't have time to do a full debate on this shit, so with Hari's permission I'm gonna give us three straight options. One, we haul ass and risk the FTL jump just before their guns are in range. Two, we try to sucker them in close and then open up on her with everything we've got and hope they aren't ready for it. Third, we let them board, kill the fuckers on the boarding team, blast the ship at close range, and then haul ass out of here.

"I'd give option three our best odds. That ship's only got a crew of around fifteen assholes, and they're gonna have to send at least a third of them over to board.

"Vote fast, guys."

• • •

"Ugh. God, I already feel gross from those anti-rads," Tanner mumbled as he got the handheld sniffer activated. He and the rest of the boarding team stood in the cargo bay, gathering up the last of their equipment while Stumpy opened the airlock hatch.

"We really need you to hold it together on this one, Tanner," Freeman warned.

"I'll be fine, BM1," he said, hoping he was right. He glanced up at Leone. "Um. Did you check that weapon?"

Leone shrugged. "I'm sure it's fine." Without thinking about it, Leone pulled the laser pistol from its holster, pressed the self-test button, and then frowned. "Huh. Freeman. This gun is bad. Or the power cell or something."

"What?" Freeman blinked. He stepped over to Leone, looked at the pistol's indicator lights, and then frowned darkly. "Goddammit. Everybody check your weapons. If you already did it, check 'em again."

Tanner didn't know whether to bathe in sweet vindication or worry about what else might be wrong with the ship's armory. He had already checked his own pistol, but went through the process again per Freeman's instructions.

"Okay, we ready?" Freeman asked. "Let's go. Head over."

As he swung himself over the airlock, Stumpy cast a wary look at Tanner. "Don't shoot me," he grumbled.

Tanner soon followed, bracing himself for the disorientation of moving through the vestibule and then coming out in an environment with an opposite up and down. On the other side of the airlock, he found Stumpy standing in front of a couple of members of the freighter's crew, both of them rough-looking men in civilian clothes. Like his shipmate, Tanner pushed up the faceplate of his helmet.

A quick look at the sniffer showed acceptable readings. No power signatures to weapons other than the boarding team's own. No traces of gunpowder. No immediate hazardous materials. Radiation readings were what they expected: significant, but within safe parameters for short-term exposure. Tanner wondered how often the crew of the freighter took anti-rads, and how unpleasant prolonged use must be.

Freeman came over next, followed by Leone. The bald Indian crewman waiting in the airlock vestibule stepped forward. "Second mate Venkatesh," he said.

"Bo'sun's Mate Freeman," said the other man, pushing his faceplate up before they shook hands. "Sorry to hold you up like this."

"Is there a problem?" Venkatesh asked curiously. "We were cleared once already."

Freeman offered a chagrinned shake of his head. "The problem isn't necessarily on your end. System regulations require a physical inspection. You guys didn't do anything wrong, but whoever cleared you did."

"Okay, then." Venkatesh nodded. "What do you need from us first?"

"Got a manifest and ship's roster we can look through?"

"Right here," said the agreeable second mate.

• • •

"There are only four of them," Kiyoshi muttered. The feed from the tiny concealed holocom camera carried by "Venkatesh" offered a clear picture of the boarding team and the two pirates who met them.

"Keep your eye on your station," Ming reminded him. "I've got this. Be ready for action as soon as I give the word." He hit a different channel on his holocom. "Hey, Tully. It's pretty much what we thought, but there are only four guys. Hari's bringing them to the port bay now. You got enough people? Everyone's at stations, but there are always plenty to spare on this boat."

"I have four of us here, plus Hari and Sam," Tully replied. "Should be fine. Ain't like we can squeeze any more guys into the passageway, anyway. Sure we can't just get 'em into the cargo bay and shoot 'em?"

"We won't get Hari and Sam clear without tipping them off, and besides, they've got a guy with a sniffer on him. Make sure nobody's carrying a gun like I told you, Tully. You've gotta do this up close."

"Yeah, I've checked. We're good. Buzz Hari to let him know we're in place."

"Right." Ming looked over to Kiyoshi. "Everybody set?"

"Damage control and gun crews ready," Kiyoshi confirmed. "Courses laid in. Engineering says give the word."

Ming checked to ensure one last thing was in place. Alfie and Ngoc waited at the airlock, ready to send their bomb through. Satisfied, the captain keyed in a code to give Hari a silent thumbs-up.

• • •

The readings on the sniffer bothered Tanner. Everything only came up in trace amounts, but they'd continued throughout their walk through the ship. "BM1?" he beckoned.

Freeman glanced over to Tanner as they walked, then held back a pace or two to look over the screen on the sniffer. "Have you guys carried weapons recently?" Freeman asked.

"We did an arms run to Moorehouse a couple months ago." Venkatesh shrugged. "Had to bring everything through the passageways because of a dumb local offloading process. Lemme guess, you're picking up chemical indicators?"

Freeman nodded. "Yeah."

Venkatesh kept leading the others along as he spoke. They passed a crew berth hatch, then came to a corner and finally to the port cargo bay hatch. "Lots of inspection crews on that job while we offloaded, too. They kept asking us to open things up right in the passageway. Now every time we get boarded, we have to explain the sniffer readings because of those paranoid bastards."

With the hatch opened, Venkatesh let his crewmate move through first, then Stumpy. Tanner brought up the end of the line. He heard something behind him and had just a split second to wonder if someone had joined them before he was seized from behind. An arm encircled his neck while his assailant's other hand grabbed Tanner's right wrist. Tanner gave a yelp.

Bodies rushed past him. Someone grabbed at his hip, snatching his pistol from his side. Tanner was then flung to the floor on his back. Shouts came from all around. His helmet, its faceplate still open, protected his head as he hit the deck. Then a long-haired, muscular man dove at him with a knife in his hand.

Tanner blocked the blade with a forearm, throwing his assailant off balance. The freighter crewman landed with his knee in Tanner's gut while an ally stabbed down at Tanner's face with another knife. Tanner turned his head more out of reflex than anything else, just in time to take the strike against the side of his helmet.

Buried in the dog pile, Tanner hardly noticed as the ship suddenly rumbled and shook.

• • •

The blast felt as if it would blow *St. Jude* in half, but the ship remained intact. Every crewman fell to the deck or against a bulkhead as the thundering boom echoed through the passageways. On the bridge, alarms blared and the ship lost all orientation as she spun away from the freighter.

Harper fell to the floor of the bridge. Reed and Gagne reeled in their chairs. The XO recovered just quickly enough to see the freighter rush away with its engines firing at full blast.

St. Jude had a hull breach. There was a fire somewhere, too, but Gagne couldn't read where because his head kept spinning. Alarms that Gagne had only heard in drills shrieked in wordless tones, warning of weapons systems actively targeting the ship.

Reacting on instinct, Gagne jabbed his fingers on the evasive computer assist buttons. *St. Jude* lurched in another direction as maneuvering jets fired across her hull, spinning just in time to avoid laser fire from the freighter's small turret—and several others that had popped up from concealed hatches. Chaff missiles fired and exploded around the corvette, further disrupting the fleeing craft's weapons.

Disorientation cleared. Automatic systems sealed the hull breach. Gagne realized it was in the cargo bay. With no one in the hold, *St. Jude*'s computer closed off the cargo bay on its own initiative to prevent the spread of flames as supplies burned. Atmosphere was quickly vented from the compartment to choke off the fire.

"Gah. Damage . . . damage control!" Gagne yelled. "Tactical! Harper, you okay? Reed?"

The older ops specialist wiped away the blood from where his nose had come down on the control panel. Harper rose, grabbing onto the astrogation worktable. "We've got her course." Harper winced.

Gagne threw on the ship's damage control network, which automatically brought to life every holocom on board. "Chief, damage report!"

"Something blew up in the cargo bay, but we're mostly fine in engineering," the chief groaned. "Engines are both live. We're not venting anything."

"*Sarah's Dream* is still—" Harper's warning was cut off by a red flash and the wail of new alarms throughout the ship. *St. Jude* trembled again, but not nearly so violently as before. "We're hit, sir. Dorsal section, starboard quarter. Think it's not bad, but they're still firing."

"Flores is hurt!" someone else announced.

"Chief, we're going to pursuit speed again," Gagne said. "Reed, give me a course and pursue. Harper, you sure that hit wasn't anything important?"

"Checking . . . yes, sir. It was your quarters, sir."

Relieved that it was only his room on the ship, Gagne brought *St. Jude* to battle stations and charged up the guns. The freighter sped away on a line perpendicular to Ophanim's orbit around

Archangel. It was the most practical course for a point far enough from the planet's gravity well to allow for a safer FTL jump.

St. Jude could beat her in an open race, but the freighter had a head start on a short track.

• • •

"Goddammit, shoot him!" growled the pirate wrestling with Tanner.

The knife had fallen loose, but only after slashing into Tanner's left shoulder. Tanner had no idea where his gun was. He fought only one assailant where a heartbeat ago it had been two. He heard screams.

His first thought had been that this must have been some mistake. That this could be talked out if his attackers just allowed him a moment to think. That maybe someone was mixed up, that this couldn't be for real, or maybe this was some misunderstanding. Then he heard the scream from down the passageway and the man tangled up with him demanded Tanner be shot.

He got an arm around the man's head as they struggled on the floor. His free hand reached for his survival knife on his leg. "Kill him!" the other man shouted. "Kill him, Ron!"

There wasn't time to process. No time to sort things out. No way out of this.

Tanner shoved his knife up under the man's jaw. He heard a terrible, gurgling half shriek, half whimper. Wrenching the knife out, Tanner lurched away and made it to one knee before he came face-to-face with a man pointing Tanner's own laser pistol at him.

The pistol beeped plaintively. Its wielder didn't wear the magnetically keyed gloves of an Archangel navy vac suit.

Tanner's foot shot out at the man's knee, which buckled with a crunch. He grabbed his attacker by the hair and laid the man's face open with the survival knife. As the crewman howled and rolled away gushing blood, Tanner scrambled for his laser pistol.

A third assailant rushed up at him from the chaotic brawl just down the passageway, brandishing an axe with a frantic expression. Tanner had the gun up and ready just as the man was on top of him. He could hardly have missed at so close a range. Thin red flashes of light burned through the axe-wielder's chest and neck, and suddenly his forward momentum wasn't under conscious control. He collapsed beside Tanner in a heap.

With the third attacker down, Tanner had his first clear look at the fight in the passageway. Freeman and Leone were both down. Stumpy took hold of his attacker's weapon and went on the offense. One of the freighter crewman had a knife in the small of Freeman's back. He yanked it out as if to plunge it in again.

Venkatesh stood in the middle of it. He had Leone's riot gun and leveled it at Tanner. It wasn't keyed like the laser pistols were. The riot gun was a real threat.

Tanner fired first. More red flashes burst from his weapon, bringing Venkatesh down with three hits before the riot gun went off. Its cloud of steel shot ricocheted wildly off the bulkheads.

Affording himself little more than half a second to aim, Tanner fired again, clipping Freeman's attacker across the back of his skull. The man jerked back out of reflex and then fell to the deck.

"Motherfucker!" Stumpy raged, slamming the wrench down on his opponent again and again.

"He's down, he's down!" Tanner shouted as he made it over to the others. Freeman groaned and coughed. Leone lay unmoving in a pool of blood with fatal holes slashed into his neck and torso. Tanner winced and turned away.

"What the *fuck* is this?" Stumpy demanded. "Where's my gun?"

"It's over there." Tanner turned his full attention to Freeman, who bled heavily. "Keep guard. I've gotta help Freeman." The young crewman tore his minimal first aid kit from its pouch on his utility belt. He found more than one serious knife wound on Freeman, along with a nasty gash on his face. "BM1, you with us? You okay?"

The boatswain's mate's eyes didn't track at first. Half-formed words fell from his lips. "Shit," Tanner said, "I think Freeman's got a concussion."

Beside them, Stumpy checked his holocom in hopes of raising their ship. "I'm getting nothing but fuckin' static. They must be jamming."

"Ship's moving," Freeman gasped as Tanner slapped skin-contracting pads over the wounds. He groaned louder when Tanner drew him up to a sitting position to wrap bandages around his lower torso. "They gotta be running from *St. Jude*."

"Right," huffed Tanner. He had been in situations like this before; they just hadn't involved so much blood and he always got a grade at the end of the simulation. At least, he told himself it wasn't that different from training. The other option was to crawl into a hole and wish it all away, and that didn't sound promising. "Freeman. Listen to me. You know how ships like this are laid out, right? You've boarded them before?"

"Yeah." Freeman's words seemed to fall from his lips. He tried to shake off the cobwebs, but it was tough going. "Listen, Tanner—"

"Which way's engineering?"

"What?"

"Engineering."

"Tanner, we've got to go . . . get to a lifeboat . . . bail out before they jump."

"No, no, think it through. They'll shoot us before we get out of range. They're jamming comms. That's gotta be because *St. Jude* is still out there. Where's engineering?"

• • •

"Hari? Hari! Son of a *bitch*," Ming roared. He'd taken his eyes off Hari's holocom projection just to make sure *Yaomo* made good time and scored a couple of hits on their pursuer, and now he saw nothing but a picture of a bulkhead.

Again, Ming turned his attention to the sensor bubble. *St. Jude* chased after them, putting on enough evasive maneuvers that *Yaomo* landed only glancing hits. The corvette's reflective armor was good; even despite her much smaller size, *St. Jude* could clearly survive serious punishment. The little corvette hadn't returned fire yet.

St. Jude poured on the speed, but even with her superior acceleration, she wasn't yet making up for *Yaomo*'s head start. Her evasive jinks and rolls cost her even more speed. Five minutes. That was all Ming needed. It would be close.

Spitting in frustration, Ming keyed a button on the ship's network. "Mansoor! Mansoor, *you there*?"

"We're here. Trying to nail this bitch, but at least we're—"

"I need you to send people to check on Hari. Anybody you can spare. I think he's down. Port cargo bay. If any of those fuckers are alive, they're probably headed for the lifeboats."

• • •

"Fuckin' suicide, man," Stumpy muttered. Freeman leaned heavily on the shorter crewman, limping as best he could. "Taking on engineering all by ourselves, three guys and Freeman's gimped already—"

Pressed up against one side of the bulkhead just ahead of Stumpy, Tanner turned to glare through the lenses of his helmet. "Stumpy," he hissed urgently, *"shut the fuck up."*

Stumpy blinked. Tanner seemed awfully scary while covered in other peoples' blood.

Swallowing his fear, Tanner crept closer to the corner. The two-minute rush from the cargo bay hatch to the corner to engineering provided just enough time for Tanner to consider things besides immediate tactics. He realized that Stumpy was chattering because he was scared. Tanner was scared, too.

He came to the lip of the bulkhead. Around his left waited either an unguarded door to engineering or men with guns watching for him. He tried to remember what they'd taught him to do in weapons and tactics school. He tried to remember what Janeka and Everett had taught him. They'd done this before. They'd done this in Squad Bay Oscar, on *Los Angeles*, in buildings and on other ships.

For a terrifying moment, Tanner's mind went blank. It was a corner. Danger lay around the corner. He was supposed to do something. He was supposed to *have* something he could *use* here. Something to throw. A grenade. He was supposed to have grenades, but he definitely didn't have any of those, even though he checked his harness for them, anyway.

Then his hand went over his belt lamp. There. That was something Everett taught. Improvise. Right.

Turning back to Stumpy, Tanner helped him settle Freeman down against a bulkhead. He realized then that neither of his companions knew any of the silent hand signals he had been taught, and so he improvised. He tapped Freeman's gun and pointed down either direction of the passageway to ask the older man to cover those directions, and then looked to Stumpy and mimed picking Freeman up. "When we're through," Tanner whispered. "Got it?"

Stumpy nodded. So did Freeman.

Tanner painted himself up against the bulkhead at the corner again. He looked back to his shipmates and hissed, "One . . . two . . ."

The belt lamp flew up and around the corner a split second before Tanner flung himself out onto the deck. Bullets and laser fire erupted from around the corner, hosing down the passageway. Most of it went high as the guards instinctively trained their weapons on the first movement they saw. Landing on his shoulder, Tanner blasted away with his pistol.

He caught a bullet in his left thigh. Another grazed his left shoulder, and somewhere in the back of Tanner's mind he wondered if that was somehow better or worse in light of the knife wound he already had there. Mostly he focused on shooting, blasting the gunner on the left, then the laser rifle–wielding guy on the right. He missed his shots on the latter. Stumpy made up for them.

"Right," Tanner grunted. He scrambled back up, rushing for the assault rifle and the dead man holding it. Pain erupted from his left leg the instant he put pressure on it, but Tanner forced it to move. It still held his weight, though he didn't want to think about how. They were almost at their target.

"They had to have heard that." Freeman winced as Stumpy brought him around the corner.

"Yeah." Tanner reloaded the rifle with a magazine from the dead man's corpse and stuffed a second into his belt. "We can't wait. You ready, Stumpy?"

His shipmate nodded. They settled Freeman down again and readied themselves. Tanner turned to the hatch, ready to throw the wheel and face whatever lay beyond . . . and then stopped. Questions came in a rush, one on top of the other: What were the people on the other side supposed to do if their guards wanted to get back inside? How did they sound an all clear? There was no porthole through the hatch, nor an intercom on the outside. Did they use holocoms? Did these guys have specific procedures?

Tanner slammed the butt of his confiscated rifle twice against the hatch. "Hey, we got 'em!" he yelled in the loudest, deepest voice he could muster. "We're both hurt! Coming in, don't shoot! Don't shoot!"

Stumpy took a prone shooting position on the deck with the riot gun. Freeman, still reeling despite stims from the first aid kit, watched their rear.

Tanner threw the wheel and pulled open the hatch. Stumpy immediately opened fire.

Two engineers fell to the deck in bloody heaps before Tanner came around the hatch. He sprayed bullets without really looking for targets, worried only about finding an emergency engineering panel in his line of sight. Everyone in the compartment dove for cover.

Tanner found the panel up against one of the giant metal machines housing the ship's main power plants. When he was first taught about emergency engineering procedures, he'd thought it was silly to put shutdown controls out in the open. Nobody needed a key. Nobody needed a code. Anyone could come in and turn a ship's engines off.

Morales had called him stupid for asking about it. The point, Morales said, was to make sure *anyone* could quickly shut down the engines in an emergency. Why would anyone want emergency procedures to be complicated? Why would you want panicking crewmembers to have to think much when seconds made the difference between surviving and exploding? Keeping it simple meant that any idiot could shut down the engines. Even an idiot like Tanner.

In that moment, Tanner could hardly argue Morales's estimation of his intelligence. He lunged forward through bullets and laser fire, diving for the big red button that any idiot could see. Even an idiot who'd caught a bullet in the ribs and a blast across his leg.

• • •

She was going to get away. Harper was good at math; ops specialists had to be. Even without the computer calculating everything for him, Harper could see where this would end. *Sarah's Dream* was too close to the edge of Ophanim's gravity well and still accelerating. She could reasonably risk a jump within another minute. *St. Jude* wouldn't be there in time.

Understanding their imminent failure didn't calm Harper's nerves at all. The freighter was still in weapons range and still shooting. Reed's cool hands at the helm coupled with the corvette's evasion programs had prevented further serious hits so far, but the freighter could still get lucky. Yet as the range opened up, the odds of getting hit decreased . . . and so did the odds that they'd ever see their shipmates again.

Then it all changed.

"XO!" Harper shouted. "She's stopped accelerating!"

"Confirm that!" the XO demanded over the comms channel.

"Confirmed, sir! She's cut her engines! We'll overtake in . . . twenty-six seconds!"

"Make sure we don't shoot past too fast," Gagne instructed from *St. Jude*'s main cannon. "I don't want to fuck this up."

• • •

"Engineering!" Ming roared in a near panic. "They're in fucking engineering! Get 'em now, now!"

It was too late. He knew it was too late. Even if the boarders were cleared out of engineering, even if there were still snipes down there alive and able to get the engines running again, they'd never rebuild enough acceleration to escape the corvette.

"She's about to overtake, Ming!" warned Kiyoshi.

"Shoot her!" the exasperated captain demanded.

"We're trying, but—"

Ming never heard the rest. *St. Jude* flew past his bridge canopy, close enough to actually see with the naked eye.

Yaomo, he realized, had gotten screwed. Again.

Then the corvette's main guns flashed with vengeful red light, and a moment later *Yaomo*'s entire bridge compartment was gone.

ELEVEN

Is This All There Is?

"That girl was a moron to pass up on you."

"Hm?"

"Back home. You know. Madelyn."

Staring up at the darkness until now, Tanner turned his head to look at Alicia's face. He couldn't make out much. The hotel room offered few amenities, but after all they'd been through in basic, the bed felt luxurious.

"Why are you thinking about her? I'm not," Tanner said, and meant it. He kissed the side of her neck. Two hours at a salon made an amazing difference for her. Tanner had found her cute with a buzz cut, but a few inches of hair made her quite pretty. He'd hardly been able to take his eyes off her.

The darkness prevented him from having another good look, but he'd had other ways to appreciate her in the last few hours.

"Hey, Tanner," Alicia began. He heard a hesitant frown in her voice. "You're not . . . I'm not saying I don't really like you, but you're not gonna get . . . you know I'm not looking for some forlorn long-distance thing, right?"

"Oh, I know." He tried to sound practical.

"If we were going to the same place, it'd be different. But I don't want you waiting around for me. I'm so happy to have this until we ship out. It's just that when we do . . . I still want to be friends, y'know? I still want to stay in touch. I just don't want it to get weird."

He took a deep breath, releasing it slowly. "No, I don't, either," he said. "You don't have to worry about that."

"So you're not gonna freak out?"

"No."

"Even if I start seeing somebody?"

"What, you've got somebody on Los Angeles *in your sights already?"*

Alicia snorted and gave him a shove. "No, you dork."

"Okay, but as long as it's a navy guy. Marines are jerks." She shoved him again. "Violent, too." He laughed.

"Says a guy who punched me in the face."

"One time! One time I got a good shot in. How many times have you kicked my ass?"

"Don't try to change the subject," she teased. "You punched a sweet, innocent girl right in the face just because she was in your way when you wanted to beat up someone else. You're all sweet and harmless and nice, but as soon as you've got the right motivation, bam. Right in the face."

Tanner sighed and tried not to dwell on it. "That was our subject?"

"No," she said. He felt her smile against his collarbone. "We were talking about other girls who could've been with you but weren't. 'Cause they were morons."

"Yeah, well. You're making that decision based on limited information. You don't know what the competition was like."

"I don't think I'd be impressed." Alicia pushed him down onto his back, sliding up on top of him. "Pretty sure I got the best of the bunch right here."

Her kisses grew hotter, as did her touch. Tanner grinned. "I'm not sure how much good I am at this point."

"I have faith," she countered softly. "Like I said . . . I know what you're capable of when you're properly motivated."

She was right.

Somewhere in the back of his mind, Tanner was still troubled by the memory of punches and kicks, of rage and blood. Her touch made short work of such worries.

His troubles almost faded away before the alarm clock beeped.

His eyes opened. The ceiling was no longer so dark, nor was it that of a hotel room. The bed was not so luxurious. No lithe, warm, affectionate companion lay against him.

He smelled spilt beer. Heard the distant sound of reveille playing over speakers outside the building. Saw the flashing light accompanying the alarm on the other end of the room and then saw it stop.

Tanner heard a groan and then a shuffle. Heifer rolled out of his bed across the room from Tanner, scratching his ass and letting out a belch on his way into the bathroom.

He was used to waking up to such things lately. Ordinarily, he just rolled his eyes and tried to laugh off Heifer's boorishness. He usually reminded himself that this was only temporary. Coming out of dreams and memory, though, Tanner could only shut his eyes and fight back the water trying to escape.

• • •

Widespread chaos made it difficult to keep up. Darren wasn't exactly trying; Jerry put out all the effort. The big pirate practically dragged Darren along through bright streets as people hustled to and fro, waving down vehicles or carrying hastily bundled belongings any way they could.

Darren would've been fine with them all leaving. Fuckers could all bail on the planet for all he cared, as long as he could go back to bed until his head stopped pounding.

"Jerry, stop," Darren complained. "Goddamn, man. I don't even have my boots on."

"I've got your boots, and your stupid fifty-grand combat jacket," Jerry said, waving the bundle in his face. "Look, you've got your gun belt, your holocom, and your money, right? Fuck the rest."

"The rest? What the hell, man? Wha's goin' on?"

"I told you. Ming's ship got pinched."

"Wha—" Darren asked. He tried to open his eyes to see if Jerry was kidding, but the sun made that uncomfortable. Darren had photoreactive contacts for that, but he hadn't time to put them in. Come to think of it, he didn't even know where the hell they were.

"*Yaomo*, remember? *Yaomo* got nailed."

"*Yaomo*? But they left. Weeks ago."

"Yeah, and they got caught weeks ago, and we only just now got the news."

Someone jostled past Darren. He almost lost his footing, but Jerry kept him up. "Assholes," Darren slurred. He looked at Jerry again. "So what's that got to do with us?"

"Means the party's over, buddy. There's no telling what those assholes will say under interrogation or what's in the ship's computers. We gotta bug out before someone decides to throw a fleet at us. We're lucky it hasn't happened already."

"Aw, hey, fuck that, man," came Darren's plaintive, sleepy reply. "I've still got so much fuckin' money to spend. Party's not over, man."

Jerry just grumbled under his breath. "All part of being a pirate. Come on," he said, towing the younger man along.

"Man," Darren fumed, "bein' a pirate sucks."

• • •

"It's a big day for you," said Chaplain Corleissen.

"Yeah." Tanner's gaze stayed on the painting of the helmsman with Jesus at his side, one hand on the troubled youth's shoulder. "I guess."

The chaplain let the silence linger. He was a young officer, well built and sharp in his dress uniform. Corleissen sat in a chair beside the couch, giving the young crewman his undivided attention.

"You know what you're getting?" Corleissen asked.

"Blood stripes. Purple Heart. Silver Cross."

"Not many non-rate crewmen going around with those," Corleissen pointed out. "Not many servicemen in general, really."

"Silver Cross is for gallantry."

"Mm-hm."

"Is that what I did?" Tanner ventured, glancing at Corleissen. "Was that gallantry?"

The chaplain smiled gently. His face was made to smile. "I can only assume you've already looked up the definition, so why don't you tell me?"

"I killed nine people."

"You did."

"I'd never been in a fight before I enlisted. My stepmother freaked out about me enlisting. She didn't want me getting brainwashed and turned into a killer. I worried about that, too. I was even afraid to hit people while sparring. Now here I am. Killed nine people. Directly contributed to the deaths of several more. Twenty-two, all told."

"We could talk about what they did to contribute to their own deaths," the chaplain noted gently. "But we've done that, haven't we?"

"Yeah."

"It shouldn't be on your shoulders, Tanner. You're no monster. It's good that you don't take this lightly. But you have to consider the whole situation."

Tanner shook his head a little. "That's not what bothers me. I mean, yeah, there's that, but . . . I killed nine people."

"Out of an entire crew who'd have murdered you without a second thought."

"Yeah." Tanner huffed. "That's kind of what I'm thinking about." He fell silent, nudging the carpet with one foot. "You know what pirates used to do to people in the age of sail?"

"All kinds of horrible things, I'd imagine."

The younger man nodded. "Still do that today, too. But they used to . . . they'd take a rope and wrap it around someone's head, and then put a stick through the back and twist it to tighten the rope 'til it fractured the skull. Made the victim's eyes pop out." Corleissen said nothing, waiting instead for Tanner to go on. "It was called 'woolding.' Happened enough that they needed a word for it, y'know?"

"I suspect they learned that from the Inquisition," Corleissen put in finally. "I seem to remember reading about that one before."

"Yeah." Tanner nodded. "Think so. People do things like that in the name of religion."

"All sorts of horrible things are done in the name of religion. Or for money, or freedom, or love. Lots of causes, good and bad."

"Sure." Tanner gestured to the painting of Christ and the crewman. "Is that what paintings like that are for?"

"Yes, probably," Corleissen admitted with a bit of a scowl. "It was here when I transferred in last month. I've been meaning to take it down. I thought that maybe I was being a bit too cynical, though, so I hesitated . . . but I guess I'm not the only one who makes that connection."

Tanner shook his head. "Not really what's on my mind. I just . . . they tortured people on Qal'at Khalil. That prince turned himself over to protect his people and the hospitals, and they said, 'Joke's on you, we didn't say we wouldn't torture people.' Didn't say how many people they'd murder. Or kidnap."

"You've been reading about this."

"Whole week in the hospital, two more on light duty. I've had time. You know how many rapes were reported out of Qal'at Khalil? Off the *Aphrodite*?"

"One would be too many, I'd think."

"Got that right." Tanner frowned. "I mean, there are women on these pirate ships. Women who just let that slide. Don't care. Probably even laugh about it."

"What did you want to talk about, Tanner?"

"These people are capable of doing all that," he said, his voice cracking. "What do you think they'd have done to me?"

"We know what they tried to do to you. And your shipmates. We know what they did to Leone. You stopped them from doing more."

"Huh. Yeah. My shipmates. Listen to how I ask that. I'm worried about what they'd do to *me*, not *us*."

"It's no crime to think about yourself."

"I'm not sure I thought about anyone else."

"Bo'sun's Mate Freeman might argue that. His wife might, too. You did all you could for your shipmates. No one thinks you did anything less. Certainly not Leone's family. I've spoken with them several times."

Tanner snorted. "Maybe. I mean, obviously I didn't want him to be hurt. Any of them. I don't like 'em, but . . ." His voice trailed off. Again, he shook his head. "I was saving my own ass."

"No one has any illusions about that."

"Oh bullshit," Tanner said to the floor. "I've seen this on the news. Heard 'em say my name. Read it a few times. Not once do they talk about what a great job Tanner Malone did of saving his own ass."

"Are you angry about that?"

"Guess not." He shrugged. "It's what I was doing when I enlisted in the first place."

"You had to know the risks when you signed up. At least on an intellectual level."

"Yeah, but there's knowing it intellectually, and then there's actually facing it."

Chaplain Corleissen allowed Tanner more silence. They'd met several times since the incident. Corleissen quickly realized that Tanner wasn't used to living in a shell. He probably never had one before he'd arrived on *St. Jude*. Drawing him out of that shell wasn't so hard; all anyone had to do was listen.

"I'm scared. I'm really scared. I had a dream last night. This morning. Whatever. There was this girl in basic, and she and I hit it off, and after basic and during weapons we spent our liberties together. She's on *Los Angeles* now. She wrote me two months ago to say she's got a new boyfriend. I'm not bothered by it. I'm happy for her. But I had this dream about our first night together, and then I woke up to Heifer scratching his ass and the room stinks and my ribs still hurt from where I got shot, y'know?

"I'm still *here*. I haven't even been here all that long. All the accidents that have almost killed me have been bad enough. Shit goes missing from my locker. Being the punching bag for the crew just sucks . . . but those people would've murdered me. Maybe done worse."

He tried to control his lower lip, going so far as to put a finger over it, but gave it up. "I'm scared. I've *been* scared, but now . . .

"And now they're gonna pin a medal on me. Third highest medal the navy has, y'know?" Tanner looked at Corleissen, who gave only the slightest nod of agreement. "They had to have stupid discussions on whether pirates count as a legitimate enemy of the state. Had to discuss whether the Silver Cross is appropriate. If it's too high."

"Those discussions happen." Corleissen shrugged. "I wouldn't place much stock in it."

"I don't. They've got standards to maintain or whatever. I get that. I don't care about the medal, sir. That's not the point."

"What is the point?"

"It's the third highest medal, sir. 'Conspicuous gallantry.' I killed nine people and got a bunch of others killed. Leone *died*, and all he gets is blood stripes and a Purple Heart. So here I am scared out of my mind . . . and I keep thinking, if that's what you do for the third highest medal, what's a guy supposed to do for number one? How many people are you supposed to kill for that?"

Corleissen didn't respond. Kill counts weren't the point, or even a necessary factor, but Tanner plainly knew that. He'd read too much not to know better.

"I'm so scared that I'm gonna die out there and that's gonna be it. No university. No girlfriend. Never see my parents again. Just those . . . just the people on my ship.

"I don't think I belong here."

• • •

"This could all be a bunch of bullshit, man!" The muscular pirate faced his comrades with his arms held wide and his chest bared by his open vest. His forceful voice quieted much of the muttering in the cargo bay.

"Hey!" Lauren barked to silence the rest. "Let Turtle speak!"

The bearded man threw her a grateful nod, then turned back to the crowd. "We don't really know anything about how *Yaomo* got pinched. You honestly think they released the whole story to the media?"

"We know they got her and figured out her name!" someone shouted.

Turtle waved his hands dismissively. "They might've blown her up and figured that out just from the wreckage. My point is, why should we assume that they know we're here? Or anything else?"

"It doesn't matter what they know," countered Casey. He stood amid the hundreds of pirates brought together for the vote. With the danger of a raid considered so imminent, there was no chance of a regular pre-voyage assembly on the other side of the planet. No one provided free booze or food this time. Every pirate not vitally needed at a ship's station crammed into *Vengeance*'s cargo bay. Those standing watches had holocom channels open to hear the meeting and cast their vote.

"It doesn't matter if we think they made all this up or if we think they opened up her astrogation logs and Ming's guys spilled their guts. The point is our suppliers think this planet is compromised. The Tongs are pulling out. The independent fences are leaving. Every whore that can pay or fuck his or her way onto a ship is getting the hell out of here. Paradise is shot, Turtle. Pretty soon it'll all just be underdeveloped real estate and a couple empty buildings.

"We've got to figure out where we want to go from here. We'll figure out a new port to call home sooner or later. Right now we need to pick a course and go, and there's no way to do that but put it to a vote."

His gaze swept the quieted crew. Turtle scowled darkly at him. "I'm sorry, buddy." Casey shrugged. "I can't keep everyone else on Paradise from pulling up stakes."

"Well, where the hell do we go, then?" someone else called out.

"Look, we can put some specific options together for you in a bit," Casey offered. "Pick a few people who want to come up with some options—"

"Jesus fuck, Casey, you want us to form a committee?" another voice yelled. Laughter ensued. Ordinarily Casey would have laughed, too, but at the moment he was too stressed to appreciate absurdities.

"Look, you got a better idea?" Casey snapped. "All we gotta do is come up with some options, all right? Let's not complicate it. I suggest that we lie low for a while until we find out if what happened with *Yaomo* makes anyone ambitious about hunting pirates."

"Are you kidding?" Turtle scoffed. "Fuck that. Hell, if I've gotta be on a ship, I want to make money, not run around with my tail between my legs."

"He's got a point," said Jerry, who stood amid the throng of pirates. Many others nodded in agreement. "A lot of us have to leave stuff behind here. Ain't like everyone can pack up all their baggage and furniture and shit and stow it on the ship."

Casey opened his mouth to counter that. Setting up houses and retirement plans on a pirate planet was stupid to begin with. Before he could say such a thing, though, he caught sight of Lauren. She had a holo screen up in front of her. He couldn't read the thing from here, but he knew a spreadsheet when he saw one.

He had encouraged her investment in the Palace. He told her it was good to find ways to grow her money rather than piss it all away like most of their comrades always did.

She had ways to protect her investment. He knew that much, though he didn't know details. Lauren had some sort of bailout arrangement with her business partners who actually ran the place. She was smart. She could think like a businesswoman, rather than just another shortsighted, greedy pirate.

Only investors didn't see the end of an investment as a finite tough break. They projected out future earnings. Any disruption of those future earnings—money they hadn't even made yet—was in their minds money they lost.

Lauren wasn't looking at how much money she had salvaged, Casey knew. When she looked up at him, all he saw was her anger at how much she'd been robbed.

Casey wanted to take his ship out of harm's way until the waters settled again. He knew, looking in the eyes of his respected quartermaster, that he wouldn't win that debate.

• • •

Presumably, some manual somewhere dictated the etiquette for large-scale awards ceremonies. It wasn't the sort of thing that Tanner would hunt down; even his bibliophilia had limits. Neither pageantry nor stage management ranked highly among his interests. Yet on that windy day on Port Augustine's parade ground, with bright lights shining everywhere to hold back the planet's perpetual night, and with the assembled ships' crews and support personnel lined in disciplined ranks and with their families seated on bleachers facing a well-lit stage, Tanner wished he had known what to expect and when.

The day celebrated much more than *St. Jude*'s moment of glory. Port Augustine's ships and personnel had been through quite a year even before Tanner arrived. There was plenty of recognition to go around. *St. Martin* had made record-breaking contraband seizures. *Resolute* had outshined all other destroyers in joint maneuvers with the Union fleet. *St. Patrick* had saved a freighter from a cascading fuel core meltdown. They all received outstanding unit citations, as did several support divisions on the base.

Though Leone's funeral had been over a week ago, his bio was still read. The base observed a moment of silence for his passing. Then the emcee returned to business.

Tanner soon realized that units had been arranged in alphabetical order. He expected *St. Jude* would get a unit citation for her refugee rescues. But then the CO of the base moved on to individual awards. Standing at the back of *St. Jude*'s two rows of men, Tanner glanced over toward Stevens up at the front. If his captain felt slighted, his body language didn't show it.

Later, he would regret not paying more attention to the rest of the ceremony. Somebody received a medal for saving two lives in a fire. Someone else was recognized for logistical feats to aid newly arriving Hashemite refugees. Tanner considered this all to be more laudable than what he had done. Mostly he thought about the awful kink in his left shoulder blade from standing at parade rest for over two hours.

His feet hurt. His collar itched. The wind, the fabric of his pants, and the hair on his legs combined to create a field of static electricity that probably could've powered every light on the parade field. Why anyone would want to make a career of this life was beyond him.

"Junior Lieutenant John Gagne, front and center," said the base CO on the stage, snapping Tanner from his disgruntled day-dreams. He watched Gagne fall out of the front row of *St. Jude*'s crew, do a right face, and then march steadily toward the stage. Tanner made a note of his path, wishing there'd been a rehearsal or something. Barely nine months after graduating basic training, Tanner had all but forgotten how to march.

Nine months since basic. Fifteen months in total since his enlistment had begun. Tanner's memory drifted to the sign above the exit to Squad Bay Oscar: "Time Passes." Just the same, he didn't enjoy thinking about how much longer he'd be at his first duty station.

". . . directed pursuit from *St. Jude*'s main cannons, personally firing them to destroy the bridge of the *Yaomo*," said the voice on the speakers. Tanner presumed this was still the base CO, but he was too far away to see. So many people stood on that platform. One of them was Gagne. The others were just nameless, faceless dress uniforms.

"With pursuit ended and having eliminated the pirates' command structure, Lieutenant Gagne made contact with *Yaomo*'s surviving crewmembers. Leveraging the achievements of *St. Jude*'s boarding team, Lieutenant Gagne forced the unconditional surrender of the remaining crew. Despite battle casualties, all of Lieutenant Gagne's personnel continued to perform throughout the incident. Lieutenant Gagne's leadership, composure, and expert ship handling serve as outstanding examples of the finest traditions of the Archangel Navy. He is hereby awarded the Silver Cross."

Applauding offered the only break from Tanner's stance. It was his sole opportunity to move his hands from behind his back, and he made as much use of it as he could. He rolled his shoulder all the while. Then he resumed parade rest as Lieutenant Gagne returned and Reed was called forward.

Several of Tanner's shipmates were decorated that day. Awards were announced by rank, meaning he'd be dead last. Reed won a Bronze Cross for his performance at the helm. Flores and Freeman went up together for their Purple Hearts. Stumpy was named for a minor citation, but no medal and no moment on stage. Then he heard, "Crewman Tanner Malone, front and center."

Despite knowing all along he'd have to go up there, his heart stopped. He hesitated. Tanner took a step back, put the wrong foot behind the other for an about face, corrected, turned, and then led off with his right foot instead of his left like he was supposed to, silently calling himself an idiot the entire time.

The CO, or appointed emcee or whoever—he'd never actually met anyone from base command—spoke as Tanner approached the stage. He repeated the same opening narrative about the date of the incident, *St. Jude*'s callout and her shorthanded crew. Tanner focused on not tripping over his feet.

"Though technically not yet qualified as a boarding team member on *St. Jude*'s roster," the high-ranking officer read from his script, "Crewman Malone volunteered to go across in order to address gaps at critical ship's stations."

He makes it sound like I planned it all out, Tanner thought. He got a good look at the speaker. The older man wore a single admiral's star. *Must be the base CO*, he figured. Yet there were two other admirals present. One was a man, the other a woman. The man had two stars. The woman had *five*.

Tanner's heart stopped. He had no idea who all these other officers were, but he immediately recognized fleet Admiral Yeoh.

The CO said something about Tanner fighting off the pirate ambush, including something about hand-to-hand struggles. It sounded official and dignified. Not much of it registered. He stood face-to-face with the highest-ranking officer of the Archangel military and a genuine war hero.

She gave a subtle smirk, tilted her head ever so slightly to her left, and then seemed to gesture with her eyes. Tanner remembered where he was again. He made a right face, turning toward the assembled crews.

He heard that he provided first aid to his team leader despite his own wounds. Something about drawing on training from weapons and tactics school. Something about assessing the situation. Rallying his comrades. Leadership. Initiative. Something about finest traditions. Blood stripes, Purple Heart, Silver Cross.

Oh my God. That's Admiral Yeoh.

She stepped in front of him with a tight smile that seemed professional and genuine. Yeoh clipped two little medals onto his chest, then offered her hand. "Congratulations, Crewman Malone," she said.

He shook her hand. "Thank you, ma'am."

Her smile remained. "Don't forget to salute," she murmured helpfully.

He blinked. Oh God. He absolutely would've forgotten. He saluted. The other admirals stepped up and shook his hand in turn, and he saluted each of them, and later wondered if he was supposed to do that or if he'd been a moron.

Tanner moved to return to his crew. His nice, safe, utterly unfriendly but predictable crew. "Crewman Malone," Yeoh said, "wait a moment."

"Aye, aye, ma'am," he replied, grateful to at least step back out of the way. The CO brought the ceremony to a close and instructed commanders to take charge of their personnel.

"At ease, crewman," she said. Tanner took a deep breath and rolled his aching shoulders. Out beyond the stage, the formal rows broke up and family members left the bleachers to join their loved ones.

"Are you nervous?" she asked.

"Yes, ma'am."

"More nervous than you were in combat?"

"I didn't have time to think about it then, ma'am. I had plenty of time here."

She nodded, still smiling. "Lengthy ceremonies like this can do that to you. When I was at the Academy, I stood through inspections with my knees locked and passed out. Twice."

Tanner smiled back a little. He appreciated her attempt at sounding like an ordinary mortal.

Yeoh turned to an aide to retrieve from him a set of envelopes. "I have a couple of things I'd like you to give your XO," she said, handing them to him. "He'll know what to do with them. These, however, are for you."

He looked down at the envelopes. They were made of rich paper, embossed all along the corners with geometric designs. All were sealed with wax. Tanner's bore his name in gold script. They didn't look remotely military. "What are they, ma'am?"

"They're letters," the admiral said, "from Prince Khalil of the Kingdom of Hashem, and from his father, the king. I understand they both wanted to express their thanks for having brought some of the pirates who attacked the Kingdom to justice."

Tanner looked up at her with wide eyes. The admiral gave a small shrug. "I imagine the letter from the king was written by an aide, but I'm sure he signed it. The prince's is probably a bit more personal in nature."

When he found his voice again, Tanner mumbled, "Thank you, ma'am."

"I understand you had some trepidation about being decorated today?"

He glanced around nervously, spotting Chaplain Corleissen not too far away. "I'm sorry, ma'am? I don't know what you mean. I'm just . . . I'm standing way above my pay grade here, ma'am."

"Don't blame the chaplain, crewman," she said. "Archangel hasn't awarded a Silver Cross in thirteen years. Certainly not one during my tenure as CNO. I took more than a little personal interest in this. So again," she said, tilting her head just a bit, "I understand you're uncomfortable."

"A little," Tanner admitted. "Yes, ma'am."

"You should be. I was."

He couldn't help but notice just how many ribbons she wore, denoting medal after medal. "Every time, ma'am?"

"They don't pull some of these things out of the boxes unless people have died," she noted soberly. "Do you know why we do this? Why we hand out medals and such?"

There was no venom or sarcasm in his voice as he answered, "I imagine it's something to do with recognition or esprit de corps, ma'am."

"There's a more practical side. The uniform is meant to tell a story, Crewman Malone. It tells the observer who the serviceman is and where he stands in the chain of command, but more importantly, it tells what he can *do*. This is why we wear the blood stripe, even on vac suits. It's to let those around you know that you can be depended on. That regardless of your rank, you know what you're doing.

"And yes," she added, "there is recognition. You had a terrible day, Crewman Malone. An awful lot went wrong on your ship and on that mission, but you and Lieutenant Gagne did the right things to get through it. You damn sure do deserve to be recognized."

Tanner didn't know what to say. He opted for the obvious: "Thank you, ma'am."

Again, she offered that quiet, professional smile. "Report back to your crew. You're dismissed," she said and sharply returned his salute before he left.

He was stopped and congratulated more than once on his way across the parade field. Tanner found that he had to keep the bundle of letters in his left hand so he'd have his right free for salutes and handshakes. It was a bit bewildering; he was used to being anonymous on the base and suspected that after today he'd go right back to it. Ultimately the biggest challenge of life on *St. Jude* and at Port Augustine was the lack of friends and social acceptance. He wondered how much of that would change.

He wondered, considering what he'd done to "earn" this day, if he could accept that without resenting himself.

Tanner found his shipmates milling around in their spot on the parade ground. None had been dismissed to meet family members or get changed out of their dress uniforms. "There he is, sir," Freeman noted to the captain, nodding Tanner's way.

Tanner saluted the captain and XO as they turned. "Sorry, sir," he said, "you weren't holding anything up for me, were you?"

"We held up for Admiral Yeoh," the captain grunted. "Don't worry about it." He gestured for Tanner to join the others in a conversational circle. "So now that this is over with, I wanted to say again that I'm sorry this all happened when I wasn't around to see it through with you, but I'm proud of you all. I think we've all learned some things from this incident about what we could do better. We need to tighten things up on this ship.

"And on that note," he said, "Miller, your captain's mast is on Monday. Dismissed."

TWELVE

Breaking Point

"Paid an awful lot for this intel." Lauren's sober observation had been repeated many times already in recent days. She didn't seem tired of it yet. Nobody else did, either.

"The crew voted their approval," grunted Casey. "Good intel isn't free." Casey stood on the bridge staring at the holographic projection of *Vengeance*'s sensor bubble. The closest contacts moved in and out of Augustine, all many light-minutes away. No patrols appeared anywhere.

"I know," said Lauren. "I'm just hopin' it pays off. We've been sitting out here for a good while."

"You think we're better off wandering around hoping we catch a random freighter?" snapped the captain. "The crew wanted to come to Archangel and kick someone in the balls. We're here, aren't we? They wanted another cruise liner. I'm making it happen, aren't I? Fucking rich people get to make their own schedule. If they want the ship to run late, it'll run fucking late."

Lauren held up her hands in a sign of peace. "Hey, I'm not trying to give you a hard time. Just antsy." She rarely saw Casey get irritable, and wouldn't have taken that from much of anyone else. Ordinarily, she wouldn't have taken it from Casey, either.

As if to show he knew it, he let out a sigh. "Sorry. Not pissed at you."

"You are, though." She shrugged. "You thought coming out here was a bad idea. You spoke against it."

"I'm making it happen," he repeated.

"You sound like a parent who's gotta break the budget on Christmas to keep the kids happy."

That got a rumble out of Casey, but not quite a laugh. "I just don't want anyone thinkin' we're gonna get to do this a third time. We pull this off, the only smart thing to do is to get our asses on the other side of the Union and stay there for *years*. Maybe even farther out than that. Sooner or later we're gonna go too far and the fat cats won't find this shit funny anymore. They'll run us down, Lauren. We can't keep coming back to the same hunting grounds. You know that, right?"

"I do," she said. "One more score out here, then we find new pastures. I'll back you." The pair fell silent, watching the sensor bubble and its complete lack of activity. Their prey was almost seven hours late. Other pirates in the crew had to know that. Some doubtlessly had to wonder if their prey would appear at all.

"Seems like you need to blow off some steam," observed Lauren. Again, the captain merely grunted. "Maybe we should swap over once they heave to. You take the boarders over. I'll run the bridge."

"That's a huge change," noted Casey. He couldn't hide his interest.

"So we'll put it to a vote. We're pirates. Fuck the rules."

• • •

"Two minutes to drop to sublight," announced Sarah Woo at the ops station. "Chief Steward, please notify our passengers."

"Aye, aye, ma'am," came the response.

Captain Aaron Kennedy listened to the routine on his bridge from his chair. *Pride of Polaris* was a good ship. Over the last few years, she had come to live up to her name. She was the highest-rated ship in NorthStar's luxury liner fleet across all indicators. She was no longer the biggest or most opulent, but Kennedy found that having a little competition only sharpened the diligence and discipline of his ship's officers. He pushed them as a good captain should, but moreover, they pushed themselves.

Smirking at the thought, Kennedy buzzed up his new chief of passenger relations. "Katie," he said, "just so you know, you'll get some angry comm calls in a moment."

"Is something wrong, sir?" In the background, Kennedy heard the band playing in the ship's main ballroom.

"No, everything's running fine. But someone always loses their lunch at a time like this."

"Certainly, sir." She smiled at him patiently. "This isn't my first rodeo."

"No, of course not"—Kennedy agreed—"nor mine. Which is why I'm about to route all my passenger communications directly to you. Have a nice night." With that, he cut the channel and input the commands into his personal comm tracker to do just as he said.

Rich people always wanted to go straight to the top when they were upset. A newer, more nervous captain on a luxury liner typically accepted that rather than deferring it to a subordinate. Kennedy was over all that.

He'd missed the one-minute warning, but didn't worry. Kennedy knew his crew could handle this even if he'd magically vanished from the bridge. He looked up, saw the clock, and gave the nod to Woo at ops. The *Pride* fell out of FTL with a brief, gentle lurch that surely upset delicate stomachs and more delicate sensibilities across the ship.

Most commercial ships had rougher drops. Military ships were typically even more jarring. Kennedy considered the *Pride* to be the smoothest ride he'd ever been on, but naturally some wealthy passengers expected to feel nothing at all.

Kennedy leaned to his right, looking over his shoulder toward Woo as she reviewed the data from the ship's sensors. "Internal systems all functioning normally. Astrogation looks good. One contact, bearing three-four-three mark three-two-seven, eighty-eight thousand clicks. Destroyer class. CDC transponder codes."

"She's hailing us," announced Bert at comms.

"CDC?" asked Kennedy. "I thought Archangel kicked them out of the system last month after they got caught letting pirate ships slide right through inspections?"

"She's giving the usual request for inspection, sir," Bert elaborated.

"Maybe they patched things up?" Sarah suggested.

"Or maybe CDC's just trying to assert themselves." Kennedy shrugged. "Can't have some random state telling a big corporate heavyweight like them who's boss. Anyway, signal our compliments and heave to per instructions. I'm sure this won't take but a couple minutes. Even they won't want to make our passengers unhappy."

• • •

He almost didn't get to see her at all. Tanner requested leave right when he learned weeks ago of the UFS *Fletcher*'s scheduled port call. He marked out a three-day window to allow for schedule changes. Morales denied it, of course, despite *St. Jude* having a full crew. Morales even refused to justify himself for it.

Stevens kept *St. Jude* on ready-alert status, able to jump into space within an hour's notice for the slightest job. Even in port, Morales came up with bullshit make-work projects for Tanner and the other non-rates.

Fletcher had been in orbit for a full twenty-one hours when *St. Jude* returned from an unscheduled patrol. The Union fleet battleship's officers and crewmen were still largely ashore on liberty, but the clock was running out. *Fletcher* would head out again in hours. Tanner literally ran from the flight line once liberty was announced. He knew the neighborhood she was in. He knew the restaurant. He ran.

Madelyn laughed when he hugged her. She wore civilian attire, her hair cut shorter than before but still feminine and flattering. She said something about the charges for assaulting a midshipman, and told him he looked good, and held him tightly. They only had a couple of hours to spend together.

It was his first hug in nine months.

"God, it's nice to see you," Tanner said when he finally let her go.

Madelyn slapped him on the shoulder, shining her ever-present grin on him. "You look good. Wow. Hey. Take a seat with my friends. This is Tammy and Rick, from my class at the Academy. And no, you don't have to call anyone sir or ma'am."

Tanner shook hands and exchanged greetings with the two young midshipmen, themselves also in civilian attire. They looked bright. Healthy. Happy.

Madelyn took the seat next to Rick, who slipped his arm around her shoulders.

• • •

"Primary engines off-line!"

"Dorsal laser mounts out! I don't think anyone's alive in there!"

Kennedy blocked out further thoughts of the gunners. He couldn't spare the time. There were thousands more to think about. "Bert, is our signal getting out?"

"Negative, sir." The bridge shuddered again as another low-impact missile exploded just beyond it, plainly more for intimidation than to do damage. If the destroyer wanted to break the *Pride* in half, at this point she could do so at her leisure. "No response to our mayday. They must've deployed jamming drones. I'm hardly getting any incoming signals at all, and what I've got is so faint—"

He paused. Kennedy tore his eyes from the holographic display of the *Pride*'s vain flight from her pursuer to look at the comms officer. "She's hailing us again. They say if we surrender now, they'll cease fire."

Kennedy's eyes drifted down to the damage control screens. One column listed damaged or destroyed systems. The other displayed dozens of medical emergencies.

• • •

Casey looked from the sensor bubble to Lauren with a satisfied grin. "See that?" He jerked his thumb to the holographic icon of the luxury liner slowing down before them. "*That's* why I let Prince Khalil go home alive."

"These guys get the same deal?" she asked.

"What, these assholes?" Casey shrugged. "Fuck no."

• • •

"I think they like you," Madelyn observed as her companions moved out.

"I think Rick likes you," Tanner countered with a smirk. "A lot."

"Yeah, well . . ." Her voice trailed off. Madelyn tugged at a lock of her short hair. "It's a lot of work making sure we keep things within regs, but I think he's worth it."

Tanner glanced over his shoulder to verify that her classmates were gone. He couldn't find any particular faults with them. As much as he envied Rick, he had to admit that the midshipman seemed like a good guy. At the very least, Rick knew that the nicest thing he could do was to clear out and let Tanner speak with Madelyn alone for a while.

The revelation didn't leave Tanner feeling jealous. If anything, he was glad to see Madelyn with someone capable of empathy. Just the same, his old fantasies couldn't die without a little disappointment.

"You're having a good time out there, aren't you?"

"Yeah," Madelyn said, her smile growing wider. "Yeah, I am. We're gonna have our asses kicked by our instructors when we get back to Earth, of course, but that's academy life for you. This patrol was supposed to end a week ago. Most of our cadre went to specialty schools or shoreside billets for their summer apprenticeship stuff. They're probably all back at the Academy waiting for classes to start by now."

"Will being late hurt your standings?"

She shrugged. "Needs of the service, right? It's not our fault if our ship doesn't get us back to school on time. They warned us when we signed on that we'd have a lot of catch-up work to do if we got back late. I don't regret it. We've learned a hell of a lot out here. But you'd know that, right?"

"Yeah, I guess."

"Hey, don't be like that. Tanner, you're kicking ass. Literally and figuratively. They don't give out those medals to just anyone."

Tanner let out a groan and put his face in his hands. "Can we not talk about the medals? God, they've only made shit worse."

"How so?"

"Every day, someone asks me if I think I'm special now. They ask if I think I'm supposed to get out of work. Morales comes up with bullshit jobs for me and says I should be able to do them on my own since I'm such a master crewman. I get treated like I'm a giant burden on everyone for months, and now they act like I'm walking around with my nose in the air when I haven't said shit about any of it. Hell, I'm still just trying to keep my head *down*."

"Tanner, I dug up the reports," Madelyn said, reaching out from across the table to touch his wrist. "You saved your boarding team. That ship was caught because of you."

"I'd say tell that to my crew, but mostly I wish they'd just forget the whole thing," he grumbled. "It's like all I did was piss them off more. Made 'em look bad. I still get reminded over and over how much I suck at my job."

"I thought you said you were fully qualified now?"

"I am now," Tanner said, "about four months late, which everyone likes to point out. I barely qualified on a bunch of deck standards. Freeman and Morales both act like they only signed off on my training sheet because they had to, and half of that they only trained me for because they were *embarrassed* into doing it after the *Yaomo* incident. I might be qualified on paper, but that doesn't mean I'm qualified *enough*. I'm still the guy nobody talks to at chow. Still the guy stuck on watch in port on all the holidays."

Tanner let out a sigh. He didn't want to be all doom and gloom in front of Madelyn in the few hours they had together. He reached for something positive. "I got along fine with almost everyone in my recruit company. A lot of us are still in touch. The rest of the people on base treat me okay. But ships' crews and shore departments all tend to stick to themselves. It's not like we all hang out together." His voice fell off as he stared at his glass with a frown. "The only one who seems to like me at all is the XO. But, y'know. Officers and enlisteds, right?"

Madelyn's head tilted. "Your XO? Gagne, right?"

"Yeah."

"He also got a Silver Cross?"

Tanner nodded. He felt her give his wrist a squeeze.

"I think I know what your problem is, Tanner," she said, her voice turning a bit firm and sounding every bit as much like an officer as a friend. "I think you're surrounded by assholes."

"It's not that simple." He chuckled. "I can't just make it all about them."

"And you haven't, and you don't, but maybe that's the answer," Madelyn pressed. "You're still beating yourself up over bombing the Test, too, aren't you? Tanner, have you considered how badly that whole thing was rigged even before your parents pulled the rug out from under you? And do you honestly think these guys on your ship are being fair to you?"

"What, you want me to blame my problems on everyone else?" Tanner blinked. "I'm not gonna go looking for easy excuses."

"That's boot camp talking," Madelyn countered, shaking her head. "If you were the type to do that, you'd have made those excuses from the start. But you try your hardest every day, right? Have you done anything crappy to these guys? Insulted them? Taken anything for granted? I didn't think so. Tanner, anytime you've got a fair shot, you do just fine. It's only when the game's stacked against you that you're screwed."

"Not everything's a game," he mumbled.

"No, it's not," Madelyn agreed, looking as if he'd proven her point. "Sometimes you gotta throw the rule book out the window. I can name a whole ship full of pirates who know better than to play with you when there aren't any rules."

She made him grin. Tanner couldn't tell if it was what she had to say or if it was just her infectious spirit, but he smiled just the same.

Then his holocom went off. He knew the tone. It was a priority from *St. Jude*.

"Crewman Malone," he answered.

"Get your ass back here, boot," Morales said. "We're going out."

"On my way," Tanner responded. "What's up?"

"Does it fucking matter? Just move." Morales snapped with much more bitterness than urgency. With that, the channel cut out.

Tanner scowled. It wasn't as if Tanner's question was out of line; usually a call-out came with at least a few words of explanation. Morales had no reason to slam the door on Tanner like that other than the simple fact that he could.

"Wow," said Madelyn. "When I'm right, I'm right."

"I have to go." Tanner sighed as he got up. "Really wish I could stay with you more today."

"Hey, no worries," Madelyn said as she stood. "I'm glad I got to see you at all. Listen, Tanner . . . hang in there, okay? You're doing good. Don't let these jerks bother you." She put her arms around him once more.

Tanner hugged her back tightly. He had no idea when he'd get to hug anyone again.

• • •

"Son of a bitch is stalling," Jerry announced from his spot on the bridge.

"Of course he's stalling," scoffed Lauren. "Doesn't take twenty-five fucking minutes to link up two ships this size."

"What's he saying?" demanded Casey.

"Guy claims his maneuvering jet system shows all kinds of bugs from the damage we inflicted," Jerry replied. "Says they're firing at random and he needs time to have his people pull 'em off-line manually."

"Oh, for fuck's sake." Casey stomped over to Jerry's station and stabbed his finger at the mic button. "*Pride*, this is the captain of the ship that owns you now. Lemme talk to your captain."

There was a pause. Finally Casey heard, "This is Captain Aaron Kennedy."

"Yeah, sure you wanna go audio only," Casey grumbled to himself. He keyed the mic again. "Kennedy, you and I both know how many redundancies there are on your maneuvering systems. You've got one minute to get this linkup done. If it takes any longer than that, you're gonna watch me murder one of your crew for every minute I have to wait. Do you fucking understand me, you little shit?"

There was another pause. "Acknowledged," Kennedy said.

• • •

"Taking off in record time for a recall," noted Gagne with a bit of a grin.

Stevens didn't share his smile. "Can't hurt that Miller's still confined to the ship." He sat in the captain's chair with his eyes on a screen from his holocom as *St. Jude* escaped Augustine's atmosphere.

"Malone could've gotten back sooner," Morales grunted. He stood with his back to the bridge canopy, watching the sensor bubble dutifully.

"Sooner than fifteen minutes?" Gagne asked casually. "He was practically out of breath when he got here. I think you're a little too hard on him."

Morales bit his tongue. "Yes, sir."

"BM2, command didn't say anything more than this when they called?" Stevens asked. "You're sure?"

"Yes, sir, I'm sure." Morales turned to face the captain. "They just said they had a partial mayday call and the general coordinates. Said there wasn't another available ship to send out."

Stevens let out an irritated breath. He touched one of the many multicolored indicators on his holo screen. "*Pride of Polaris*, mayday," someone said through an awful lot of static. "We are . . . dest . . . location . . . several casualties . . . mayday . . ."

"They don't say anything about being under attack," Stevens thought aloud.

"They don't say they aren't, either," put in Gagne.

"No, they don't," the captain concurred. "Still. Computer says the *Pride* is a luxury liner run by NorthStar, so she'd be armed. Their arrival points are randomized. If someone was going to jump her, it'd have to be either amazing luck or amazing planning."

"Happened with *Aphrodite* last year."

"It did, but that was a year ago. What're the chances of the same thing happening in the same system twice? We'll go in ready for anything, but they've probably just had some sort of systems crash." Stevens turned to Morales. "Prep the cargo bay to send over damage control parties."

"Aye, aye, sir," said Morales before heading off the bridge.

"Reed, you have a course laid in for me?"

"More or less, sir," the astrogator mumbled. "We don't have an exact fix on the signal because of the interference. Best we can do is ballpark it. And we're still technically within the system."

"I'll take full responsibility for going FTL here," Stevens said. "Go ahead and log that and transmit it to command. How soon before we're fully clear of Augustine's gravity well?"

"Three minutes, sir."

Stevens keyed on the PA. "Attention all hands: let us pray."

• • •

Casey strode onto the liner's bridge and shot Captain Kennedy without a word. The bullet tore through Kennedy's midsection with an ugly explosion of blood, sending him staggering against the back of his captain's chair and then to the deck. Screams and yelps burst from the other uniformed men and women all around them.

"*Stupid* asshole!" Casey spat. The liner captain clung to life, though with great pain. Casey kicked him in the head repeatedly.

The other pirates watched their prisoners. Some of the *Pride*'s bridge crew witnessed Casey's brutality against their patient, skilled captain. Others couldn't bear to look.

"Oh, get a grip," Casey snapped at them, "he's not dead yet. You. You're the first mate, right? What's your name?"

"S-second mate. Woo. Sarah Woo," she answered as calmly as she could. Her boss and mentor lay bleeding out on the deck in front of her.

"Where's the first mate?"

"Dead. He's dead."

"Huh. Tough shit. Have you assembled the passengers on the promenade deck?"

"Yes. We've done all you asked of us. You didn't have to shoot him."

"Didn't have to?" Casey snapped. He stepped forward, bringing his face threateningly close to hers. "You're right, I didn't have to. I don't have to do any of this at all. Hell, I could get a fucking job and a wife and all that other bullshit. But clearly I'm not here to just do what I have to do, so maybe you'd better concern yourself with what I might do just 'cause I feel like it."

At that, a thought struck him. He spun around, looking over the bridge, and found the astrogation station manned by a young woman. "You're not the senior astrogator, are you?" he asked.

"N-no," she stammered.

"Good." Casey smiled. He snapped up his gun again and put a bullet through her leg. The young woman lurched over in shrieking pain. "That felt good," he said.

Casey gestured to a couple of fellow pirates, who dragged the bleeding captain off the bridge. Then he keyed up his holocom. "Chang," he said, "you guys in the engineering room yet?"

"We're here," came the response. "Wilson's looking over the engines now. He says we need some time to get things rolling again, but hopefully no longer than an hour or two."

Casey's mouth twitched. "Cutting it close," he muttered. He moved over to the holo projection of the *Pride*'s sensor bubble. They were over eight light-minutes away from Augustine. If the liner's distress calls made it out of the jamming field, any ship underway and ready to jump on the crisis would have arrived by now. Any ship taking off from the planet would need time to get itself together and launch, let alone cover the distance. An Archangel corvette could perhaps do all that within two hours, but *Vengeance* would overwhelm any corvette.

He turned his attention to his holocom again. "I know I don't have to tell any of you guys to hurry up," he said in a friendly tone, "but I'm gonna say it, anyway. We've got our asses out in the wind until this ship's ready to jump."

"Gotcha. Wilson and his guys are on it."

Casey cut the connection. This had been the plan all along: jump the liner outside of Augustine's immediate sensor range, fix her up, and do a short, simultaneous FTL run with *Vengeance* into deep space, and then wring every last cent out of the passengers before dumping them. All they needed was time to get the liner running again and for her passengers and crew to be kept cowed and compliant.

"This ship has retractable hull panels over its promenade, right? Gives you a big skylight window so people can look out at the stars or planets or whatever bullshit's out there?"

• • •

"Contact from drone delta," Jerry announced on the bridge of *Vengeance*. "Just dropped out of FTL, bearing zero-three-three mark zero-zero-nine, distance—"

"I see it," Lauren interrupted. She shifted from *Vengeance*'s sensor bubble to the bubble on the perimeter drone. The expensive drones offered an extended immediate bubble and a certain degree of information control. Deployed in a net around the *Vengeance*, they provided jamming interference for any signal within the sphere while continuously looking outward. Their presence meant that the newcomer likely hadn't detected *Vengeance* or the *Pride* . . . yet.

"Dial down the jamming on the drones," she ordered. "Helm, put us on the other side of the liner relative to that target. Do it delicately; don't break our tethers or the gangway tubes."

"She's an Archangel Navy corvette," someone said.

"Figured as much. Somebody get Casey on the line. Jerry?"

"Yeah, boss?"

"How's your manual targeting?"

• • •

"This is serious bullshit, man," grunted Stumpy as he dumped off another bag of equipment in the cargo hold.

"Seriously," Heifer concurred. He, too, was burdened with multiple canvas bags containing damage control gear.

Tanner waited for Heifer to get out of his way, then put down the bundle of tools and kits filling his arms. His helmet tumbled from its spot slung over his shoulder as he tried to set everything down. "I'd have an opinion," he huffed, "if I knew what the hell was going on."

"Doesn't fuckin' matter," Stumpy complained. "Should still be someone helping us carry all this shit. Would've been Leone if he wasn't dead."

"Yeah. He used to get it worse than you before you got here," Heifer agreed.

Tanner had almost tuned them out. "Wait, what?"

Stumpy and Heifer glanced at one another uncomfortably, but then Heifer just shrugged. "Just sayin', he was the one who caught all the shit before you did. I mean, it was all just pranks and teasing. You know. Harmless stuff."

"Harmless stuff," Tanner repeated.

"Yeah, what about it?" Stumpy asked. "New guy always gets shit on. It's not like he ever said anything about it."

"He never said . . . ?" Tanner didn't move. Ugly things roiled around in his stomach; he couldn't be sure if they were of anger, or guilt, or both. *Oh God*, he thought. *I never talked to Leone, either. He was so quiet.*

"Leone wasn't the newest on the ship before I got here," Tanner said quietly, staring at them both. "Wells was the newest. I know. I've looked. The newest guy was your drinking buddy, Wells."

"Yeah, but . . . Wells is cool." Stumpy shrugged.

Tanner's face set in a grimace. He felt a faint burning sensation across his shoulders, trailing down to his hands, which clenched into fists.

Bad enough that they treated him this way. Bad enough that Tanner had to live with it. But Leone died with it. Tanner never considered that someone else on the ship might suffer from the petty bullying and harassment.

The sound of footsteps cut off the conversation. Morales and Freeman appeared through the hatch. "Okay, so here's the deal," Freeman began. "We're responding to a garbled mayday. Captain thinks it's a ship having an internal emergency, which is why you're loading all this gear in here. We may have to send over damage control parties to help that ship."

"It's gonna be Stumpy, Heifer, and me outside if we do a linkup," Morales added, "because we don't have time for fucking around or puking or whatever."

Something inside Tanner snapped. "Well, thank God there's always time for you to be a *dick*."

• • •

"ANS *St. Jude*, we read you. This is CDCS *Osprey*. We are on scene and linked with NSS *Pride of Polaris*. She has suffered damage in an attempted pirate attack. We responded and the attackers fled. *Pride*'s comms are down. We are providing assistance. Over."

Jerry snorted as soon as Lauren's hand came off the mic. "You think they'll buy that?"

"For sixty seconds? Why not?" asked Lauren. "We've got transponders and markings. We've even got the right paint job."

"Lotta fun that was to put on," muttered a crewman.

"Worth the work if it saves your ass here," she countered. "Now shut the fuck up. Twenty ways this could go wrong. Jerry, how're they coming?"

"Turned and closing."

"Watch 'em as they get in weapons range."

"*Osprey*, this is *St. Jude*," came the response. "Acknowledge your status report. Request you open visual communication, over."

• • •

"CDC? They're supposed to be gone," Gagne noted after he unkeyed the mic.

"Supposed to be cleared out weeks ago," muttered Reed. "Could be they were transiting through on another job?"

"Sure looks like the liner took a pounding," observed Harper. He stood at the helm, watching the video screens intently as they closed in. "There's a debris field, too. Can't tell if the destroyer's been hit much."

"*St. Jude*, *Osprey*," said the woman's voice over the speakers. "Those bastards had deployed an ECM drone net to cut off transmissions. Still a few of 'em out here. Not all the static has cleared out of our systems yet."

Skeptical glances and frowns appeared across *St. Jude*'s bridge. Stevens didn't notice. He watched the range decrease. "Helm, stand by to cut speed," he ordered. "XO, tell 'em we'll link up to aid in recovery ops."

• • •

Heifer and Stumpy both looked on with mouths agape. Freeman was speechless.

"What did you just say, boot?" Morales growled. He stepped forward.

"You've been a dick to me since I came aboard for no discernible fucking reason," Tanner fumed. "I do my job. I'd do it better if you people would *teach* me, but instead I have to learn it practically all by myself. I do the best I can every fucking day, and all you do is scapegoat and bitch."

Heifer nudged Stumpy. "The fuck does 'discernible' mean?" he asked. His shipmate just shrugged.

• • •

Casey watched the direct feed to his holocom with growing tension. "That thing could fuck us up if she goes hot," he warned. "She'll be tricky to hit and she can punch back pretty hard for her size."

"I hear you, boss," Lauren said. "Stand by."

There was nothing else he could do. The pirate captain put his faith in his crew and watched in silence.

• • •

"We acknowledge your intentions, *St. Jude*," Lauren replied calmly over the comm. "Glad to have the help."

Her eyes stayed glued to the tactical screens. "We only get one real shot with this, Jerry," she warned. "Steady aim. Steady. You ready?"

"Soon as you take your hand off my shoulder, hon," Jerry replied coolly.

Lauren blinked. She pulled her hand away.

• • •

"Cap'n, it looks like their weapons are still hot," warned Reed.

"They said they're trying to bring down the remaining drones." Stevens shrugged.

"With the main cannon?"

Stevens blinked. He looked up from his screens through the canopy, where the liner and destroyer floated tens of thousands of kilometers away.

For a brief instant, the entire world around Stevens went red. Then it was gone.

• • •

"Tanner!" Freeman barked. "This is not the time for bullshit!"

"Tell that to him," Tanner snapped back. His eyes stayed on Morales. "What the fuck is your problem with me, anyway? What did I ever do to you?"

"I think those medals really did go to your head," Morales sneered. He stepped closer, providing a wordless reminder of just how much bigger and stronger he was than the young crewman. "You've got two seconds to apologize."

Tanner had no idea where he was going to go with this. There was nothing for it but to keep swinging. It was what he'd been taught. "I'm just sorry I can't think of anything worse to call you right now . . . *dick*."

The bigger man's eyes flared. Morales tensed at the shoulders, like a man who was about to either shout or throw a punch.

Bright-red light flashed through the compartment immediately behind Morales, so intense that Tanner couldn't see a thing through it. The light stretched from the deck to the overhead, blotting out everything behind Morales, including Stumpy and Heifer behind him and Freeman off to the big man's right. It lasted less than a second. In that time Tanner heard a terrible crackle, and then nothing.

In the blink of an eye, everything behind Morales became endless night.

Tanner watched in shock as Morales fell slowly away into the void.

THIRTEEN

Oscar's in the Water

Cheers erupted across the bridge on *Vengeance*. Casey heard them perfectly over his holocom. The scene on the bridge of the *Pride of Polaris* was somewhat less unified. Pirates hooted and hollered with bloodthirsty joy. Some of their prisoners wailed; others bowed their heads and wept.

"Jesus fucking Christ." Lauren laughed. "We wiped more than half of that thing right out of space."

"We see it, Lauren," replied Casey. He watched the wreckage on his video screen. Everything from the starboard wing to most of the corvette's center had all but disintegrated. The port wing and a portion of its fuselage rapidly drifted closer under the ship's original momentum, tumbling through space without anything left to control it. Casey thought he could even make out a body floating off on its own.

"Out-fucking-standing, all of you," Casey told her. "Damn good job. All right. Someone's gonna miss them on their communications net soon. Let's get our act together and get out of here before any other trouble shows up."

• • •

There was no air out here. There was no heat, no gravity. Nothing protected him from the void. Not even coherent thought.

Freezing terror gave way to training and instinct for ten crucial seconds. He dove left for his helmet, which he found floating off the deck right where he'd laid it. Tanner slammed it down on his head and activated the seals as he had a thousand times in basic training. His eyes flicked left, then right, then around, trying to orient himself to what was left of *St. Jude*'s cargo bay.

The tiny remaining patch of ship filled him with horror. Emergency track lights provided just enough illumination to guide him to the oxygen capsule panel at one remaining bulkhead. Tanner scrambled for it, flailing about in zero g as if he'd never experienced it before. He reached for anything he could push off of to propel himself along. He floated with agonizing slowness to the panel, tore it open with trembling fingers, and somehow managed to shove a fresh oxygen canister into the back of his helmet.

He tried to paint himself to the deck and bulkhead, sitting down against a corner with his legs pushing him back and his shaking hands searching for something to hold. He feared floating away and then realized he'd activated the magnetic strips in his vac suit without even thinking about it. Stars watched him without emotion or mercy. Morales floated farther away into the void.

Imminent death dominated his thoughts. The nausea that usually accompanied sudden shifts in gravity didn't even register. The fact that he'd survived at all seemed like some unimaginably cruel twist. Everyone else had died instantly. Tanner was left to stare eternity in the face until his air ran out.

That thought led him to another, and though it did little to relieve his panic or give him hope, he followed it. Tanner activated his holocom and called up the comms net for his shipmates. If anyone had survived at all, even if their bodies floated out in space, their holocoms would register within fifty kilometers.

Morales. Morales was the only one left on the net. He was half a klick away already, without a helmet and well past the maximum thirty seconds a human could possibly survive unprotected in space. Tanner's eyes shut tightly. The last face he would see was that of Morales. That was the last person he'd ever speak to before he died out here, so very far from home.

He didn't even have a home, he realized. Not really. He had a barracks room on Augustine with a boorish, unfriendly roommate—now dead—and a bunk on this ship that was now just so much dismembered metal floating in space. His family lived in another star system. His friends from school chased their futures at universities, his shipmates from basic scattered to other billets, all unaware of where he was or what happened to him. Many would probably never know. Even Madelyn might not know about this for weeks or even months.

He was just shy of twenty years old. No university. No career. No girlfriend. Nothing. Exactly like he'd told the chaplain.

I don't want to die out here.

Something inside him demanded, in a familiar voice he could practically hear, *Quit sandbagging, recruit.*

Tanner blinked away his panicked tears.

No. I don't want to die.

He slowly, gingerly unglued himself from the bulkhead, crawling across the deck out to the edge again to assess his situation.

It was exactly as he'd feared. The laser blast had gone straight from the bow on through the aft, wiping away everything it touched. *St. Jude* had done nothing to blunt or mitigate the damage. No electrostatic reinforcement of the hull, no evasive maneuver.

In the distance far ahead, Tanner could make out lights shining differently than the other stars. He called up the optics suite on his helmet, trying to bring his short, quick breath under control as he worked. The computer in his helmet locked onto the lights and enhanced the image.

He saw two ships, a cruise liner and a destroyer with CDC markings, bound together by multiple tethers and gangway tubes. *St. Jude*'s wreckage still maintained much of its momentum, rapidly approaching the ships at something close to her original intercept course. The corvette's corpse wouldn't collide with either ship, but it would come within a few dozen kilometers.

He tried to think the situation through, once again cursing Stevens and his refusal to brief anyone on anything, ever. *St. Jude* came out alone and in a hurry and was now off the communications and tactical grid. Augustine Harbor would notice that, but Tanner didn't know how far out he was. The other corvettes on the station weren't in alert standby mode and therefore couldn't be out here for several hours at best. Madelyn's ship wasn't even scheduled to leave for another two hours, and who the hell knew how long it would take a Union battleship to get its ass in gear for a local emergency.

It seemed obvious that *St. Jude* had been suckered. No one even sounded an alarm before the blast hit. There was no telling how that had been arranged, nor whether or not it could be done again.

The likelihood of a destroyer taking out a battleship seemed remote. But then, Tanner considered, at least one pirate destroyer had pulled off an awful lot of audacious things in the last couple years. It had been in Archangel space before . . . and CDC had been given the boot.

None of that reduced his fear. To the contrary, Tanner felt his chances of survival diminish further if it was that same pirate destroyer out there. He'd read everything he could find about recent pirate activity after his day on the *Yaomo*. Chances were that practically everyone on that liner was as good as dead, if not dead already.

Tanner looked out at the two ships again. He'd gotten a good deal closer already. *St. Jude*'s corpse would likely pass by the ships before his oxygen ran out.

He thought back to the piracy reports. If it *were* the destroyer that hit *Aphrodite*, they might put the crew out in lifeboats again. Even lifeboats had airlocks—tiny ones, but airlocks nonetheless. If he could get to the liner and hang on to the outside of one of the lifeboats until it launched . . .

It was beyond crazy, but the thought provided a much better chance of survival than he would find on a gutted and dismembered corvette.

• • •

For the first time, Nathan Spencer regretted taking a gap year. He also regretted going to the pool on the promenade deck to do his writing.

He'd been thrilled when his grandparents first proposed it. "Keep your educational debts down below twenty-five thousand," they said, "and we'll cover some travel after graduation. It'll be good for you."

Nathan didn't quite hold up his end of the bargain—his final financial obligations were more like twenty-eight thousand—but his grandparents decided that it was close enough, and his parents agreed. It wasn't lost on Nathan that his grandparents simply wanted to give him this experience regardless of how well he did, but he couldn't fault them for wanting to motivate him. They had paid his way into the Society of Scholars in the first place, after all.

His experience turned out to be longer than a year, and more fun than he'd expected. Nathan saw Columbia and New Beijing, toured the palaces of Delhi Prime, and went on an expedition through the canyons of Wushan. He spent more than six months on Earth soaking up history, culture, and alcohol. As it happened, he remembered the partying the most, but it wasn't like he'd spent the entire gap year on aimless celebrations and cliché tourism.

Nathan volunteered for several charities. He even worked a little along the way, enough to save up for a ticket on the *Pride of Polaris* so he could ride home in style. He also followed a specific travel itinerary, which together with the report he'd been writing on his holocom up until an hour ago, earned credits at Raphael University, where he would begin his studies in just a week . . . if he made it there alive.

That seemed increasingly unlikely with each passing minute.

"Ladies and gentlemen, this is your new captain speaking," announced a gravelly, energetic, frightening voice over the ship's PA system. "As you've been told, your ship has been taken by pirates. We are on board and in control. If anyone happened to be looking out a porthole or an external view screen five minutes ago, you just saw us wipe out your one shitty chance of rescue.

"If you cooperate, this will be over soon and you will be allowed to disembark on a lifeboat or escape pod. If you do not cooperate, you'll be shot. If you resist or try to hide, you and everyone around you will be shot. This is what happened with the passengers of the *Aphrodite*, though I'm sure the media didn't tell you that.

"You should also know that every inch of this ship is monitored. Do not try to hide valuables. This will only make us angry. Do not try to reason with us. We will shoot you for wasting our time. Do not try to get to an escape pod or a lifeboat. They are all locked down. Just do what you are told and remain quiet and no harm will come to you.

"Passengers will assemble on the promenade deck. Go there with your hands above your head, find a place to sit, and wait there quietly."

Nathan glanced about the promenade. He, and everyone else around the broad, spacious pool, had been trapped there when the attack began and the emergency doors had slammed down on every exit to compartmentalize the ship. He sat waiting for the pirates wearing nothing but swim trunks, a towel, and a very worried expression.

The doors opened again. Nathan wanted to run, but there was no place to run to.

• • •

"Abandon ship" had its place on any ship's station bill, just like battle stations, damage control, or search and rescue. Every officer and crewman had a responsibility. Everyone had equipment they were expected to salvage and bring off the ship if at all possible. Tanner had endured abandon ship drills in Squad Bay Oscar many times. He'd participated in a half dozen much more realistic drills on *Los Angeles* during his apprenticeship phase, and even a couple during weapons and tactics school.

On *St. Jude*, Tanner knew his responsibilities from reading the station bill. Training for his ship began and ended there.

Obviously the call to abandon ship would be made only in the worst, most chaotic circumstances. It was understood that a given crewman might not be able to carry out his or her responsibilities. The equipment they were expected to salvage might be destroyed, or it might be impossible to get to one's regularly assigned lifeboat. One was expected to improvise and do the best job one could. If a crewman's regular responsibilities were impossible to execute, he should do the next best practical thing.

Tanner's regular responsibilities were out of the question. He was supposed to go forward and collect the boxes of personal power cells from a gear locker that no longer existed. The next best thing was to grab whatever might possibly be useful, be it a weapon or a sniffer kit or even a blanket. Any equipment was better than no equipment.

One of the damage control bags hadn't floated out into space. He had that. Searching for more gear, Tanner found a spacewalking harness in the surviving locker, complete with its nitrogen capsules for zero-g maneuver. "Oh, thank you, God," he said out loud. Finally, one real piece of luck.

Then again, he figured, he'd had the dumb luck to be in this situation in the first place. *Is it good luck to get shot but survive*, he wondered, *or bad luck to have been shot at all?*

Tanner donned the harness before slinging the bags over his shoulders like a backpack. Then he pulled the magnetic tape from his utility belt and wrapped it around himself and the bag to keep it under control. He didn't want all that mass flopping around and throwing him off while executing such a risky maneuver.

The numbers on his holocom spun down. He glanced around the side of the bulkhead, noting that *St. Jude*'s remaining hull panel was already starting to break apart. He didn't need it to hold together much longer, though; if his math was correct, he would soon come as close to the linked-up ships as *St. Jude*'s corpse would carry him.

Tanner waited. Salvage work had gotten his mind off his terror, but for two endless minutes all he could do was wait. For the moment, he wasn't so overwhelmed by the certainty of impending doom. He was possessed instead by the ordinary fear that he would make a mistake, that either his calculations or his physical strength and finesse wouldn't be enough to do the job.

Either he stayed here and spun off hopelessly into space, or jumped for it only to screw it up and hopelessly spin off into space . . . or, just maybe, he could do it right and go from one longshot chance to the next. It would be a miracle if he could do any of this at all without filling his helmet with vomit.

He triple-checked the course on his helmet and his holocom. Both systems were tied in to his EVA harness. The time spun down.

Tanner fired the nitrogen capsules on the harness, blasting him away from the remains of *St. Jude*.

Dozens of kilometers separated Tanner from his target. He had little fuel. There was also a limit to his oxygen, which, while sufficient for the job, wasn't enough to make him comfortable. Tanner kept the capsules firing until they dwindled to fifty percent of their capacity, hoping that he would build enough momentum to get the job done. Then he cut the power. The vibrations of the harness capsules ceased to resonate through his suit and in his helmet.

Then there was nothing around him but the void.

• • •

"Attention, crew of the *Pride of Polaris*," Casey said into the mic on the bridge. "This is the acting master of your ship speaking. You have heard instructions for passengers to assemble on the promenade. You will not go with them. You are to assemble in the main ballroom. Go there immediately. Do not stop to aid passengers. Let them aid themselves. Failure to follow instructions will be dealt with severely. Do not test us. Do as you are told and you will live through this."

Casey dropped the mic handset and looked to Carl. "There," he said, "that short and concise enough for you, professor?"

The big man shrugged with a grin playing at his face. "I'm just sayin', we're the ones holding guns to their heads. Why coddle them?"

"Coddle 'em? 'Cause every fuckhead crewman's wondering to himself, 'Wait, you want me to abandon the passengers?'" Casey said in an exaggerated tone of bewilderment. His frown reasserted itself. "Besides, we don't want to kick potential recruits any harder than we have to, right?"

Carl shrugged. “Surprised you want to pick up recruits at all given our situation. Guess it gives you a good chance to practice your speech again.”

Casey nearly retorted, then bit it back. “You know what?” he said. “Just for that, you get to stay on the bridge.” He gave Carl a feigned salute, then turned toward the exit. “Everyone’s a fucking critic,” he grumbled.

• • •

Fourteen minutes of agonizing nothingness turned over to fifteen. Then sixteen. Seventeen. The tiny glowing numbers in the bottom-left corner of his heads-up display rolled on, minutes counting up while distance counted down. He had to use optic measurements alone, since he couldn’t risk bouncing any sort of signal off the ship lest it be detected. That meant for less reliable measurements, but soon the hulls of the liner and the destroyer beyond it grew larger and closer.

Tanner controlled his breathing, his nausea, and his fear.

He wouldn’t run out of oxygen before he hit the ships. That much was certain now. He’d have a good twenty minutes left at least. More if he could keep his breathing to a slow, measured pace and keep his activity to a minimum. All he had to do once he was at the liner was to walk across its hull to one of the lifeboats and wait—and hope he chose the right one, and hope it would be released before his oxygen ran out.

Maybe there would be other opportunities to extend his dwindling lifespan. Maybe not. One problem at a time.

• • •

“Casey, I’m here with the passengers,” Chang announced on *Vengeance*’s open comms channel. “They’re sitting tight.”

"Good job," replied Casey. He stood just outside the main ballroom, receiving a final few reports before he went inside to launch into his monologue. "You got enough manpower?"

"Yeah, I think we're set here," said Chang. "We could hose 'em all down right now if we had to. Hell, I'd be inclined if it wasn't such a fucking mess."

"Now, now," cautioned Casey, "let's not get carried away. Anyone goes off half-cocked, I'm makin' 'em clean up the mess personally and by hand. Anyway, we've got a good object lesson set up for 'em already. Carl, you there?"

"Yup," replied another voice on the comms net.

"Is the captain in position?"

"Looks like it."

"Then how 'bout you open up the curtains?"

• • •

Nathan could hear the apparent leader of the group of pirates on the promenade talk to others on his holocom. He couldn't make out every word, but the meaning and emotion were obvious enough. The Asian man and his compatriots carried guns Nathan had only seen in movies. He knew just enough to understand how dangerous their weapons were. He saw little chance for a passenger revolt.

The bulkheads at each end of the promenade began to hum, and soon the hull panels above broke open and retracted. Thick, transparent plastics so polished as to be practically invisible kept the ship's atmosphere inside. The *Pride of Polaris* offered spectacular views from its promenade. The overhead frequently opened up to the sights of planets, comets, and the like, offering visions most people never got to see with the naked eye.

Tonight, all that was in view was the shark-shaped pirate ship looming above, attached with tethers and gangway tubes.

Its hull blocked the view of anything beyond. Nathan wondered if the pirates just wanted everyone to see their big, scary ship. Intimidating though it was, the ship was no more threatening than the armed men who stood right among them.

Then Captain Kennedy floated lifelessly between the two ships.

People screamed. Others whimpered. Nathan heard several of the pirates laugh. "Just a reminder, folks," the lead pirate called out. "Anyone feels like putting up a fight or a fuss, they're welcome to join the captain out there."

• • •

He made it.

Tanner was only off on his trajectory by a few hundred meters, easily corrected with short bursts of the nitrogen capsules. He had to expend much of his remaining nitrogen to decelerate before he splattered against the ship's hull, but altogether he got the job done. Drifting a few short meters away, he gave it a final microburst and then activated the magnetic relays on his boots. Nineteen minutes after abandoning *St. Jude*, Tanner stood on the hull of the *Pride of Polaris.*

Tanner kept low, hoping not to set off any sort of sensors or security equipment on the outside of the hull. He looked around to get himself oriented. Nothing in his surroundings looked like a lifeboat bay. He'd have to walk around.

One foot came down in front of the other. Tanner tried not to overthink things, but with no one to talk to and no instructions to follow beyond whatever he made up as he went along, Tanner's worries provided the only available company. His plan wasn't much of a plan. He had no idea when the pirates would release a lifeboat, assuming they released one at all. And what were the chances those inside would risk opening an airlock to let him in? What were the chances they'd be picked up before they all perished from the lack of oxygen? What if his presence were detected long before then?

Was there something more important he should be doing? He couldn't think of anything, but the thought nagged at him.

Movement in the corner of his eye caught his attention. Tanner crouched low, realizing even as he did it that such a move could make little difference out here on the hull. He was completely exposed.

The object passed through a shadow. Tanner waited, and then swallowed hard as the body floated back into the light.

• • •

"So first off, I'd like to apologize for this rough treatment and all the fright we've put you through," Casey said loudly as he strode into the ballroom. The hundreds of crewmen and attendants before him sat in silence, just like so many other ships' crews, colonists, and other assorted prisoners before them.

"You've got to understand that this ain't personal. Hell, we can prove it ain't personal, 'cause you don't know any of us, and we don't know any of you. But I separated you working folks out from those rich sons of bitches out there on the promenade deck because I wanted to ask you all a question.

"How much debt do you people carry?"

• • •

The man wore a wedding band.

His bloody uniform indicated high rank, presumably the liner's captain. The ugly hole through his belly looked as if it may have ended him well before he was cast out of the ship. But what caught Tanner's attention was the wedding band. Somewhere out there was the man's widow, and she didn't even know.

His face seemed like it should normally be set in some kind expression, though at the moment it bore only shock. Tanner reached out with trembling hands to pull him down to the hull. It was a useless gesture, of course. The man floated back up.

He looked like a kind man. Respectful. Married. He was a total stranger, but at a glance, this was all Tanner could know of him, and now he was dead. If everything Tanner had seen and read were any indication, the captain wouldn't be alone. For all Tanner knew, the captain had never done any harm to anyone, and now he was dead.

St. Jude's crewmen were all dead. In eighteen more minutes, Tanner's oxygen would run out, and then he would be dead. Nothing in Tanner's plan made any difference in that.

Rage began to drown out fear. Rage decided what Tanner would do with the remaining minutes of his life.

He crouched down, cut the magnetic relays on his feet, and jumped for the destroyer looming above its captured prey.

• • •

"Daddy," hissed Elizabeth.

"Hush, honey," her father whispered back. He kissed her on the head and held her tight. "It's gonna be okay. Don't you worry."

Elizabeth frowned. The men with guns were frightening, sure, but she wasn't nearly as frightened as her father. "No, Daddy, look," she said. Elizabeth was a sensible little girl. She knew when to keep something quiet. "Look up."

"No, honey, you shouldn't look up at the man," her father said. "Look at me, Elizabeth. Just look at me. Don't look up at that poor man."

Her frown only deepened. "Daddy, the dead man's gone." She kept her voice low, speaking only just over a whimper. She didn't want the bad men to hear. "There's someone else out there, Daddy."

"Oh no." Her father shuddered. "God, how many people are they going to take?"

"Daddy, no, it's not that," hissed Elizabeth. "There's a man walking on the outside of the other ship."

• • •

Tanner made it to the destroyer in seconds. He had to correct his jump with a burst from his EVA harness, but he didn't beat himself up over it. He barely noticed his nausea, either. At the moment, he cared only about finding an airlock or access hatch on the stern of the ship.

His first thought had been to try to find the bridge and then some entryway close to it, but that wasn't practical. Much could be said for the value of a ship's bridge, but in the end, every large ship had backups and redundancies for helm and control in or near engineering. The reverse was never true. Ships didn't have a backup engineering section.

Tanner found a likely spot not far from the port-side thrusters. The hatch spanned two meters in diameter, with warning labels and markings all around. It had no control pad, nor key slot, nor set of latches. The metal was likely about as thick as the hull around it. Military ship designers wanted a ship to survive a pounding from other ships' weapons, and they didn't want to create weak points a computer could target. The only way to be let in was via the controls on the inside.

That, or with the tools in the damage control bag slung and taped to Tanner's back.

He cut the tape with the survival knife that he had once considered a hokey relic of the age of sail, then used the tape to secure the bag against the hull. Careful to prevent other tools from floating free, Tanner pulled out the electromagnetic breaching kit. He spooled out the magnetized contact cable, carefully ensuring that it covered the full circumference of the hatch. He double-checked the instructions printed on the side of the controls to make sure he didn't blow this.

"For internal use only," it read. "Check for fire, hazardous gas, or hull breaches on the other side of a hatch before use. May result in explosive decompression if placed improperly."

Tanner skipped through all that to check the directions. Whether the breaching kit was the appropriate tool to override the seals on an external hatch was irrelevant; he had nothing else. Whether the compartment on the other side contained atmosphere or not was also irrelevant; the compartment beyond it surely would, and he only needed this hatch open long enough to pass through.

He took a deep breath. If nobody knew he was out here yet, they'd likely know soon enough.

Power surged through the control box and the cables when Tanner keyed the activator. At first, nothing happened; then the seam running down the center of the hatch split open. Atmosphere vented out. Tanner tore the bag loose from the side of the hull and heaved himself inside.

Seconds later, the relays on the hatch reset automatically. The hatch slammed shut, leaving Tanner in a darkness marked only by his helmet's optic displays and a single, tiny red light up against one bulkhead. Gravity reasserted itself instantly; his damage control bag was suddenly very heavy, with its tools now spilling out all over the deck. Tanner's sense of up and down returned.

He didn't allow himself time to recover. Tanner slammed his hand down on the red light before activating the lamps on his helmet. As he had expected, his hand covered a small, recessed video camera.

Opposite his entry point was a second hatch. It, too, lacked any sort of controls or handles. That was as Tanner had feared;

Los Angeles had been designed the same way. He had to leave the breaching kit outside. He couldn't open this second hatch.

That said, there were more sensors on an airlock than the single camera covered by his hand. Someone had to know that something strange had happened in here. He reached for the now half-empty damage control bag and placed it over the camera, securing it with the frayed tape.

Tanner plucked the crowbar from the pile of tools, took up a spot beside the internal hatch, and waited.

• • •

Selection for boarding parties turned out to be a popularity contest, and one that Darren Mills deliberately, gladly lost. He was perfectly happy to remain aboard *Vengeance*. The thought of capturing a luxury liner and bleeding it dry pleased him, of course, but he held little interest in doing the actual bleeding. Even if the *Pride*'s passengers and crew were dramatically less likely to put up resistance than the militia of Qal'at Khalil, Darren had already seen enough blood and gore to last a lifetime.

His approach had trade-offs, of course. Engineering on *Vengeance* was down to a skeleton crew, since every technically inclined hand that could be spared was needed to get the *Pride*'s FTL drives up and running again as fast as possible. Combined with the need for general boarders, *Vengeance* was left with less than a score of engineers on board. Only one of them was completely sober and vigilant.

"Hey, airlock nine's showing some funny readings," Darren announced from his station. He brought up the internal sensor suite, finding the airlock's atmosphere almost entirely depleted and its internal camera off-line.

"Maybe someone bumped into something in there," suggested one pirate.

"No, they aren't using nine for boarding." Darren frowned. He keyed a few more options on the controls. The camera showing the passageway outside the airlock revealed nothing out of the ordinary. The external hatch remained sealed per normal. No further loss of pressure, no wavering of other indicators. Everything was quiet.

"Betcha I know what happen'," someone else slurred. "Fuggin' piece of that ship we blew up might've hit us. Right inna airlock hatch. Boom."

Darren rolled his eyes. The great thing about serving on a pirate ship was that there were few bullshit rules. The downside was that there were few rules at all. There were penalties for serving out a watch while drunk, but many pirates tried to get away with it, anyway.

He looked left, then right. Minor projects preoccupied some of his comrades. A couple others were wrapped up in their own conversations. Several more had their holocoms linked in a game that they played against one another with fierce intensity.

Darren let out a sigh. He could make a big deal out of this, but if it turned out to be no big deal at all, he'd just annoy comrades who were only now beginning to forget his disastrous first week. His performance in Khalil City had gone a long way to repairing his reputation. The last thing he wanted was to wind up back in the doghouse again over something stupid.

Something told him not to go alone, though. "Hey," he said, tugging at the dozing engineer next to him. "Hank."

"Huh?"

"Hank, something's up with airlock nine. We gotta go check it out."

The middle-aged pirate sniffed. "Hm. Okay. Sure," Hank said, rubbing his eyes. "What's wrong?"

"Pressure leak inside the airlock, but it looks like it's all sealed up tight outside," Darren told him. "Think it might be something internal. Hey, Lance!" Darren called to the head of the engineering watch. "We're gonna go check out a thing!" From behind a desk, Darren saw a hand wave in acknowledgment. That was as formal as things got around here.

"Y'know," Hank mentioned blearily as Darren stood and donned his combat jacket, "you don't gotta wear that fuckin' thing everywhere."

"I do if I don't want it stolen. Thing cost me fifty thousand bucks."

Hank made a face. "Who's gonna steal that?"

Darren shook his head and tugged Hank along.

The airlock of concern lay only a few minutes away, up one level and down a passageway. With *Vengeance* conducting boarding operations, most of the crew still on board remained at battle stations. Darren and Hank passed no one on their way.

Coming to the airlock, Darren made sure that the hatches leading to the compartment were all shut. He then checked the external gauges and controls, finding the readings steady but very low, just as they had been when he first noticed the problem. A small porthole offered a view of the airlock compartment at eye level. Darren peeked inside and found nothing but a sealed external hatch. The vantage point didn't offer him a view of the video camera.

"Looks like everything's fine in there," Darren said. "Guess we can open her up. Call it in to the bridge, will you?"

Hank shrugged. "Bridge, this is Hank from engineering. We're gonna check a busted sensor in airlock nine. Don't freak out if the readings go weird."

"Gotcha, Hank," came the response. "Knock yourselves out."

Hank gestured for Darren to lead the way. Darren keyed the hatch controls and peered inside.

The crowbar that swung out from around the corner shattered Darren's nose and his cheek.

Hank let out a yelp as Darren tumbled back. The helmeted man in the vac suit came on, swinging the crowbar across Hank's face. He stepped out of the airlock, bringing the crowbar down on Hank's head twice more as the engineer fell.

Tanner looked left and then right. No other enemies occupied the passageway. He spun around again to find the first pirate he'd struck looking up at him with wide, shocked eyes over a bloody face. The man fumbled with his gun. Tanner swung the crowbar down several more times.

Not fair, Darren objected in panicked, silent thoughts. *This just isn't f—*

The crowbar came down on Darren's head again and again until Darren stopped moving.

Thinking quickly, Tanner dragged one fallen man into the airlock, then the other. He tore off their gun belts, amazed at the degree of firepower these two guys casually carried around on board their ship. *A plasma carbine? Seriously?*

Then he realized what the first one was wearing. Archangel marines didn't wear combat gear that good. It was simply too expensive.

He didn't stop to contemplate his good fortune. Tanner tore the combat jacket from the pirate's corpse. As he finished stripping the bodies of useful gear, he discovered the first pirate's holocom. Tanner tried to activate it, but the earring simply beeped at him with a disapproving tone. He tried activating it again, this time using its owner's lifeless yet still warm thumb and forefinger. The holocom flared to life, but the menu screen demanded a personal security code before it would open up further.

Tanner sighed. "Guess you're not quite as dumb as you look," he said to the dead man. He shut the airlock once more, leaving Darren Mills and Hank Bruning behind him.

FOURTEEN

No Such Thing as a Fair Fight

Not a single soul occupied the passageways leading from airlock nine to main engineering. No alarm rang when he opened hatches along the way. Tanner held his breath at every portal and junction, sure that he would be spotted. Every encounter with a pirate brought with it the danger of more pirates. Numbers would tell.

The entryway to main engineering was the most nerve-wracking point yet. He expected to be spotted immediately, to be sucked into a fight where the best he could do was to throw around as many blasts from his plasma carbine and slag as much important equipment as possible before being cut down. Tanner slipped open the hatch, keeping it to his side like a shield as he looked inside. There he discovered why his movement thus far had been so easy.

Two men not far from Tanner's age sat turned away from their stations while engaged in a holocom game. Another seemed to be reading a book. Across the spacious, noisy hall of plastic and metal pipes and machinery, three more pored over a gutted power generator laid out on a worktable. One man sat with his feet up at his station, his hand hanging down from his seat to ineffectually cover the bottle of whiskey sticking out of the bag on the deck beside him. Like the pirates Tanner fought at the airlock—indeed, just like the pirates on *Yaomo*—not one of them wore a vac suit. And not one of them looked up to see who came in.

Discipline on *St. Jude* had been poor, but compared to this scene, Tanner's old ship had been a fascist dream.

He didn't risk thinking about it long. Tanner spotted a serviceable bit of cover behind a power distribution box. He closed the hatch behind himself and slipped over to the box, careful not to move so fast as to attract attention. Crouching low and looking around carefully, Tanner took the time to orient himself to *Vengeance*'s main engineering space.

Huge pieces of self-contained machinery dominated the large compartment, each providing a portion of primary power and propulsion for the ship. Arranged in the spaces between were gear lockers, workbenches, computer consoles, and storage tanks. Tanner needed to get at the consoles. He kept low, stuck to the shadows, and steered clear of everyone, crawling under racks and benches to get around to a single U-shaped desk.

Someone sat with his feet up on the desk. A plain ceramic coffee mug occupied one corner of his space, bearing the name "Lance" in handwritten letters. Some of his monitors displayed airlocks connected to their captured prey. Others depicted graphs and charts for power, life support, and other systems. The center monitor screen played the highly pornographic antics of several different people on an absurdly large bed. Tanner put aside his awe at the lax attitudes all around him as he crawled forward.

Though not completely absorbed by the video, Lance gave it enough attention to leave him oblivious to approaching danger. His right hand slipped under his waistband as the action grew hotter. The engineer wondered, briefly, if he could get away with more than simply scratching himself without anyone noticing.

Then the knife came into his throat. A strong hand pinned his left wrist to his chair's armrest. Lance tried to let out a yell for help, but his throat no longer carried sound.

Engineering was a loud place. People banged around all the time. No one noticed as Lance expired.

Tanner slipped up to the console, turning off the sex scene on the main screen with a blood-soaked finger. He called up a main file directory and searched for a set of the ship's schematics. It was easy enough to download the information to his holocom in case he needed it later. He would be thrilled to survive long enough to even have a "later."

He'd come aboard *Vengeance* with little more than an angry, vague desire to inflict harm. Though his rage still propelled him, Tanner understood the need for a plan. Whether or not he could pull it off was irrelevant; a failed attempt at accomplishing something significant was better than causing random chaos. Tanner traced out pathways from engineering to the bridge. He'd never make it through all those passageways if anyone knew he was coming.

There had to be alternate routes. He looked for other systems in the ship and found, as he had suspected, that the ventilation systems weren't practical. Apparently, the shipbuilders had all seen those movies where people snuck around inside the air ducts and made sure it couldn't happen on this destroyer. The engineering crawl spaces throughout the ship ran for only short distances. Tanner would frequently have to traverse open passageways.

Then Tanner hit upon his solution. He couldn't get all the way to the bridge, but he could get close, and no one would detect him coming. Ordinarily it would've been ridiculous—but then, he wore a perfectly serviceable vac suit and helmet. There was no reason he couldn't apply it to this particular task.

Main engineering had provided almost all he could hope for. There was only one other matter to address. With his path set,

Tanner tugged Lance's body down to the deck, gave it a pat down and confiscated his automatic pistol and ammunition. Then he began his low crawl out from the monitor suite.

Little had changed over the last few minutes. He saw one engineer leave the compartment, mumbling something barely audible about the head. Tanner froze until the man passed, then resumed his quiet withdrawal.

Several meters away from the dead engineer and his monitor console, Tanner found a broad, heavy storage locker. It was a permanent fixture in the engineering space, designed as an integral part of the compartment's layout. Its thick metal housing and bright warning labels made its purpose quite plain.

Though considered remarkably stable and safe under normal circumstances, the solid fuel cells used in starships still had to be handled with care. Each cell, charged up by the ship's reactor and stored for emergency use, contained a remarkable amount of energy. Ship's designers went out of their way to ensure that fuel cells would not be subject to violent treatment. Moreover, designers, engineers, and technicians all took steps to ensure that cells were never stored en masse, preferring to limit the potential scope of an explosion by spreading out the necessary fuels. Storage units such as this one protected their contents from accidents.

They were not meant to be opened by unauthorized personnel like Tanner. Nor were they intended to be left open. Nor, certainly, was anyone supposed to run down to the other end of a passageway and then, once behind cover, fire off a carefully aimed blast from a laser pistol into the open locker.

The instant explosion went beyond Tanner's expectations. Fire and shredded metal erupted in every direction with a boom heard throughout the ship. Though thick sheets of metal housed the most vital machinery, a great deal of other systems and gear enjoyed less protection. The blast knocked out control panels and generators, cut cables and pipes, and annihilated no small portion of the engineering watch. Survivors were plunged into further chaos as damaged systems went haywire, flames roared from the wreckage, and fire-retardant gasses spewed from their pipes.

Though protected by cover and distance, the blast still knocked Tanner off his feet. His ears rang despite the audio protection offered by his helmet. He didn't waste time in assessing the damage he'd inflicted. As soon as he was on his feet again, Tanner rushed for the hatch labeled "Water Distribution Space."

• • •

"What the fuck was that?" demanded Lauren.

"Checking!" answered Jerry. He grimaced. "I was afraid of that. Something blew up in engineering. They've got a fire and casualties. Look, it's on the monitor here."

Lauren leaned in over Jerry's shoulder. Men and twisted metal lay strewn about the compartment, which rapidly filled with smoke. Not everyone was dead; some were already at work recovering. She could see at least one man rushing for a still-functional communications panel to call the disaster in.

The acting captain didn't wait. Automated fire control systems plainly couldn't handle that on their own. She hit her holocom and put out an emergency signal to the section leaders of the boarding parties. "Boarders, this is Lauren on *Vengeance*," she said loudly. "We've got an explosion and fire in engineering. Plenty of injuries. Cause unknown, but I need damage control over here right fucking now. Wilson, you copy?"

"I hear you," Wilson came back. "We're still a little while away from getting the *Pride* going again, but I'm releasing people. Casey, you listening?"

"Yeah, I'm here," Lauren heard Casey reply. "*Vengeance* is more important than the liner. Keep working on this ship with anyone you can spare, but *Vengeance* has priority. Lauren, I'm gonna release plenty of boarders, but I need at least a couple hundred guys to keep this ship secure."

Lauren couldn't argue with that. The information coming in on the monitors and comms channels indicated a single fuel cell locker had exploded, but that naturally led to other problems and further possible danger. With enough people on the job, though, they could prevent any sort of cascading catastrophe. If she couldn't handle this mess with six hundred men and women, she couldn't handle it at all. "Good enough," she said. "Get 'em over here. *Vengeance* out."

"Christ, what a mess," grunted Jerry. "Any idea what could've caused that?"

Lauren let out a tense breath. "This is why you can't slack off on a ship," she fumed. "People get careless, get complacent, then shit like this happens at the worst possible time. I'll bet you anything if we could autopsy a couple of those bodies we'd find all sorts of fun stuff in their systems. *Dammit!*"

Yet even as she spoke, Lauren wondered if she relied too heavily on conventional wisdom and experience. She had survived her share of shipboard accidents in her time, but there was always the possibility of another explanation. *Could this be deliberate?* she wondered. *Could one of Wilson's snipes have lost his marbles?*

"Give me a rundown on who's coming back on board as they get here," Lauren said. "Let's make sure we cover all our bases."

• • •

"Two-six-zero mark two-one-three to Augustine, approximately three point five minutes at quarter speed. No inbound contacts to destination. Three outbound contacts, all clear of our path."

"Midshipman Carter, I don't think I saw you plug the numbers into the computer," observed Lieutenant Sharma. He stood behind the young woman's shoulder, taking her and her classmate through the lookout routine as UFS *Fletcher* pulled out of orbit.

"No, sir, you did not," answered Madelyn.

"And yet your numbers are exactly correct," added Sharma.

The midshipman beside Madelyn groaned. It wasn't the first time she had shown Rick up. "How do you make this look so easy?"

"I'm just smarter than everyone else," Madelyn joked as if it should be obvious. Rick groaned again, eliciting a laugh from his classmate.

Sharma rolled his eyes. "Enough with the flirting." Madelyn and Rick both blinked, looking up at the lieutenant with surprised expressions. "Oh, come on, everybody knows. It's not a problem. This isn't the eighteenth century. Just focus on the task at hand."

Madelyn turned beet red. Her gaze shifted from Sharma to the screen in front of her as her back stiffened. She didn't need to look at Rick to know he was staring down at the console in front of him with a mortified expression.

"Lieutenant Sharma, we've got a change of plans," someone announced. The astrogator and the two midshipmen turned. Captain Catherine Leigh stood behind them, leaving Madelyn doubly mortified at Sharma's advice. Had the captain heard their discussion?

"Ma'am?" asked Sharma.

"Augustine Command lost contact with one of their corvettes while she responded to a possible distress call just past the FTL line," explained Leigh. "We're the closest ship in the area, and since we're almost ready to move they've asked us to go take a look. Lay in a course."

"Ma'am?" piped up Madelyn. She'd hardly spoken to Leigh in the entire three months she'd been on board. A great many steps in rank separated them, not the least of which was the difference between commissioned officer and midshipman. This time, she couldn't help herself. "Did they say which corvette?"

Leigh tilted her head a touch, not answering right away. "That's right," she said, "you're from this system, aren't you? Michael, was it?"

"Yes, ma'am."

The captain nodded. "They said it was *St. Jude*," she answered. "I wouldn't get too worried. If they were really concerned, they'd have authorized an FTL hop. We'll get there soon regardless. Lieutenant Sharma, the coordinates are in the system. If you could double-check the course and approaches for hazards?"

"Right away, ma'am," Sharma said. He turned to Madelyn as the captain left. "I'll need my seat back, but don't go anywhere. You should see how this is done."

• • •

Well, shit, Tanner thought. *This is awkward.*

The main water distribution tube had carried him two-thirds of the way across the ship. He didn't swim so much as push himself along the inside of the tube, kicking when he had room and wiggling free when stuck. With few internal markers in the tube and a limited file of the layout of the ship's plumbing copied to his holocom, navigation proved difficult. His helmet and harness provided the only light he had.

For all that difficulty, though, he made good time. Only twice did a grate or a filter block him, and that was easily resolved with the simple tools he had on him. The real difficulty had been in getting into the tube without making a giant mess that would give him away.

But now he came to the end of the watery road. His shoulders were stuck. The tube had been only barely large enough for him to enter, and now it was too thin to move around. *Just as well*, he decided. His oxygen cartridges, depleted already by his time in the void, would run out in another couple of minutes. It was time to leave.

He had the perfect tool for accomplishing that, but getting it out of its large holster on his right hip proved difficult. There was barely room to draw it out all the way, and not nearly enough room to hold it away from his body. Tanner took one last stab at orienting himself, watching the bubbles in the water to confirm which way was up and which was down.

He made a final check of the schematics. They hadn't changed since the last time he looked. There was only one practical direction to go, and sadly it wasn't up, left, or right. Tanner put the plasma carbine up against the bottom of the tube, tilting it to the most favorable angle he could manage without blowing off his own feet, and pulled the trigger.

Green light and impossible heat flared up all around him. He was lucky he didn't boil himself alive, but then, the water heated by his plasma blast escaped almost instantly. His gun created a large hole in the tube, disintegrating plastic well beyond the actual diameter of the plasma blast. The water in the tube followed gravity. Tanner was washed out instantly, falling two and a half meters onto the hard tile of an open bay shower.

He took the fall as best he could. The padding of his combat jacket and the vac harness helped, but ultimately the only part of his body left unhurt by the impact was his head, protected by his helmet. His rough, sudden landing forced an inglorious sound from his throat.

Tanner lay on the tile as water gushed down on him from above. He moved his arms, then his legs, starting with small motions just to make sure he hadn't broken anything. Then he rolled out from under the ruptured tube, looked around to orient himself, and got to his feet. His expectations held true; with the ship in the middle of both a boarding action and an emergency in main engineering, nobody was taking a shower. Coming out of the head, he found no one in the large crew berth.

It all went to hell the moment he stepped out of the compartment.

Four armed men stood at the junction just to his left. He had the drop on them for all of half a heartbeat—just long enough for his brain to process the horrid, terrifying development—before someone down the passageway to his right yelled, "Hey! Who the *fuck*—"

Tanner snapped the plasma carbine in his hands to hip level, one hand on the trigger and the other under its barrel, and let loose the widest possible blast of green destruction into the pack of sentries a mere couple of meters away. Smoke, gore, and screams resulted while Tanner immediately spun and dropped to one knee to fire at the voice down the opposite end of the passageway.

Bullets and lasers flew past him, largely aimed too high by rushed, startled hands. Tanner afforded himself a half second to aim and fired another blast that expanded as it flew down the corridor at this second batch of foes. Then he spun back to the first group once more, falling onto his left shoulder. Tanner had already annihilated one man and dismembered another with his first shot. Of the two remaining, one had enough of his wits about him to leap behind the contour of one bulkhead. It wasn't enough to save him from Tanner's weapon. Superheated green plasma partly melted the edges of the bulkhead as well as the half of his body that hadn't gotten around it for cover.

A hail of friendly fire cut down the fourth pirate in the nearer group. Tanner rolled away from him, scrambling for cover. By the time the remaining pirates corrected their fire, Tanner had rounded the corner. He heard the frightening ping of a grenade ricocheting off the bulkhead close to him. Spotting the thing just in time to see it land alarmingly close, Tanner had no real time to think. He reached out with one hand in the shape of a hook, scooped it up, and hurled it back down the passageway.

Had he stopped to listen, he might have heard the pained screams that blended with the echo of the resultant explosion. Tanner didn't stop. He glanced around quickly to orient himself, picked a direction, and ran, keeping his weapon up and at the ready all the while.

Weapons and tactics school emphasized the need to control oneself and avoid casualties by friendly fire. No such concerns burdened Tanner here. He was quite ready and willing to shoot anything that moved, as the next pirate to step into his path found out to his instant regret.

• • •

Jerry couldn't believe his eyes. The mess in engineering already held plenty of his attention. Now this. "Lauren, we've got trouble!" he shouted, pointing to the action in the passageways. The violence displayed over the monitors was soon accompanied by a cacophony of weapons fire close enough to be heard on the bridge.

Lauren hit the emergency signal on her holocom. "Recall! Recall! All available hands, we've got hostiles aboard *Vengeance*! Get the fuck back here now!"

Within seconds, her holocom erupted with rapid responses. Boarding teams from all across the *Pride of Polaris* announced their imminent return.

"Christ," breathed Jerry, "they're already closing on the bridge."

"How many are there?" someone demanded.

"Fuck if we know yet," the acting captain snapped.

"Chopra's team says they've got casualties!" called out another bridge hand.

"Where the fuck is Paco? Weren't they covering deck three?"

Then the ship shook. "Second explosion in engineering!" reported Jerry. "That mess still isn't under control!"

"All available hands!" Lauren repeated into her holocom. "All available hands, return to *Vengeance* now!"

• • •

Had Casey's holocom been on a handset, he'd have thrown it down onto the deck. It was bad enough to be interrupted. Doubly aggravating for its timing, coming right as his recruiting pitch left his mouth. But for the interruption to announce *this* . . .

"Chang! Castillo! Yadav! Hold firm on your positions! Carl, you button that bridge down, and if anyone blinks wrong, fucking shoot 'em!" Casey's orders came without much thought. Whether the action on *Vengeance* required a few dozen guns or literally every single crewman, they couldn't let the *Pride* go now. Even if this disruption was eliminated in the next two minutes, it had already revealed a crack in the pirates' image of unassailable strength in front of their captives.

Naturally, Casey wanted to charge back to his ship, to take control of the situation or at least find out from Lauren what the hell was going on so he could help her deal with it. But he'd left her in charge, and he had to maintain his faith in her. She was the most experienced pirate he knew; if she couldn't deal with whatever danger had appeared, chances were no one could. Casey had to concern himself with other matters.

Glaring viciously at his captive audience of the ship's crew and junior officers, Casey drew his pistol and fired randomly. His bullet caught a young man in the shoulder. It might have been better to kill the man outright, but then, his cries and whimpers of pain would serve as useful background noise.

"Forget it!" Casey snarled. "Forget what I said! Not one of you is coming with us. You'll be lucky to get out of this alive! Up! On your feet, all of you!"

He switched over to a direct line on his holocom as his frightened audience got ready to move. "Chang," he said, "we're bringing the crew out to the promenade. I want all these assholes in one place until we get shit sorted out again."

Chang gave some sort of acknowledgment, but Casey didn't listen. He was already looking for someone else to shoot.

• • •

It was exactly what they had taught Tanner not to do. Everett and Janeka put Oscar Company through frequent simulated small arms combat at the tail end of basic training, both in the squad bay and on *Los Angeles*. They showed the recruits how to find and use cover, how to move forward, and how to retreat as a team under covering fire. Weapons and tactics school elaborated on all such topics. All of Tanner's instructors instilled a sense of aggression and urgency in such matters, but they also wanted their people to survive.

Headlong charges with weapons blazing were strictly for the movies, they said. Wild exposure provided nothing but dead comrades. A crewman or a marine had to rely on his teammates to stay alive.

He had no teammates here. No covering fire. Nothing but a thin margin of surprise and whatever aggression he could dish out. Every passing second provided another chance for the enemy to realize that he was all alone. Yet as aggressive as his enemy could be, they apparently weren't used to being on the receiving end.

Alarms rang throughout the ship. Tanner raced around a corner to find three men at the base of a ladder, each of them with their weapons raised and their eyes wild. He let his feet fly out from under him, willingly falling down onto his back as they spun and opened fire.

Tanner's plasma carbine was set to maximum spread. The bursts wouldn't travel far, but they didn't need to. He pulled the trigger half a second after his shoulder hit the floor with the gun aligned as close to parallel to the deck as he could manage. The trick worked; two of the men shrieked in sudden agony as their legs dissolved in a green flash.

The remaining man hosed down the corridor with bullets. Tanner felt something strike against his right calf. Slugs hit the padded armor of his jacket. Then his head jerked sideways involuntarily, almost rolling his body over with sudden force. A high-pitched ringing tone overwhelmed his hearing. He lost his gun. Black and red spots clouded his vision.

By the time it cleared two seemingly endless seconds later, he couldn't believe he was still alive. He thought he'd been lying on the deck for an eternity. Yet the alarms still blared. No weapon filled his hands. He heard frantic, panting breath and the sound of metal sliding and clicking against metal.

Tanner forced himself to roll back up to one knee and then rise. In the middle of the passageway, standing amid his mortally wounded comrades, a panicked young man frantically tried to reload his assault rifle. The bullet that clipped Tanner's helmet had been the last from his magazine.

Lunging forward, Tanner got his left hand around the pirate's neck. He shoved his foe up against the bulkhead, grabbed for the pistol tucked into the pirate's belt, and pulled the trigger the instant his finger was around it. Only two inches of air and the lenses of Tanner's helmet separated their eyes as the bullets tore through flesh, bone, and lungs.

Stepping back, Tanner found his right leg much weaker than his left. Blood flowed from his calf. It had to have been from a ricochet; at full force, a bullet from that rifle should have done more damage. All those bullets, only to hit a glancing blow across his helmet and a ricochet through his lower leg. The combat jacket stopped the rest. His luck held.

There was no time to deal with the wound properly. Tanner limped over to retrieve the plasma carbine still lying on the deck. Two steps told Tanner all he needed to know about his leg. Seconds mattered, but so did blood loss.

Tanner paused to pull the electrostatic tape from his belt.

• • •

"Where the fuck is Shango's team?" growled Jerry.

"Not gonna be here in time," answered Lauren. She let the screen from her holocom fall away. "Have we still got a fix on only one assault element?"

"So far, yeah. Such a fucking mess in here I can't even tell, but there's gotta be more than one," her ops boss grunted. "And goddammit, I've already got two different teams with friendly fire casualties. They're rushing back so fast they don't even know who they're opening up on, and I can't tell—dammit! Look! Hector just got wasted! He's on this deck!"

Lauren bit back a curse. One of Jerry's view screens relayed images of smoke and debris from yet another small security team's demise. There were only three men with Hector to begin with, but now all she could make out was a smoky mess of blasted corpses and bulkheads with the paint melting off. At least one of their attackers was awfully liberal with some sort of plasma gun.

That sort of firepower presented a real problem. Lauren considered her options. Jerry all but read her mind. "Seal off the bridge?" he asked.

"Not yet." Lauren scowled. She strode away from him, heading for the only hatch in or out of the compartment. "I want a shot at these fuckers first. Ted, Sarah, c'mere. Grenades. Mike, you're on the hatch." Lauren pulled the scattergun from its holster on her back.

• • •

The bridge sat just down the end of the passageway. It had a single broad hatch. Two more hatches lay before it to either side of the passageway, both only a few meters from his goal. The layout reminded him just a little of *St. Jude*, where the captain and XO both had their quarters near the bridge.

Crouched at the top of a ladder well at the opposite end of the passageway, Tanner considered his options. The lack of obvious defenses unsettled him, but he couldn't allow time for attackers to come up from behind him. His limp wasn't too bad now; electrostatic tape had it wrapped tight while adrenaline blunted the pain.

He kept his gun trained on the bridge hatch. They had to see him out here on some sort of security camera. There had to be an ambush ready. *Bridge at the end of the passageway, hatches to either side before I get there . . .*

Clearing those two compartments had to come first. Tanner picked the hatch to his left more or less at random. He rushed up and had his hand on the large, wheel-shaped handle when the bridge portal flew open.

Gunfire followed. Tanner hid behind the heavy metal hatch he'd only just opened. Then the grenades flew from the bridge, one, then two more, then another. He leapt through the open portal, trying to shut the door behind him in time. Though the bulkheads and the door held against the series of explosions that followed, the hatch wasn't quite closed. The shock waves knocked him to the deck.

His only look at the compartment came as he got to his feet again. It had to be either the captain's or XO's quarters, but the living area was a shambles. No one else occupied the compartment in that moment, though; nothing else mattered.

Tanner pushed the hatch open, swinging his plasma carbine around it while using it as cover. He heard quick, cut-off words as he moved: "Did we—fuck!" Lasers and bullets struck against the hatch, which Tanner answered with a half-aimed blast from his much heavier weapon. He heard a scream. Someone shouted out, "Seal it! Seal the bridge!"

That was his cue. Tanner charged, firing a last blast of his weapon before it clicked dry. As before, the wide ball of plasma left smoke and screams in its wake, searing the bulkheads and passing straight through the limbs and flesh of humans who weren't far enough out of the way. Tanner followed the same path.

Haste made all the difference. Heavy metal panels slid up from the deck and down from the overhead around the bridge portal, coming into place over the bridge hatch. Tanner dove headlong through the space between the thick walls, landing unceremoniously on his faceplate and belly in the bridge just before the entrance slammed shut. His weapon fell from his hands, clattering off to one side.

The chaos created by his plasma blasts had not yet abated. "My arm!" someone shrieked in anguish. "Oh God, my arm!" Another voice howled in even greater pain, unable to form words. Sparks burst from a ruined control panel.

He rolled without thinking about it. Left was as good as right when he had no real clue where danger was yet. His legs collided with someone standing over him, sending the surprised pirate stumbling to the deck.

"Shit! Get him!" a woman behind Tanner demanded. "Jerry, fuck him up!"

Bullets ricocheted across the deck as Tanner scrambled away. He got to his feet, finding himself moving toward a tall, balding man at a control console. "Lauren," Jerry barked, getting out of his seat, "I'll get—"

A fist loaded with rage and fear cut Jerry off. It landed forcefully against his jaw, eliciting a popping noise from the pirate. Tanner grabbed the stunned pirate by the shoulders, pulling him around to get something between him and the woman shooting at him. Jerry collapsed as soon as Tanner was past. The younger man dove for cover behind the control console, trying to get a sense of his surroundings, his opponents, and his prospects. He had only a second, perhaps two.

There was a pistol tucked into an underarm holster sewn into his combat jacket. He remembered that. Tanner grabbed for it just as he looked up, spotting two more pirates behind yet another set of consoles just beyond the one sheltering Tanner. They both rose from their desks, eyes wide and hands drawing weapons. Shouted commands and screams of pain filled the bridge from every side.

Tanner got off the first shot. The pirate to his right jerked back, blood and bone bursting as Tanner's bullet passed between his collarbones. His comrade fired away, shooting with more urgency than control. Janeka had taught her people to aim. A red flash of the enemy's laser cut a line through the console above Tanner's head. A second, straighter shot bit through his jacket across his left shoulder. The heartbeat Tanner spent training his pistol on his opponent proved worthwhile. He shot the pirate squarely in the face.

His shoulder burned with worse pain than anything he'd experienced, but the hit was blessedly narrow and cut a straight line through his flesh. He hadn't lost feeling or control of his arm.

Sudden movement drew his attention to his left. Lauren appeared right next to him, stepping around the wrecked console to level her scattergun right at Tanner's head. His left arm swung up immediately, pinning the weapon against the side of the console and pushing himself away as it went off. He could feel the heat of its blast rush by inches from his back, but more than that he felt Lauren's foot as it swiftly came up into his side. The jacket did nothing to soften the blow. She kicked him away, but by then he had his gun pointed at her and fired.

Lauren saw it in time to dodge behind Jerry's console again. Tanner scrambled away. There was another pirate in his way then, a swarthy man in thick leather and silks with a pair of pistols that weren't up in time to stop Tanner from tackling him. Again, Tanner spun around his opponent, using him for cover.

His foe wasn't as hesitant to fire this time as she had been when Tanner first tried this. The shot from Lauren's scattergun blasted the pirate forward onto Tanner in a bloody mess, sending both men to the deck under a rain of gore.

Once again, Tanner's helmet had saved his skull from a nasty landing against a metal floor. Falling on his back, Tanner found that he'd come nearly full circle around the main control console. Jerry still lay on the deck, knocked out cold by Tanner's punch. Lauren appeared from around the other side again; Tanner fired off two more shots from his gun to send her back behind cover while he rose. By the time she risked another shot, he was gone.

Lauren couldn't decide on a foul enough exclamation. Practically her whole bridge crew was down, most of them dead, all at the hands of a single guy. Her opponent moved with more urgency than grace, evading her next shot solely by virtue of slipping on the blood on the deck and landing on his side. Then he rolled behind the command and control table. Yet another of her bridge crew had hidden on the other side of that; once again, she heard shots ring out and saw that same pirate fall away with holes blown through his chest.

She paused for only a moment, but it was enough to assess the situation. One guy on the bridge, half-rushing and half-stumbling around. The pirates were used to having the initiative, accustomed to being on the offensive and following at least some loose sort of plan. They had no time to regroup here. No time to regain their balance. They were on the defensive, and as a result they were dying and the bridge was getting smashed.

He didn't come out from behind the command table again. His gunfire ceased. He had to be reloading. Fully fed up with this shit, Lauren rushed forward and launched herself over the command table.

Just as he slammed his fresh magazine home into his pistol, Tanner was tackled to the deck from above. He and his assailant tumbled. She recovered first; still on his side, Tanner swung his pistol around at Lauren only to have it kicked painfully out of his hands. Her next kick came straight for his head. Her boot heel slammed into the left lens of his helmet with a crunch. The jarring blow put Tanner on his back once again. Pain shot through his left eye, which now refused to open.

She sprang to her feet, drawing a long, laser-heated knife. Tanner had a leg up in time to return her stomp to the face in kind as she lunged in. Lauren shrugged it off, slashing downward through the fastening straps of his jacket.

Tanner kicked again, sending her stumbling back. She lost her blade. It gave him enough time to get to his feet. His left eye finally opened again, only to leave him looking through a badly shattered helmet lens. Tanner popped the seals on the helmet to remove it. His jacket fell open.

He flung his helmet at Lauren as she recovered. Blood trailed from it as it flew through the air to strike against her shoulder. His cheek bled freely, cut by shards of his broken helmet lens. Lauren came on, swinging feet and fists with frightening speed.

Tanner blocked, dodged, and gave ground. He couldn't avoid every blow, nor did his open jacket absorb them all. He took a blow to the chest, one against his injured shoulder, and another on his cheek. He thought he felt one of his ribs crack under a kick. Tanner immediately understood who was the superior combatant.

She was kicking his ass. It was like fighting Janeka, only worse. Lauren intended to kill him.

No, he realized. He stayed on the defensive, keeping his guard up and doing all he could to stay alive. *It's not worse than Janeka. She's not as strong.*

He looked for an opening. Lauren came on, driving him farther back, but finally he blocked and twisted her into a tangle. Tanner went for broke: his forehead came down hard on her nose.

Rocked back by the blow, with shapeless bursts of red and green exploding behind her tightly shut eyes, Lauren swung one arm out wide to fend off her opponent. It wasn't the first time her nose had been broken. She needed only a moment to recover.

Tanner didn't give it to her. He pressed on, throwing punch after punch, driving her off balance until finally he risked a slow, powerful roundhouse kick. His foot came right into her center, sending her practically flying back into the main control console in the center of the bridge.

The tall fixture shook as Lauren bounced against it. She took a right hook to the face and fell down onto her back. Her eyes opened just in time to see the wrecked console's shattered, laser-blasted top half slide down on top of her. Lauren let out a sharp, sudden scream as hundreds of pounds of metal and sparking, ruined circuitry pinned her arms to the deck.

Though nearly doubled over from the beating he'd endured, Tanner jerked back with wide, shocked eyes. Her howl of pain bit into his ears. Tanner's gaze swept the bridge, looking for the pirate who was certain to shoot him dead as he stood there dumbly.

No such pirate threatened him. Every one of his opponents lay broken or dead. He was the last man standing on the bridge of a pirate ship.

The thought helped him stand a little straighter.

• • •

"Lauren? Lauren, talk to me, goddammit!" Casey stared at the holocom on his wrist, so angered by the blank screen of his comms channel that he wanted to put a bullet through it. No reply came. It didn't bode well.

His mind raced. He had to do something. "Fuentes!" he barked over the main channel reserved for boarding teams. "Harrison, Bell! Get your asses up to *Vengeance*!"

Chang looked on with a frown. Unlike most of his comrades, he gave no outward sign of stress. Though just as concerned as the rest of the pirates, he didn't let it show. "That's gonna leave us really thin here," Chang warned quietly. "There can't be that big a fight going on over there."

"Do you wanna take that fucking chance?" snapped the captain. Then he bit back his next comment, forcing himself to take a breath once confronted with Chang's calm expression. "It can't be any security teams or other bullshit from this ship, 'cause our guys at the airlocks didn't see anything get by them. It's gotta be some faction of our own crew making a play."

"Gonna be tough sorting out the friendlies from the traitors if that's the case," observed Chang.

Casey grunted. He looked out across the promenade deck, his gaze sweeping across the hundreds of passengers and crew and their comparative handful of captors. "We've got this ship," he said. "We've got everyone under guard, we've got the bridge, the shuttle bay, and engineering covered. We don't need more than that until this mess is straightened out."

• • •

"Wow. Those really are some thick doors," huffed Tanner. He tapped at them with his reloaded plasma gun, impressed by how solid the metal sounded.

The only other conscious person on the bridge said nothing in response. She lay with her arms buried under the wrecked control console, biting back her pain. Her eyes darted this way and that, looking for any sort of opportunity but finding none. Even Jerry, though still out cold, lay securely bound in electrostatic tape.

Tanner limped around in a circle at the center of the bridge to assess the damage. The command and control table was smashed, and with it the usual three-dimensional sensor bubble was gone. Still, Tanner didn't need to operate the destroyer by himself, even if he could. He just had to make sure nobody else took control of the bridge, and to hope engineering would remain too chaotic for anyone there to override his control.

"Those blast seals aren't too thick to cut through with the right tools," Lauren said bitterly. "They'll get on that as soon as they realize they've lost the bridge. Probably right now," she added, hissing through her pain.

"Yeah. Figured that part out already." Tanner made his way to the communications station, which thankfully had suffered only minimal damage. The controls weren't too different from the setup on *St. Jude*; there was certainly more to work with, but some of the basic equipment was about the same.

"What's . . . drones?" he blinked at the status board. "You're using jammer drones?"

Lauren looked at him with disgust. "What kind of idiot are you, anyway?"

"Not gonna argue that, but at least you have idiot-proof controls," he muttered as he deactivated the drones. Tanner called up the broad-frequency distress channels and keyed the mic.

"Mayday, mayday, mayday, this is—" He stopped. There was a protocol for this. Mayday three times, ship identification three times, position, situation, passengers . . . only how should he identify himself? *St. Jude* was gone. *Pride of Polaris* was the one in trouble, yet he wasn't actually on the *Pride*. And *Vengeance* was a pirate ship . . . Tanner frowned. *What the hell,* he decided. *Tell it to them straight. If I die, at least there'll be the recording.* He keyed the mic again.

"Mayday, mayday, mayday, this is Crewman Tanner Malone of ANS *St. Jude*, mayday. My position coordinates ride this signal. *St. Jude* is destroyed. I say again, *St. Jude* is destroyed. I am on board the Centurion-class pirate destroyer *Vengeance*. I have taken the bridge. Pirates from *Vengeance* have boarded NSS *Pride of Polaris* at these coordinates. I say again, pirates have taken NSS *Pride of Polaris* with approximately twenty-five hundred passengers and crew on board. Mayday, mayday, mayday." With that, he keyed the "repeat message" button.

"You'll be dead before help gets here," spat Lauren.

"Probably, but at least I ruined your day." Tanner pointed to a relatively unscathed bridge station against the opposite bulkhead. "Is that damage control?"

"What," sneered Lauren, "you plan on running this ship all by yourself?"

"Take that as a yes." He limped over to the station. "Oh, thank God, there's a first aid kit here."

"Fat lot of good it'll do you."

"Y'know," said Tanner, "I've had to hold my tongue for over a year while people were shitty to me. I'm not obligated to be polite to you." He paused with the first aid kit only long enough to put some clotting gel in the freely bleeding gash under his left eye. There wasn't time for more than that. He had to figure out the console layout in front of him.

"They're gonna break you before they let you die, motherfucker!" Lauren seethed. "You don't even know what pain is yet. Hell's gonna be a relief when you finally get there."

"Your friends don't sound very nice." Tanner's eyes stayed on the controls. The locked panel above the main console looked like it held what he needed, but he had no idea what the security access code might be. "Bet they're not very trustworthy, either."

"What the fuck would you know about it?"

"Realistically? Not much," Tanner grunted as he tried to pry the panel open with his multitool. The clasps held fast. "But I read a lot. Read everything I could find on what you guys did to *Aphrodite.* Qal'at Khalil. That stuff. Seems to me you probably wouldn't want to turn your back on friends like yours for even a second."

"Figured that out all by yourself?"

"Yeah, well"—Tanner shrugged—"I'm book smart. Not very good with tools, though."

Tanner drew his laser pistol, turned his face away, and shot the clasps on the locked panel. Sparks and smoke flew. He pulled the remaining debris off and waved away the fumes. He found exactly what he'd hoped for. Tanner looked from the panel back to the thick metal barrier sealing off the bridge.

"I figure if I was on a ship full of guys like that, I'd want some way to deal with a potential mutiny, y'know?"

• • •

"Casey, this is way bad, man!"

"Carl, just get ahold of yourself," Casey said to the projection of his deputy on the *Pride*'s bridge. Several screens from his holocom floated in front of him, each one displaying the faces of different team leaders. Most were back aboard *Vengeance.* A couple other teams were still aboard the *Pride*. The last of Casey's screens displayed the computer-generated text of Crewman Malone's mayday call. "Can you jam it?"

"With *what*?" snapped Carl. "This is a fucking luxury liner. You think they've got jamming equipment on this thing?"

"Okay, fine. Guys, here's what we're gonna do. Wilson, keep working on this ship. Sankersingh, cut through to the bridge and murder that little shit. Fuentes, Bell, you keep going and get in there to back Sankersingh up. Metcalf, you're in charge of finishing the sweep on *Vengeance*. Make sure there isn't another one of these assholes hiding somewhere. Carl, you still with me?"

"Yeah," he said, "yeah, I'm here. Sensor bubble still doesn't show any contacts, by the way."

Casey nodded. "That's good," he reassured Carl. "Okay, Carl, here's what you do. Route me into the *Pride*'s ship-to-ship comms system and put me through as a mayday response. Let's see if we can't talk his way into a bullet." He looked up to Chang, then gestured out at the massed hostages a few meters beyond him. "Chang, pick out something tragic."

He pulled the video capture capsule off his holocom, set it to focus on his image, and then tossed it to the floor in front of him. He heard the beep of his holocom as the capsule synched up, and a second beep as Carl put him through on the ship's systems. The pirate captain waited for Chang to drag a frightened young girl over to him.

A response screen flickered to life just past the capture capsule, ready to project the image of whomever answered his call. "Attention, Crewman Malone," Casey said. "I say again, attention, Crewman Malone."

• • •

Tanner immediately snapped his laser pistol up toward the image on the screen of the comms station. He recognized the gravel-voiced pirate from the Qal'at Khalil files. The man had a pistol in one hand. Tanner had a sinking feeling he knew exactly where this would go.

"Better answer that," warned Lauren.

Trying to think of how to counter the inevitable, Tanner limped over to the comms station. There was a chance this guy would pull something new, but he doubted it. So far his MO had worked out just fine. Why wouldn't he continue it? The last thing Tanner wanted was a hostage negotiation.

No. The *last* thing he wanted was for some innocent person to die right in front of him.

He pressed the button. "This is Crewman Malone," he answered.

"Malone. I'm not gonna tell you my name. I will tell you that I'm the captain of the ship you're on. We need to talk. But first things first." The pirate gestured to someone offscreen with one hand. Tanner heard a yelp and saw a young girl in a blue dress shoved toward the captain.

Tanner promptly shot out the comms station.

• • •

Casey had his gun on the back of the girl's neck. He was just about to say, "Just so we understand each other," when the punk on the screen cut off the image with his pistol. Chang and another pirate nearby stared as their captain blinked in surprise.

"Son of a bitch!" growled Casey, shoving the girl back to Chang without even thinking about it.

• • •

Wide-eyed and sweating, Tanner stared at the smoking remains of the comms station. His breath was quick and heavy. That little girl may have just been murdered. Perhaps she was still alive but probably not. He never should have opened up the channel. Stupid. So stupid.

"Point's made, kid," Lauren growled. "You know the score. You're all alone on a ship you can't even run. We've got a couple thousand hostages. If you don't want them to start dying ten at a time, you'd better get back on the line and surrender right fucking now."

"You mean he'll kill all those people you guys were gonna murder, anyway?"

"Maybe not," pressed Lauren. "Maybe you oughta try making a deal." She gave a little nod of her head toward the comms station. "Backup system is right there. Better make the call."

Negotiating was pointless, and Tanner knew it. Moreover, he knew there was no further point in speaking with his prisoner. He lurched across the bridge to the damage control station, momentarily forgetting all his pain.

Without a word, Tanner threw the first large switch on the emergency venting panel. And then the next. And then the next.

• • •

"We're on it, Casey, we're on it," called a voice over Casey's holocom. "We're at the bridge now. We'll cut through and get the bastard. Don't worry."

"Almost got engineering under control again," piped up another.

"Fuentes here. We're on board *Vengeance* now."

"Bell here, ditto that."

Casey paced back and forth in front of his hostages and his men, listening in to the reports. The quick end to his conversation with Malone left him almost speechless. Casey was stuck on the luxury liner with no enemy to fight and his forces too far away to effectively direct. All there was to do was to keep his captives in check.

The thought stopped him in his tracks. He looked out over the faces of his hostages. They remained gathered in a single mass that began a few meters away, just down a handful of steps from the landing. "Don't anybody get any fucking ideas," he warned in a loud but calm voice. Their whispers and murmurs ended as he spoke. "Sit quietly and cooperate and you might get out of this alive. You don't have any other options. Nobody even knows you people are in trouble. Nobody's coming to help."

His gaze swept the crowd once more. The silence reassured him.

Then he heard the soft, distant thump from up above. And another.

Casey, Chang, and everyone else assembled on the promenade looked up through the luxury liner's transparent canopy shell. *Vengeance*'s grappling cables and enclosed gangways had retracted; the ship was already drifting away from the *Pride*.

Dozens of pirates flew helplessly out of open airlocks, access hatches, and bay doors all across *Vengeance*. They floated off into the void in all directions.

Casey's heart leapt into his throat, choking off the scream that threatened to escape his lips.

• • •

Silence held across the bridge. Even Lauren had been cowed. Her natural aggression would soon reassert itself, but for at least this brief moment, her mind struggled to accept the reality of what the man at the backup comms panel had just done.

Tanner stared at the controls, too wrapped up in his own thoughts to notice her silence. He found his hands trembling again. All this blood and insanity and he could still feel fear—and despair.

He'd already accomplished so much more than anyone could ask of him. He was already hurt. He was still utterly alone and outgunned. Getting this far was nothing short of miraculous. No one could blame him if he sat tight and waited for help. It was probably even the wisest thing to do from a tactical standpoint.

Somewhere out there was the corpse of *St. Jude*. Somewhere out there floated Morales. Tanner had escaped all that. He made it all the way here.

He could live through this if he just stayed put.

That uniform means that if there's gotta be a fight, you want it to come to you and not to someone else, Janeka repeated in his head. *You ready for that, recruit?*

Tanner shut his eyes tightly. He saw the face of a scared little girl and an angry man with a gun. He took a deep breath, flicked the red switch on the panel, and threw away his hard-won chances of going home alive.

"Mayday, mayday, mayday, this is Crewman Tanner Malone of ANS *St. Jude*, mayday. My position coordinates ride this signal. *St. Jude* is destroyed. I say again, *St. Jude* is destroyed. Pirates have boarded NSS *Pride of Polaris* at these coordinates. I say again, pirates have taken NSS *Pride of Polaris* with approximately twenty-five hundred passengers and crew on board. I am on board Centurion-class pirate destroyer *Vengeance*. I have taken the bridge and vented the majority of *Vengeance*'s crew out into space. I am abandoning *Vengeance* to attempt rescue of *Pride of Polaris*. Mayday, mayday, mayday."

FIFTEEN

Monsters

"Course heading confirmed. ETA twenty-nine minutes at current speed." Madelyn's voice trembled as she spoke. It wasn't pronounced, nor loud, but Rick noticed. He also noticed the way she stared at the yellow circle on the astrogation chart marking the last estimated position of *St. Jude*. Sharma double-checked her findings, then input them in the computer.

"He wouldn't be out here if it wasn't for me," Madelyn said. She bit her lip.

"What do you mean?" Sharma asked. "Who?"

"Her friend on *St. Jude*," Rick answered for her.

"I talked him into it. Talked him into enlisting."

"Madelyn, he made his own choice."

"He was supposed to go off to an ecology lab for an internship before university, but it got all fucked up and he didn't know what else to do," she went on. To her credit, there were no tears in her eyes. This was the military. It was risky business. There was every likelihood that she would someday have to say good-bye to friends whose lives ended much too soon. But she could steel herself against only so much. "He's gentle. Nice. I never saw him hurt anyone. All he wanted to do was work with furry animals and estuaries and stuff. I talked him into this."

Sharma glanced at her, unsure of what to say. "Why'd you encourage him to do this?" he asked, figuring maybe it would be good for her to get it out now.

Madelyn swallowed. She didn't answer right away. "I thought he'd be good at it." She tapped at a couple of buttons. "He's smart. Really smart. Tougher than he knows. I thought . . . I thought he'd be good at this."

Rick gave her shoulder a small squeeze. "Who says he isn't?"

Madelyn huffed.

"Captain!" a voice called out across the bridge. "We've picked up a mayday call."

Heads turned toward the communications watch officer. He had one hand over his ear, covering his headset out of habit. A pair of enlisted specialists beside him wore similar expressions of disbelief. "It's—this is weird, ma'am," he explained. "I don't know whether I believe this or not."

Standing at the center of the bridge, Captain Leigh gestured for her comms officer to put the message on speakers. Madelyn's breath caught in her throat.

". . . Crewman Tanner Malone of ANS *St. Jude*, mayday. My position coordinates ride this signal. *St. Jude* is destroyed. I say again, *St. Jude* is destroyed. I am on board Centurion-class pirate destroyer *Vengeance*. I have taken the bridge . . ."

Sharma blinked. "You've got to be kidding."

"That's him," said Madelyn, who was more astonished than anyone. "That's his voice."

Sharma focused on his station. He nudged Madelyn out of her chair. "Get over there and tell the captain."

She blinked. "What? But—"

"Midshipman Carter, I would think that's a prank or a lunatic talking, except you're here telling me he's legit. Get over there and tell the captain now."

Following his instructions more out of reflex than sense, Madelyn walked over to the communications station. Both the captain and XO had moved over there as well, listening in and evaluating the message with their comms watch section. "It's the right band for distress calls, ma'am," said one of the enlisted technicians. "Nothing on the signal is out of place. We're riding up on it, too. Almost a reciprocal of our course."

"Yeah, but listen to what he's saying," countered the ensign standing beside her. "The hell kind of mayday call is that?"

"The kind you put out when the protocol goes out the window, sir." The tech shrugged. "I mean, if that's the truth, what else would you say?"

"I don't know." The captain crossed her arms thoughtfully. "We'll have to check it out, but it sounds awfully fishy to me. What if this is a wild goose chase?"

"Captain?" asked Madelyn. She waited for Leigh to turn around, taking a breath as she realized once more how far beyond her station she was reaching. "Ma'am, I know that crewman. I went to school with him. He's a friend. This is for real."

Leigh raised a curious eyebrow. "You think it could be any kind of a setup? Could he have snapped?"

"No way, ma'am. Not him."

The captain's eyes stayed on her. Madelyn held her gaze.

"Captain," piped up the ensign, "the call has changed."

"Headset," Leigh said, reaching out with one hand while her eyes stayed on Madelyn's. She held up the earpiece to listen. "XO," she said finally, "bring the ship to battle stations. Tell Major Kading to ready his marines for a boarding action." She returned the headset and then strode away from the station, calling for the helm to increase speed and for Sharma to plot out an emergency FTL jump.

Madelyn glanced down at the comms techs. One of them held the headset up to her without a word. Madelyn listened, once again feeling the breath knocked out of her.

"Midshipman Carter," she heard the captain say. The captain faced another direction entirely, her attention on another matter as she said, "If I was in that kid's shoes, I'd be shooting everything that moved. Might be best if we had a friendly face over there to talk him down. Suit up for boarding and go get your boy."

• • •

He allowed himself three minutes with the first aid kit. Localized painkillers provided minimal relief. Clotting gel stopped the bleeding. Microweave bracing bandages ensured nothing would open back up.

The last of his electrostatic tape plugged the holes in his vac suit. The roll ran out before he could tape his combat jacket closed again. With its shattered eyepiece, his helmet was a loss. Fortunately, he found a couple of spare helmets on the bridge—nothing as good or combat-worthy, but enough to get the job done.

Tanner looked over the external passageway monitor again. A mob of pirates lay dead just outside the hatch. They had been considerate enough to bring a plasma cutter with them. Tanner would need that.

"You don't really think they'll fall for that bullshit," said Lauren. Her voice had gone dry, which only made her sound all the more bitter.

"Fall for what?"

"That mayday correction. Going over to the *Pride*."

Tanner shrugged. "They'll know when I show up on the ship." He adjusted his new helmet's seals and made one last check of his weapons.

"Christ, you really think you're some kind of knight in shining armor, don't you?"

"Yup. That's me. Speaking of chivalry," he added carelessly, "here you go." He tossed the open first aid kit down to her. It landed on the deck beside her, its contents scattering all around and on top of her where she lay with her arms trapped by the wrecked console.

Lauren screamed in rage, trying to wrench her arms free once more only to suffer further pain. "Fuck you, asshole!" she howled. "Go to hell!"

"Probably on my way," Tanner said as he got to the bridge hatch. "You might want to hold your breath."

Lauren blinked, then realized what he meant. She inhaled deeply just before the blast seals opened. Air rushed out into the empty passageway as Tanner walked through. More air pumped into the bridge from its independent emergency supply, replenishing the atmosphere until the hatch closed behind him.

Then he was gone. Lauren had only the pain of her injured arms and the endless loop of Tanner's mayday call to keep her company.

• • •

"Oh Christ, Jesus *fuck*, Casey," Carl ranted, frantically looking from one sensor readout to the next on the bridge of *Pride*, "there's gotta be five hundred guys out there just floating in space! *Our* guys! I can't get goddamn anyone on a comms channel over on *Vengeance*. I think they're all dead!"

"Calm down, Carl," he heard Casey say in an even tone. "You're still alive and you've still got the bridge. We're still in control of this ship. They might not all be gone on *Vengeance*. We had guys fighting a fire, right? They'd be suited up for that. Right, Wilson?"

Carl turned to his comms screens then, looking to the one dedicated to Wilson and the engineering boarding team for some reassurance. It wasn't forthcoming. "If he emergency vented the whole ship from the bridge, it might not matter," answered Wilson. "The system's designed to expel everything from engineering that isn't welded or bolted to the ship, so—"

"Okay, never mind," Casey interrupted. "Don't worry about them. Either they made it or they didn't. Nothing we can do about it from here. Carl, do another security monitor sweep of this ship. Make sure none of our hostages have slipped away and gotten squirrely without us noticing. And keep the bridge crew up there in check. Wilson, I need an estimate on how long it'll take to get this ship's propulsion going again. FTL and sublight. How do we look?"

"We've almost got the thrusters online. Just give us a few more minutes to button things up the rest of the way, and we should be ready to run tests on the sublight drives. FTL should be ready in another ten or fifteen."

"Can't you work any faster?" pressed Carl. "Maybe we oughta grab some snipes from the *Pride*'s crew and force 'em to help?"

"And give them a chance to sabotage us?" Wilson shot back. "It would be one thing if someone volunteered, but pressed for time like this? Too tempting for some snipe to be a hero. I know what I'm doing, Carl!"

"But—"

"Excellent," Casey broke in. "Keep at it, Wilson. See, Carl? We're gonna be fine."

There was a moment of silence. Then, "Boss, I don't like the way the bridge crew up here is looking at us. Should I just smoke 'em?"

"Christ," Casey muttered under his breath. Then he turned his voice back to the comms channel. "No, Carl, don't smoke 'em. Don't kill anybody you don't have to. Every one of these fuckers we kill might be money down the drain. We're gonna need ransoms to buy our way back out of this hole." He cut the audio on his holocom and looked over to Chang. "I've gotta go up there and settle his ass down before he does something stupid. Probably should be on the bridge, anyway."

Chang merely nodded. "Keep the channels open."

The pirate captain walked out.

As soon as he was gone, Chang turned to Turtle. "You thinking what I'm thinking?"

• • •

Despite the destroyer's uncontrolled drift, *Vengeance* and the *Pride* hadn't yet come far apart. Tanner stood on the destroyer's outer hull, held in place by the magnetic pads in his boots as he assessed the distance by eye. His fear had not abated so much as grown familiar. This was no less insane than everything else he'd done today. Suicidal or not, though, his work was not done. Every minute the two ships remained stranded was another minute for help to arrive. With that in mind, he pointed himself toward the aft quarter of the *Pride of Polaris*, inhaled deeply, and jumped.

Too hard, he realized as soon as his feet left *Vengeance*. *Way too hard. Shit. Shit.* Tanner scolded himself bitterly as the *Pride* rushed up much faster than he'd expected. He had strapped a portable (as if!) plasma cutter to his back along with two or three more weapons. That much extra mass would make for a rough landing if he weren't careful. He realized as he crossed the empty space that he hadn't been careful at all.

Nothing for it. Tanner unstrapped the plasma cutter from his back, holding it well away from his body as he closed on the liner's hull. He couldn't risk bouncing off, either; he'd just have to suck this up and hope he didn't break any bones. Tanner put the magnetic pads in his vac suit on full strength and hoped for the best.

"Ooof!" He fell against the hull about as roughly as he'd feared. Tanner landed on his feet, knees bent loosely and ready to fall backward as inertia, momentum, magnetics, and his body mass came together in a mess of physics he didn't want to think about. He bounced despite the magnets in his vac suit, but he didn't float far before being pulled back to the hull once more. He didn't hear the plasma cutter hit the deck, and then he remembered why he couldn't hear anything out in space. It took only a moment to regain his jarred senses.

He risked several long jumps along the hull, feeling sore all over as he moved and wishing he'd allowed himself more in the way of painkillers. Somewhere in the back of his mind, Chief Everett scolded him for his bitching. He kept moving.

At the edge of the *Pride*'s starboard main thruster, Tanner inhaled deeply to brace himself for what really made zero-g ops unpleasant. He took a step over the side, magnetic treads meeting with the hull to reorient his personal sense of up and down, and then with two more steps he did it yet again. In those few meters of movement, he turned himself completely upside down from where he'd stood a moment ago. Tanner walked into the gaping maw of the *Pride*'s thruster, keying up the power sequence on his plasma cutter along the way.

She suffered damage here. Nasty gouges had been cut into the metal by *Vengeance*'s lasers. The *Pride* had been built with automatic sealing chemical jets all across her vital areas; as soon as breaches occurred, the affected area filled up with foam. He saw the remnants, and he could see where new plating had been hurriedly welded in place from the inside.

Tanner only knew the very basics of ship propulsion, but now he felt desperately grateful for all the sadistic repair chores Everett dreamt up in basic training. A common crewman like him had no idea how to fix a starship engine, but he knew a damage control patch when he saw one . . . and he knew how to use the tools he had to get through it.

"Hope they don't have any of the ship's engineers in here working for 'em," Tanner said to himself as he got to cutting.

• • •

Casey sank into the captain's chair at the center of the bridge, looking over the shoulders of three of his people at the control consoles arranged in front of him. Not every station on the bridge was manned, but not every one of them needed to be.

Off to one side sat Carl, doing his best to keep his hands steady as he drank from a mug. Opposite Carl were the hostages from the bridge crew. Someone had seen to the junior astrogator's wounded leg. Wisely, they kept quiet. Casey could see plenty of fear in their eyes, which was good, but it wasn't the sort of fear he normally saw from hostages. These weren't people facing a dreadful but unavoidable unknown. These bastards suddenly had hope.

He tried not to think about that. He focused instead on settling the issue. Casey called up main engineering on his primary view screen. "Wilson," he said, "talk to me. How we doing?"

Wilson looked up from his control bank at the two-way view screen above him. "Running through our checklists now. Systems are all buttoned up, breaches are all sealed. Main power is online and stable." His eyes darted from one area to the next as he spoke, reviewing data screens and gesturing to his crew of techs and machinists. "Power flow checklist from drives to thrusters complete. Main thruster ignition safety check is good. Stabilizers look . . ." Wilson frowned. "Shit."

"What is it?" Casey asked, but he could already hear someone beyond Wilson shouting in alarm.

"Shit!" Wilson spat.

"Talk to me!" demanded Casey.

"We've got a hull breach on the starboard thruster. Radwell, you and Ron told me you had that buttoned up!"

"We did!" someone shouted. "Air pressure recovering—wait, there's another breach! What the *fuck*?"

"Main thrusters going into auto safety shutdown!" someone else yelled.

"Breach sealing system firing again!" another voice called out. Alarms flared, both in engineering and on the bridge, to announce much the same warning.

Casey's eyes went wide as a sensation of dread threatened to drown him. "Wilson, get someone in there now! Somebody armed!"

"On it," Wilson said, already turned away from the view screen and waving his arms as Casey spoke. Then he turned back to him. "Wait, what did you say?" he asked. "Somebody what?"

"Armed!" Casey shouted. "Somebody—"

Shots rang out in engineering. Casey could hear them almost as clearly as Wilson. Endless bullets streamed and ricocheted across the bulkheads and the machinery. Men screamed. Others leapt for cover, pulled weapons, and returned fire. Someone shouted, "Grenade!"

There was a burst of light and a high-pitched sound so loud that the audio baffles cut in. Casey watched in horror as Wilson reflexively put his hands over his ears, staggered out into the open, and was then torn apart by a burst of bullets.

• • •

Shift to cover. Stay low. Advance. Advance.

The grenade did its job beautifully. Tanner's ears rang as loud as ever; he crouched several meters out of the effective radius and wore a sealed helmet, but even so the blast was shockingly loud. Had that grenade been used to retake *Vengeance*'s bridge as its owner had undoubtedly planned, it surely would've done the trick. Instead, it provided Tanner with a vital edge.

Given the labyrinthine environment, Tanner decided not to be stingy. He had three more such grenades and no reason not to use them.

He moved forward, ducking and slipping behind every bit of cover he could. Each corner that might hide trouble got one of his grenades. He took only a split second to assess each moving target. None wore anything remotely like a passenger liner's uniform. All carried weapons. He had no time to secure prisoners, nor even to ask for surrender, and no backup.

Tanner shot men in the back, men who struggled just to get to their knees, even men who looked up at him in a dazed, confused manner. The kick of his assault rifle and the roar of its fire didn't blot out their faces or their screams. He had no time to invent a less lethal solution. He fired, moved, reloaded, and fired. The helmet interfered with his aim. It was bulky and fit poorly. He ditched it and kept shooting.

Little more than a minute later, Tanner ran out of targets. The last of his opponents disappeared through a hatch at the other end of the compartment.

Stop and think, Tanner, he told himself. *Think.*

Luxury liner. No idea how many pirates remained. They were long on guts but short on tactical firearms training. Few of them used cover to full effect. They kept taking chances to get clear shots, and Tanner kept cutting them down for it. Yet Tanner had the drop on them in most of his clashes. Even here, he was lucky not to be flanked. He couldn't count on that to continue.

He moved to a console with a map of the ship on one screen. It was as bad as Tanner had expected. Choke points, blind corners, vaulted ceilings, and wide-open passageways lay all over the place. There would be distracting decorations everywhere, too.

And passengers. Panicked, unarmed passengers. Tanner was up against career criminals without a shred of conscience. He looked around at the dead bodies on the deck, looking for options. Precision weapons would be vital.

"Tanner!" demanded a gravelly voice. He froze in his tracks, then swung his rifle around this way and that before he realized the voice came over the PA. "That's your name, right? Tanner? Figure we ought to be on a first name basis by now. Don't try shooting out the speakers this time. Won't do you any good. You did realize that there'd be cameras all over engineering, right?"

He hadn't thought of that, actually. He should have. Tanner scowled, turning back to his search for weapons. None of the dangers of conversation with the pirate captain had changed in the last ten minutes.

"So you've shot a bunch of my guys in the back and run the rest out of engineering for the moment. Good for you. What's your next move?"

Stiffening at the taunts, Tanner looked over his surroundings again. "I don't think I have to go any farther," he answered loudly, unsure whether he'd be heard or not. "This ship isn't going anywhere while I'm in here."

"Well, you've got a good point there, but we've still got plenty of guys to dig you out. Only we don't have to do that. We could just, I don't know, start executing hostages. You remember them, right?"

Tanner reloaded his weapon. He didn't answer.

"You wanna maybe make sure nobody else gets hurt, then?" Casey pressed. "Any opinions on that?"

"You mean all these people you plan to murder, anyway?" Tanner scowled. "Yeah, I know how you played Prince Khalil. No dice."

Someone yelped. Tanner heard sounds of a struggle. Then he heard the gunshot, and the terrified scream of a man in pain. More panicked screams erupted. Tanner tried to blot it out.

"So if you've got the balls to check the monitor, you can see Senior Astrogator Boren on the deck here bleeding out from a stomach wound," the gravelly voice said. "He won't die right away, but he'll sure as shit die if nobody helps him. Now, you want me to pop a few more of these guys? Maybe do one in the head right now, just to make sure we're clear?"

Tanner's eyes shut tightly. He took in a long breath of air full of the smell of gun smoke and dead men. The killing would continue regardless of his surrender. He knew that. The pirates would keep killing. Turning himself over would do no good.

"How many more dead people you want on your conscience, kid?" demanded Casey.

"Don't try that bullshit with me! You're the one pulling that trigger," Tanner replied. His voice shook. "That's all on you. I know I can't save everyone . . . but if you get away, you keep doing this shit. As long as you're stranded here, the number of people you can kill has a finite limit."

"What?"

Tanner opened his eyes. Straight across from him stood vital relays that managed power for the FTL drives. He raised his rifle and unloaded the magazine into the system, reducing it to a pile of broken circuitry and scrap.

"Mother*fucker*!" Casey fairly shrieked.

"I said, 'finite.' I'm sure there's a dictionary program on the bridge computer. See if you can find it before I come shoot your ass."

Tanner started for the hatch. He heard the pirate captain's gun click again, somehow loud enough to overcome the thumping of Tanner's heart. He opened his mouth to yell something, anything to delay the next shot for just another second.

"Casey, contact!" yelled out another voice in range of the captain's mic. "Union battleship, less than one light-minute—" The PA cut out.

It stopped Tanner in his tracks. His emotions surged up in a jumble again. Help was here. That had to be Madelyn's ship. There was no way the *Pride* would go anywhere now. Casey, if that was his name, could buy time with hostage negotiations . . . but in the end, they'd never let him actually take this ship anywhere, would they?

He tried to think it through. Putting himself in that battleship captain's shoes seemed easy enough. Contain the situation. Don't let the bad guy escape. Negotiate to save as many lives as possible. He knew next to nothing about hostage negotiation. Was that something you tried to do quickly? Was it in the negotiator's interests to stretch things out? What would the pirates think of all that?

Casey had hostages and a stranded ship. He had to know that he wouldn't get away with much loot by this point. He couldn't possibly want anything more than his freedom. How could he maintain it? Tanner rushed over to a console to look over the map of the ship again.

They weren't entirely stranded. There were shuttles. Shuttles, hostages, and pirates who wanted their freedom more than anything else.

Tanner rushed to the hatch.

• • •

"NSS *Pride of Polaris*, this is UFS *Fletcher*. Report your status immediately."

"Oh Jesus fucking Christ, that's a goddamn battleship, Casey!" Carl's voice shook. He was on his feet at his station, pulling on his hair. As if the sight of the thing on their sensor bubble and view screens wasn't intimidating enough, the battleship closed to visual range.

"I see it, Carl," said Casey, his reassuring tones now giving way to annoyance. "Calm down. Stand over there. I need you out of my way, Carl. Move." He gestured to a spot at the rear of the bridge, near the exit. It was the only place where Carl wouldn't be right next to Casey, or a pirate who hadn't lost his shit yet, or the *Pride*'s huddled bridge officers. If Carl wanted to open up that hatch and run screaming down the passageway, Casey figured, that would be just fine at this point. Carl stepped over the wounded, wheezing astrogator as he obeyed.

With his formerly trusted yet now more or less expendable deputy out of the way, Casey took a long, steadying breath to assess his situation. His boarding crew had dwindled from hundreds to a few dozen. Engineering was lost. The liner was stranded.

"The fuck do we do, Casey?" asked Lonnie. Unlike Carl, the muscular pirate held his cool. The handful of others likewise remained calm, keeping their emotions in check. Casey selected for strong nerves among his bridge crews. Apparently Carl had been a mistake, but the rest of his people were solid. They trusted him.

"They're gonna try to stall for time," explained Casey. "They might not have a negotiations specialist, but a ship that size oughta have at least one officer who's been to a class or two. Or they'll read what to do from a fucking manual. Regardless, the protocol is for them to drag this out, calm everyone down, get us to see the inevitability of defeat, and all that bullshit. It gives them time to consolidate their control of the situation. They'll also want to have someone separate from the CO doing the negotiating so the CO won't have to split his attention. So," he said, calling up the comms system, "we're not gonna let 'em do any of that to us."

"What about that asshole shooting up the ship?"

"Yeah, that's a problem," Casey grumbled. He opened up the channel. "UFS *Fletcher*, this is Jolly Roger. That's the only name you get. As the annoying recorded message from the destroyer has informed you, this liner is under new management. Please open one-way visual communications so I can see who I'm talking to."

A moment later one of the view screens changed, presenting the image of a Union fleet commander sitting at a bridge station. "This is Commander Trinh," he said. "Visuals open. Please reciprocate."

"Fuck you, no. You don't rank command of a battleship. Put the captain on."

"Negative, Jolly Roger. Captain is unavailable. You speak through me."

Casey sighed. "Okay. I'll open up visuals long enough for you to see me kill a hostage. I've got a lot of these fuckers to burn through." He waved to Lonnie, who roughly grabbed one of the *Pride*'s bridge officers by the arm as Casey stood. He dragged the man over to Casey's console, slamming his head down on the desk and holding it there. Casey keyed the video feed, pulled out his gun, and held it to the man's head.

"Stop!" he heard someone yell. A dark-haired woman immediately replaced Trinh on the view screen. She wore captain's pips on her collar and shoulders. "This is Captain Leigh."

"Oh good," replied Casey. "Normally, I'd shoot this fucker anyway just to make a point, but I should probably establish some good faith." He pushed the hostage back out of the way, cut the visual feed, and sat back down. Casey wondered how many times he'd be interrupted from shooting someone today. He let the thought pass.

"So I've got about two thousand rich, influential tourists and another six or seven hundred crew as hostages. We haven't spaced anyone yet. All those bodies floating around out here are my own guys. I'm having a very shitty day and I'm in no mood to fuck around."

"You also aren't going anywhere in that ship," Leigh observed. "Surrender without hurting anyone else and we'll see to it that you get a fair trial. Cooperating now will mitigate—"

"Hah! Again, fuck you, no, thanks. You don't dictate shit here, lady. Here's the only deal you get: this ship has two FTL-capable shuttles, and we're taking them. We will take hostages with us. Obviously we can't take anything close to the number of hostages we have here, so we'll leave you with the rest. Naturally, I'm going to pick all the children and anyone else that it'd be especially tragic to see die. You will back off out of weapons range and allow us to leave. Your only other option involves wasting shitloads of hostages, and we both know you can't do that.

"When we reach a safe spot, we will release the remaining hostages. Don't call us, we'll call you. That sort of thing. No ransom, no bullshit. I kept my word on Qal'at Khalil, and I'll keep it here, too. But if you fuck with us, you'll be the captain with all the innocent blood on her hands, you got me?

"Make a choice. Thirty seconds. Think fast." He cut the channel, and then hit the comms link on his holocom. "Chang, listen up, we gotta move. Pick the most tear-jerky hostages you can and head for the shuttle bay. Make sure the rest know that we'll vent the whole promenade if they get squirrely. Got that?"

"Casey," Lonnie murmured, "you can't actually vent that deck on a ship like this. It's not built to—"

"I know that, Lonnie," groaned Casey. "Chang, you there? Chang?" Silence followed.

"Casey!" barked an unexpected voice on his holocom. He could hear gunfire in the background. "Casey, it's Takashi! We've got trouble!"

The pirate captain's mind raced. Takashi was on the lower decks, maintaining small sweeper patrols of the passageways and the shuttle bay. "Keep him pinned down!" Casey ordered. "Kill the fucker if you can, but at least keep him contained!"

"Casey, you don't understand!" Takashi shouted over increasing gunfire. "It's not the Malone guy! It's Turtle and Chang!"

Casey's face grew dark. He stood from his chair, moving quickly over to the internal security station to check the promenade monitors.

The passengers and crew were still there. He spotted a few of his pirates, standing in isolated twos and threes, looking confused and nervous. Yet he could not find Chang, or Turtle, or any of the rest of their section. The hostages on their portion of the promenade looked agitated and unsure. Their watchers were plainly long gone.

"Backstabbing sons of bitches," he breathed.

"Jolly Roger, this is Captain Leigh. Your terms are acceptable under certain conditions."

Casey growled in frustration. He tapped a few buttons on his holocom, tying it in to the bridge comms system. Then he drew his gun and waved it at the hostages in the compartment with him. "Up! On your fucking feet! Everybody I haven't shot yet, get the fuck up! Nobody make a goddamn sound!" He clicked on his holocom once more. "No conditions, lady. We do it my way and we do it right fucking now. I will call you when I'm ready to launch. Jolly Roger out."

• • •

Murray whipped around the corner with a cut-down assault rifle in each hand, sprayed wildly, and got perhaps a third of the way through either weapon's magazine before he was blown away. He fell back on the broad, undecorated service passageway in a bloody mess. Crouched behind the corner, Chang bit back a curse. Murray may have been yet another idiot with more liquid courage than brains, but he was also another gun down on Chang's team.

Chang wanted to talk Takashi into going along. The *Pride* wasn't going anywhere, not with a firefight in her engineering space. Casey had plainly lost control of the situation. Any idiot could see it was time to abandon ship. Yet leave it to good old Takashi to choose blind loyalty over any sense of self-preservation. Chang had already forgotten who fired the first shot, but it hardly mattered; all it took was a single minute for both packs of pirates to shoot one another to shit.

Turtle held his rifle around the corner opposite Chang, firing off several laser blasts without exposing his head to aim. "I always hated this guy, anyway!"

"Never gonna get anywhere like this," observed Chang. He sent a burst of bullets down the passageway, trying to work out effective tactics. Takashi's crew had better cover, hiding behind service carts and overturned storage lockers farther down the passageway. Chang glanced over his shoulder at the three guys remaining with him. Frank was wounded with a nasty burn through his shoulder that would probably cost him his arm. The other two could still fight.

On the other side of the intersection of passageways, Turtle had five guys left. One of them was committed to keeping watch over the dozen or so hostages they'd taken from the promenade in their retreat. In the middle of the intersection itself and on the floor behind both corners lay dead pirates. Chang spared an irritable thought for how the hostages were the safest ones in this mess. They were the only people that nobody had any reason to shoot.

"Turtle!" Chang shouted. He gestured to two of his comrade's men, then gestured for them to fall back and around through the passageways. Turtle nodded, relaying the instructions while Chang turned his attention back to suppressing the enemy. Their only hope of ending this mess was a flanking maneuver. Wild-assed bravery wouldn't win this fight.

The minute the flankers were off, though, Takashi's guys came to exactly the opposite conclusion. Sensing that the fire of their opponents had diminished, several of them charged. They leapt out from behind their cover, shooting and screaming as they charged up the passageway. Chang had equally feared and hoped for this. Pirates relied on bravery and aggression, taking big risks that exposed them to danger but often won great gains for the survivors.

It wasn't always as easy to cut down onrushing men as it looked in video games. The designers rarely took into account smoke, or awkward cover, or nerves.

Chang and his men emptied their weapons into the charging men. Bullets and blasts flew everywhere. Far too many of them went wild as excited, frightened pirates sprayed and prayed. Chang held his cool, putting down one, then another, as the rush came on. One of his mates gurgled and fell back. Chang didn't look. He focused on the enemy. In a rush, it was over; the charge was defeated, but not without cost.

The passageway went quiet. The charge left Takashi with only one or two more guys at the most. Chang shrank back behind his corner, pulling out a fresh magazine. He looked to Turtle.

Gunshots rang out through the passageway beyond Turtle and the hostages. Ricochets sparked against the bulkheads. Turtle didn't see it; he fired his gun toward Takashi again, risking a look around the corner this time. "Turtle!" Chang screamed.

Turtle didn't look up from his shooting. Someone down the passageway screamed in pain as he took a hit from Turtle's rifle. "What?"

"Behind you! Shit, behind you!"

The guy watching the hostages behind Turtle understood. He turned to look, brought his gun up and ready, but hesitated when someone appeared around the far corner. The newcomer didn't. A single bullet blew through the pirate's chest. The hostages pressed themselves to the bulkheads and the deck.

Then the new attacker in Darren's stupid combat jacket aimed and fired again. Turtle went down with his head left in a bloody ruin. The last man standing on Chang's side quickly followed suit with a wounded cry.

The newcomer's weapon ran empty. He charged. Chang gave up on reloading his rifle, knowing he'd never have it ready in time. His opponent rushed across the intersection, heedless of incoming fire from Takashi's remaining guns.

Chang threw up a fist and then elbow into the face of his attacker. Tanner tried to block but had committed too much to his charge. The blows threw him off balance, sending him past Chang to land on his back. Chang brought his foot down into Tanner's gut in a punishing stomp.

Tanner latched onto Chang's foot and knee, fiercely twisting Chang's leg with both hands. The pirate tumbled to the deck beside Tanner, leaving both in a violent pile. Chang struggled to recover, but Tanner came out on top. Roaring with anger, Tanner pulled his knife and went straight at Chang's face and neck. Blood flew. Tanner didn't let up.

"*Tanner?*" someone asked. "Oh my God, Tanner, is that you?"

He stopped stabbing. Tanner looked up from his grisly work to find Nathan Spencer there among several other total strangers, all of them clinging to the edges of the passageway. Nothing concealed the shock in Nathan's eyes as he stared at his classmate.

Breathing heavily, shaking with pain and anger, Tanner turned away to find a gun. Plenty of them lay on the floor around him. Tanner spotted an expensive, tricked-out laser rifle, snatched it up, and forced himself to his feet. People spoke around him, but he didn't listen. The rifle had his attention.

Full power cell. Computer-enhanced scope. His enemies had an awful lot of top-dollar weaponry. This would work.

"Tanner, wait! Where are you going?"

"Shuttles," Tanner grunted as he lurched around the corner. He limped down the corridor dripping with blood. Two men appeared at the end of the passageway, stepping out from behind cover to greet their apparent ally.

"Oh man, Darren," Takashi said. "Thank God you showed up, I thought we—"

Tanner cut him off with a blast from his rifle, did the same to Takashi's comrade, and kept moving.

• • •

"Shuttle Alpha has docked with the destroyer. Marines have boarded," announced Commander Trinh. "Nothing different from what we can see from here. Ship seems to have been vented, most systems powered down."

Captain Leigh nodded. She looked to her comms officer. "No response from the pirate?"

"No, ma'am."

The captain frowned. "This isn't good. If they want to jump out in a shuttle, we can't risk firing on them, but if something's gone wrong on their end . . ."

Trinh looked up at her. "Ma'am?"

"Grapple and board," Leigh ordered. "Helm, bring us in. Marines, stand ready for boarding."

• • •

All of his successes, all of his power and influence, and it came down to this. Half a dozen pirates, himself included, rushing a handful of hostages to a getaway vehicle like he'd just fucked up a simple bank robbery. Casey hurried his companions, willing and otherwise, down the corridors to the shuttle bay.

Disaster or not, he would get away. No fleet captain would fire on a ship carrying hostages just to eliminate a handful of fleeing pirates. He would get away, and then he'd start anew. Rebuild. He'd taken things this far. He still had his cash, his connections, and his reputation. The loss of *Vengeance* would hurt the latter, of course, but eventually he'd recover. He could cook up an explanation. There would still be pirates who remembered him as the man who'd led the Qal'at Khalil raid.

The *Pride* shuddered. His group stopped, looking around nervously. Casey stole a look at his holocom and its ties to the bridge monitors. "They're linking up to board," he said. He pointed to the passageway leading to the shuttle bay. "That puts the battleship on the other side from us." He looked at his men, hoping to inspire all the determination he could. "We're going to make it."

At the bay hatch, Casey and Lonnie took to either side of the portal with weapons at the ready. The shuttle bay was a wide, spacious area, kept clean and inviting for the high-paying passengers who might charter one of the small craft for a jaunt during the luxury liner's stops. Legally, the shuttles were there for the use of ship's business, but, as anywhere else, money talked. The shuttles were ideal for Casey's needs.

"Dennis, Kiyoshi, you guys take the helm," he said. "Shouldn't take more than a minute to get her warmed up. Go," he urged. As the two rushed out, Casey turned to the others. "Lonnie, Travis, you're bringing up the rear. Any more of our guys make it down here, we'll take 'em with, but you've gotta watch for hostiles. Anyone looks the least bit unfriendly, waste 'em. Chad and I have our guests," he finished, looking at the handful of others menacingly. "Don't anyone try anything clever. You run, we waste you, and if we can't, we'll just waste one of your friends here."

He looked out at the shuttle bay again. Dennis and Kiyoshi were halfway there. Casey shoved one of their hostages through the portal, then another. "Go! Get going!" he shouted.

They ran. Kiyoshi and Dennis were already inside the shuttle, firing up its engines. Casey looked left and right as he and Chad brought up their hostages, watching for anything that might screw up their escape.

All the other doors remained shut. No one else was about. Fifty meters or so off to the left sat the second shuttle, resting in its launch bay all alone, except for the blood-soaked guy crouched underneath its fuselage with a plasma carbine.

"No," shouted Casey in an instant of panic. "Christ, no!"

The plasma carbine went off, striking near the main thrusters of the shuttle. Sparks flew as metal melted and burst. Casey, Chad, and all their hostages instantly dove for whatever cover presented itself. The plasma carbine went off again, striking the shuttle in the same spot.

It was only a simple civilian craft, with nothing anyone would call armor to protect its hull. The boom of its exploding thrusters shook the entire shuttle bay.

• • •

He didn't expect an explosion. Tanner's heart leapt into his throat when the blast hit, more so for the screams it elicited from the people in the starship liner uniforms than anything else. He hadn't even seen them before he fired. All he saw were the two pirates climbing inside a vehicle he had to keep from leaving.

That job was done. Whether or not the pirates inside were down would have to wait; there were more outside. Tanner spotted them amid the liner crewmembers through the smoke.

"Casey, what—" shouted one.

"Chad," the other barked with a familiar, gravelly voice, "grab her! Now!"

The other pirate reached for one of the liner's officers. Without thinking, Tanner dropped the plasma carbine on the deck and took up his laser rifle, bringing it to his shoulder. "Human male," he said to the targeting computer. "Beard. Headshot."

Circuits in the weapon hummed to life. Tanner looked down the scope, training the crosshairs on the face of his enemy as the pirate wrapped one arm around the woman's neck and placed a gun against her head. The outer brackets of the crosshairs flashed green. Tanner pulled the trigger.

A second later, with the rifle's computer correcting for Tanner's aim, Chad fell away from his hostage with a hole burned through his forehead.

Sudden, overwhelming force struck against Tanner's chest. Tanner felt himself rocked off his feet by the impact. It felt as if the whole left side of him just collapsed. He didn't hear the boom of Casey's shot.

The world seemed to go fuzzy. Everything slowed down. Soft, rhythmic tapping brought him back, increasing in volume and clarity as the world cleared up again. Tanner realized he'd been shot. His combat jacket hadn't entirely blocked the bullet. He didn't know how bad it was.

His eyes fluttered open. The pirate captain ran toward him, dragging along the same woman the other pirate had tried to hide behind. Just the pirate and his hostage, running for Tanner—no. Not Tanner. For the shuttle. For the only means of escape.

Tanner's mind still felt fuzzy. He genuinely considered lying down. He was badly hurt. There was just one hostage left. It would be sad, but nobody could hold it against Tanner after all he'd been through. He might not even live another minute. He'd been hurt. Casey had hurt him.

He'd hurt lots of people.

More than anything else in the world, Tanner needed to hurt him back.

Casey ran with his hand on Sarah Woo's collar, half-shoving and half-dragging her along. The other hostages scattered away too quickly after the shuttle blew to corral them, and he didn't have time to fuck around with that, anyway. Lonnie and Travis would either get a clue and catch up before he had the bay doors open or they wouldn't. Casey had a way off the ship and something to shield him from reprisals. That was all that mattered. Fuck the details.

Then Woo yelped and fell out of his grasp. She nearly pulled Casey down with her. Casey stumbled, recovered his balance, and turned to grab her again. Instead, he saw Tanner let go of Woo before he tackled the pirate captain.

They tumbled to the deck together. Casey absorbed most of the fall, feeling the breath knocked out of him. He swung his gun around even before he tried to rise; Tanner caught him by the wrist just in time to ward off a bullet. Tanner's free hand came into Casey's side once, then again, but as he cocked it back for a third punch Casey wrenched his gun-hand free and pistol-whipped Tanner across the side of his head.

Angry hands grabbed both Casey's wrist and the pistol before Casey could shoot, twisting them away from one another. Casey gasped in pain as his thumb broke under the sudden strain. Then an elbow came up against his chin, knocking him back. The gun fell away. A solid punch landed on Casey's jaw, and then another.

The pirate tried to retaliate. He stepped back to get space, bumping into the shuttle but ignoring it, then lunged forward with a fist. Tanner caught him at the wrist, twisted, and pulled him forward, and then stepped slightly behind Casey to bring his elbow down on Casey's shoulder with a pop. He heaved Casey's wrist up again, hyperextending the pirate's arm before slamming his elbow down against Casey's. Casey let out a scream.

Tanner didn't stop. He shoved Casey against the shuttle, punching again and again into the other man's gut, then his chest, and then his face, as Casey slumped to the deck.

Though he wanted to fight back, Casey quickly found his options torn away from him. His right thumb and elbow were broken, along with the shoulder popped out of joint. He withstood the pounding of Tanner's fists long enough to wrench a knife from his boot, but the enraged younger man spotted it before the weapon could be put to use. He seized Casey's arm, tore the knife from his hand, and plunged it into the pirate captain's left shoulder.

Then he slammed his fist down on it, eliciting a second cry of agony.

It wasn't good enough for Tanner. He kept pounding. Casey felt his jaw smashed, felt an eye socket crack, and soon couldn't even muster enough coherent thought to curse at his foe.

Tanner forgot all about the other pirates. He just kept hitting, pouring out hours and months of fear, pain, and loss as if Casey had been the author of it all.

Shots rang out once more. People screamed, some in fear and others in pain. Loud voices shouted out commands. The woman near Tanner called out for help. He barely noticed.

"Over here!" someone yelled. Tanner kept hitting.

"Hey, he's down, he's down!" someone else yelled. Strong hands grabbed Tanner's shoulders and pulled him back. Tanner struggled at first, still fixated on punching and hurting, but then Casey was out of his reach. Men and women in vac suits and combat gear stood all around him.

"You got 'im, buddy," one of the marines said. "You got him. Relax."

The words passed him by like another language, meaning nothing. "Shit, he's been shot. We need a corpsman over here!"

"Gonna need a couple. Christ, look what he did to this guy."

"Not even sure he'll make it. Corpsman!"

None of it registered. Then someone said, "Tanner?"

A woman in full combat kit knelt in front of him. She pulled off her helmet. "Tanner, it's me," Madelyn said. She put a hand on the side of his face. "It's over, Tanner. We're here. It's over."

Tanner blinked at her. She went blurry. "I tried, Madelyn. I tried." Talking became difficult. Something large and heavy welled up in his throat, trying to force its way out. His mouth refused to stay straight.

Tears streamed down his face.

"I don't belong out here, Madelyn," he sobbed. "I can't do this for four more years."

SIXTEEN

Above and Beyond

"The drugs won't erase memories or anything like that," explained the ship's doctor. He sat on a stool beside the bed, pointedly not touching the hypo spray injectors as he spoke. "But when someone experiences the sort of trauma you just did, it can be hard to get your brain and your body to realize you're on the other side of it."

Tanner gave a slow nod. The muscles in his neck ached, much like all the rest of him. He had no idea how he could've been running and fighting yesterday when he hurt so much today.

"Nobody's going to force it on you," continued the doctor, "but I can't recommend enough that you talk to someone in mental health about what you went through once you get home. I imagine you've got a lot to work out. If you don't feel it today, you probably will sooner or later."

"It's okay," said Tanner. He'd have shrugged, if he didn't have both of his shoulders partly restrained by gel packs. "I'm not gonna try to be a tough guy. You probably already gave me some of that stuff to get me to sleep last night, anyway, didn't you?"

The doctor nodded. "A little, but you didn't need help falling asleep. You were exhausted. Again, it's about making sure your brain doesn't develop triggers. This is just the biochemistry, though. The hard part comes later."

"Yeah. It's okay. Do what you gotta."

The doctor stood, picked up his hypo spray, and placed it against Tanner's neck. The injection hardly hurt at all.

The sound of knuckles rapping against the open door caught their attention. "Am I interrupting anything, sir?" Madelyn asked the doctor.

"It's fine," he said, picking up his tray of equipment. "We're done here."

Madelyn took up the doctor's stool as he left. "How're you feeling?"

"Ow," replied Tanner. "I feel ow."

"Well, I hope you're ready to walk out of here. *St. George* just rendezvoused with us to take you home. I asked if I could escort you down."

"That was nice of you."

"Yeah, well. I'm wonderful like that." She smirked. "Figured I'd come give you a little update. Let you lean on my shoulder. Be supportive. Hold your hand in your time of need. Send my boyfriend into a jealous fit."

"He didn't seem like the jealous type. If he wants to be with you, he'd better get used to other guys paying attention to you."

"Other guys aren't usually famous." Madelyn shrugged. "Which you are. Already."

"Well, if you want, you can jump in bed with me and we can fool around until someone comes looking for us. Might be a while, but I'm game."

"You wish. Did I mention he's seen me naked?"

Tanner sighed. "Go get the doctor. I need more drugs if I have to deal with you."

"Poor baby. Anyway. You'll be happy to know Senior Astrogator Boren and passenger Doris McArtle came out of surgery in the last couple of hours. They'll both make a full recovery. You officially saved every-fucking-body."

Tanner's lips twitched but fell again before they formed a full smile. "Not everybody. Not the captain. Or the ones who died when they first took the ship."

"No, but you can't hold those against yourself, Tanner. You weren't even there yet."

"I know, I just . . . I get that. It just seems kind of crappy to do a victory dance when there are gonna be a lot of funerals."

"That's fair. I just don't want you beating yourself up over shit beyond your control. You saved the day, Tanner," she said gently. "You walk off this ship with your head held high, or I'll slap you around until you do."

"Yes, ma'am."

"You should also know that one Lauren Williams has demanded we file a civil rights charge against you. She claims you threw a first aid kit at her when she lay helpless and injured, which I think was gloriously shitty of you." Madelyn grinned. "Captain Leigh told her to shove it up her ass, but sooner or later some lawyer somewhere might try to make a thing out of it. I wouldn't worry, though."

"So she lived?"

"Yeah, she did. Her and another guy on that bridge. Jerry somebody, the guy you taped up. A few others survived on *Vengeance* by stuffing themselves in airtight lockers or whatever. A bunch of others had the sense to surrender when we boarded the *Pride*. That Casey guy pulled through, too.

"Since this was all in Archangel space and technically they were apprehended by an Archangel Navy crewman, that means they all get to face trial here. Which ultimately means no executions," she added. "That'll be a big diplomatic mess soon enough, given how many systems with capital punishment will also want a piece of these guys. Oh, and Archangel has laid claim to the destroyer and that'll likely stick, too."

"How many were caught?"

"Sixty-seven. Already been transferred off ship." She looked at him warily, knowing what question would come next.

"How many died?" he asked quietly.

"Tanner . . ."

"I'm gonna read it somewhere sooner or later, anyway."

She couldn't argue that. "Seven hundred ninety-six." He closed his eyes. "Hey," she added, "I took out four of them myself. You should've seen me. I was pretty badass."

Tanner's eyes opened again, turning toward her skeptically. "How do you feel about that?"

"Fine," she answered. He waited. "Shitty. Both. I don't know, Tanner." She sighed. "They were scum and they were going to rob and murder people, and they had done that and worse to others. Do I feel bad about pulling the trigger on another human being? Yeah, kind of. I'd have preferred to take them alive. But I keep looking at the after-action analysis and I can't see anything else I could've done differently. And the same goes for you. It's not like anyone was gonna talk them down. You did the right thing.

"And I'll tell you something else. You remember that talk we had on Augustine before this mess happened? I felt bad. I felt really bad that I had a part in getting you to enlist."

"I made my own decision, Madelyn."

"Hell, yeah, you did, and we both know that, but still. You've been miserable, and I could tell and I felt awful. But I don't now. I don't feel a damn bit sorry, and I'm not gonna worry about you anymore. And I can give you a list of about twenty-five hundred people and their families who feel the same way. So don't go all angsty and guilt-ridden and mopey on me or I'll never forgive you."

Tanner broke the silence that followed her statement. "Wow."

"Yeah. I know. Tough love."

"You marines really are jerks," he deadpanned.

"Yup."

"I mean, I used to tease Alicia about it, but Jesus," Tanner continued, plainly not bothered. "That's your idea of counseling?"

"Yeah, it is." Her holocom chimed, followed quickly by the ringing of a bell. "That'll be *St. George*. C'mon, get your ass out of bed, crewman."

"Yes, ma'am," Tanner grunted. He started to rise but found his way blocked. Madelyn leaned in to kiss his cheek. "Isn't that fraternization, Midshipman Carter? I don't know who to tell first, your captain or your boyfriend."

"You have no proof," she said, helping him out of bed. "Let's go."

Tanner had nothing in the way of belongings to collect. He wore only loose hospital pants and a shirt, barely more substantial than pajamas. Madelyn put one of his arms over her shoulders at the door. Though his stride was stiff, he could walk. He was mostly glad for the emotional support.

"Oh man," he said in the hallway. "All these painkillers they put me on . . . I'm definitely gonna puke in the airlock this time."

"Don't worry about that," Madelyn assured him.

Tanner appreciated her easy confidence in him, but he knew better. His head cleared during the walk, but his stomach remained queasy. It was only when they were nearly at their destination that Tanner realized a ship the size of *Fletcher* had more than one option for linking up with a mere corvette.

St. George sat waiting in the battleship's open, spacious docking bay. Lined up at her loading ramp stood two side parties, the smaller of them made up by *St. George*'s crew. The larger party consisted of officers and crewmen from *Fletcher*.

Captain Leigh stood at *St. George*'s gangway, calling the assembled men and women to attention. The docking bay fell silent.

"You've got to be kidding," Tanner said under his breath.

"C'mon, Tanner," Madelyn urged. "Let's get you home."

The walk seemed longer than it should have been. Tanner felt his legs tremble as they drew close. The moment they were between the ranks of the side parties, he heard Captain Leigh call, "Present arms!"

Tanner blinked. Every single person present outranked him, yet every hand came up in salute as he passed. So did the hand of Lieutenant Duran of *St. George*. So did Captain Leigh's.

Madelyn brought him to the captain, then stepped back, turned, and offered her own formal salute. Tanner turned, holding back a well of emotion as he returned the gesture. He did the same for Captain Leigh then, wondering briefly if he'd done this properly, and then deciding he didn't care. He was in hospital pajamas. He could be forgiven a breach of military courtesy or two today.

All the hands came down. Tanner felt marginally less awkward.

The captain smiled. "It's been an honor to have you aboard, Crewman Malone." She offered her hand, which Tanner took gratefully.

"I don't know what to say, ma'am."

"You don't have to say anything," she replied. "I know you don't exactly have much gear left to transfer aboard," the captain continued, "but we wanted you to have this, at least."

The XO stepped forward, holding in his hands a familiar, battle-scarred Archangel Navy helmet.

"The computer kept working the whole time," said Leigh. "It recorded pretty much everything up through the moment my marines found it on the destroyer." Tanner accepted the helmet with a trembling hand. "Damn fine piece of work, crewman."

His throat went dry. "Thank you, ma'am," he managed. He looked to Lieutenant Duran, whose face bore a kind, patient expression. "Sir?" he asked, wondering what if anything he was supposed to say or do.

Duran took it from there. "Permission to depart, Captain Leigh?"

"Permission granted, captain," Leigh responded. They exchanged salutes. Duran gestured for Tanner to head up the gangway.

Halfway up the ramp, he looked into *St. George*'s cargo bay. It looked identical to the cargo bay of *St. Jude*. He stopped, released a shuddering breath, and then boarded the corvette.

• • •

"Due respect, Mr. President, this is bullshit."

President Aguirre lifted his gaze from the holo screen on his desk. The hair stylist at his side instinctively stepped away. All conversation in the busy office ceased. "I'm not sure I hear much due respect in the way you say 'Mr. President,' Frank."

NorthStar's appointed political adviser to Archangel looked for a moment as if he might be cowed by the president's stern glare. He gathered his courage and pressed on, though with a barely softer tone. "Your system is almost a *year* behind its primary debt payments, sir," complained Frank Andrews. "You have the ninth strongest system economy in the Union. Every indicator out of your system shows that you could absolutely afford those payments as originally scheduled. It's not like Archangel is experiencing major financial hardships."

"And yet why are so many of my people completely broke, Frank?" President Aguirre asked casually. His eyes drifted back down to his speech. "We have numerous hardships. Per capita debts are as high as ever. Pirates plague our region. Our closest neighboring system has fallen into civil war, leaving us with significant security and humanitarian crises and forcing us to further expand our militia, while our corporate partners have repeatedly failed in their security obligations—"

"Mr. President, are you just reciting your speech at me?"

Once more, Aguirre's eyes turned on Andrews, then flicked to his press secretary. "Yeah. It's a good speech."

Standing to one side of the president's desk in a black-and-crimson business suit, Andrea nodded with a tight smile. "Thank you, sir," she said.

Aguirre turned his attention back to Andrews again. "You've been provided with a VIP seat, as has your corporation's vice president. You'll get to hear the whole thing soon. This being the most important speech of the year, I don't exactly have time to give you my full attention. Sorry about that," the president added without conviction.

Andrews swallowed hard. He knew perfectly well when this meeting was "squeezed" in before the Annual Address that it wouldn't be a serious discussion. Still, he rarely got in at all these days, and he couldn't tell his bosses he'd turned an opportunity down. He had to try. Moreover, the president had to know whom he was dealing with.

"If your address includes a statement on a swift resumption of debt payments and renewal of security agreements," Andrews said, growing stern once more, "we won't need to discuss the matter again."

The president's eyes flicked over to his chief of staff. Victor Hickman stepped in. "As the president said," he interrupted, "you've got a good seat. We're about to head over to the capitol. I recommend you get there before us, or security will probably hold you up."

Andrews held back a growl. "Thank you, Mr. President," he muttered as he turned and walked out. Silence reigned until he was gone.

"We might want to have an extra medical team ready to go for that man's inevitable coronary tonight," Aguirre said. He took a last look in the mirror, then glanced at Andrea once more. "It's a great speech."

"Thank you again, sir," she replied.

"You look good, by the way."

"I'll look wonderful in my ball gown later, sir." Andrea shrugged with mock arrogance.

"Oh yeah? You know, I'm looking for a date for that."

"Pretty sure your wife has you covered, sir, and I'm already spoken for."

"Oh right. I forgot. You're cradle-robbing tonight."

Andrea huffed. "After twenty years in politics, cradle-robbing is the least of my sins, Mr. President."

Aguirre grinned at her, then signaled to his aides and staffers that he was ready to go. "You're not playing politics as usual, Andrea," he said as they walked. "You're helping me liberate our system from corporate oppression."

Her face grew serious. "Are we ready, sir?" she asked quietly in the hall. "Are we ready for what comes next?"

The president stole a look to David Kiribati, one of the night's "designated survivors." The intelligence minister would not be in attendance tonight; if some disaster struck the capitol and claimed the lives of most of Archangel's top officials, he would be among those to provide continuity. "Not yet, no. But we will be."

Kiribati followed the president to the car. He offered up his good wishes as they departed, exchanged quiet nods with Aguirre, and then departed for his own transport.

• • •

"Nervous?" Andrea asked.

Not for the first time, her date seemed momentarily tongue-tied. Tanner stood in his full dress uniform, with several shining medals pinned to his chest and another that hadn't been awarded in half a century hanging from his neck. They waited in a small, somewhat dark alcove to be announced as they entered the ball.

Andrea stayed at his side all night, both through the president's address and the ride over. She only parted from him to change for the festivities, and found him suitably awestruck when he saw her in her red gown.

Andrea personally took charge of vetting him before he was awarded the Archangel Star. She quickly got to know Tanner better than anyone. Some of her staffers joked that her maternal instincts had finally kicked in at long last, but she reminded them that he was no child. Then they suggested she had other instincts at work.

To all appearances, she was only a few years older than Tanner. In truth, she was three times his age. Good longevity treatments could do that, if one had the money. She made a point of drawing as little of Tanner's attention to her real age as possible, distracting him instead with charm and wit. She had plans for him after the ball.

She'd committed graver sins in her life. Young or not, he was no child.

"No." Tanner shrugged. "Sorry. Just thinking." He seemed distant.

"About what?"

He didn't answer at first. "I hated those guys."

"I'm sorry?"

"The crew. *St. Jude.*" He frowned quietly. "I hated them. Practically all of them. They were shitty to me. Treated me terribly. So I hated them." Some other dignitary's name was called in the ballroom beyond them. Applause resounded not far away. Tanner looked down at the floor. His tone held steady; this was no breakdown, no moment of self-pity. His tone was almost casual. He just had to get it off his chest.

"They pushed me around, they insulted me all the time, they even stole from me, and I didn't have it in me to do anything about it. I keep thinking about that. The president's speech . . . he said nice things about them. I guess it was deserved. But every time I see Morales's widow, or the captain's, or any of the other families, I just keep my mouth shut because I don't want to make them feel worse.

"They didn't deserve to die. They did their jobs. They were brave. All that's true, and I'm not trying to take that away. Maybe it's petty of me to care about anything else. But all that talk about honor and virtue and . . ." He shook his head. "They were jerks."

Andrea watched him with concern. "Do you feel like you need to say that to anyone else?" she asked.

"No. I don't. I won't," he added with a smirk. "Just you and my military therapist."

"Why didn't you tell me before?"

"What would've been the point?" He shrugged. "Nobody needs to hear all that. Not now. I just . . . felt like sooner or later I had to say it. Maybe that means I'm not so great, either."

An aide popped his head around the corner, waving to Andrea with a questioning look. She frowned, held up two fingers, and waved him off. She turned back to Tanner.

He offered a small, apologetic smile. "I'm grateful to be here with you. But I know I'm just on my fifteen minutes of fame here. I'm still not even sure I belong in the navy, and I'm positive I don't belong *here*. I'm just a guy who screwed up on the Test and couldn't get into college. So I just wanted to say thank you for tonight, in case I don't get a chance to say so later."

"Tanner," she said, taking his hand, "you know it wouldn't have been hard to set you up with someone tonight, right? There are an awful lot of pretty, famous women who'd love to be seen with you in that uniform of yours right now."

"There isn't anyone in the Union I'd rather be here with than—"

She waved off his concern. "Thank you, but that's not my point. Tanner, I wouldn't have had trouble finding a dazzling celebrity date for this, either. I've done it before. I didn't ask if you'd be my date out of charity. I wanted to go out with the guy who had the nerve to make a pass at the president's press secretary a year ago while he was a nameless recruit holding a mop." She squeezed his hand and watched her words sink in.

"Important people jockey all year long for an invitation to this. Heads of state. Corporate presidents. Celebrities. Scientists. Royalty. Famous, powerful people from all across the Union. They're all here tonight. Every one of them knows you're the coolest guy in the room. I think it's going to be that way for you for a long time."

He blushed, which didn't surprise her. He blushed—and smiled.

• • •

He'd been in worse spaces.

The cell was clean and warm, with metal walls and adequate ventilation. His sleeping space had an actual mattress of sorts, and sheets. The plumbing all worked. Moreover, he had the cell to himself.

None of that made it any less of a prison.

"Look, Aguirre wouldn't make claims like that if he didn't mean them," said one of the voices around the corner from his cell. The sound carried loud and clear through the transparent fourth wall. "I just don't think it'll pass the senate."

"Are you kidding?" countered the other. "You don't go up for the Annual Address and say the government's permanently revoking all the corporate education charters *and* system security contracts unless you've already got the votes sewn up."

"Oh, I'm sure he thinks it's all sewn up, but there's backroom dealing, and then there's public reaction. How many of those senators are gonna suffer big blowback from their constituents for this? How many of 'em are way deep in Lai Wa's pockets? Or NorthStar's? This is no done deal, my friend."

"Hey, you assholes wanna shut the fuck up?" Casey shouted.

Silence fell in the hallway. Then Casey heard the approach of footsteps. A husky man in security armor came around the corner. "What," said the guy through his helmet, "you don't like to talk politics?"

Casey snorted. "Not with Frick and Frack the Ignorant Prison Guards."

"You didn't complain when we played the president's Annual Address."

"Professional oratory is fine, but I can feel brain cells die every time one of you talks like you know anything."

"Fair enough." The guard Casey called Frack shrugged. He activated the holocom on his wrist. A screen appeared before him. The guard tapped a few of the holographic buttons, bringing up media videos from some sort of red carpet event. "If you wanna talk about something a little less highbrow, I'm game. See, this is the celebrity news feed for the after-party of the speech or whatever, right?"

Casey groaned. "Just fuck off and die already."

"No, no, I want to hear your expert opinion on this. You look like you've been around the block a few times, right?" Frack kept poking at buttons, bringing up an alternate screen and then zooming in on images as he spoke. "See, this woman here is the president's press secretary. Gorgeous, right? I mean, they say politics isn't a game for beautiful people, but I guess there are always exceptions. Look at that figure, huh?"

Casey glared at the image of the woman getting out of her luxury ride. His eyes narrowed as he saw the next figure emerge from the hovercar.

"And I guess they said this guy's her date. You know him, right? He's the guy who killed all your buddies and left you pissing blood. I heard he made you cry and everything. That true?"

Casey said nothing. The guard went on in his friendly unbothered tone. "So he's her date, which has gotta be just a political photo op. Goodwill gesture for the troops. All that sort of shit. But still, check out that look in her eyes. That's some predatory, older woman, I'm-gonna-eat-this-kid-for-dinner shit there, isn't it? Don't you think?"

Casey scowled deeply at the guard, whose face remained hidden behind his helmet. "I think she's gonna fuck him. My buddy out there disagrees. What do you think? You think he's getting laid tonight? I think he's getting laid. Hell, this is an hour old. Maybe she's fucking him right now. You think?"

The sound of a door opening for newcomers provided a slight distraction. The guard didn't look right away. "I mean, really," Frack said, "what else have you got to think about right now other than which gorgeous celebrity is sleeping with the guy who put you in here?"

"Markinson," interrupted the familiar voice of the other guard. Casey's tormentor looked back down the hall, nodded, and walked away. Casey sat back down on his thin bed.

Minutes passed before anything changed, but then Casey heard footsteps outside his cell again. The tone was markedly different from those of the guards. His gaze shifted toward the hallway as he waited.

"Didn't think you'd come down here in person," he said once David Kiribati stood within view.

"Not everything can be trusted to an intermediary," replied Kiribati.

Casey raised an eyebrow. "That some sort of sarcasm?" he asked. "I did everything you asked. Turned up the pressure. Let the ship crews escape. Hit the fucking Hashemites where you suggested—and you *knew* that would cause a civil war, didn't you? You knew it. This is what I get for all that?"

"And I held up my end of the deal. I fed you all the information you asked for. But I asked you not to come back to Archangel space." Kiribati's tone remained calm and cool in contrast to Casey's obvious anger.

"I told you, it's a fucking *democracy* with my guys," snarled Casey. "How much control did you think I had?"

"Calm down, Casey. You know perfectly well I didn't set you up for this."

"No, but you could get me out of here!"

"Don't be ridiculous." Kiribati shook his head. "You're one of the most notorious criminals in the Union. You aren't going anywhere, except to trial and then to prison. Give it a couple of weeks after that. Let the attention die off."

Casey's eyes narrowed. "And then?"

"Archangel is going to need starship captains with combat experience," Kiribati said. "Recent fiascos aside, a man like you might be worth his weight in gold very soon."

"You're really going to keep pushing the corporations?" Casey asked. Kiribati gave a short nod. "You'd give me back *Vengeance*?"

"No," huffed the other man, "no, not on your life. There's too much attention on our newest destroyer. But we have other ships that aren't on our books. You might find one of them very familiar. It's amazing how easily certain luxury liners can be converted to combat ships."

Curiosity shone in Casey's eyes, followed quickly by understanding, and then anger. "Son of a bitch," he muttered. Kiribati merely shrugged. Casey had to let it go; he was in no position to make issue of it now. "Some of my crew survived. I want them."

"Well, you certainly can't have all of them. But you could probably have a few. I'll get you a list. Two names, three at the most."

"Done."

"And you forget about revenge," Kiribati warned. "You aren't a pirate anymore. This isn't an exchange of favors. You work for me now. Don't think I won't have plenty of leverage."

The pirate shrugged. "There are more important things in life than revenge."

AUTHOR'S NOTE

If I were one of those (very cool) authors who do a whole ton of research for a novel, I would have bibliographies at the end of my books. Instead, I'm the type to rely on only a few sources for inspiration and/or fact-checking. Google and Wikipedia have certainly been good friends of mine for this purpose.

For *Poor Man's Fight*, I talked with a high school physics teacher (don't laugh, the dude's brilliant) to double-check myself on some of my zero-gravity stuff. I frequently went online to fact-check things I remembered from my astronomy classes in college (well, really just "intro" and the accompanying lab). Very little drives me more nuts when it comes to sci-fi than the way Hollywood can't understand the difference between "interstellar" and "intergalactic"; these words actually *mean something, dammit.*

I also crowd-sourced a few small details with friends via my personal Facebook page. The debate over whether a particular can of whup-ass should be opened with A) a knife, B) a crowbar, C) a blowtorch, or D) surprise strangulation turned out to be a great way to liven up a Thursday night.

Ultimately, I wouldn't call my novel "hard" sci-fi. I tried hard to create a setting and rules that make sense, but it's not like I did a whole lot of math, and I didn't plumb the depths of current theory about space travel and technology. I have a lot of admiration for authors who do that, but in the end I knew the focus of my story would be elsewhere.

There's one thing I really wanted to get right, though: space pirates.

I hold a bachelor's in history, and I'm a genuine nerd. I care about these things.

While I wanted to retain the freedom to innovate and adjust, I wanted my space pirates to work like real, historical pirates. I've always been fascinated by the subject. Since the first book I read about pirates as a kid in elementary school, I knew that Hollywood tends to get pirates all wrong.

Empire of Blue Water by Stephan Talty is a fascinating book about Henry Morgan and the pirates of Port Royal—which, incidentally, was pretty much the polar opposite of what one usually sees in films. It's a history book, but it largely reads like a novel; there's not much in the way of dialogue, mind you, but Talty knows how to pace and how to keep his readers immersed. If you enjoyed the pirates of my novel, I highly recommend checking it out. *Under the Black Flag* by David Cordingly is also a great book on pirate history and lore.

Poor Man's Fight had a good number of beta readers, for whom I'm exceptionally grateful. Thank you all, again. It meant the world to me.

ABOUT THE AUTHOR

Photo © Sean Young

Elliott Kay grew up in Los Angeles and currently resides in Seattle, Washington. He has a bachelor's degree in history and is a former member of the US Coast Guard. Kay has survived a motorcycle crash, severe seasickness, summers in Phoenix, and winters in Seattle.